LEXI HODGES

Cross Her Heart

First edition

ISBN: 979-8-9920172-1-2

This book was professionally typeset on Reedsy.
Find out more at reedsy.com

For the obsession Twilight created and The Vampires Diaries solidified

Contents

Preface

Long before Violet Ashwood met Sebastian Kieran, before the Phoenix Massacre, and even before the Night Realm saw the light of day, a set of twins were born. In an ordinary village, in an ordinary kingdom, but with extraordinary gifts. Well, it was the *lack* of gifts that truly made what they could do extraordinary.

Born in the kingdom of Joveryn in the mortal realms—a short boat ride from Alentara if you could survive the storms and the creatures lurking beneath the surface—the twins couldn't have been placed in somewhere more opposite than Alentara. Where magic prospered and ruled in Alentara, magic was forbidden in Joveryn. And what could be worse than living in a place with no magic? Having gifts and being forced to hide those gifts because you lived in a place where magic wasn't allowed.

Whether it was a price to pay or a punishment from the gods, no one will truly know why the twins weren't given a natural connection to magic. Instead, they were given the ability to pull magic from others.

Most called the twins abominations while a few believed they were exactly what the coven needed. To save them from the creatures of the night.

The vampires.

1

Chapter 1

Bronwen

Weeks had passed since I'd last encountered one. I'd nearly given up hope until a laugh drifted from just beyond the trees to my right. My pace quickened, my heart leaping into my throat. I pulled my hood tighter around my face, blending into the shadows as I moved closer. I wasn't ready to be seen, not yet.

The towering pines whispered in the breeze, their gnarled branches swaying above me. I came to a stop when I noticed a clearing with a small cottage sitting in the middle. Its stone walls were overtaken by wild jasmine, the vines crawling up to the roof as if the house itself were consumed by nature. I'd passed this place countless times, wondering who could live here—someone who let flowers overrun their home, or perhaps someone who had long since disappeared.

I supposed my answer might be no one now, considering the lifeless body that had just fallen to the ground with a dark figure standing above it. Only the moon and stars in the sky gave me just enough light to see what took place before me, but it wasn't enough to know exactly what they looked like. Not until they were closer.

The soft crunch of leaves behind the cottage drew the figure's attention. My body tensed, and I ducked behind a nearby tree. The figure took a step toward the noise, crouching and patting the ground. I squinted, trying to make sense of their actions. Moments later, a dog ran from the side of the house, tail wagging furiously as it jumped into the figure's arms.

I stood frozen for a moment as I watched the figure pet the dog and say unintelligible things to it. What was it doing? No—what was I doing watching this?

I exhaled, lowering my hood. The warm night air kissed my skin, and I could feel the figure's attention shift as its back stiffened. He tilted his head back, drawing in a deep breath. Then, in the blink of an eye, he was standing before me. The hairs on the back of my neck prickled. No matter how many times I'd witnessed it, their speed always caught me off guard. But I showed no fear, keeping my chin high as I met his gaze.

It was then that I could see who I was dealing with. A male who looked to be not much older than me. He was taller than me—taller than my father, who was no small man. His short blonde hair gleamed almost white in the moonlight, his pale skin showed no blemish, and his eyes . . . his eyes glowed an eerie red.

A vampire.

Exactly what I had come to find.

"It must be my lucky night," he said, his voice smooth as velvet, with a sinister edge that made the hairs on my arms stand on end. He raised a hand, brushing my dark hair aside, exposing the tanned skin of my neck.

I stood tall, gripping the sleeves of my cloak as I waited for his advance.

He leaned in, inhaling deeply, his lips brushing against my skin. "And you . . . what are you?"

I didn't answer. I never did. Let them think they had the upper hand—that they had what they wanted before I took it all away.

But vampires usually didn't talk. If anything, it was a few nonsense words that would keep me confused for days trying to figure out what they meant. Bloodlust consumed them, leaving only one thought: to drain the human in front of them.

But this one . . . this one was different. He had control. I could feel the restraint in his movements, the calculated way he held back, even after feeding. That made him far more dangerous than the others.

His eyes came back to meet mine. Glowing red to match the blood of his last victim that still stained his lips, a woman foolish enough to hang her laundry out at night. She should've known better. We all knew better than to leave the safety of our homes after sundown.

I could have stopped him. No—*should* have stopped him. But I didn't care enough to.

That, I suppose, was what made me more dangerous than the rest.

"Come on, green eyes," he said as he poked his lip out. "You're taking all the fun out of it."

I locked eyes with him, holding my ground in silence. A faint hum seemed to ripple from him, like an unseen current vibrating in the air between us. It called to me, pulling at the core of my being, a forbidden temptation I could barely resist.

3

But I had a ritual that I liked to keep that somehow made it all even better.

He cocked his head to the side. "Fine. Be that way."

In an instant, his face shifted, the playfulness replaced with a dark intensity. Beneath his eyes darkened, and his fangs extended as he sank them into my neck.

I waited. Just long enough for my vision to blur, for the pressure of his bite to overwhelm me. I slid my hand up his stomach, then his chest, until I made it to his neck. I wrapped my hand around his throat, forcing the magic that made him what he was to leave him and come into me. The vampire's breath caught in his throat, and his eyes widened in shock. He pulled away from my neck, but it was too late.

I squeezed harder, not just around his throat but around his magic. It was mine now.

He gasped for air, his face contorted in pain, but it didn't matter. The power I had stolen from him—his magic— coursed through me, making me feel alive in a way nothing else ever could.

He fell to his knees, staring up at me, helpless. I raised my other hand, and with a thought, fire bloomed in my palm—a crackling ball of heat, ready to reduce him to ash.

"Come on, *red eyes*," I said, mocking him, my voice low and laced with venom. "You're taking the fun out of it."

The flames reflected in his red eyes, but he didn't flinch. His lips curled into a grin, his sharp teeth still covered in my blood. It was as though he welcomed it, as though he found some twisted joy in my defiance.

But as I brought the fire closer, his expression shifted, just slightly—an almost imperceptible flicker of something behind his arrogance. Fear? No. Something darker, something that made my pulse stutter. His grin widened as if he knew a secret I didn't, a glint of malice dancing in his gaze.

The flames licked the edges of his shirt, and the acrid scent of singed fabric filled the air. He didn't move, didn't scream. Instead, he leaned forward slightly, his voice a low rasp as he fought against my control to speak. "You don't know what you've started."

A chill raced down my spine, despite the fire burning in my hand. I hesitated, the words replaying in my mind. What did he mean? What was he trying to say?

The hesitation cost me.

A faint rustling reached my ears—too deliberate to be the wind. My grip faltered, and just as I turned my head to investigate, a force like a battering ram slammed into my side. The fire in my hand extinguished instantly as I was thrown into the air, crashing hard against the unforgiving earth. A jagged rock jutting from the earth tore through my side. A sharp, burning agony ripped through me as my skin split open, the wound dragging down my torso like an unrelenting claw. Warm blood seeped into my clothing, sticking fabric to flesh as a fresh wave of pain surged through me, leaving my vision spotty. Every breath sent white-hot agony shooting through my ribs, the injury deeper and more vicious than any before.

I struggled to push myself upright. The world around me was a blur of shadows and moonlight, the towering pines looming like silent sentinels. I blinked hard, forcing clarity, and froze when I saw him again.

The vampire was standing tall, his focus fixed on me. But he wasn't alone. Another figure emerged from the shadows, shorter and darker, with an air of malice that made my stomach churn. Their movements were fluid, predatory, and their glowing eyes burned through the darkness like embers.

The blonde vampire raised a hand, halting the new arrival mid-step.

"I don't share," he said to the new vampire, his voice colder now, each word laced with deadly intent. His gaze flickered to the blood pooling beneath me, a cruel smile playing on his lips.

My teeth clenched as I gathered the last remnants of magic from deep within me. The air around me grew hotter, sparks snapping at my fingertips until a flame burst to life once more. My body screamed in protest, but I ignored the pain, channeling every ounce of my remaining strength into the fire. The fire streaked toward the blonde one, its heat distorting the air between us. Just as it was about to reach him, a blur of motion intercepted it—the new vampire leaped in front of him, shielding him with his own body. Flames roared to life, consuming him instantly. His agonized scream shattered the night, his form contorting as fire licked hungrily at his flesh. He thrashed for a moment before collapsing, his body turning to ash that scattered into the wind.

The blonde smiled and let out a wicked laugh as he looked around at the ashes floating in the wind. I pointed my hand towards him again but before he met the same fate as his friend, he disappeared into the darkness.

Panic gripped me. I scanned the woods, my vision dimming with every passing second. The magic I had stolen was slipping away, just as the blood from my side soaked into the earth. I had to leave before it was too late. I thought of home—of the front door to the cottage my family lived in for generations—and willed myself there.

The next thing I knew, I was on my knees, the door before

me. I hit my hand weakly against it, gasping for breath.

The sharp sting of the bite on my neck reminded me of what my family was about to discover. Even if the secret of me going into the woods at night was about to come to light, no one could know I let one bite me. I healed it quickly, using the last remnants of the magic I had stolen.

I slumped against the door, and the world went black.

***

"How could she have been so reckless?" Papa's voice thundered through my room as his heavy boots stomped across the floor. He hurled a trinket from my dresser, and I watched it shatter against the stone wall. His long, now graying hair that he always wore neatly in a bun brushed against his shoulders. He hadn't taken the time to pull it back since he found me on the steps in the early hours of the morning.

"Henry, please." Mama's voice was softer, but no less filled with worry. She moved toward him, placing a hand on his shoulder in an attempt to calm him. She had always been the steadier of the two, but even she could only do so much when Papa's temper flared, which I understood more than most. That same temper ran through me.

Papa let out a sharp breath. His green eyes flickered with barely contained fury. "She knows better than to go into the woods after sundown."

The healer pushed the needle deeper, and I bit back a hiss, swallowing the sting. Papa could heal me with a few words, but he wanted me to feel it. To punish me. To make me understand the pain the townspeople endured when the vampires came for them, though they would hang us in the square without a second thought if they ever learned what we were.

He had stopped the bleeding and healed my punctured lung when he found me, but left the open wound exposed, ensuring that each time the needle pierced my torn flesh, I would feel the raw, searing pain. The slow, careful stitching sent jolts of agony through my side, each pull of the thread a reminder of my mistake, of my vulnerability. The sensation of torn skin being pulled back together was unbearable, but I clenched my jaw, refusing to let the pain show.

"She's too young for this," Papa muttered, the words thick with frustration.

I scoffed, though the motion made the room spin.

Twenty-two. I was nearly twenty-two.

"Winnie, what were you doing out there?" Mama asked softly. "You should have been in bed."

"I was out there for the same reason that any other witch goes into the night, Mama."

"Hunting? But Winnie, you—how did you—" She glanced at Papa, her voice trembling.

I pushed myself up slightly, wincing as the pain in my ribs flared. Since he wouldn't heal me, he was going down too. "Tell her about the vampires, Papa."

"Henry?"

As Papa opened his mouth, the door creaked open. My twin, Adar, stepped inside, his wild black hair in disarray, his eyes— my eyes—locked onto me with that sharp, knowing gaze of his. His shirt was untucked, buttons mismatched, exposing some of his golden skin, and one leg of his pants was tucked into his boot while the other hung loose.

"B, you alright?" Adar reached his hand out as he walked towards me. He didn't have to say anything for me to realize what he was doing.

I winced as I shifted, trying to sit up. The healer's hand came down on my shoulder, but I pushed her away, desperate to reach out to my brother.

Just as our hands were about to touch, Mama yanked him back by the collar, her voice sharp. "Oh no, Adar. You are not helping her this time."

He glanced at me. "Sorry, B. I tried."

I let out a huff as I leaned back against the pillow, the small movement causing me to tense.

Mama looked down at the disheveled mess that stood before her. "And who was the unfortunate one this time?"

Adar plopped down in the chair opposite my bed, lounging as if the chaos swirling around him didn't exist. He crossed his arms behind his head, his grin a mix of mischief and defiance. "Charlotte Gentry," he said with a casual shrug. "Though I wouldn't call her unfortunate. Let's just say she got more out of it than I did."

He waggled his eyebrows for effect, and I couldn't help but roll my eyes. Mama sighed, clearly unimpressed, but Adar didn't care. He leaned back further, a smug smirk on his face. "She even thanked me when it was over. Can you imagine? A grateful witch—who knew?"

My brother had many talents. Wooing a witch for a little magic being one of his favorites. He could also sell anything making him the preferred child to go to Market with Mama in town square, and beat anyone that challenged him to a sword fight, though I wasn't too far behind him on that.

Papa groaned. "Adar, I have told you not to—"

"Oh, no. You can yell at him later. We aren't done," Mama cut in.

Papa shot me a glare before turning to Mama. "I wanted to know what their gift would do to a vampire."

I scoffed at the word gift. No natural connection to magic, but the ability to pull magic and wield it in any way we wanted. Some gift.

Mama paled. "When?"

Papa grabbed her hands. "Odelia—"

Mama turned to me. "When?"

"We were six or seven."

Mama ripped her hands away from Papa.

"What happened?"

"We both placed a hand on it and pulled until her veins bulged and her skin went gray." I remember that moment all too well. The magic surged through me like a lightning strike, setting every nerve in my body alight. My breath hitched, and I felt my heart hammering against my ribs, as if it, too, was desperate to escape the sheer force coursing through me. My hands trembled, not from fear, but from the sheer energy that felt too vast to contain. "But within minutes her magic seemed to regenerate, bringing life back to it once again, and Adar—"

"B," Adar warned.

"Adar nearly cried as he ran to hide behind Papa when the vampire shot up." I started to laugh but the moment brought pain so strong that the laugh turned into a scream.

"Henry! They were only children. They could have died."

"No, Winnie set the vampire on fire with one pointed finger before it took a step toward her."

"So what? You've turned our daughter into a hunter? Without telling me?"

"No." Papa ran his hand through his hair. "I had no idea

she was doing this."

"Then why, Winnie? That one vampire has caused all of this?"

I glanced at Papa.

He sighed. "After that, she begged me for weeks to bring another vampire home. I dismissed her every time until I got so aggravated with her relentless begging. So we made a deal."

"A deal?"

Papa sighed, his voice low. "A vampire every birthday."

He thought it was harmless, just a way to help me understand my abilities, but it was never enough. Once a year wasn't enough.

That was why I had been in the woods last night. And the night before. And every other night for the last two years.

Mama turned and ran out of my room. Papa chased after her, leaving Adar and me in silence.

He let out a low whistle. "Well, that was dramatic."

I ignored him, my fingers ghosting over my neck as an odd tingling sensation crept across my skin. My stomach twisted when I felt it—the raised scars where the vampire's mouth had been just hours ago. It shouldn't be there. I had healed it, just as I always did. There was never a trace left of what had happened. But this time was different.

I didn't kill him.

He was still alive.

And I was marked.

2

Chapter 2

Bronwen

I hadn't slept in the same room with Adar since we were ten. He snored, muttered in his sleep, and—worst of all—woke me up as soon as the sun crested the window. And yet, here we were again, our beds only a few feet apart.

My side throbbed, and each breath sent a flare of pain through my ribs. Despite the bruises, the cuts, the broken bones, Papa still thought I'd try to sneak into the woods tonight. I didn't argue. Not because I thought I needed to be locked away—no, all I wanted was sleep. But more because I feared what would come of being marked.

Not many had been marked. The idea alone made my skin crawl. My fingers drifted to my neck, tracing the faint scar that seemed to pulse with its own heartbeat. The stories I'd heard were enough to make anyone shudder. Usually, vampires couldn't control themselves, draining their prey before the thought of stopping even crossed their minds. But in the rare cases of markings, the consequences were far worse. There was the story of a man who swore he could feel the vampire's presence—even in his dreams—every night, he experienced death, over and over, until he couldn't bear to close his eyes. In the end, it wasn't the vampire that killed him, but the weight of a stone tied to his waist as he sank into the icy embrace of the river.

Then there was the woman who willingly gave herself to a vampire—nights spent in his arms, her body a canvas for his fangs. When her sister found out, she had her committed, hoping to save her from whatever madness had taken hold. But madness wasn't what came for her. The vampire stormed the asylum, leaving a trail of bodies in his wake before vanishing into the night with her, never to be seen again.

But I knew one thing: I'd never tell anyone. Least of all Papa. If he knew, he'd risk his life—and the whole coven's—for me. I also didn't want to give the coven one more thing to talk about. I could handle myself.

I just needed a few days to heal.

I squeezed my eyes shut as a sharp jolt of pain shot through me. All I could hope for was a full night's sleep without being haunted by a vampire.

"Wake up, B. Mama made your favorites for breakfast." Adar's voice carried an edge of teasing, as if he knew exactly how much I hated mornings. I squinted as the light poured into my room, catching sight of him perched on the edge of his neatly made bed. He was tying his boots, dressed in his fighting leathers.

I rolled to my side, letting out a gasp as my sore side reminded me of my injury. Moments from that night raced through my head, but I felt a little relief when I realized I had

13

slept through the night without a nightmare.

"Why are you dressed like that? You don't go back today," I said, my voice cracking slightly as I tried to sit up.

Though there were no wars or outside threats, Adar joined the Legion the moment he was old enough. But his time with the Legion would eventually come to an end when Papa decided to step down as the coven's Father—though the true reason for Adar leaving could never come out.

"No. I have something else I have to do today." He avoided my gaze, his tone carefully measured. I narrowed my eyes. Adar wasn't the best liar, but he rarely gave me enough to catch him outright. Still, I didn't press him. I was too hungry to argue, especially if sweet bread and grape jam were waiting.

It took me a while to make it to my wardrobe, considering every step I took sent pain radiating throughout my body. I silently cursed Papa for the torture he was forcing me to endure. He may have stopped the bleeding as soon as he found me on the doorstep, but he left every other injury.

Quite possibly the worst part: I couldn't fix my hair. Thank the gods I had no plans to see anyone today.

It took me even longer to walk down the small hall to our kitchen. The smell of baked sweet bread, warm and inviting, wafted through the house and pulled me forward despite the ache in my side. The kitchen was small but comforting, with a large wooden table in the center, its surface worn smooth from years of use. Copper pots hung from the walls, catching the morning light that streamed in through the small window above the wash basin. Herbs—lavender, thyme, and rosemary—dangled from the rafters, their earthy scents mingling with the sweetness of breakfast.

"Good morning, Winnie!" Mama chimed as I shuffled into

the room. Her voice was bright, her hands busy arranging plates on the table. She moved with precision, her skirt swishing softly as she leaned over to set a glass of water at my spot. Her black hair, neatly braided down her back, moved with every motion of her hips as if they were connected.

I took another step forward as I studied Mama. She had been so upset yesterday and yet here she was, acting like her usual self.

I glanced at Adar who leaned casually, a knife in one hand and a half-eaten apple in the other. He shrugged his shoulders as if he knew exactly what I was thinking.

"Where's Papa?" I asked.

"He's meeting with the coven," Mama replied, her voice softer now, almost distracted. She turned to stir something on the stove, the clang of the spoon against the pot punctuating her words.

"The entire coven?" I slid onto a chair, wincing as the motion sent a jolt of pain through my ribs. The wood beneath me felt hard and unyielding, a reminder of my bruises. My fingers brushed against the glass of water, its coolness grounding me.

"No, just a few men from each of the areas."

"Why aren't we at the meeting? Or at the very least Adar, if this is some men only thing," I pressed, ignoring the throb in my side. The savory and sweet scents around me did little to calm my growing frustration.

"You need to heal," she said firmly.

"Well, what is it about?" I asked, narrowing my eyes.

Adar let out a soft snort, quickly muffled by another bite of his apple. The faint crunch of the fruit echoed in the otherwise quiet room, grating against my already frayed nerves.

"Vampire hunting," Mama said after a brief hesitation.

15

I shot her a glare. "What?"

She placed the spoon down before walking to me. "Your father thinks the witches have slacked on their duty of hunting. He is creating assignments and having them go out more."

Why did I tell them what I was doing?

I lathered a piece of bread with grape jam, the sticky sweetness clinging to my fingers as I spread it thickly across the slice. The tangy burst of grape hit my tongue as I shoved it into my mouth, the texture rich and comforting, even as my thoughts churned.

"Are you sure you aren't going to Market with me today?" Mama asked Adar, turning her attention to him.

"No. I think I should stay and take care of B."

I cut my eyes at him. I did not need anyone taking care of me.

Mama kissed his cheek before she nodded and walked out of the door.

Adar walked over to me and placed his hands on my wound.

"Ow! What are you doing?" I said just before a tingling sensation went over the wound, healing it immediately. His palms were warm, roughened by years of training and swordplay, but there was a gentleness in his touch that surprised me.

I took in a deep breath, something I had been avoiding, but it had never felt as good as it did now. The air was cool, sharp as it filled my lungs, yet it carried a strange sense of relief that coursed through my body.

I let out a sigh. "You held onto that magic since yesterday?"

He nodded, slicing another piece of the apple before tossing it into his mouth. "You're welcome."

I glared at him. "And you couldn't have healed me before

now?"

He shrugged his shoulders. "Papa said to wait. He said you needed to at least suffer for a little while. Especially after what you told Mama."

I scoffed and put another piece of bread in my mouth.

"Go change."

"What?" I asked as I glanced down to see what could possibly be wrong with what I was wearing. Not to mention I'd never ask Adar for his opinion on my dresses.

"Go put on your leathers."

Those words had me jumping out of my chair without another word.

"What are we doing, Adar?" I asked as I stepped into the sunlight, tying my hair back into a braid.

Adar tossed a sword my way, and I barely caught it by the hilt. Had he lost his mind? If I would've been a second off with my catch, it would've sliced my fingers off.

"Considering you got knocked on your ass, I'd say I've slacked on our lessons," he said. His words stung, not because they were harsh, but because they rang true. My grip on the sword tightened as a flicker of frustration coursed through me. I couldn't stop picturing that night—the helplessness, the cold fear creeping up my spine.

"You need to be better." He motioned me to follow him to the small open area of our yard that wasn't overgrown with hawthorn bushes.

"I don't think a sword would have stopped what happened last night," I replied as we stopped.

He came down with his sword. I barely blocked it, realizing I might have become a little rusty. I blamed that on him, though.

17

"No, but your instincts were off." He swung again, and I turned just before contact.

"Why does it matter? I might as well ask Papa to build me a tower and lock me up with the horses. At least they don't judge me for sneaking out."

He dropped his arm that was holding the sword and shook his head. "You know Papa better than anyone. His main goal is to get rid of the vampire problem we have. Why would he prevent one of his best assets from hunting them now that he knows you want to? He just needs time to cool off. So until I go back to camp, I'm going to make you a little more prepared."

"But this doesn't matter." I waved the sword in my hand. "I can use magic."

"And if you come across a human that sees a witch and wants to kill you?" Another hit, but I dodged it and hit him in the side with the flat part of the blade.

I shook my head as I mentally noted that the score was me: one and annoying know-it-all brother: zero. "The only humans I have come across in the night are being drained of their blood, and I don't think they could put up much of a fight."

"So you've never seen a . . . member of the Legion during your hunts?"

I took a step back. "What are you talking about?"

He ran a hand through his hair, the movement slow and deliberate, as if he were untangling more than just his thoughts. His eyes flicked to the trees, then back to me, a flicker of something—hesitation?—crossing his face. It wasn't like him to hold back, and the silence stretched between us, gnawing at my patience. He used to tell me everything.

Back then, it felt like we were conspirators against the world, laughing at Papa's rules and whispering secrets under the moonlight. But now? Every word felt carefully chosen, every glance like he was measuring whether I was ready to know more. Since he'd joined the Legion, it was like a wall had grown between us—one he didn't seem interested in tearing down. And yet, here he was, training me, guarding me, as if trying to shield me from something I couldn't see. I hated him for it, but I hated needing him even more.

But how angry could I truly be when I made sure I chose a top with a high collar to cover the scars on my neck?

He rubbed the back of his neck, his eyes scanning the ground as though the answers he sought were buried there. The silence stretched, thick and heavy, until finally, he spoke.

"Do you really think we spend all of our time drinking?" he asked, his voice quiet, almost reluctant. "The threats may have stopped from outside the kingdom, but it has only gotten worse within. The vampire population is growing, and the Legion's priorities have changed. And if a member saw you in the night . . . You don't have the ability to just disappear unless you have a source."

"Does Papa know this?" My voice was sharper than I intended. My mind raced, piecing together the implications. The coven hunting vampires was dangerous enough, but if the Legion was watching . . .

I swallowed hard. If they ever saw magic—

"Of course he does, B!" Adar's tone snapped me out of my spiraling thoughts. He shot me a look, half disbelief, half exasperation. "Who do you think had me join the Legion in the first place?"

My stomach twisted, the answer settling in before he said it. I stared at him, waiting for the final blow.

"He needed someone on the inside."

3

Chapter 3

Bronwen

The cool night air clawed at my throat with every ragged breath. The metallic tang of blood, faint but unmistakable, mingled with the earthy scent of damp moss. My lungs burned, the searing pain spreading through my chest as I pushed forward. The shadows between the trees shifted and warped, as though they were alive, watching me with unseen eyes.

The briers scraped at my legs, their sharp thorns tearing through the fabric of my skirt and biting into my skin like tiny needles. My foot caught on an exposed root, and I stumbled. The ground rushed up to meet me, the impact jarring my bones as I slammed into the cold, damp earth. My hands stung, the rough texture of the forest floor cutting into my palms.

When I tried to push myself up, a searing pain twisted through my ankle. A sharp cry escaped my lips, and I bit down hard, trying to stifle the sound. The joint throbbed with every attempt to move, the ache spreading like fire. I was trapped, pinned to the ground by my own body's betrayal.

The silence around me felt deafening. No rustling leaves. No chirping crickets. Just the pounding of my own heart, loud and unrelenting in my ears.

Then it came—a blur of motion in the corner of my eye. A cold breeze stirred the hair at my neck, carrying a faint metallic scent. The creature was fast, too fast, slipping through the shadows like smoke. My pulse quickened as I scanned the trees, my eyes darting desperately for any sign of it. A shiver ran down my spine. I wasn't just being hunted—I was being toyed with.

I should have left Sarah's house sooner. I'd stayed longer than I should have, caught up in her sister's poetry reading, and now I was paying the price. Sarah's mother had begged me to stay the night, but I promised to make it home before sunset. The sun had just disappeared behind the trees when I'd started my walk, but somehow, this one was already out.

The hand that gripped my chin was as cold and unyielding as stone. It forced my head upward, and my gaze locked onto eyes the color of fresh blood. They gleamed with malice, their intensity pinning me in place. The faint scent of iron wafted from his breath, sharp and bitter, as his cruel smile widened.

"Shhh, it's okay. You're safe now," he whispered, his voice low and soothing, a contradiction that sent every instinct in my body screaming.

Before I could recoil, his fangs flashed in the dim light, sharp and glinting like a predator's. They pierced my neck, and a cold, searing pain erupted at the point of contact. It spread quickly, like ice shattering through my veins, numbing and paralyzing. The pull was overwhelming, a sensation so strange and consuming it left me breathless. My limbs felt weightless, detached from my body as the world tilted and spun.

I tried to push him off, but his strength was too much. My vision

blurred, my body trembling. The world faded, and the darkness
swallowed me whole. It wasn't a quiet darkness—it felt as if the
shadows themselves were alive, pulling me deeper into their grasp.

I woke with a jolt, gasping for air, my chest heaving. My heart
pounded against my ribs, each beat a painful reminder of the
nightmare I couldn't shake. My hands instinctively pulled the
blanket tighter around me, a futile attempt to shield myself
from the lingering dread.

No. No, no, no.

It wasn't real. It couldn't be real.

But it felt real. Too real. The weight of the vampire's hand
on my chin, the piercing sting of his fangs as they broke my
skin, the way my body froze as his cold breath brushed my
neck—it was all burned into my memory. My mind churned,
replaying the scene with agonizing clarity. And his eyes—
those blood-red eyes—were unmistakable. I'd seen them
before.

It was him. The vampire that marked me.

I clenched my fists beneath the blanket, trying to ground
myself, but the trembling wouldn't stop. I thought I was safe,
but the nightmares had begun.

Was it just fear playing tricks on me? Or was this the effect
of being marked? My thoughts spiraled, each question heavier
than the last.

A cold sweat broke out along my neck, and I wiped it away
with trembling fingers. I wasn't even sure who I was in the
nightmare. When I'd fallen, the skin on my hands was lighter
than my own. What did that mean? Was I losing control of
myself completely? The thought sent a shudder down my
spine.

I glanced at the bed beside mine. Adar was still fast asleep, his breathing slow and steady. At least I hadn't woken him. The last thing I wanted was to see the worry in his eyes, the same worry I saw in Mama's every time she looked at me yesterday.

Adar's words echoed in my mind, cutting through the haze of fear. He had been training me, reminding me of skills I had let slip in his absence. When he left to join the Legion, it was like a piece of me had been torn away. I had felt abandoned, betrayed, and for a long time, angry. But now, I understood. He left because he had to. Because Papa asked him to. The perfect son, doing his duty once again.

He wanted someone on the inside, to learn their routes, when they went out into the night, their methods, and anything that could help protect the coven.

Although there wasn't much of a pattern to when or where they went, when Adar was with them, he could sense the magic that radiated off witches and was able to steer the Legion in the opposite direction.

I now understood that he didn't choose to leave me, he only did what was asked of him. The perfect son in every way just doing one more thing to appease Papa.

Still, it didn't make the loneliness any easier to bear. All that was left for me to focus on was the hollow, aching pull deep within me. It gnawed at me day and night, a constant reminder of what I was. An abomination. Defective.

A siphoner.

The words the coven whispered about me had etched themselves into my soul, but no amount of cruelty could dull the truth: I needed magic. Without it, I felt like a ghost, half-alive and half-empty.

I knew my brother felt it too. I saw it in his eyes whenever he used magic. The pull, the temptation, the way it made him feel stronger, more powerful. He fought it, though. He had more restraint than I did. He could go weeks, months, without giving in. But I couldn't. I needed it.

It made me feel alive in a way nothing else ever could.

I shut my eyes tightly, trying to block out the images of my nightmare gnawing at me. The bed creaked as I shifted, pulling the blanket tighter around my shoulders.

***

The needle's sharp end pierced the skin of my thumb. I hissed, dropping the pair of pants I'd been working on all morning onto the floor of Mama's small sewing room.

Rolls of cloth, some new and others frayed from years of use, were stacked neatly against one wall, their colors muted in the dim light. A wooden worktable sat in the center of the room, its surface scattered with half-finished garments, spools of thread in every color, and delicate lace trims waiting to be stitched. The faint creak of Mama's rocking chair added a soothing rhythm to the space, blending with the soft rustling of fabric as she worked.

Mama let out a quiet laugh before covering her mouth to attempt to hide it before I noticed.

"What?" I asked, slightly annoyed that my pain was amusing to her.

Mama chuckled quietly from across the room. "You can dodge a sword but not a needle," she teased, her voice warm and light.

I shot her a glare, but the smile that tugged at my lips

betrayed me.

Mama had sewn three dresses in the time that it had taken me to finish the pair of pants I had been working on for a week. She was right: I was not a skilled seamstress, but I always helped her any chance I got. With all of the action and fighting I enjoyed, time with Mama seemed to balance me.

She sat gracefully, her small frame barely making a dent in the cushioned chair. Her long, curly black hair cascaded over her shoulders, framing her tan skin and dark eyes that held an effortless warmth. She always wore a pastel-colored dress, the soft hues complementing her gentle nature perfectly. Every movement she made was fluid, delicate—so distinctly feminine that it almost felt like she belonged in a world untouched by hardship. But I knew better. I knew the strength behind those steady hands, the quiet resilience that had carried her through the years without magic. And despite everything, she still radiated elegance, as if nothing could steal the grace she carried in her very bones.

Though with the warmness and love she had always given me, I felt immense guilt when I looked at her. Her steady hands with a needle were the same that once summoned fire with a whisper and a flick of her wrist. A witch without magic— because of me. Because of us.

Mama hesitated for a moment, her fingers trembling slightly before she steadied herself. "I have something for you," she said as she walked to the trunk she kept under the window of her sewing room.

She pulled out a new pair of pants, just like the ones Adar wore while we trained yesterday: black with some sort of holster on the right thigh, except there was one thing different about them.

They were exceptionally smaller than anything my twin could fit in.

I jumped up as excitement rushed through me, my heart pounding with gratitude and disbelief. Pants were a rare gift for me—something practical, something freeing. But I could only wear them at home, and the few pairs I owned were threadbare and patched beyond recognition. But these . . . these were new, untouched by wear, and tailored just for me.

"Oh thank you, Mama!" I wrapped her in my arms.

"You should wear them when you are out at night," she said softly, her voice steady but tinged with an edge of unease.

As I pulled away, I noticed the way her fingers lingered on my shoulders, as if reluctant to let me go. Her gaze was heavy, filled with a mixture of pride and fear that made my chest tighten.

"What?" I asked, unsure if I had misheard or if this was some kind of test.

"Winnie, I know better than to try and stop you. Even if part of you is like me—content to stay close to home—you're your father's daughter, too." Her lips twitched into a bittersweet smile. "You're just like him. You'd walk into fire if it meant proving yourself. And nothing I say could stop you from doing what you want."

I stared at her, my throat tightening. "Mama—" My voice was barely above a whisper, guilt pressing against my ribs. "I'm sorry for how I told you everything. I shouldn't have said it out of anger."

Mama's expression softened, and she reached up, brushing a strand of hair from my face. "I'm not mad, Winnie. I needed to know. I just wish your father hadn't kept it from me."

I swallowed hard and nodded, guilt still pressing heavily

against my ribs.

Her hand lifted to my shoulder, squeezing gently. "Just promise me you'll be careful. That you'll come back."

The weight of her words, of her quiet acceptance, settled over me. I nodded, unable to speak. Her dark eyes searched mine for a moment longer before she released me and turned back to her sewing.

The door creaked open, and Adar stood in the doorway, his wide frame filling the space. His smirk was cocky, as always, and he had a turkey leg dangling from one hand like it was some kind of trophy.

"Finished being useful for the day?" I teased, raising an eyebrow.

He took a slow bite, exaggerating the motion, before leaning lazily against the frame. "You're welcome, by the way. That barn didn't fix itself."

I rolled my eyes. "If you're here to gloat, you're wasting your time."

"Who said anything about gloating?" He gestured for me to follow, his smirk widening into a grin. "Come on. Time to see if all that sewing has dulled your reflexes."

I hesitated, glancing at the pile of mending beside me, but the challenge in his eyes was impossible to ignore. He knew exactly how to needle me, and I hated how easily it worked.

I glanced at Mama who gave me a small nod.

"Fine," I muttered, rising to my feet. "But don't cry when I beat you." I brushed loose threads from my new pants. If I was going to train, I was going to wear them. They were made for this.

Adar chuckled, already heading out the door. "Big words, little sister. Let's see if you can back them up."

"I am older than you!" I yelled at his retreating figure.

4

Chapter 4

Adar

"And how was that? Hope I wasn't too gentle that time." I stood over Bronwen, fighting back a smirk. Frustration shone in her eyes as she pushed herself off the dirt. Her bright green eyes—just like mine—almost seemed to glow under the late afternoon sun, burning with stubborn determination. Strands of dark, wavy hair clung to her sweat-dampened face, and streaks of dust smeared across her tan skin. She was small, but she never let that stop her, always making up for it with sheer force of will. That will, however, wouldn't save her in a real fight if she kept making the same mistakes. Her pride was stung, and I couldn't help but enjoy the small victory.

But beneath the satisfaction was the constant worry gnawing at me. She needed to learn. Not for my sake or Papa's, but for her own survival.

Yesterday, I held back, letting her think she was gaining ground. Today? She had pushed too far. She said I swung like a lady at court fanning herself—*soft and delicate*. She didn't realize how much she relied on my patience.

Her next swing came low and quick, the blade cutting through the air with a sharp whoosh. I turned my foot sharply, the ground shifting beneath my boot, and avoided her strike.

"Your eyes are giving you away," I said.

"What?" she snapped, her voice thick with irritation. She lunged again, her movements fast but imprecise. Our swords clashed in a harsh, ringing note that echoed through the yard, the vibration tingling up my arm. There was no strategy in her strike, just raw frustration.

"You're looking at your target spot before you swing. That'll get you gutted," I warned, my voice steady but firm.

Her scowl deepened. Bronwen's shoulders were rigid, her hands tightening around the hilt of her sword. Sweat beaded on her forehead, a testament to her effort, but it was clear she was pushing herself past her limit. This time, she missed completely. And again. Same outcome.

I shook my head. "You can't just look me in the eyes either."

Her hands tightened around the hilt, the tension in her shoulders making every swing more erratic. She was seething, her breaths coming faster.

"Then what the fuck am I supposed to do?" she spat, her voice rising with frustration. "Look at your feet? No. Look where I intend my sword to make contact? No! Shall I close my eyes? Is that what you want?"

She squeezed her eyes shut, jabbing the sword toward me in a reckless burst of anger. If I hadn't been paying attention, she would have skewered me then and there.

But that might have been her goal.

With one quick movement, I sidestepped, the dry earth crunching under my boots, and knocked the sword clean out of her hands. It clattered to the ground, the metallic sound cutting through the tense air. She froze, her fists clenched, her jaw tight, as she stared me down.

She didn't need to say it—her anger was written across every inch of her face. Without a word, she turned and stormed toward the house, her steps sharp and forceful. Dust kicked up in her wake, swirling in the golden light of late afternoon.

Her stubbornness would either get her killed or make her a queen.

And I'd gladly sacrifice myself if it meant she would be ruling a kingdom one day . . . unless she decided to kill me first.

I sighed, bending over to collect her sword. The polished blade felt cool against my palm, the weight a familiar comfort. I ran my thumb along its edge, testing its sharpness, before slipping it into the sheath and following her back toward the house.

As I walked, my thoughts lingered on the tension between us. Bronwen didn't see the bigger picture, not yet. She thought I was trying to control her, to shape her into something she didn't want to be. But that wasn't it at all. Every sparring session, every harsh word—it was for her. Because if she wasn't ready, the world wouldn't give her the time to learn.

Something was coming for her. I could feel it.

I tried to brush it off, to dismiss it as nothing but me being too protective over her. But when Papa's yells and Mama's screams filled our home after they found her on the steps, those worries became real.

And if something happened to her because I didn't push hard enough . . . I wouldn't forgive myself.

The house felt quieter when I stepped inside. The dim light filtering through the small windows cast long shadows across the creaking wooden floorboards. Bronwen had retreated to her room, and the faint sound of a drawer closing reached me as I walked down the narrow hall. She was at her vanity, her back to me.

Carefully dabbing something onto her cheeks, she was completely absorbed in her reflection. It was so . . . *Bronwen*. She could be covered in dirt, bruised from sparring, and still insist on perfecting every detail of her appearance.

Her vanity wasn't just pride—it was armor. I knew that. Bronwen always needed to control something, and if it couldn't be the chaos of our world, it would be herself.

"You're out of practice," I said, leaning casually against the doorframe.

She continued patting too much of that pink stuff onto her cheeks. Her brows furrowed with concentration, as if her appearance was the only thing that mattered in that moment.

"You're out of practice," I repeated, not moving from my spot.

Her only response was the sharp clink of the powder container slamming onto the table, the sound echoing against the walls.

She didn't look at me, but I knew she was seething—her back stiffened, her lips pressed tightly together.

"You haven't been here," she snapped, her voice hard and raw. "What did you expect? That I'd practice with a tree? Papa's too busy, and no man around here would ever give me the chance. You haven't been here, and I needed you."

Her words cut deeper than her blade ever could. I hadn't chosen to leave, but I couldn't deny that I had left her to face things alone. I wasn't prepared for that level of bitterness, but I pushed the sting aside, keeping my tone steady. "I wasn't

33

given a choice. You know that."

Her hands clenched into fists, her nails biting into her palms.

I pushed off from the doorframe and took a step into the room. "I have to do this. For Papa and for the—"

She whirled around to face me, her eyes blazing with a fire I hadn't seen in a while. "Do not say the coven."

I took a slow breath, trying to keep my composure instead of matching her with the anger I felt brewing inside of me. "They are our responsibility whether you accept it or not. You know that."

And I knew I couldn't protect her forever. But for now, I could prepare her. Even if it meant she resented me. Even if it cost me the relationship we once had.

***

The next day, after the tense silence had stretched thin between us—which our parents noticed immediately at supper—I found myself pacing the yard, waiting for her. Our practice area was nothing more than a patch of worn dirt surrounded by wild grass. The ground bore the scuffs of countless hours spent training, the marks of sparring etched into the earth like a testament to our struggles. A light breeze carried the scent of damp soil and the faint tang of iron from the swords. This wasn't a grand arena; it was our yard—a simple, rugged place shaped by Papa, Bronwen, and me. Several minutes had passed, and I was starting to wonder if I would have to face Papa to explain why the *light of his life* still couldn't land a proper strike.

She had the swiftness and the unnerving ability to kill in

a sword fight without giving it a second thought. It was impressive, but it unsettled me too.

I let out a sigh when the back door swung open, and Bronwen marched over to the practice area, sword in hand.

"You still want to do this?" I asked, raising an eyebrow.

She didn't answer but raised her sword in challenge.

I nodded, raising my own blade in readiness. "Alright, give me your best shot."

She came at me faster than I expected, her movements sharper than before. This time, she wasn't swinging wildly. Every strike was more focused, more controlled. I had to work to keep up with her pace.

"You've been holding back," I said between parries, blocking her thrusts as she continued her assault.

"I haven't been holding back. I'm just more annoyed now," she shot back.

I grinned, parrying another attack. "You're improving. But your footwork is still sloppy."

She huffed and swung again, but I saw it coming this time. I stepped to the side and knocked her blade out of alignment, making her fall to the ground.

"You need to flow with your movements, B. Footwork, precision, timing," I said as I offered a hand to help her up. My hand hovered for a moment, hesitating as I watched her expression. Pride flickered beneath the frustration in her eyes, a subtle reminder of how far she had come. But the weight of my responsibility loomed just as heavily.

Could I push her hard enough to prepare her without breaking that fire?

As she finally reached for my hand, I gripped hers firmly, pulling her up. "Like this." I showed her how to step fluidly, how to move with her sword instead of against it.

This time, she struck with more confidence, adjusting her stance as I'd taught her. Every move wasn't perfect, but it was far better than before. We sparred for a while longer, sweat dripping down our foreheads.

"You're not there yet, but you're getting closer," I said, breathless but pleased with the effort. Watching her now, I couldn't help but feel a swell of pride. She was determined, relentless even. I hoped she'd find the balance before the world demanded it from her. She nodded, wiping her brow.

"I'm not done yet," she muttered. "I'll never be done."

I smiled, watching her carefully. "Good. Never stop."

5

Chapter 5

Bronwen

I brushed through the gray mane of my horse, Shadow. There wasn't a tangle in his mane because I had been obsessively brushing it for the past hour. It was the only thing that seemed to calm me over the last few weeks.

Shadow snorted softly, shifting his weight, his muscles rippling under my touch. I buried my face in the curve of his neck, his coarse mane brushing against my cheek. He smelled of warmth and familiarity, a reminder of simpler days when the world outside hadn't felt so heavy.

"You keep me sane, don't you?" I whispered, my voice barely audible above the barn's quiet creaks and groans. Shadow flicked his ears back toward me as if he understood, his steady breathing matching the rhythm of my own.

The nightmares came every night, and though each one was different, they all ended the same way. I, well my soul in the body of someone else, was bitten and drained of blood by him every time. Every night, they became more vivid and the feelings, the fear I felt, the pain from the bite, the feeling of dying all grew stronger. I felt the person's panic, their need to get back to their family and every time I woke up, I felt like I had lost someone I knew. They were real people. They weren't made up scenarios that the mark had created. They were his victims. And I was going to experience dying through every one of them. Gods I'd hoped there weren't too many, though the hope I had was slim.

Shadow jumped as if he felt the panic run through me as I recalled all of those nightmares. I ran my hand down his black back. His gentle snort broke the quiet, and I couldn't help but smile faintly.

He was a wild horse we found when he was only a foal. He was frail and weak, and if anyone else would've found him, they would've left him to die but Papa wouldn't do that. Papa brought him back to our barn, and I grew attached immediately. I hand fed him until he was back to health and even spent the first week sleeping in the barn with him. He grew so attached to me that I could let him out of the barn, and he would follow me everywhere without trying to run away—that's how he got his name. He was my shadow.

As I leaned into his warmth, I closed my eyes and let the steady rise and fall of his breaths pull me back from the edge. Shadow wasn't just my horse. He was my tether, my constant. And in moments like these, he was the only thing keeping the darkness at bay.

I reached for Shadow's saddle, lifting it with ease as I draped it over his broad back. He shifted under the weight, snorting softly, his hooves stamping against the barn floor with growing impatience.

"Easy there," I murmured, running a hand along his neck.

Shadow's ears flicked forward, and he pawed the ground as if urging me to hurry.

"You're as impatient as ever," I said with a faint smile, grabbing the bridle. He lowered his head obediently, letting me guide the bit into his mouth. As I fastened the straps, he tossed his head, his energy practically vibrating through him.

When I reached for the stirrup, Shadow let out an excited whinny, shaking his mane as though he could barely contain himself.

"All right, all right. Hold on," I chuckled, stepping toward his side, ready to mount. Just as I placed my hand on the saddle, the barn door creaked open.

Papa walked in carrying a stack of wood. Even though Adar had spent most of his time away from the Legion helping Papa fix the barn, there were still a few tasks to be done.

Papa nodded his head, bidding me to come help him.

"Just a minute, Shadow," I mumbled as I walked out of his stall.

I took a deep breath as I walked over to Papa. I had always been close with him, but I had done my best to avoid him these last few weeks. But one way I didn't want to spend time with him was working on the barn. Sword fighting? Yes. Riding horses? Yes. Building a barn? *Gods, no.*

He dropped the stack of wood before picking up one to fill the small area that was exposed to the outside. I grabbed the other end and held it to the wall of the barn. Did I want to do it? No. But now was not the time to argue when he was already upset with me.

"How many times?" he asked as he hammered another nail into the piece of wood on the wall.

"What?" I asked as he kept his gaze on the task at hand.

"How many times have you gone out at night?" Papa's question cut through the steady rhythm of his hammer. His tone was calm, but there was an undercurrent of something heavier—disappointment, maybe. Or worry.

I hesitated, my heart thudding in my chest. "I—I don't know."

He stopped, turning to face me, his green eyes boring into mine. "How many, Winnie?"

"Too many times to count," I whispered, the truth spilling out before I could stop it. The words felt heavy, like a confession, and I braced myself for his response. It had been nearly two years, and besides the times that I was too exhausted to get out of bed, I went every night. Sometimes for an hour or so and other times I stayed out until dawn.

"And how many did you find?"

That I knew the answer to.

"Twenty-seven," I said quietly, avoiding his gaze.

His eyes widened. I should've lied.

"And you pulled all of their magic before killing them?" he asked, his voice quieter now, but no less intense.

I nodded, my throat tightening as guilt and defiance warred within me.

His jaw tensed and he closed his eyes as he shook his head. "It is my fault. I've darkened your mind. For whatever reason you weren't given a connection to magic, it happened and the gods do not make mistakes. You are playing a dangerous game and it has to stop. The more magic you get, the more you want and it will eventually consume you."

"What has made you change your mind? None of this seemed to bother you on my birthdays."

"I've seen it in the stars."

It took everything in me not to scoff at what he had said. I had never believed in the signs in the stars. If the gods wanted us to know something, I feel like they would be a little more obvious than putting discreet messages in the stars.

He handed me the hammer, and I tapped a nail into my end of the wood. We stayed silent for a while.

"I've had visions of you covered in darkness, Winnie. And you'll take your brother with you."

I swallowed hard, adjusting my grip on the hammer before driving another nail into place. The words settled over me like a heavy cloak, but I kept my gaze on the wood, focusing on the task in front of me.

"So are you going to forbid me from hunting?" I finally asked as we moved on to the next piece of wood. I ran my fingers over the grain, buying myself a moment before picking up another nail.

Papa exhaled slowly, wiping sweat from his brow before positioning the board. "Do you only go for the magic?" he asked. "Or do you see the good you are doing by killing vampires?"

I handed the hammer to Papa and pressed my palms against the cool wood. His question lingered, heavy with expectation. My thoughts churned, the weight of his words pressing against the call I felt deep within me. I traced a knot in the wood, the rough texture grounding me. When I first started, the rush of power was all that mattered. The night had become my escape, the darkness a solace that shielded me from feeling powerless.

The hammer finally struck, breaking the moment of still-ness. The sharp sound brought me back, my fingers curling into fists against the wood. The weight of what I'd done—and what I might yet do—hung in the air between us.

Do I see the good I'm doing? Of course. Do I care that I am saving the naive humans? No. They should be smarter.

But I did enjoy the power I felt from killing vampires.

"I know you well enough to know you have been going with the goal of pleasure, and I will not support you with that. You have to change your mindset. Magic distracted you and nearly got you killed. If you can promise me that you are going with the purpose to kill vampires, and not for magic, then you can go."

"I will go to kill vampires."

I stepped back after the words left my mouth, unsure if I even believed them. The truth was murky, tangled in the rush of power I felt when siphoning magic and the faint satisfaction that came from the kill. I had wanted so badly for his approval, to prove I could be what he expected of me. But could I really change? The night whispered promises of strength, a freedom that felt impossible to deny. And yet, here he was, looking at me as if I could be more than what I had let myself become. His gaze lingered, heavy and hopeful, making the weight of my promise feel like another chain binding me to expectations I wasn't sure I could meet.

He let out a huff of frustration before grabbing me by both shoulders. "Winnie, promise me you will take when necessary but only take the amount you need. Nothing more."

I hesitated, the words sticking in my throat. Could I promise that? The magic had a pull that was impossible to ignore, a hunger that grew with every drop I siphoned. I wanted to tell him I could change, but deep down, I feared the truth.

I nodded, forcing myself to meet his gaze, even as the doubt clawed at me. "I promise."

He kissed my forehead before walking to an old wardrobe he kept in the far corner.

"Here." He handed me something wrapped in cloth.

The weight pressed against my palms as I unwrapped the fabric, revealing the stakes. Their rough, unpolished surface seemed to hum with purpose, as if they carried the burden of every life they would end. I ran my fingers along the grain of the wood, feeling the jagged edges where they had been carved. This wasn't just a weapon—it was a reminder of the responsibility I carried every time I stepped into the night. Papa's eyes lingered on me, heavy with unspoken words. "I know you like fire, but it doesn't hurt to have other options."

Shadow struck his stall door, letting out a loud huff. "Now go ride Shadow before he decides to break the other barn wall."

His words clung to me as I mounted Shadow. Visions of darkness, taking Adar with me—what did he mean? The questions lingered, pressing against my thoughts as I rode into the midday sun.

***

"And where were you when Papa had me hammering wood to a wall?" I narrowed my eyes as Adar walked into the kitchen. I'd grown used to my brother disappearing for hours and returning with messy hair and flushed skin, though the thought always made me nauseous.

"I thought the two of you could use some alone time to discuss some things." He laughed which did nothing but irritate me further. He walked to the counter and looked through the jars of various fruits and vegetables Mama had been working hard to put up the past few weeks to ready us for winter.

My anger quickly dissipated as I watched him fill his satchel with sweet bread and jams. I had tried to push back the thought that he would be leaving again, but it couldn't stop the inevitable. And today was that day.

"How long until I'll see you again?" I walked over to a small cabinet and grabbed the grape jam I had hidden from him.

Adar paused for a moment, his hand resting on the strap of his satchel as his eyes softened. For a moment, he seemed almost hesitant, his fingers brushing the worn leather of the strap as if weighing something unsaid. "I'm not sure," he said finally, his voice quieter than usual. "Several months if I had to guess."

A lump formed in my throat, but I pushed it down, forcing a smile as I handed him the jar. "Just . . . come back," I whispered, the words slipping out before I could stop them. His eyes met mine, and for a fleeting second, the teasing facade he always wore cracked. There was something there— regret, maybe, or worry. It made my chest tighten.

He rested a hand on my shoulder, his grip firm but warm. "Always," he said with a small, reassuring smile tugging at his lips. But the flicker of doubt in his gaze didn't fade.

Before he could step away, I pulled him into a hug, holding on tighter than I meant to. He stiffened for a moment before exhaling and wrapping his arms around me. Neither of us spoke, the weight of his departure settling between us in the silence. Finally, he pulled back, his hands lingering on my shoulders for a second longer.

It lingered until he turned and walked toward the door. The sound of his boots on the wooden floor echoed in the silence, and for a long moment after he was gone, I stood there, staring at the empty space where he'd been, wondering what he wasn't telling me.

6

Chapter 6

Bronwen

He bit me, taking enough blood to leave me disoriented before disappearing into the night. I clasped my hand over my neck and looked around for anything familiar so I could find my way back home. The willow tree—the tree I played under as a boy and brought my wife to when I asked for her hand in marriage. It was only a hundred or so yards from home. I headed that way but had to grab on to trees to keep myself from falling over.

My vision started to blur when a sinister laugh rang through my head, low and guttural, as if it were crawling up my spine. The sound was close—too close—sending a shudder down my back. It held a cruel edge, sharp and taunting, the kind of laugh that reveled in fear. My breath hitched as I spun around, my heart hammering against my ribs, but there was nothing there—only darkness stretching endlessly around me. I started to move again, trying to make my way home, to my wife who begged me not to search for the cow that went missing right before sunset. I hadn't believed anything would happen. There hadn't been any vampire incidents in months, and I thought I would be okay.

I made it through the trees to see my wife standing in the yard. She smiled with relief when she saw me before her smile disappeared and her eyes widened.

Snap! A sharp, unbearable pain tore through my thigh as something struck the back of my leg with brutal force. I hit the ground hard, my vision tilting as a strangled cry ripped from my throat. A sickening crunch followed as the bone was forced through the front of my skin. My pulse pounded in my ears, drowning out everything else as waves of dizziness crashed over me.

"Go inside!" I screamed at my wife before a blur ran in front of me. Then, he was standing with his hands on my wife's neck. "No!"

The vampire sank his teeth into my wife's neck, and I watched as the color drained from her skin. He let go, and she fell to the ground in a lifeless pile.

I turned my body around by gripping the ground and pulling myself away. Between the blood loss and the tears, I could barely see what was in front of me. The ground beneath my palms felt slick with blood, my own warmth pooling around me.

I stopped, my breath hitching as realization crashed over me. The world blurred at the edges, dark spots creeping into my vision, but the sight before me was unmistakable. Black boots. Polished and still, standing just inches from my face. My heart pounded in my chest, a dull, frantic rhythm against the numbing ache spreading through my body.

He crouched down and grabbed me by the chin forcing me to look at him. A bloody smile was on his face as he assessed me with wide eyes. "She was a sweet little thing."

I spit in his face, and it only angered him more.

He wiped his face with his fingers, dragging them across his lips. "Here. Have a taste," he murmured.

While he kept his grip on my chin, he forced my lips open, his bloody fingers prying past my clenched teeth. The metallic tang of blood flooded my mouth, thick and warm, coating my tongue in something sickly and bitter. The taste clung to my throat like iron and salt, making my stomach churn. I gagged, trying to twist away, but his grip was unrelenting.

"Please," I gasped, my voice barely above a whisper. "Let this be over."

"Oh, you are going to beg me now? But we were having so much fun."

I swallowed hard, my throat raw. "Please."

His eyes darkened, the amusement in them vanishing as his grip on me tightened. I felt the slow press of his breath against my skin, a cruel moment of anticipation before his fangs scraped over the tender flesh of my neck. The pressure built, the inevitable bite hanging between us like a drawn-out promise of pain. My pulse hammered wildly, my body screaming for escape even as I was held immobile in his grasp. Then, finally, he sank his teeth into me. The pain was immediate and searing, a cold emptiness spreading from the wound as he pulled my blood into his mouth, draining away every last shred of warmth I had left.

I gasped for air as I jolted awake, my chest heaving as if I had been running for my life. My skin was damp with sweat, and my hands trembled as they gripped the thin blanket tangled around me. The room felt too small, too suffocating, the faint smell of wood smoke and lavender doing little to ground me. My heart pounded in my ears, drowning out the silence of the early morning.

That was nightmare number twenty-two.

Even though I knew it wasn't real, my throat ached as if I had been screaming. The memories of the nightmare clawed at my mind, refusing to fade, and I couldn't shake the feeling that I had truly been there. He had gotten more twisted with his kills, growing bored of the simple ways. This one wasn't completely unfamiliar, though. I had lived through it last night from the wife's point of view. So stupid, she was. Leaving the safety of her home for love. Though I may never know the reason, vampires do not go into homes.

Papa has our cottage spelled, not for fear of them entering at night, but more for the fear of them lurking outside. We have learned through the years that witch's blood has a distinct smell, and it seems to be more attractive to vampires. Good for hunting—bad for the unsuspecting.

Though still well before sunrise, I knew I wouldn't be able to go back to sleep. Once I was jerked awake and felt like I was coming back to life after dying, there was no way I would shut my eyes again.

I pushed myself out of bed and quietly crept down the hall, hoping not to wake up my parents.

"Oh you're awake already." Mama's chipper voice caused me to jump back and hit the wall. "I would love it if you would go to Market with us today."

I scrunched my nose but thankfully it was still dark enough in the hall that Mama couldn't see. I had forgotten what day it was and that the long trip ahead had Mama awake well before usual.

"I don't know. That is more of Adar's thing." I regretted saying his name as soon as it came out of my mouth. The lines that had gradually formed over recent years were more

49

pronounced from the candle's flames that she was carrying, showing her sadness that Adar wasn't here.

I bit the inside of my cheek, trying to talk myself out of saying the words I knew I would regret. "Actually, I would like to go with you today." Her eyes widened, and then the smile I loved to see spread across her face.

She came to me and placed her hand on my cheek. "It will be fun. A girl's day—well besides your father but I'm sure we will barely see him once we get to town."

As I walked back into Mama's sewing room to grab another stack of clothes to take to Market, I saw the pair of pants I had finished sewing the other day placed to the side. I grabbed them and set them on top of the various men's tunics, doublets, and pants before carrying them to the wagon.

Mama was checking over everything I had already brought out to ensure we had everything we needed. Even though I could make it to town in half an hour on horseback, pulling the wagon would take us much longer, so if we forgot something, we wouldn't be going back for it.

She turned to me as I placed the last stack next to her, immediately noticing the pair of pants I added and picked them up.

"What are you doing with these?" she asked, trying her best to hide the judgment that showed all over her face.

"I am taking them to sell," I said as if me bringing them to the wagon wasn't obvious enough.

"Winnie, I don't think—"

I cut her off. "I can sell them." I hadn't thought much about bringing them, but now that she said something, I saw it more as a challenge. I could sell them.

She nodded before closing the wagon door, careful to ensure the latch was in place, and heading to the front to sit next to Papa. I had considered riding with them, but the thought of being smashed on the small bench with the two of them for over an hour sounded terrible.

After they left, I went to the barn and readied Shadow for the trip. He was restless as I strapped the saddle to him, knowing it meant excitement was to come. At least he would have an eventful day of travel and finding new grass to eat.

Town was strict about what was allowed past the gates to keep the winding cobblestone streets in pristine condition. No horses and anything with wheels which left walking on foot and making several trips to the town square with everything you wanted to sell at Market from the gates. All of the streets led to the back where an even larger gate sat in front of the castle where the Joveryn King lived. I had grown to believe he was more of a fairy tale than an actual king. He stayed in his castle only giving orders to the Legion on how to execute things. And no one had ever seen him.

Though all paths led to the castle, I avoided that direction if I could. Because to the right of the large gate was where they persecuted the witches.

I had forgotten just how much I despised Market days. It didn't take but a few customers to remind me.

The first one, a rather large lady in the most atrociously patterned dress I had ever seen, didn't hide the fact that she was disappointed to see me in the place of my twin. I had no doubt that with his obsessive need to charm and please anyone, he would've told her that her dress was the prettiest thing he had ever seen. I, on the other hand, said nothing.

51

Though I had no doubt that my face said enough.

The second one, an older witch from our coven, practically screamed when my hand brushed across hers when we reached for the same cloak. I can assure you, Genevieve Drotini, the one who uses her magic to cloak herself and lure younger men into her bed before sending them back to their wives reeking of perfume, the little bit of magic running through your veins would do nothing for me.

And the third one, as if the first two weren't enough, was Lowen Reeves, a man my age that I had found myself kissing more times than I'd like to admit. Lowen was . . . uncomplicated, predictable even, and that was part of the problem. He was handsome, with his curly brown hair and deep blue eyes, and his easy smile made it far too simple to lose myself in fleeting moments of affection. But it was always just that—fleeting. For a time, his attention felt intoxicating, a distraction from the weight of everything else. Then it became suffocating, a reminder of the kind of life I wasn't ready to live. I'd kiss him, let him touch me, and when his gaze started to hold too much hope, I'd push him away and ignore him for months. But no matter how many walls I built, Lowen always found his way back to me, like a persistent echo of something I wasn't sure I could escape or embrace.

"What did your mother have to promise you for you to come to Market?" He smiled his perfect smile, the one that made a few young girls who stood close by giggle, and I had to force myself to smile back.

"Adar left for camp yesterday and her sulking did nothing but damper my mood. One day of helping her at Market seemed like the best way to bring her spirits up."

His eyes drifted down my body, but before he could ask if

he could walk me home after Market, I quickly turned and grabbed the pair of pants I had sewn.

"Here." I shoved them into his hands. "I made these for you." A small lie, but if anyone was going to buy the poor excuse of pants that I made, Lowen would.

"You made these for me?" His face lit up at the thought that I was thinking of him when I had been sure to avoid him for the past few months.

I placed my hand in front of him. "That will be ten coins."

That should fix it.

He looked at me for a moment as if he was waiting for me to say I was joking, but I stood still and kept my hand extended. He reached into his pocket and grabbed a handful of coins, but before he could count out ten, I grabbed what I could and thanked him.

Another customer came—my mother's stitching was always a popular item, but Lowen stood by and waited for me to finish with the customer.

With my first attempt clearly ineffective, I decided to try one more thing. "Do you think you could find me some of those sweet chocolates you got me for my birthday?"

"Oh, I don't know. They are brought in on the ships during summer and usually sold only in the southern coastal villages."

I poked my lip out, knowing exactly what I was doing. "I just really liked those," I said as I reached over the table and grabbed his arm, "and I would be so happy if you got them for me again."

His eyes widened before he quickly ran his fingers through his hair, trying to hide his reaction. "Then I will do my best to find them." He leaned over and kissed my cheek before saying goodbye.

At least that will keep him away for a few days.

After Lowen, I had managed to scare off more customers than I sold to. Mainly because the familiar faces I saw, I didn't like but Mama didn't seem to care. She was just excited that I agreed to come.

Market was just as it was years ago when I came with Mama. The air was thick with the smell of roasted nuts, freshly baked bread, and a hint of leather from the cobblers' stalls. Merchants shouted their wares, their voices weaving together into a chaotic symphony that made my head ache. Children darted between booths, their laughter mixing with the sharp clang of a blacksmith hammering metal in the distance. Every cobblestone seemed to hum with life, the town square pulsing like a living, breathing thing.

Until a face caught my attention and I completely stopped breathing.

Only a few feet away was the face that crept into my dreams and turned them into nightmares. Only now, his eyes were brown, with no trace of the red that once burned in them. His short, icy blonde hair was neatly combed, though a few strands had fallen out of place, making him look unsettlingly normal. His sharp jawline was more pronounced in the daylight, giving him an air of refinement. His clothes were simple but well-fitted—a plain cotton shirt with the sleeves rolled up, tucked into dark trousers that looked worn but sturdy. His skin . . . it had more color, more life in it than the image engraved in my mind.

He looked . . . *human*.

He looked nothing like the monster in my nightmares, yet the way he carried himself, the subtle control in his movements, sent a chill down my spine.

I had to be hallucinating. Was he somehow able to haunt my reality now, too? He stood at the booth selling beeswax candles, but never took his eyes off of me. When he realized I saw him, he nodded to the candle maker and made his way to me.

I shoved the green dresses to the bottom of the stack, quickly moving things around to ensure there wasn't any sign of them.

"Mama, I think I left the green dresses in the wagon, and Mary Simon just came by asking for one. Could you go get them?" I asked, trying to stay calm and hide the urgent need of getting her away from the booth as quickly as possible.

"Are you sure? It is a long walk, and I thought I saw you carrying them up here."

He was only a few feet away now.

"Please, Mama." This time, the shriek in my voice gave me away completely.

She looked at me concerned, but nodded. "Sure, Winnie," she said.

The air at Market, once bustling and alive, felt stifling now, thick with the weight of his presence. My chest tightened as he approached, his movements smooth as silk. The clamor of merchants and townsfolk blurred into a distant hum, as if the world had narrowed to just the space between us. My breath hitched, and I gripped the edge of the table so tightly my knuckles turned white.

He reached our table and ran his long, slender fingers over a few shirts, pausing on one as if considering it. He picked it up, turning it over in his hands. Then, with an almost careless flick of his wrist, he tossed it back onto the table, ruining the pile I had just folded.

Vampires couldn't walk in sunlight. It was a fact I had clung to, a rule that had kept me sane. But here he was, standing in the midday sun, his skin glowing with the kind of vitality that mocked everything I thought I knew. My pulse raced, every instinct screaming at me to run, but my legs felt rooted in place, frozen by the sheer impossibility of it all.

When his eyes met mine, the familiar flash of malevolence sparked in them, and I knew. This wasn't a hallucination or some cruel trick of my mind. It was him.

"Winnie, is it?" His voice slid through the chaos, smooth and sharp, cutting straight to me.

The sound of that name from his lips sent a shiver down my spine. My throat tightened, but I forced myself to speak. "Do not call me that," I snapped, my voice trembling despite my effort to keep it steady.

His smile widened, and he tilted his head, the motion eerily predatory. "Oh, you prefer green eyes? My apologies." The words dripped with mockery, each syllable like a taunt.

"What do you want?" I demanded, though my voice came out weaker than I intended.

He leaned forward, his hands braced on the table, his height towering over me.

"I've come to collect what is mine," he said, his gaze dropping to my neck that I had purposely covered with a choker I made out of fabric to match my dress. His mouth parted slightly, and I could see the hunger flickering in his eyes, barely restrained.

My hand flew to my neck, instinctively covering the spot where the mark was. "I am not yours," I hissed.

"Oh you're not, are you?" His chuckle was low, almost a purr, and it sent chills racing down my spine. "Tell me, have

I already crept into your dreams? Do you see my face the moment you close your eyes? Shall I add a name to the face you see? It's August, and believe me when I say it will only get worse from here."

"I could tell what you are," I whispered.

His eyes widened and he smiled once again. "Yes, and I could breathe one word and have you hung before nightfall. What is it? W-w-wi—"

"Stop," I said louder than I intended. I glanced around to ensure no one was looking our way.

He leaned forward. "Face it, *Winnie.*"

I gritted my teeth, digging my nails into the underside of the table, ignoring the pain as I scratched away, pushing splinters into my fingers.

"In no world will you be the one coming out of this alive," he said softly. "But I am going to have so much fun dragging this out."

A sliver of wood finally broke away, and I reached across the table and stabbed it into his hand.

He let out a sharp breath, but he didn't move.

My confidence that had seemed to be lost in the moment of seeing a vampire out in broad daylight ripped through me once again. I leaned in close, to the point I knew the smell of my blood would have him questioning whether he could keep up with the public appearance he had somehow created.

"I can't wait to watch you burn."

7

Chapter 7

August

"Again!" her father yelled.

She staggered, clutching her thigh where his wooden practice sword had landed a brutal blow. The sting already promised a bruise by morning. She rose to her feet, eyes burning with the need to prove herself, and this time, she blocked his swing, deflecting it just enough to come back with a quick jab to his ribs using a smaller piece of wood. It was shaped like a dagger—one I hadn't noticed before.

Her father let out a loud laugh, the sound booming with pride, before dropping his sword, picking her up, and spinning her around. His joy was palpable, his eyes shining with the satisfaction of seeing her strength.

"Are you ready for your gift?" he asked, setting her back down on her feet.

She nodded eagerly, her vibrant—almost glowing—green eyes practically shining with excitement.

Her father motioned to the men holding me at the edge of the woods, their chains woven with spells that bound my strength, reducing me to nothing more than a weak human. The spells crackled faintly against my skin, a buzzing, stinging sensation that made every movement feel like wading through thick, icy water. My limbs, once so capable and powerful, felt as though they were weighted with lead. Each attempt to move was met with resistance that seeped into my bones. I couldn't fight my way out; the magic had stripped me of everything that made me dangerous, leaving a hollow ache where my strength used to be.

The men dragged me toward her, and she could hardly contain the smile that stretched across her face, knowing exactly what was to come. But she didn't wait for them to bring me all the way. She ran to me, and her small, childlike hand found my shoulder.

The world seemed to stop. The air left my lungs, and what felt like acid burned through my veins, spreading with an agonizing slowness, as though fire had replaced my blood. It wasn't a sharp pain—it was molten, relentless, crawling through every nerve and igniting them one by one. My ears rang with the phantom sound of something tearing, like fabric being ripped apart, matching the rhythm of my own unraveling. It was as though she were siphoning the very essence of my existence, ripping every bit of my being from me. My mind screamed in agony, a piercing, endless wail, but not a single sound passed my lips.

Without warning, she raised a hand, her fingers curling around a small ball of fire. The heat that radiated from it was excruciating, and she brought it closer, closer until my skin began to blister.

Then, I felt every part of myself burn to ash.

I woke up covered in sweat, my skin flushed and burning as though I had truly been engulfed in flames. The nightmares were getting worse.

I had heard the stories of marked ones, how their dreams were plagued by the one who had marked them. The pain, the relentless torment, driving them closer to madness with each passing night. But I never heard of it happening the other way.

Luckily, I'd never truly felt sane, so there wasn't anything to take from me.

The dreams started a little over a week ago. The same nightmare, night after night, but each time, it was a new year. Her birthday became a twisted tradition—a dark gift she seemed to take pleasure in getting. Each year, her father was prouder, her skills sharper. Yet, every year, he made sure to be tougher on her.

It was the same every year. She would spar with her father, she would eventually beat him—I'm still unsure as to if she truly beat him or he finally let her win every time—and he would give her his birthday gift to her. A vampire.

Except now, I was the fucking vampire.

Burned alive every night.

I'd just hoped that once we made it through her birthdays, the dreams would end. Though I was sure it wasn't that simple.

I had decided the moment I left her in the woods that I was going to drag this out. She was different. A witch, except she managed to suck the life out of me—literally. I thought it would be a fun way to pass the time, terrorizing her, driving her insane, letting her attempt to kill me. But each night, I found myself hesitating, caught between my hunger and something deeper. The thought of her growing stronger, of meeting me as an equal, both thrilled and unnerved me.

I couldn't ignore the hunger, though. It gnawed at me constantly, a relentless pull that was as maddening as it was intoxicating. Her blood had become an obsession, a need that clouded every rational thought. I'd never craved anything like this before. She was in my veins now, whether I wanted her to be or not.

And yet, part of me held back. Part of me wanted to see how far she'd go, how much she'd fight, how strong she thought she was. The tension between my hunger and my curiosity was unbearable, and the line between torment and fascination grew thinner by the day. She was just as crazy as I was. She just didn't know it yet. And I was going to see just how far I could push her.

But these dreams had me questioning that decision.

I'd never gone out during the day. With hunting much easier at night, I usually slept while the sun was out. That was the plan for today until the smell of her blood—the only fucking thing I thought about—filled my lungs. I had searched for that smell since the night I first tasted it, but every night I fell short. I had thought she'd died from the injuries she'd sustained that night—because I couldn't smell her anywhere for miles into the woods—until the dreams started.

If she was dead, she wouldn't have been marked and that connection wouldn't have formed for her bloody memories to force themselves into my dreams.

But no matter how far I searched, I couldn't find her, making the need only grow stronger. Until this morning. On Market day. So fucking *close* to my home that I could practically taste her in the air.

I was glad it happened this way, though. If we were alone when I found her after weeks of searching, I didn't think I could've controlled myself. But seeing how easily she went from the initial shock to stabbing me in the hand in front of dozens of people just reassured me that I was going to drag it out.

I rose from the bed and poured water into the washbowl before splashing my face as I was still drenched from sweat.

I looked into the mirror to see red eyes staring back at me. I closed my eyes and with nothing more than a thought, I brought them to brown. A simple trick I had always been able to do, though I never had a choice in the color. They were familiar eyes that I hadn't seen in over a century.

I rubbed the bridge of my nose trying my best to get the smell of her blood out of my mind, but I knew it would take a miracle to do so.

I had to feed before I went looking for her again tonight if I wanted any chance of being able to restrain myself. I just hoped she wouldn't hide herself like she had somehow been able to do these last few weeks.

I put a shirt on and headed out of the door to see what options I had in town tonight. As I stepped into the sunlight, I squinted as my eyes adjusted to the brightness. A sharp pain raced through my head before it disappeared just as fast as it came. I'd take that over being forced into the darkness any day.

Market was over, and the sun was quickly going down, leaving the number of people outside growing scarcer by the minute. I walked a while, examining my options. A gentleman with hair that was beginning to gray: no. Another man who was pushing a cart of vegetables: no, he seemed busy at the moment. An older woman with a rather distinct odor to her: *fuck*, no.

I continued my walk, dipping around a corner as I made my way closer to the district of the much more . . . giving type of people until I saw a young woman with dark hair who had seen me before I saw her. She stood there twirling her hair, a playful yet nervous smile on her lips as she waited for me.

Perfect.

"Looking for something?" she asked, her voice soft but laced with something like amusement, as if she knew exactly what to do to get what she wanted.

I gave her a slow, deliberate once-over, drinking in the sight of her. She had no idea what she was walking into, but the smell of her blood . . . It was almost too much to ignore.

"Perhaps," I said, my voice darker than I intended. "But I think I've found exactly what I need."

Her gaze flickered, something shifting in her expression— nervousness, curiosity, fear? I couldn't tell, but it didn't matter. She was mine now.

I stepped closer, allowing my presence to close the space between us. She didn't flinch, not even when I reached for her arm, pulling her just a bit closer. I could feel her pulse beating beneath the soft skin of her wrist, pounding in my ears, the rhythm of it driving me mad.

"I've been hunting for someone like you," I said softly, brushing a lock of hair from her face. She didn't pull away, and that only made the hunger grow.

I took a step back, pulling her with me until we were in the deep shadows of an alley from the rapidly lowering sun.

She smiled then, a tiny, unsure curl of her lips. "What makes me so special?"

I pushed her against the brick wall, a startled gasp escaped her lips.

I brought my lips close to hers. "You're not," I whispered, my voice low and dark. "But you're here."

Her eyes flickered, and for a heartbeat, I thought she might have realized what was coming. But she was too late.

With a speed that would have terrified her had she been any more aware, I pressed against her, my fangs scraping her neck as I leaned in.

She gasped, and for a brief second, her hands flew up to push against my chest. But her attempt was futile. I sunk my teeth into the soft flesh of her throat, and the moment her blood hit my tongue, I nearly lost control. It was sweet, better than anything I've come across in days, but it wasn't *her*.

This wasn't the girl from my dreams. This wasn't the one I marked. This was nothing more than a substitute.

Her blood rushed over me, warm and rich, a fleeting moment of pleasure. But with each drop, I felt the edges of my sanity slip further away. My hunger grew stronger, but I pulled myself back. This wasn't the time to lose myself.

Not yet.

I drank slowly, drawing out the pleasure of her life slipping away, though I stopped just before her legs gave out. I pulled away, my fangs retracting, leaving bloody marks on her neck. She stood there, her legs trembling, the blood still dripping down her skin, but she wasn't dead.

"Go," I murmured, barely above a whisper. "Run."

Her eyes, wide and filled with fear, met mine as she staggered back, almost tripping over her feet. Just as she turned to make her escape, I slammed her back into the wall and wiped a tear from her cheek.

I placed a soft kiss on her forehead, leaving her blood from my lips in its place. "If only it could be that simple."

I sunk my teeth in her once again and drank deeply. Her breath came in shallow gasps, a desperate, broken rhythm.

Her legs trembled beneath her, but she couldn't escape me now. I could feel her life slipping away, the pulse in her neck growing weaker with each swallow.

I drank until she was still, until her body went cold in my arms and the warmth of her blood no longer flowed.

When I finally released her, she crumpled to the ground, a lifeless heap.

I tilted my head up and looked at the stars that had begun to shine in the sky, unable to stop myself from smiling.

"Here I come, *Winnie.*"

***

The forest was quiet, as if even the nocturnal creatures had decided to stay hidden tonight. I expected her to come here, and the soft crunch of leaves under a hesitant step confirmed it.

I turned toward the sound, my eyes scanning the darkness until they landed on a faint shadow moving between the trees. She was creeping through the clearing where we first met, her movements cautious. My lips curled into a smile. She came. Brave or foolish, I wasn't sure which.

I inhaled deeply, but her scent wasn't there. The air was clean of her, free of the intoxicating pull I'd come to expect. My brow furrowed until I noticed the cloak she had pulled tight around her. Of course.

Witches and their spell-laden cloaks. I'd come across them before—enchanted to mask their wearers, granting them an edge over creatures like me. Clever, but not clever enough.

She paused near the center of the clearing, her head tilted slightly as though listening for something. I watched her, hidden in the shadows, as she slowly turned in a circle, scanning the darkness for any sign of me.

She thought she was alone. The thought made me grin.

I moved silently, circling her as she moved through the clearing. Her breathing was steady, but I could hear the faint hitch in it every few moments, betraying her nerves. She was on edge, every muscle in her body taut, like a bowstring ready to snap.

She stopped abruptly, her body tense as she stood perfectly still. Her frustration was obvious in the sharp way she exhaled, her fists clenching at her sides. She muttered something under her breath, the words too faint to catch, but her rigid posture and the quick shake of her head told me everything I needed to know.

I leaned against a tree, watching her with quiet amusement. This game of cat and mouse was more entertaining than I'd anticipated. She had no idea how close I was, how easily I could close the distance between us. But where was the fun in ending it now?

Her cloak shifted slightly as she moved again, the faintest glimmer of light catching on its fabric. She adjusted the hood, pulling it tighter, and the brief motion gave me a glimpse of her face. Her green eyes burned with frustration, her jaw clenched tight. Even in the dim light, I could see the fire in her expression, the determination that made her so different from anyone else I'd ever hunted.

I stayed where I was, letting the moment stretch. The longer she stayed out here, the more frustrated she'd become. And the more frustrated she was, the more mistakes she'd make. It was only a matter of time before she slipped.

For now, I was content to watch. To see how long it would

take her to realize she was the one being hunted.

8

Chapter 8

Bronwen

With Adar back with the Legion, I could leave during the night without anyone knowing. Not that I was sure he'd have tried to stop me if he were here.

But now that I had seen him—August—and he'd seen my mother, knew my name, or at least the pet name my parents have always called me, I had to end this. End him. Before something worse happened.

Too bad it had been days since I saw him at Market. Days of restless searching and finding nothing. Physically, he remained absent, but every time I closed my eyes, there he was. His voice played tricks on me, his words filled with riddles that always left me utterly confused.

Every night before I attempted to sleep, I spent hours scouring the surrounding woods, hoping to find him. The night after Market, I returned to the place where he had marked me. Nothing. The next, I wandered toward town. Still nothing. Last night, I ventured farther than ever, ending up at a quiet pond under a canopy of stars. Still no sign of him. Just disappointment. He had bested me again, haunting my nights as I returned home, exhausted and defeated.

But tonight would be different. *It had to be.*

Every step felt heavier than the last, the weight of sleepless nights and constant failure pressing down on me. I hated him—his smugness, his power—but most of all, I hated the fear he had carved into me. I wasn't going to let it win. Not tonight.

I waited until my parents were fast asleep, their breathing soft and steady through the walls of our home. After dressing in my leathers, I strapped a wooden stake to my thigh—one of the few Papa had trusted me with—and a small knife to my forearm. I avoided the sword. My brother would have demanded I carry it, but it felt too clumsy for this kind of hunt.

Finally, I tied my spelled cloak around my shoulders. The enchantment hummed faintly against my skin, a subtle reminder of the magic woven into its threads. It wasn't as sturdy as Papa's, but it carried my own touch. A regular cloak wouldn't suffice; I learned that lesson quickly. A witch's blood was potent, an irresistible lure for vampires. If I wanted to hunt, I had to mask my scent. The spell was born of necessity, a small act of defiance against my own vulnerability. The magic felt like a part of me now, born from desperation and determination alike.

Fortunately, my abilities with magic made the process easy. I hadn't been taught the specific spells for cloaking, but it didn't matter. A touch of stolen magic and the right intention, and the enchantment was mine.

I wanted to spell my cloak to hide my scent, so I did.

With the hood pulled snug over my head and my hair tucked

away, I slipped out of the window and into the cool night air.

Tonight, I headed toward town again, though I stayed off the main path, weaving between trees until I found a small clearing with good cover. My heart pounded as I crouched low, knife in hand.

The plan was simple: bait him.

I pricked my finger with the knife, wincing as a bead of blood swelled and dripped onto the ground. I quickly tucked my hand beneath my cloak to hide the scent and moved several feet away before pressing my back against a large oak.

The minutes stretched long, the stillness of the forest sharpening every sound. My pulse thundered in my ears, but I held my breath, scanning the darkness for any sign of movement.

The night went on, leaving me disappointed and ready to accept another night of defeat, until the crunch of leaves shattered the silence.

I turned just in time to see August crouched over the spot where my blood had fallen. The moonlight turned his pale, icy blonde hair into a silver halo, a cruel contrast to the darkness in his crimson eyes. Just as I had expected, gone was the human man from Market and in his place was the vampire that had consumed my thoughts. He brushed his fingers against the ground before lifting them to his lips.

I pressed my back tighter against the tree, willing my breath to still, but my heart thundered louder with every passing second. He inhaled deeply, his chest rising as though he were savoring a long-forgotten memory. The silence of the forest seemed to press in around us, broken only by the low, guttural hum that escaped his throat—a sound that sent chills rippling down my spine.

His lips curled into a slow, satisfied smirk. "Oh, we're playing games now, are we, Winnie?" His voice cut through the quiet, low and mocking, each word a taunt that seemed to echo in the stillness.

I fought to steady my breathing as his head snapped up, his movements precise and unnervingly sharp. His crimson eyes swept the clearing, unseeing yet searching. He tilted his head slightly, as if listening to the rhythm of the forest itself, and my pulse quickened further, betraying me.

The corner of his mouth twitched. "You may have masked your scent," he said, his tone light and almost playful, "but you didn't quiet the sound of your heart.

Before I could react, he was on me. His speed was inhuman, a blur of movement too quick to track. One moment, I was hidden in the shadows; the next, his iron grip pinned my wrists above my head with a precision that spoke of years spent honing his hunt. His other hand clamped over my mouth, silencing the scream that tore from my throat.

Without a free hand, he brought his mouth down, gripping the tie of my cloak between his teeth and pulling it loose. My cloak shifted and exposed my body to him.

The scent of my blood hit him like a storm, a tide that drowned every hint of composure. His head snapped back, his chest rising sharply as he inhaled. His red eyes burned brighter, flickering with a hunger so visceral it felt like the air around us thickened with his need.

Dark veins webbed under his eyes, then receded, only to return again, deeper and more pronounced.

Frantic. He was frantic. My blood was driving him mad.

He shuddered violently, every muscle in his body coiled like a predator holding itself back from a fatal strike.

When he finally stilled, his lips quirked into a dangerous smile. "A witch without her mouth is like a carriage without its horse," he whispered, his voice a low, mocking purr against my ear. His breath was cool, sending a shiver down my spine. "Useless."

I squirmed against his hold, but his grip only tightened, his strength unyielding.

I let out a scream, but it was muffled by his hand. If he squeezed any harder, he would snap my wrists.

"And you without your hands?" His voice dropped into a dark, feral growl as he dragged his nose along my neck, savoring every tremble that coursed through me. His breath was hot and unnervingly steady. "Defenseless."

His teeth scraped against my skin, and I thrashed harder. Desperation gave me clarity. My mind raced as I adjusted my stance, aiming with precision. I slammed my knee upward with every ounce of force I could muster, targeting the vulnerable spot I knew would cripple him, at least for a moment.

His growl transformed into a strangled gasp. His body folded as he crumpled to the ground, his hands instinctively clutching the point of impact. The brief sound of pain he made was both satisfying and chilling.

I lunged for him, ready to grab his magic, my movements fueled by the adrenaline surging through me. But just as my hands grabbed his shoulders, Papa's warnings echoed in my mind.

I've had visions of you covered in darkness, Winnie. And you'll take your brother with you.

For the briefest moment, I hesitated.

And that was all he needed.

With a flash of movement, August vanished into the shadows, leaving me breathless, shaken, and alone. My hands trembled as I pressed them against the rough bark of the tree, my mind racing to steady itself against the chaos he left behind.

I wanted to collapse, to let the fear finally overwhelm me, but I couldn't. Not now. Not when he was still out there. Each shaky breath I drew only strengthened my resolve. He was faster, stronger, more calculated than I had imagined, but he wasn't invincible.

This wasn't over. Not by a long shot.

I straightened, the cool night air chilling the sweat on my skin. The hunt would continue, and next time, I wouldn't let him escape. Fear still lingered in my chest, but it was a fire now, feeding the determination that coursed through me.

I would find him again. And next time, I would end it.

9

Chapter 9

Bronwen

After I made it back home last night, I fell asleep only to be awoken from a nightmare not long after. I paced the halls of our home until the sun began peeking through the trees. Every muscle in my body felt heavier with each step, but I forced myself forward, refusing to let anyone see the cracks forming beneath my mask. This had been my routine for days now— endless pacing and fractured sleep, the nightmares coming quicker and cutting deeper into the hours meant for rest. I was lucky to get a few hours of sleep each night, but even those left me more exhausted than before.

The circles under my eyes had darkened, swollen and heavy, evidence of sleepless nights that weighed on my body like a burden. Wrinkles I hadn't noticed before framed them, aging me beyond my years. If the nightmares didn't drive me mad, having to look at myself might. I painted my face with makeup, applying more layers than I ever had before.

But today, *today* may have been the worst day of my entire

life. It wasn't the day I nearly died when August marked me. Nor was it the day Adar gashed my arm open while we were sparring. As I sat at my dressing table and ran my brush through my hair, a clump of my black hair came with it. My long, luscious *beautiful* black hair.

I swore under my breath, tying my remaining hair back into a braid before heading to my wardrobe. As I reached up to open the door, the bruises on my wrists caught my eye: purple imprints in the shape of fingerprints. I clenched my fists.

"Fuck!" I hissed, rummaging through my dresses to find something that would cover the marks.

"Winnie!" Mama called. "Is everything okay?"

"Yes, sorry! I, um—I hit my toe on the bed corner."

"Well, ladies do not use such words."

"*Ladies do not use such words*," I muttered under my breath. "Sorry, Mama!"

I pulled out a deep blue dress. Its sleeves extended over my hands, with small loops to hook over my middle fingers. It wasn't a favorite, but it was my only option to keep my parents from noticing the bruises.

I tightened the corset a little more than usual, hoping my enhanced figure would distract any lingering eyes from my face, and cut a small piece of fabric from the bottom layer of my dress to tie around my neck.

Gods, what kind of fashion statement did it look like I was making?

Papa sat at the table shuffling through a stack of papers, and Mama leaned down to kiss his cheek. Breakfast was long gone; I'd spent the morning in front of the mirror, and now my stomach growled at the lack of food. I sifted through the fresh fruit, the selection bare as the season was coming to an end, and settled on a pear.

As I took a bite, Papa cleared his throat, catching my attention. "I have to go to Bodaira. Would you like to come with me?"

I whipped my head around, thinking my brother must have been home for him to ask that question.

Papa rolled his eyes when I looked back at him. "I'm leaving in half an hour if you want to come."

I bit into the pear again, trying my best to do anything to hold my tongue.

"You can always stay and join me for tea at the Reeves," Mama offered as she wiped down the chopping block. "Lydia and I have so much to discuss."

Go with Papa to listen to the coven's latest problems or sit through tea while Lydia Reeves and Mama talk about how good it would be for me to settle down and marry Lowen?

I'll take the witches.

***

The road to Bodaira stretched ahead, its monotony broken only by the occasional rustle of leaves. Shadow's unease mirrored my own, his ears flicking toward the shadows as if sensing a presence neither of us could see. His tension brought August to mind—a thought I'd rather avoid today.

The memory of August's hand clamped over my mouth crept in, his fear of me evident. In the moment, I thought it was to silence my screams, but it was the middle of the night. If someone heard, they wouldn't have left their home to help. He covered my mouth to prevent me from speaking a spell. He hadn't realized I couldn't practice magic without a source, but why would he? Unless he'd heard about us from other witches—unlikely, given vampires and witches didn't mingle—he couldn't know. That ignorance was an advantage. I just needed another way to get to him.

I could pull magic from a witch today, but that would bring down Papa's wrath. Another vampire might suffice, but it could take days to find one, giving August time to strike first. Market tomorrow might present an opportunity. If he showed up, I could siphon just enough to prepare for a confrontation. But that plan relied on chance—a flimsy hope at best.

"Did you go out last night?" Papa's voice broke through my thoughts.

I nodded.

"Well?"

Shadow's head flicked to the side, and I gave him a quick pat to calm him.

"Well, what?" I asked.

"Did you find one?"

The last thing I wanted was to tell Papa about August.

"No," I lied.

He cursed under his breath.

"Why are you so worried?"

"Because it is our duty to protect humans."

I looked ahead and tried to bring my focus to something else.

The trees. Pine. Pine. Pine. A small oak. Pine.

Our duty. Gods!

"You risk yourself to protect the same people who would hang us. Why?" I snapped. "We can protect ourselves, and if they kill a few hate-filled souls, it's less for us to deal with."

Papa glanced around, as if someone might overhear us,

though we hadn't seen anyone this entire time.

"Do you remember the story of how vampires were created?" he asked, his voice carrying the weight of a lesson I had heard countless times but never quite understood fully. There was something different in his tone now, something heavier, as though the story wasn't just a tale but a confession.

I nodded. "A witch wanted to become immortal, so she cast a spell that granted her immortality but at the price of bloodlust."

He shook his head. "There are parts of that story no longer taught."

"What parts?"

"She was our ancestor," Papa continued, his voice quieter now, as if the weight of the truth made the words heavier. "Her father, the leader of the coven, was incredibly powerful. The kind of power our bloodline had then was something we could never fathom now. He had two children. Twins. A boy and a girl. Just like you and Adar. But the father didn't plan on them leading the coven together. He was giving the coven to his son. The daughter grew to hate her family for that, so she wanted a way to become more powerful than them to prove she was the better choice. She knew what she wanted to do, but her gifts weren't strong enough to complete the spell alone. So she went to Alentara."

I frowned, listening closely. "But you can't travel through the Sea of Mavrola," I countered, my voice hesitant.

"The Sea of Mavrola used to be a river."

I whipped my head to him. The motion caused Shadow to slightly jump. "What?"

"There was a bridge between the two kingdoms of Alentara and Joveryn, allowing anyone to travel between the kingdoms just as we do with the other human kingdoms. But with the power our coven possessed, faeries and creatures tended to stay in Alentara. Our ancestor went to Alentara and found a cunning human-like faerie to help her. He promised to help her in exchange for his own immortality. He knew how to do it, but he didn't have the magic to do it. And no one in Alentara would help him.

"The faerie came back to Joveryn with her, and they stood on the bridge while she completed the spell. She needed the magic in the nature in Alentara and wanted to bring it into Joveryn. Nature fought back. During the spell an explosion threw her and the faerie off of the bridge, our ancestor into Alentara and the faerie into Joveryn. The water between the two grew, pushing the kingdoms farther apart. Our ancestor became trapped in Alentara because the vicious sea would never let her come back. The spell created the first vampire through the faerie. With its immortality came the need for blood, and he created an army of vampires.

"So that is why I try to get rid of the vampires. Not for the humans, but to right the wrong our ancestor committed," Papa said, his gaze fixed on the horizon coming into view. "I believe this is why the gods have made you and your brother the way you are."

His words struck a nerve, and for a moment, I wasn't sure whether to feel honored or trapped. "As punishment?" I asked, the skepticism in my voice hard to mask.

"Not as punishment," he said, his tone softening. "As redemption. You and Adar are gifted more than the two of you realize. Your way with magic is exactly what is needed to finish this. To fix what was broken."

I stared at him, the enormity of his belief pressing down on me. This wasn't just a mission—it was a destiny, one I hadn't asked for. One I wasn't sure I wanted. "So we are supposed to kill every vampire?"

"No, we kill until we kill the first vampire. The one that started this is the one the gods want punished."

"That seems like an impossible task. How do we even know he is still in Joveryn? And how would we know if we killed him?"

"We'll know," he said firmly, his conviction unwavering. "When the gods grant us the power we were meant to have, we'll know we've succeeded. And when we have our power, we will stop the persecution."

Papa's words settled like stones in my chest, each one heavier than the last. It wasn't just a story of a witch's wrongdoing; it was the legacy of our family, a burden passed down through generations. Was that why Papa was so insistent? Why he risked everything for a mission that seemed impossible? To right a wrong we hadn't committed but were still bound to?

The weight of his words lingered, pressing heavily against my thoughts, but the briny air filling my lungs offered a sharp reminder of where we were. Whatever this legacy meant, whatever destiny Papa believed in, it would have to wait until later.

My stomach churned as the familiar discomfort of Bodaira settled in. The people here had always been nasty to me during the few visits I'd made with Papa. But the older I'd gotten, the less it bothered me. One day, I would be above them. One day, they would have to submit to me, whether they liked it or not.

We walked onto the wooden deck that was built over the rocks where land met the wild waters of the Sea of Mavrola until we reached a small apothecary. A bell overhead rang as Papa opened the door, gesturing me inside. As my eyes adjusted to the dimly lit room, the eyes that met mine were nothing but unwelcoming. I had never seen the woman before, but witches always seemed to know me when they saw my green eyes.

She quickly changed her expression when Papa walked in. "*Father*, I am so glad you came. Though I didn't realize you would bring someone with you."

That reminder of Papa's title as coven leader gave me the best idea I'd had in a long time.

"Well, this is my daughter. She is getting older, and she needs to learn these things."

I walked to the counter that stood between me and the woman before I extended my hand to her. A quiet gasp escaped her lips as her magic brushed faintly against my skin, like a whisper begging to be heard.

"I am Bronwen, one of the siphoners," I said, my tone snappy. I kept my hand out where she looked at it like it held the plague. "But you can call me your future *Mother*."

The word brought her widened eyes back to mine, fear pouring from her face, but she placed her hand in mine. I smiled as I gripped tightly and shook, every nerve in my body alive with the hum of her magic under my palm. The temptation clawed at me, a siren's call urging me to take it, to feel its power coursing through me. But I held back, forcing myself to focus on the fear in her eyes instead of the energy at my fingertips.

Papa came to my side and placed his hand on the small of my back, his touch grounding me. It was a silent instruction, a reminder that this wasn't the time to lose control. I released her hand, letting the magic slip away, leaving only the echo of what I could have taken. I gave the woman a smile—though my eyes may have told her a different story—before I turned to look at the various bottles of liquid that were shelved across the wall.

"I came as soon as I got your letter. You said it was urgent. What is it?" Papa said low. Though we were the only ones in the room, he was always worried someone else could be listening.

"The vampires. They seem to be," the woman paused as if she was choosing her next word carefully, "evolving."

"Evolving how?"

The woman tapped her finger on the counter. "A few nights ago, a few witches that were assigned to hunt were . . . well, I guess you could say *ambushed*."

"What do you mean?"

"They found a vampire and right before they attacked, other vampires attacked them. Two died, but one managed to get away and tell us what happened."

My stomach twisted into knots. The weight of my silence pressed down on me, heavier than I could bear. I should have told Papa that I wasn't attacked by one vampire that night, but two. The memory of the second figure—how it had loomed in the shadows, waiting—played over and over in my mind. If I had spoken up, warned him, maybe those witches wouldn't have been ambushed. I could have prevented this.

"The vampires are traveling in groups now?" Papa asked.

"Yes, which makes hunting even more dangerous."

Papa sighed. "We will have to change our hunting tactics. We will do larger groups with a few that stay hidden in case there are other vampires lurking around."

The apothecary's walls closed in as Papa continued his

discussion, but my attention shifted to the window. Outside, two men close to my age stood watching, their whispered words drawing smirks that made my stomach twist. The redhead's mocking laugh echoed faintly through the glass. My grip tightened on the bottle I held, the motion tipping it into another with a sharp clink. Papa glanced at me before nodding towards the door. His silent request was unnecessary as I had already made my mind up on what was to come.

I slung the door open, the bell hanging above reacting to my harsh motion, but it didn't slow my pace.

"What is it?" I yelled as I made my way to them, my voice sharp enough to draw the attention of passersby.

"Well, I was just telling my friend here what a shame it was." The redhead's tone dripped with mockery, his smirk daring me to react.

"What?" I demanded, stepping closer, my fists clenched at my sides.

"It's a shame how beautiful you are," he sneered, his gaze sweeping over me like I was something he owned, "and you come from such a powerful bloodline. And yet, you shouldn't be allowed to procreate. No one would want that contamination."

My blood ran cold. Coven members.

I forced myself to laugh, the sound cold as I locked eyes with him. "Is that really a way to talk to the one you'll be submitting to soon enough?"

The two exchanged glances, the quieter one clearly uneasy. He shifted his weight, looking like he regretted every moment of standing here. The redhead, however, tilted his chin up, his sneer deepening. "I wouldn't be so sure of that."

"Really?" I stepped closer, my voice lowering to a dangerous whisper. "Do you realize I could make you believe you're a mermaid, have you jump over the railing, and you'd drown yourself trying to breathe underwater before anyone could save you?"

His smirk faltered for just a moment before returning, brighter and more forced. "You can't. You don't have magic. You're an . . ." He paused, savoring the insult he was about to deliver. "You're an abomination."

Before he could blink, I had his forearm in a vice-like grip. His wince was immediate as I siphoned, just enough to remind him who held the power here.

The quieter one opened his mouth to intervene, but with a quick wave of my hand, his eyes glazed over, and he fell silent.

The redhead opened his mouth to scream, but no sound came out. His eyes widened in panic, and I leaned in close, my voice dripping with venom. "All it takes is one thought, and you'll be diving into the deep oblivion. Or better yet—perhaps I'll have you strip down first and parade along the boardwalk, let you lose every shred of dignity before you lose your life."

Tears welled in his eyes as his bravado crumbled. His confidence, so carefully built, was gone in an instant. I glanced toward the apothecary window, ensuring Papa was still deep in conversation.

His magic pulsing beneath my palm hummed faintly, but nothing compared to the magic I was used to feeling. If I pulled too long, I could rip his connection to magic away completely. And if I did that, Papa might just throw *me* over the railing.

"Here's how this is going to go," I hissed. "I'm going to let you go, and you're not going to tell anyone about this. I'm sure you wouldn't want people knowing how easily you were bested by a woman. And if you do talk? I'll kill you in your sleep. Got it?"

He nodded frantically, and I released him. With another wave of my hand, his friend blinked out of his daze, looking around in confusion.

I turned to walk back toward the apothecary but stopped, throwing a final glare over my shoulder. "Oh, and one more thing. I'd like to see you or anyone else try to take the coven from my brother and me. There would be hell to pay for anyone who dared to go against us."

I didn't pull much from him, just enough to make sure he wouldn't forget.

The magic I'd taken buzzed under my skin, a steady hum of energy that sharpened my thoughts. It wasn't much, but it was enough to face August again. Enough to end this game once and for all. I just had to refrain from using it before I saw him again.

Bronwen with self-control? Patience? That would be new.

10

Chapter 10

Bronwen

The silence was suffocating. Every rustle of leaves, every snort from the horses, and every bird flying above seemed louder than it should have been. The magic flowing through me had me jumpy, its constant hum a relentless presence in my mind. Every moment was a battle to keep it contained, to stop it from spilling out. We were nearing home, and Papa hadn't said one word to me yet.

I knew it was coming. Anytime Papa was this quiet, it was because something was bothering him. And I knew what it was.

He didn't want me to go out alone.

As our barn came into view, I tapped Shadow's side lightly to have him move a little faster. Just a little closer and I'd be away from the conversation that I knew was coming.

"Winnie," Papa mumbled.

I pretended like I couldn't hear him.

"Bronwen."

Great. He used his *Father of the coven* tone, and he said my real name.

I pulled on the reins and brought Shadow to a halt. Whipping my head around, I said, "I am not hunting with others. I'd rather die."

He stayed silent for a moment. "Winnie."

"You can either put bars on my window and lock me in my room or let me hunt alone. Those are your options."

He stared at me a moment, and something that was almost a smile formed on his lips. "I know."

What?

"You . . . *know*?"

He nodded. "Please just be careful. That's all I wanted to say."

I tried to form the words, but nothing came out. With the click of his heel, his horse jolted forward and left me stunned.

At least he knew.

I stared at myself in the mirror in my room, barely recognizing the face that looked back. My reflection seemed foreign, haunted by dark circles under my eyes. I ran my fingers along the dark circles under my eyes, but quickly pulled my hand away before I did something I'd regret.

Any other time I had magic, getting rid of the blemishes would have been my first priority, but priorities change, unfortunately.

Mama stuck her head into my room. "Lowen is here to see you."

I tilted my head and ran my fingers through my hair. Maybe he was what I needed right now. A distraction.

"Tell him I will be out in a moment."

Mama nodded and left.

Before walking out of my room, I added a little lipstick and perfume. I smoothed my hands over my dress, ensuring it sat just right before adjusting a loose strand of hair behind my ear. Taking a deep breath, I glanced at my reflection one last time, forcing a small smile.

Mama gave me a knowing look when I walked into the kitchen before nodding toward the back door. Her lips twitched as if she wanted to say something but decided against it.

I rolled my eyes but couldn't help the small smirk that tugged at my lips. She always saw more than she let on.

As I stepped into the shade of the barn, I saw Lowen petting Shadow. He had a small box tucked under his arm.

"Lowen," I said, drawing his attention away from Shadow.

His face lit up with a boyish smile as he turned to me, his excitement evident. "I got you the chocolates," he said, extending the small box toward me, his fingers gripping the edges like he was afraid I might refuse.

"Thank you."

I reached out, my hand lingering a moment atop his as I took the box. My fingers brushed against his, and for a brief second, neither of us moved. My eyes trailed over him, taking in the way he had chosen the blue shirt I once complimented. The top few buttons were left undone, revealing the warm tan of his skin. He had styled his hair differently today, slightly tousled but in an intentional way, as if he had taken extra time to make sure it looked effortless.

When I met his gaze again, he was watching me carefully, uncertainty flickering in his expression. I didn't blame him. I was unpredictable, and each time he saw me, he never knew which version of me he would get.

And today he'd get the one he wanted.

I needed to feel him. To feel something that would make me feel real again. I was balancing on a short wall between reality and the part inside of me that was a mix between stolen magic and lack of sleep.

I took the chocolates from him and placed them on the old wooden work table. Taking a slow step closer, I let my hand rest on the waist of his pants, my fingers tracing the fabric lightly.

"I've missed you," he murmured, his voice softer now as he cupped my face, his thumb brushing against my cheek.

I met his gaze through hooded eyes before sliding my hand up his chest, feeling the warmth of his skin through the fabric. "I've missed you too," I whispered, my voice barely audible between us.

His fingers lingered at my temple, tucking a loose strand of hair behind my ear before trailing down to my jaw. The touch was light, hesitant, before he finally pulled me into him. His lips pressed softly against mine, a slow, testing kiss, but I refused to let hesitation linger. Reaching up, I tugged him closer, deepening the kiss, feeling the urgency rise between us.

In one swift motion, he lifted me, his hands firm against my waist as he set me on the table. The chocolates slipped from the edge, the small box tumbling to the ground. I bit my lip as they scattered across the floor, forgotten in the moment.

At least I had another reason to bid him away when I grew bored of him again.

He brought his hand up my leg, pushing my dress along with it. As we continued to kiss, his fingers slid inside of me. I moaned under his touch as I gently rocked against him.

I slowly unbuttoned his shirt, my fingers grazing over the fabric, eager to feel the warmth of his broad chest beneath my hands. He met my pace, shrugging it off his shoulders before returning to me, his lips trailing up my neck, lingering at my pulse.

"I want all of you, Bronwen," he murmured against my skin, his voice rough with desire. A quiet clink filled the air as he unfastened his belt, the sound sending a shiver through me.

"No. Some things need to be left until—" I stopped myself before I almost said something I'd regret. I didn't want to further our relationship, and in the beginning I thought he felt the same way. It was fun.

That was all it was.

Until one day I could see his feelings change. The gifts he brought me, the compliments he gave me—more about my laugh or my stubbornness and less about my looks. I blamed myself. I should have stopped this the moment I began to notice.

He leaned back, his brows knitting together. "Until what?" His tone was softer now, hesitant, but there was a sharp edge of hope clinging to his words, one that only deepened my unease.

I pulled him back to me, our lips meeting again.

"Marry me," he managed to say through the kisses, his voice trembling with a vulnerability I hadn't expected.

I pushed him off of me. "What?" My heart sank as his words hung in the air, their weight pressing against my chest. This— this was what I was trying to avoid. A relationship was one thing, but a promise like that? It wasn't just about marriage; it was about what I'd lose. Lowen wasn't a witch. If I tied myself to him, I'd have to give up a side of me. I'd never feel magic coursing through my veins or even the small thrill of hunting vampires. It wasn't a compromise I was willing to make.

Lowen looked at me a moment before grabbing my hand and getting on one knee. "Bronwen, I love—"

"Get up." I rolled my eyes.

His brows knit together in confusion as I cut him off, hesitation flickering across his face before he finally stood up. "What is this?"

"What?" I pushed my dress down covering my legs once again.

"Us. I have done nothing but try and yet every time I feel like we are getting somewhere. You push me away."

I hopped off the table and walked past him, making my way to Shadow. As I reached out to pet him, he flinched slightly, his ears flicking back as if sensing the unsteady rhythm of my heartbeat. I ran my fingers through his mane, taking slow, measured breaths, trying to steady myself as the weight of the moment settled over me.

"I've never said there was an us," I mumbled, my voice barely audible as I turned to him. "This is fun. Isn't that enough? Why does it have to be more?" The words tasted hollow, even to me, but I wasn't ready to give him anything else.

"I have turned down many advances for you," he said, his voice shaking with frustration. "I've chosen you, Bronwen. Doesn't that mean anything?"

I shrugged my shoulders. "I never told you to do that."

His expression turned cold. "Have you been giving your time to others? Is that why you push me away?" He stepped closer to me. "You—you're *whoring* around?"

Before I could stop myself—though I'm not sure I would've

done it differently—my fist made contact with his face. He grabbed his cheek and looked at me with wide eyes.

Shadow stirred in his stall, letting out a loud snort, his ears flicking back at the tension in the air.

I bent down, snatching Lowen's shirt off the ground, and tossed it at him with a sharp flick of my wrist. "Lowen, leave before I do something you'll regret." My voice was steady, but the heat rising in my chest was anything but.

His jaw tightened, his hands clenching at his sides. He stared at me for a long moment, something dark flashing behind his eyes—something I hadn't seen from him before. Then, without another word, he turned on his heel and stormed out, his footsteps echoing in the quiet barn.

***

I scoured the woods for hours, the magic pulsing through my veins like a second heartbeat. A melodic tune hummed in my mind, soft but insistent, growing louder with every step I took.

Use me. Use me. Use me.

The words looped in my mind, a seductive chant that wrapped around my thoughts, squeezing tighter each time I resisted.

"Go away," I mumbled as I hit my head with my hand. I had never heard that before, but I also had never held on to magic for longer than a few hours before I would use it to have our baron fruit trees bare fruit in the middle of winter, or make my hair a little shinier, or even just to do something to scare Adar.

I wanted to use it so badly, to release the pressure building inside me. The need was suffocating, like a weight pressing down on my chest, begging for relief.

August just had to come find me tonight. I pricked my finger, leaving a trail of blood to entice him more, and yet—*nothing.*

It was like he knew how bad I needed to see him tonight. So he didn't come.

I made my way home, jumping at every small sound in the woods that I heard before collapsing on my bed.

He placed a gentle kiss on my neck. "Come on. It's getting dark. We shouldn't be outside."

"I need to go home."

"You can stay with me tonight."

He took my hand, leading me through the streets at a hurried pace. I giggled, breathless, as he glanced nervously at the darkening sky, more concerned about nightfall than I was. I wasn't sure why—I'd never stayed out this late before. But he gave me attention, and that was enough. For weeks, I had tried to talk to him, only to be met with indifference. Yet tonight, he looked at me like I was the only person in the world. I couldn't walk away—not when I finally had what I wanted.

We turned into a narrow alley, the walls closing in as shadows deepened with the fading light. Steps loomed ahead, leading to a dark green door adorned with a golden fox, its eyes gleaming as though it knew what was about to happen. My heart quickened as he opened the door, pulling me inside.

Once inside, he pushed me against the cold wall, the air thick and stifling. I closed my eyes, anticipation fluttering in my chest, but instead of a kiss, sharp pain exploded in my neck. The sting sent a shockwave through me, freezing me in place.

I struggled, my hands clawing at his chest, but his strength was unrelenting. The room seemed to spin as panic overtook me, my vision blurring as he laughed. I twisted, trying to break free, but his grip tightened, and I felt myself growing weaker with each second.

Just when I thought hope was gone, he released me. I stumbled toward the door, but before I could reach it, I was thrown across the room and slammed onto the bed. His weight pinned me down, his hands trapping mine above my head as his grin widened.

His once deep brown eyes that I had grown so fond of were now a searing, burning red. The warmth that had once made them familiar was gone, replaced by something inhuman, something predatory. His short, tousled hair fell slightly over his forehead, a deceptive echo of the man I used to know. He loomed over me, his breath shallow, his clothes—once neatly worn—now slightly disheveled, his shirt unbuttoned just enough to reveal the pale stretch of his collarbone, smeared with the remnants of fresh blood.

My blood.

Tears streamed down my face, hot and unending. "Please," I choked out, my voice trembling. "Let me go. I won't tell anyone. I promise." The words felt fragile, like glass about to shatter under his gaze.

"You see." He bit down on my arm, only taking a small amount of blood before bringing his face back to mine. "I don't believe you."

I shook my head but before I could say anything, he bit my other arm.

I kicked him with my legs but all he did was smile. "I wouldn't do that if I were you."

I kicked again, and he lowered himself as he pushed my dress up and bit my inner thigh.

"Stop!" I screamed but he came back up and kissed my cheek

before biting my neck one more time.

I startled awake, my chest rising and falling in rapid, uneven breaths, as if I had just sprinted for miles. My skin was damp with sweat, my heart pounding so violently that it drowned out the silence of the room.

I knew sleep wouldn't find me again, but I still rolled over, pulling the blanket up in search of comfort. That's when I felt it—something wet against my skin. My brows knitted together as I reached down, fingers brushing against the damp patch on the bed. I lifted my hand to my face, but in the darkness, I couldn't make out what it was.

With trembling hands, I fumbled for the candle beside my bed and struck a match. The flickering light illuminated my palm, and my breath caught in my throat. Blood.

A chill spread through my body as I inspected my arms, the candlelight revealing deep, bloodied marks marring my skin. Not just scratches, not mere cuts. No—*bite marks.*

My pulse roared in my ears. This—this can't be real. I must still be asleep. Squeezing my eyes shut, I willed myself to wake up. But when I opened them again, nothing had changed. The blood was still there. The wounds still burned.

My breathing quickened as the mattress shifted beneath me. A slow, creeping dread curled around my spine. I wasn't alone.

I turned my head, every muscle in my body locked with fear.

August.

He was lying beside me, his pale face serene, the candlelight kissing the blood smeared across his mouth.

A scream ripped from my throat as I threw myself off the bed, my heart slamming against my ribs.

August's red eyes flashed open, confusion flickering across

95

his face before a slow, twisted smile spread across his lips.

"You—" My voice faltered, my eyes darting toward the door just as Papa stormed into my room.

I gasped, looking down again—nothing. My bed was empty. My arms, smooth and unblemished.

"Winnie! What's wrong?" Papa's strong arms wrapped around me as he pulled me close.

"I—I just had a nightmare." My voice was hollow, my eyes sweeping the room again. Nothing was out of place.

But I knew the truth. The nightmare had bled into reality. And with each passing hour, the line between the two was dissolving. Was it the magic coursing through my veins? Or would this torment continue until I finally ended his game?

11

Chapter 11

Bronwen

August was still alive, and because that wasn't torture enough, I was at Market again. I couldn't let my parents go without me. Not until the threat was gone.

As I looked for a tree to tie Shadow to along the other horses, the wind blew, carrying with it the rustling of leaves and something that sounded eerily like the word Winnie. I glanced around, hoping it was the magic playing tricks on me until I saw him.

The horses grew restless, pulling at the ropes that tied them to the trees as August walked past them.

"Hello, Winnie." His voice was smooth, almost pleasant, but there was an edge to it that made my skin crawl. Shadow shifted uneasily beneath me, his ears pinning back as August drew closer. I tightened my grip on the reins, trying to calm him, but it was no use.

I scanned the woods. No one was around—at least, no one that I could see. The weight of the magic inside me pressed against my ribs, pulsing, waiting. If I was going to use it, I had only one chance. One moment to strike before he had the chance to stop me. But what if someone was here and watched me practice magic?

"Where were you last night?" I needed to keep him talking, to stall until I could figure out what to do.

August chuckled, a low, rumbling sound that made my chest tighten. "Oh, I had . . . other things to attend to." His eyes swept over me slowly, his gaze lingering like a physical touch. "But I smelled you. It was hard to stay away."

My hands clenched around the reins. "You should have come," I said through gritted teeth. "I waited."

"I know," he said, his voice dropping to a near whisper. "And I drained six people trying to stop myself from finding you and ending our little game so soon."

He reached out toward Shadow, his fingers hovering near the horse's muzzle. Shadow reared back suddenly, throwing me to the ground before bolting into the woods. The sharp crack of my wrist breaking as I landed sent a wave of nausea through me.

August stood over me, his smile widening as he crouched just out of reach. "Oops," he said, his voice dripping with mock innocence.

I bit down on my lip, refusing to give him the satisfaction of hearing me cry out. He tilted his head, watching me intently. "You know, Winnie, no one's around. You could heal that wrist with a single word."

I stared at him, trying my best to control myself. The pain was overwhelming, my vision blurring at the edges. Nausea came from the pain, and I couldn't bear it any longer. I closed my eyes as I gave in, feeling the warmth of the magic over my wrist.

I had allowed the magic to eat me alive from the inside—all for nothing.

August's smile turned sharp. "Hmm," he murmured. He rose to his feet, brushing off his coat. "See you around, Winnie." With a wink, he disappeared.

With the magic gone and the pain subsiding, my mind cleared again.

But one thing stayed the same: I hated August.

I looked in the direction Shadow fled and let out a sigh of relief when I saw him eating grass not far from where I was. Making my way toward him, I ran a hand down his neck, feeling the tension still lingering in his muscles. "I need you to stay here, boy," I murmured, gently taking the reins and leading him toward a sturdy tree. I tied him securely, giving him a final pat before stepping back. "I won't be long. Stay put, alright?"

I made my way to town square, pulling twigs from my hair and brushing the dirt from my dress, seething. I pushed through the crowd, not bothering to apologize to anyone I bumped into. Anyone who looked at me the wrong way was testing me right now.

As I made it to our booth, the back of a tall man in a long black coat with almost white hair blocked my view of Mama.

Are you fucking kidding me?

I quickened my pace until I reached the booth. Without hesitation, I stepped in front of Mama, pushing her gently behind me as I planted myself between her and August.

His amused stare met mine, a smirk tugging at the corner of his lips, but I didn't waver. My glare was sharp, unwavering, and filled with all the hatred I could muster.

"Get away," I spat, my voice low and venomous, my teeth clenched so tightly my jaw ached.

Mama gasped. "Winnie!"

"I'm sorry. I was interested in a new pair of," August paused as he picked up the first thing he could grab from the table, "women's stockings." He couldn't stop himself from smiling at his own mistake.

"Then buy them and leave."

Mama came to my side looking over the mess that I must have been. She brushed her hands against the back of my dress. "What happened, Winnie?"

"Yeah, what happened, Winnie?" August asked, innocence painted across his face.

Mama stopped what she was doing and glanced between the two of us with scrunched eyebrows.

August gave Mama a smile that infuriated me. "Hello. My name is August."

"Odelia Delvaux. It is nice to meet you. I apologize for my daughter's behavior." Mama extended her hand to which August glanced down before shoving his hands into the pockets of his coat.

"Odelia, I am terribly sorry, but I was a very sickly child. I nearly died from a fever so I promised my dear, dear mother before she died that I would do my best not to ever get sick again, so I tend to steer clear of the touch of another."

My mouth fell open at the amount of trickery that just came out of his mouth.

"Oh that's quite alright, dear."

I shot a look at Mama.

"It looks like Winnie may need to freshen up. I will come back later and finish my shopping." And with that he turned around and waltzed his way to another booth.

Mama turned to face me, her lips pressed into a thin line. "Winnie, where are your manners?"

I couldn't tell her the truth. "I just don't like him."

"Well the poor boy has been through enough. You should be nicer."

That poor boy just broke my wrist and wishes to drain me of my blood, but okay.

Mama made me change, and unfortunately the dresses I like to wear usually didn't sell very well at Market—because no one has taste—so I had to settle for something more common which meant more fabric covering my chest and a fuller skirt. It was like women didn't want to show what they actually looked like.

When I made it back from changing, August was back at our booth talking to Mama. I kept having to tell myself that he wouldn't do anything in public, and Mama never left home after dark. She was safe. He was just doing this to annoy me.

"Winnie! You changed." His eyes swept over me, lingering a moment longer on my now covered chest. He snorted like he knew what I had on was something I didn't prefer. "Wonderful."

He lifted a goblet to his lips, the deep red liquid swirling inside catching the light. I hadn't noticed it before—he must have acquired it in the brief time it took me to change.

"It's quite early to be drinking, don't you think?" I asked.

"It's never too early for a drink, Winnie." He glanced down at my neck, and I dug my nails into the palm of my hand, less at what he meant and more at that nickname.

"I am going to grab more men's shirts from the wagon. They are selling fast today," Mama said as she squeezed my arm.

I gave her a small smile before shifting my attention back to August.

Stepping out from behind the booth, I folded my arms. "What about that story you told my mother?"

August raised a brow, his smirk unfaltering. "And what's to say it isn't true?"

He held my gaze for a lingering moment before, with a flick of his wrist, he tilted the goblet in his hand. The deep red liquid cascaded over my new dress, the sharp scent of wine filling the air.

"Apologies, weak muscles from the illness." He winked as he turned and walked away.

If there ever was a day that the rage inside me was at the point where one more thing would have me explode, it was today.

I didn't just want to kill August anymore. I wanted him to suffer.

Immensely.

The crowds grew lighter, and the sales slowed as Market day began winding down. The air felt heavier, a suffocating tension settling over the streets as people moved sluggishly toward their final purchases. Then, the bell rang.

The sound sliced through the hum of Market like a blade, sharp and jarring. My breath caught in my throat, and for a moment, the entire square seemed to freeze.

It tolled again, deeper this time, reverberating through my chest. Each chime felt like a hammer blow, driving a spike of dread into my heart. I glanced at Mama, her face pale as she clutched my arm.

I pushed through the gathering crowd, dragging Mama with me. Every toll echoed in my ears, louder than the last, until the weight of it became unbearable. It was the sound of death, the sound that haunted my childhood.

They found a witch.

I remembered every night it had kept me awake, the times it had left me trembling with fear that someone I loved would be next. We had to find Papa.

I let out a breath when I saw Papa. He met us at the star etched in the stone below our feet, something that had become a tradition whenever we heard the bell tolling. Relief came over his face when he saw us. Mama gripped my arm tightly.

We stood, all clutching each other while we stared at the stage. It was a large wooden podium that sat much higher than the ground. The wood was darkened with age, its splintered edges stained from years of use. Across the stage hung ropes above trapdoors, each one ready to deliver its gruesome promise with the pull of a lever.

Above the platform, banners fluttered in the faint breeze, bearing the king's insignia: a black raven with its wings spread wide over a blood-red background. It was a stark reminder of the crown's complicity in the centuries of persecution. The king, safe within the fortress of his castle, upheld the laws that sanctioned these executions, yet he never had to witness the horror himself. The thought churned my stomach. He ruled over death with impunity, his hands never stained by the blood.

The stage was the centerpiece of the town's fear-driven theater, a grotesque spectacle that drew the bloodlust of the crowd like moths to a flame. Papa said they used to burn witches, but over the years, we evolved. Fire could no longer touch us, so they adapted.

A few Legion soldiers stood on the stage, but one in particular caught my attention.

Adar held tightly to a woman with a sack over her head. His grip was firm, his knuckles pale, and his face a mask of stoicism. Yet, I could see the tension in the set of his jaw, the flicker of something unspoken in his eyes as he stared out over the crowd.

My chest tightened as I watched him. I hadn't seen or heard from him since he left, and for a fleeting moment, I wondered if he might be the one about to face death. But here he was, draped in full Legion attire, carrying the weight of his role like a burden he couldn't shake. I felt every emotion he was trying to bury—anger, shame, regret. It was as though I were on that stage with him, feeling the same suffocating pressure.

This wasn't just another duty for him. It was a battle within himself. Though I was not sure what all he had done during his time with the Legion, this was the first time he was on the stage.

As the final toll of the bell faded, I glanced around and realized the entire town had gathered. The oppressive silence that followed was thick, broken only by the hushed whispers rippling through. They all stood, eyes fixated on the hooded witch, waiting to see who it was—the one who had lived among them, tricking them every day.

Another soldier approached the witch and ripped the hood off of the woman. Gasps followed by whispers ripped through the crowd when they saw who it was. Cloth was wrapped tightly around her mouth, and her hands were bound behind her back to ensure there was no way she could fight back.

The woman shook her head violently, her eyes wide with terror as tears streamed down her face. Muffled pleas escaped through the fabric gag, but they were ignored. Adar grabbed her by the shoulders, forcing her to stand still as another wrapped the coarse rope of the noose around her neck. She twisted against his grip, her silent cries growing more desperate, but it was no use.

The sickening snap of her neck echoed through the square, cutting through the heavy air. For a moment, there was silence—an unnatural stillness as the reality of what had just happened settled over the crowd. Then, the cheers erupted, a wave of triumph fueled by fear and hatred. They celebrated the death of someone's daughter, someone who had been loved, as if it were a victory worth cheering.

This had to come to an end. My hatred for the coven burned bright, fueled by their disdain and cruelty, but watching the execution unfold twisted something deep inside me. They didn't deserve this.

The genocide had to end. I had to push past my anger and find the first vampire, to restore the balance before we all ended up on that stage, condemned by the very people we tried to protect.

12

Chapter 12

Adar

I stared at her limp body swaying slightly on the stage, her blue-tinged hands marked with desperate scratches where she had fought against the binds. Her lifeless blue eyes stared blankly out at the thinning crowd, empty of the fire that once made her so intolerable.

Diana Blackwood.

She had been a thorn in my sister's side, one of the cruelest voices mocking Bronwen and me for years. And yet, as I stood there, watching the vultures circle above, I felt no satisfaction in her fate. She didn't deserve this. No one deserved this.

The future Father of the coven stood on the stage and did nothing.

My chest tightened with the weight of my actions. I had been part of this. I had torn down her door, stormed through her home, and found her hiding beneath the floorboards. I bound her hands, shoved the cloth into her mouth to prevent her from speaking a spell, and drug her to the square. When her eyes met mine, they burned with betrayal, and I knew she would have exposed me in a heartbeat if given the chance.

But what did that make me? A coward? A hypocrite? I hated the Legion for what it stood for, but here I was, wearing their uniform, playing my part in the very thing I despised. It was a role I hadn't chosen for myself, and it hollowed me out with every step. Even if I'd wanted to save her, I couldn't have. Diana had trusted the wrong person, shared her secrets with a boy who feared witches more than he cared for her. It was a mistake she couldn't take back, and the town had made their judgment.

The crowd buzzed with morbid excitement. They cheered the snap of her neck as though it were a festival. To them, witches were monsters, evil incarnate. Diana was no longer human in their eyes. I glanced at my family in the crowd. Mama's tears streaked her face as she clung to Papa's arm. Bronwen stood stiff, her green eyes cold and distant, likely imagining what she would do if anyone dared lay a hand on her.

And me? I stood on the stage, the perfect Legion soldier, wearing my mask of indifference. My face gave away nothing, not my disgust at the crowd's bloodlust nor the shame clawing at my insides. But inside, every instinct screamed at me to do something—anything—to end this. I could feel the weight of my failure pressing down on me, choking me with its silence.

"Adar!"

I turned to see Rhydian motioning to me, a wide grin plastered on his face as he lingered near a group of young women. Of all the Legion soldiers, he was the only one I tolerated. He was here because of his father, a punishment to make a man out of him. It hadn't worked. His mask of humor

107

hid his discomfort well, and that made him bearable.

One last glance at Diana's body, and I forced the guilt down like a bitter drink. I needed a distraction—anything to escape the weight of what I'd just witnessed. Her death would haunt me, I knew that much, but there was no sense in dwelling on something I couldn't change. At least, that's what I told myself.

Rhydian's grin widened as I approached. "Ladies, this is Adar. He's the most disciplined soldier among us." He shot me a wink, knowing full well how false that statement was.

The blonde closest to him turned her attention to me. Her fair skin and soft curls framed striking hazel eyes that sparkled with mischief. She stepped closer, her gaze roving over me in a way that left no room for interpretation.

"Is that true?" she asked, her voice smooth and teasing. "Disciplined?"

I smirked, letting the mask of a soldier slip into something easier. "Only when I have to be."

Her lips curled into a sly smile. "And when you don't have to be?"

I stepped closer, lowering my voice just enough to draw her in. "Then I'm exactly what you want me to be."

Her cheeks flushed slightly, though her confidence didn't falter.

"Do you know where the Legion camp is?" I asked.

She nodded, and my smirk grew. "Come tomorrow. I'll make sure you have a memorable visit."

She grinned, biting her lip before nodding again. "Tomorrow, then."

As she walked away, I let out a breath I hadn't realized I was holding. For a brief moment, I had escaped the weight of Diana's death, the judgment of the crowd, and the expectations of my family. But I knew it wouldn't last.

***

The next day, the camp buzzed with activity. The clang of swords against shields echoed across the grounds, a rhythm as familiar as my own heartbeat. Fires crackled in scattered pits, their smoke curling into the air and mingling with the pungent smell of sweat, leather, and steel. Soldiers barked orders, their voices sharp and cutting, while rookies scrambled to obey.

Nearby, a blacksmith worked tirelessly, the rhythmic pounding of his hammer punctuating the chaos. Sparks flew with each strike, briefly lighting up his determined face before fading into the haze.

I moved through the camp, my steps heavy, each one an effort to ignore the oppressive energy around me. The camaraderie that others found here felt hollow to me, a facade that barely masked the weight of what we did. Laughter rang out from a group gathered near the mess tent, their amusement grating against my nerves.

This was their reality—a cycle of drills, bloodshed, and distractions. And I was part of it, even if every fiber of my being wanted to be anywhere else.

"Did you see the way her eyes popped?" A soldier's voice cut through the yard, followed by cruel laughter.

My grip tightened on the hilt of my sword as I turned toward the sound. Two rookies stood near the training circle, their smirks widening as they mimicked Diana's struggle on the stage. Fury boiled in my chest, spreading like fire through my veins, but I forced my breathing to remain steady.

"You think that's funny?" I asked, my voice cold and measured as I approached.

The taller one met my gaze with a smirk, his confidence brimming with ignorance. "What, you feel sorry for the witch? She got what she deserved."

My jaw tightened as I stepped closer, my knuckles white around the hilt of my sword. "Careful," I said evenly, though my voice carried a warning that hung heavy in the air. "Keep talking, and you'll find out what I think you deserve."

The smirk faltered, but the shorter one laughed nervously, glancing between his friend and me. "Relax, Adar. It's just a joke."

"I'm not laughing," I snapped, my tone sharp enough to make the taller one take a step back. My hand itched to unsheathe my sword, to silence their mockery with the edge of my blade, but I couldn't. Not here. Not now.

From the corner of my eye, I saw Rhydian approaching. His usual grin was gone, replaced with a wary expression as he placed a hand on my shoulder. "Let it go, Adar," he said quietly, his voice low enough that only I could hear. "They're not worth it."

My gaze remained locked on the rookies, my muscles coiled with tension. He was right. A confrontation here would only draw more attention, and I couldn't afford anyone questioning my reasons. I released a sharp breath and dropped my hand off of my sword.

"Get back to training," I said over my shoulder, my tone leaving no room for argument.

The rookies muttered under their breath but turned away, their laughter replaced with a forced focus on their drills. Rhydian gave my shoulder a light squeeze before stepping back.

As I walked away, the tension in my chest remained, each step heavier than the last. Their words echoed in my mind, stoking the fire I couldn't seem to extinguish. Diana's lifeless eyes flashed before me, a reminder of my failure and the inescapable truth: no uniform, no mask of indifference, could erase the weight of what I'd done.

The rest of the morning passed in a blur of drills and exercises. My body moved automatically, blocking, striking, parrying, but my mind was elsewhere. The guilt I had tried to suppress clawed its way back, and I needed a distraction better than sparring.

The hum of conversation grew louder as the visitors arrived. Women from the nearby villages filtered into the camp, their laughter and chatter filling the air. It was a common occurrence, a distraction encouraged by the commanders to keep morale high. The men's attitudes shifted, their postures relaxing as they abandoned their drills to mingle.

Among them was the blonde from the day before. She stepped into the camp with a confidence that drew eyes, her hazel gaze searching until it landed on me. A smile spread across her lips as she approached, her steps unhurried.

There was my distraction.

"Adar," she greeted, her voice soft but teasing. "I hope you haven't forgotten our arrangement."

I sheathed my sword, my lips curving into a smirk. "I wouldn't dream of it."

She tilted her head, studying me. "Good. I'd hate to think I'd come all this way for nothing."

"Not a chance," I said, stepping closer. "Let me show you around."

As we walked, the other soldiers watched with envy and amusement, some offering remarks that I ignored. The blonde stayed close, her arm looped in mine as we moved through the camp. She asked questions—about the Legion, the training, the battles—but her eyes lingered on me more than anything else.

When we reached a quieter corner of the camp, she turned to face me, her expression softening. "You're not like the others, are you?"

I raised an eyebrow, amused. "What makes you say that?"

She hesitated, her confidence faltering for the first time. "You just . . . seem different. Like you don't want to be here."

For a moment, I considered brushing her off, but something in her gaze made me pause. "Maybe I'm just good at hiding it," I said, my tone lighter than I felt.

Her lips parted, as if she wanted to press further, but she let it go. Instead, she smiled and reached for my hand. "Then maybe you can show me what else you're good at hiding."

I chuckled, letting her pull me closer. For now, I allowed myself to enjoy the distraction, pushing thoughts of Diana and the weight of my guilt aside. The world outside the camp could wait.

13

Chapter 13

Bronwen

The woods seemed darker tonight, the dense canopy of leaves swallowing what little moonlight tried to break through. Each step I took stirred the forest floor, the soft crunch of twigs and leaves underfoot a reminder of how exposed I was.

The silence was oppressive, broken only by the occasional hoot of an owl or the rustle of unseen creatures in the underbrush. Shadows danced in the corners of my vision, shapeless and fleeting, keeping my nerves on edge.

I had walked at least a mile tonight in search of a vampire— not August, honestly anyone but August. After losing that magic, I wanted to find another one before him so I could be prepared. I felt like I was running out of time. The longer I let this go on, the deeper I'd be in this mess. Because of the hanging, I didn't go out last night. Or the night before.

Everyone was on edge. Mama checked in on me constantly, though she never said anything, and Papa—

"Oh, now where is Winnie off to tonight?"

He flew past me in nothing but a blur. I stopped walking. I gritted my teeth at the sound of the voice I didn't want to hear just yet.

"You made it easy for me tonight." If I had wanted to see him, he wouldn't have come. It was almost as if he knew I didn't want him here, which was why he chose to appear. Other nights I could try my hardest to lure him out to no avail.

"Did I?" I asked.

This time he came in quickly from behind, not giving me a chance to grab him before he was gone again. I looked around, but the night had grown cloudy, leaving no bit of light to help. The trees I knew I had walked past only moments ago were nowhere to be seen.

"Is it just you, or do you have another waiting to save you when a woman brings you to your knees?"

"You wouldn't be the first to have me on my knees, Winnie." His voice was close and far all at the same time.

My cheeks reddened, and I started walking again. "You didn't answer my question."

The incident in Bodaira had me worried. August was with another vampire the first time we met, but I thought it might have been a one-time occurrence. But he also came out during the day somehow and was more controlled than I had ever seen a vampire before. He was different, or extremely old, or vampires really were evolving. And I was just assuming it was him again in Bodaira. But it could be another. They could all be changing faster than we could stop them.

"You killed that other vampire, remember?"

"Was he your friend?" I asked, trying to make sense of it all.

"He was a nuisance, and you ended the problem. So I should

be thanking you, actually."

"Pity, I'd love to break your heart," I mumbled, my frustration boiling beneath the surface.

"In due time, Winnie."

I stopped walking again as I squinted my eyes, trying to get a glimpse of where he could be, though I knew it was no use.

"Do you not know a spell to make it easier to see me?" His voice was behind me, and I whipped my head around, met with nothing but darkness again.

I kept silent, not wanting to admit the truth.

"Oh, Winnie, you're taking all of the fun out of it."

"Bronwen!" I yelled, turning around once more to the direction he spoke from. Hearing that name from his lips ignited something deep inside of me. "My name is Bronwen. Stop calling me Winnie."

I waited a moment, but he didn't say a word. It was a nice change, and for a moment, I thought he had left. I began to walk again, the tension easing from my shoulders slightly.

"Did you dream of me last night?"

I threw my hands into the air. The sweet peace I was given ripped away from me, leaving me more irritated than before.

"Do you ever say anything of value?" I yelled into the darkness, glancing around to find an idea as to where he could be. I just wanted it to end. He had turned my dreams into nightmares, leaving me restless and on the brink of insanity from the lack of sleep. And now, now he had ruined the one part of my life that I enjoyed.

"Witches are tools and tools are for power, and when the tool is useless, the witch is the world's to devour." The words blew like wind around me. Some from my left while others came from my right.

What the fuck did he say?

I rubbed my fingers on my temples, the cryptic words ringing in my ears. "That is not what I meant."

"Did you know the one that was hung the other day?"

His question caught me off guard. "Yes," I said carefully. "She tripped me when we were young, causing me to fall into a mud puddle. It ruined the new dress my mother had just made for me, so I took some of her magic and made her believe she was a dog. The coven spent a week trying to find a spell to reverse what I had done but to no avail."

I tried to bite back a smile. I shouldn't think of such a memory and feel . . . proud of what I had done.

She's dead.

"Did they make you fix her?" he asked.

"You can't make me do anything."

"Well? It didn't end there. She wasn't barking when she was begging for her life."

I kept silent as I continued walking, trying to block out his taunts, but the memory hung heavy in the air.

"Did your brother fix her? Funny . . . a witch in the Legion. Capturing and killing his own kind."

I stopped and turned around, looking everywhere for him. He may have met Mama at Market and possibly seen Papa somewhere in the crowd, but there was no way he would have known the man in armor on the stage was my brother. Or that I even had a brother.

Yes, my father made Adar fix her, but August shouldn't know about him.

My breathing grew quick as the thoughts raced through my head with Adar possibly being out in the woods at night with the Legion. He was perfectly capable of protecting himself, but if August had even tried to hurt him . . .

"Come out. You want to drag this out? Well, I want to turn your insides into liquid and have you beg me to kill you." I yelled, pulling my hood down to tempt him more. Anger filled me from the thoughts of how he could know of my brother.

"Come out!" I screamed.

I had to put an end to this.

"Come out!"

I pulled the blade from my arm and raised it with my other hand, ready to draw blood to force him to me.

His arm wrapped around my neck, taking away my ability to breathe. I dropped my blade, dug my nails into his skin, and grabbed a hold of his magic, forcing him to release me. I spun around, ready to finally end this when I locked eyes with those familiar red eyes, only they were on a different face, a more delicate face. A woman's face framed with wild blonde curls.

The magic pulsated through me, intoxicating and danger-ous, a steady thrum that seemed to sync with my heartbeat. I could feel it, raw and potent, ready to consume.

But Papa's voice echoed in my head, louder than the magic's whispers. *Darkness will consume you.* His warning was a tether, pulling me back from the edge. I took a sharp breath, forcing myself to focus. This wasn't the time to lose control—not with August lurking nearby, waiting for a moment of weakness.

Forcing myself to breathe, I grabbed the stake from my leg and plunged it into her chest.

Her lifeless body crumpled to the ground as I pulled the stake out. I didn't pull much magic, but I could feel it running through my body, begging to be used.

And I knew just who I wanted to use it on.

I scanned the woods, my vision sharpening with the faint

pulse of the stolen magic. A flicker of movement caught my eye—leaves trembling on a high branch. My gaze snapped up, locking on him. August stood on the branch, staring down at me with a look of fascination on his face. As I kept my eyes on him, he tilted his head as if he was trying to figure out if I could see him or not.

I smiled faintly and raised my hand. With a flick of my wrist, a branch shot toward him, impaling the tree inches from his head. His grin faltered.

Before he could move, I froze him in place. Invisible ropes of magic wrapped around him, pinning him to the trunk of the tree. His eyes widened, the amusement draining from his face.

"How do you know about my brother?" I demanded, my voice low and sharp.

He squirmed against the bonds, his struggles sending sparks of satisfaction through me.

"How!" I shouted, tightening the magic around him.

August's laugh rang out, defiant and maddening.

I let the invisible ropes grow hotter until they burned into his skin.

"Dreams!" he gasped, his voice strained. "The dreams!"

"What dreams?" I hissed, loosening the hold just enough to let him speak.

"You dream of me, and I dream of you. Every night. A new year, a new birthday, and you kill me every time. He is there some nights."

Relief washed over me as his words sank in. He was suffering too—haunted by the same torment. A twisted smile spread across my face as I realized he couldn't escape this any more than I could. But the satisfaction was fleeting. My chance was here, now, and I wouldn't waste it.

I reached for the magic again, summoning another branch to strike. But nothing happened. The stolen power drained from me, leaving an empty ache in its place. My vision blurred, the last remnants of the magic fading as darkness took over.

I stumbled, cursing under my breath. I was so close. It was almost over, and I had failed. I let him get under my skin.

I turned around and started walking back to the direction I came from, not even attempting to see where he was now.

"Where are you going?" he called from behind me, his voice taunting as it echoed through the trees.

I didn't stop. "Home," I said, my voice steady. I reached for my hood but hesitated, letting my hand drop to my side. He knew of my family, and if he was foolish enough to follow me, he'd face a far worse fate than I could offer tonight.

"But the night is so young," he said, his tone dripping with mockery. "And you almost had me. It was quite thrilling."

I glanced over my shoulder, not to see him but to let him know I wasn't afraid. "I'm over your games for now. Unless you plan to fight me, I have better things to do."

The woods fell silent, and for a moment, I thought he was gone. Then a soft breeze whispered past me, carrying his voice. "Goodnight, Winnie."

14

Chapter 14

I had seen this home maybe hundreds of times and never knew what lived inside. Or should I say *who* lived inside. The bane of my existence, and yet—the only thing that motivated me now.

She had never put her hood back on, so her scent was strong—until she stepped close to her home, where it was as if she had disappeared. Except I still saw her. I just couldn't smell her.

I had come across witches before, but none had masked their homes the way this one did. Though I also had never come across a witch that could suck the life out of me.

On the nights I could come to her, I did. In the beginning, I wanted nothing more than her blood. The scent of it—rich, potent, and unlike anything I'd ever encountered—drew me to her like a predator to prey. That's all she was supposed to be: prey. Another meal.

But she wasn't like the others. She was hunting me, too.

It wasn't just the magic, though that was enough to send a chill down my spine. It was her fire, the defiance in her eyes that dared me to try and break her. I hated it.

I hated her.

But that hatred wasn't the cold, hollow thing I was used to. It burned, sharp and consuming, so different from the suffocating void I had drifted in for decades.

Winnie ripped me out of that void so quickly that I could barely catch my breath.

She had become the one thing I didn't understand. The more she resisted, the more I craved her—not just her blood but her fire. She made me feel alive in a way I hadn't in centuries, and that was the cruelest game of all.

I left her home down the beaten path, not worrying about anyone seeing me. The moon cast pale light through the trees, and the scent of distant prey teased my senses. I hadn't fed in days, and the hunger clawed at me, sharper than usual after being near her.

I heard the crunch of leaves underfoot before I saw him— a man walking alone, a heavy pack slung over his shoulder. He wasn't from here; his clothes marked him as a traveler, likely from another kingdom. His steps were weary, the way someone walks when they've been on the road too long.

I smiled at the welcome visitor and closed my eyes, shifting them to a human brown. The transformation was effortless but always left a fleeting, almost hollow sensation, as if masking my nature drained something deeper within me.

I stepped into his path, my sudden appearance making him stumble back. His wide eyes darted to the sides, looking for an escape.

"You must not be from here," I said, my voice smooth,

almost conversational. "No one local would be foolish enough to travel at night."

The man straightened, trying to mask his fear. "I'm just passing through. I mean no harm."

I let out a low chuckle, taking a step closer. "Harm? No, you wouldn't mean harm. But harm will find you, all the same."

He clutched the strap of his pack, his knuckles whitening. "I . . . I have nothing of value."

"Oh, but you do," I murmured, my eyes locking onto the vein pulsing in his neck as I could feel the red creeping back into my eyes. "You have exactly what I need."

Before he could move, I was on him. My hand clamped over his mouth as my fangs sank into his throat. The warm rush of his blood was instant, intoxicating. His struggles weakened as I drained him, the fight leaving his body until he was limp in my grasp.

I let him drop to the ground, wiping my mouth with the back of my hand. I crouched beside him, tilting my head as I studied his lifeless form.

"A shame," I muttered, almost to myself. "But you really should have known better."

Leaving the body where it fell, I continued on my way. The hunger sated but the lingering taste of his blood was dull compared to what I truly craved. It was never enough.

It would never be enough.

***

The following night, I found her again, though it wasn't hard considering her scent flooded my senses as soon as I stepped into the woods. Tonight, the woods led her to a pond I'd seen her find before. She sat next to the water with her cloak folded neatly next to her. She was waiting for me.

Her black hair flowed into the black of her shirt and . . . pants. I hadn't noticed it before. A woman in pants.

Tight fucking pants.

What the fuck was she doing to me?

The moonlight reflecting off the water made her skin look like liquid gold, and yet her eyes . . . her emerald eyes were the most precious thing on her.

I lingered in the shadows, moving silently as I studied her. She wasn't relaxed, though she pretended to be. Her shoulders were rigid, her hands resting on her knees but ready to move at the slightest sound. She wasn't just waiting. She was hunting.

I didn't show myself, but I stayed close, letting my voice carry on the breeze. "You're back again, Winnie."

She stiffened, her head turning slightly, just enough to catch my words without giving away her full attention. "Don't call me that," she snapped, her tone sharp and unforgiving.

I smiled, even though she couldn't see me. "Your family is no concern of mine," I said smoothly, addressing the thought weighing on her. "You don't need to worry."

Her voice hardened, cutting through the stillness. "Lest you forget, I've lived through your victims. I've seen the games you play. Tormenting a husband by killing his wife first. Chasing girls through the woods, letting them think they're escaping you when we both know no one could outrun you."

I cocked my head, weaving closer but keeping to the shadows. My movements were fluid, each step calculated to keep her guessing. "Oh, I love games," I replied, my tone light, teasing. "But not against a family of witches. I'm not so

123

arrogant that I don't know my odds against that."

She turned toward my voice, her jaw tightening.

"As long as you don't tell them what I am," I continued, my tone dropping slightly, "there's no reason for you to worry."

She stood, wiping her hands against her pants before putting her cloak back on.

"What do you know of the first vampire?" she asked suddenly, her words laced with frustration. The shift in topic caught me off guard.

"The first vampire?" I repeated, feigning disinterest. Her teeth clenched, and I had to fight the urge to laugh. Everything I did seemed to drive her mad.

"Did I stutter? Yes, the first vampire," she hissed, her voice taut with annoyance.

I moved faster now, weaving through the trees, ensuring my steps were deliberate and just loud enough for her to hear. I stayed out of her reach, keeping the game alive.

"I know nothing of the first vampire," I said, flying past her close enough that her hair stirred in the wind.

She spun around, but not fast enough. Her hands darted up, her sharp eyes scanning the woods for any trace of me.

"You're a coward, August," she called, her voice echoing.

I let out a low, amused laugh that rippled through the clearing, relishing the way her shoulders tensed at the sound.

She started walking toward the trees, away from where I was hiding. "How old are you?"

I watched as she nearly tripped over a fallen branch, shaking my head in silent amusement. She should've seen that. A simple spell could fix her vision.

"So many questions tonight, Winnie," I teased.

Her exasperated sigh was as satisfying as her irritation.

"Well? How old are you?"

"Old enough."

Her eyes snapped toward me, and for a brief moment, our gazes locked. She couldn't see me clearly, but I could feel her suspicion, her curiosity. She was testing me, just as much as I was testing her.

"So you're old, and yet you know nothing of the first vampire?"

I let my voice drop lower. "I know a witch created a vampire, which in turn created many more. But that's all I know." I moved closer as I spoke, circling her. "Why are you asking?"

She didn't hesitate. "Because I want to kill him. Almost as much as I want to kill you."

Her words brought a grin to my lips, sharp and full of promise. "Good. Keep that fire, Winnie. You'll need it."

15

Chapter 15

Bronwen

"Good morning, Winnie," Mama said with a soft smile as I entered her sewing room. Her voice was warm and familiar, making the nickname feel less grating. Only she and Papa could call me that without stirring some part of my frustration.

"Good morning," I replied, rubbing the sleep from my eyes. Or rather, the lack of sleep. My nights were still filled with restless nightmares—August taunting me at every turn, his laughter echoing through the darkness.

Mama seemed to notice the dark circles under my eyes, though she didn't comment. Instead, she gestured to an empty chair by her side.

"Come, help me with this hem," she said, her tone gentle but firm.

I sat beside her, smoothing the fabric she handed me. The needle always felt awkward in my hands but the rhythmic motion of stitching calmed me. For a while, we worked in silence, the sound of scissors and thread filling the space.

Sunlight streamed through the window, casting a warm glow over the sewing room. It felt safe here, as if the troubles of the outside world couldn't touch us.

"You should take more care of yourself, Winnie," Mama said softly after a while, her eyes never leaving the fabric. "A good night's rest does wonders."

I nodded but didn't respond. I just hoped she only thought it was because of the hunting.

"I need you to deliver some items to Miss Georgia sometime today," she said, nodding to a small bag near the door. "She's far too pregnant to come to Market, but she's requested new dresses."

"Alright," I said, stifling a yawn. "I'll take it once I've changed."

Mama gave me a knowing look but said nothing. She knew my routines well enough. I didn't let anyone see me until I was properly dressed and composed.

Back in my room, I stood before the mirror, frowning at my reflection. The dark circles under my eyes stood out sharply against my skin, a testament to my sleepless nights. With a determined sigh, I reached for a jar of powdered pigment, carefully dusting it under my eyes to mask the signs of exhaustion.

My hand grazed over the scar on my neck, right above my shoulder. Its dark lines shined brightly against my tan skin. I dabbed a little powder on it and succeeded in making it less noticeable, but it did nothing to hide the raised skin. If anyone looked hard enough, they would see it.

I took my time choosing a dress, settling on a soft green one that complemented my eyes. The fabric hugged my form just enough to be flattering. I pulled my hair forward to do my best to cover the side of my neck.

Satisfied with my appearance, I made my way down the hall and grabbed the bag Mama had prepared. The morning light was bright, and I squinted as I stepped outside, the cool air brushing against my skin. The road was quiet, lined with towering trees that swayed gently in the morning breeze. My steps were steady, my thoughts scattered as I let the crisp air clear my mind.

Further down the winding road, I spotted Talia, a girl I had known since childhood, walking in the opposite direction with a basket tucked under her arm. We had once been inseparable, spending countless afternoons climbing trees and sneaking treats from Market. But as we grew older, our paths had shifted. She had been with Adar for a while—long enough for everyone to see how deeply they loved each other. But Adar knew the truth neither of them could escape. She wasn't a witch, and because of that, he couldn't give her forever, no matter how much he wanted to. When he ended things, it wrecked them both. She believed he had simply fallen out of love with her, never knowing the real reason, and that misunderstanding built a wall between us. She drifted away, not out of hatred, but out of hurt, and though we still exchanged pleasantries, the closeness we once had never returned.

She paused when she saw me, a smile brightening her deep brown face, her freckles standing out against her dark skin. Her thick curls were tied back with a simple ribbon, though a few rebellious strands framed her face, catching the morning light.

"Bronwen! You look lovely today," she said, her eyes drifting to my dress. "That color suits you so well."

I ran my hands down the fabric with satisfaction. "Of course it does. I always look good."

Sophie chuckled, shaking her head. "And humble as ever."

"Confidence and humility don't always go hand in hand," I said playfully. "Besides, if you had Mama sewing your clothes, you'd always look this good too."

She rolled her eyes, shifting the basket in her arms. "Making a delivery?"

I nodded, adjusting the bag on my shoulder. "Mama made some dresses for Miss Georgia. Figured I'd enjoy the walk while I can."

Sophie glanced up at the sky. "Well, don't let the sun ruin your perfect dress," she teased. "See you later, Bronwen."

I waved as she passed, watching her disappear down the path before resuming my walk. The momentary distraction had been pleasant, but as I walked further, an unsettling quiet settled over the road. The chirping of birds and the rustle of leaves ceased, replaced by an eerie stillness. My fingers tightened around the strap of the bag, and I glanced over my shoulder. Nothing. Yet the familiar prickle on the back of my neck told me I wasn't alone.

"Running errands, Winnie?" His voice slithered from behind me, laced with mockery.

I froze, closing my eyes for a brief moment to steady my breathing. "Not today, August," I muttered, continuing down the path without turning around. It was too early for this.

Too early for him.

"Such a dutiful daughter," he mused, his tone light and taunting. "And here I thought witches didn't bother with neighborly kindness."

Ignoring him was futile, but I tried anyway. My grip on the

bag tightened. Miss Georgia's home wasn't far now, and I could only hope he would leave me alone when I got there.

Surely he had something better to do.

"You know, I thought after last night that nothing could be better than those pants on you."

I stopped.

"But that dress . . . One gust of wind and I could see exactly what was under it."

He's just trying to get under your skin.

I took a deep breath before turning to him, allowing my gaze to slowly rise to meet his. He stood effortlessly, his tall frame leaning just slightly to one side as if he were completely at ease. The sunlight caught the sharp angles of his face—his high cheekbones, the defined curve of his jaw. His short blonde hair, tousled just enough to look intentional, framed his features perfectly. But it was his smirk that made my stomach twist with irritation, a slow, knowing curl of his lips that made it painfully clear he was enjoying this. He was waiting, reveling in the moment, pushing me just enough to see how I'd react.

But gods, why did he have to be so tall?

Focus, Bronwen.

I bit my lip, letting my gaze drop slightly before flicking back up to meet his. I knew exactly how to play this game. My voice dropped just enough to make it sound like a secret between us. "If I show you, will you leave?" I tilted my head slightly and bit my lip, teasing the line between amusement and challenge.

His smirk dropped from his face. A crack in his centuries old armor that made him almost look . . . human.

I let out a short before turning away and resuming my walk.

The moment of calm shattered as my bag was yanked from

my grasp, soaring through the air before colliding with a tree and landing in the mud with a dull thud. My fingers curled into fists as I spun around, my jaw tightening.

August leaned lazily against a nearby tree, his arms crossed over his chest, watching me. His expression was so infuriatingly smug, it made my blood simmer.

"Oops," he said, feigning innocence.

"You're insufferable," I snapped, my hands balling into fists as I walked towards him. "Pick it up."

He tilted his head, his grin widening. "Make me."

That was all the invitation I needed to lunge toward him. He moved to dart away, but not fast enough. My hand closed around his arm, grabbing his magic. His playful expression shifted to one of surprise—and fear. I could feel his pulse quicken under my grip, a faint and fleeting sign of life that only made the magic within him more tempting. The surge of power coursed through me in a heated wave, leaving him unable to fight back.

He dropped to his knees, and I grabbed his neck.

"Do you think because the sun is out that I won't kill you?" I hissed, tightening my grip. "No one is around. And if someone saw, I'd just kill them too."

The words that spewed out of my mouth shocked me, but I meant them.

His hands clawed weakly at mine, his nails scraping against my skin, but it was futile. The life drained from him, and with it came a rush of energy that filled every inch of me. It was intoxicating, an unrelenting pull that threatened to drown out all reason. I tightened my grip, savoring the fleeting moment of control.

I raised my hand, watching as flames danced at my fingertips, the heat radiating from them in waves. I brought my hand closer to his chest, stopping just short of contact. The scent of singed fabric reached my nose, and I knew the delicate skin beneath was blistering. His strained gasps filled the silence, each one a reminder of the power I held.

"C—" he choked. "Carrow."

My brow furrowed. The name hung in the air, heavy and unfamiliar, yet it struck a chord deep within me.

"What?" I demanded, my grip loosening slightly as his words echoed in my mind.

He closed his eyes, gasping for air. "First vampire," he whispered hoarsely. "Carrow."

The name felt like a stone dropped into the still waters of my thoughts, sending ripples of questions I couldn't ignore. Carrow. The first vampire. Was this another one of his games? Another distraction meant to throw me off course? I couldn't trust him, but what if he wasn't lying? What if this was the lead I had been searching for?

I released him, letting him fall forward as I stepped back, my heart pounding. My mind raced, caught between skepticism and a growing determination. If this Carrow existed, if he was truly the first vampire, then finding him could be the key to ending all of this—the hunting, the endless fear, my . . . defect.

I clenched my fists, forcing myself to focus. "What do you know?" I demanded, raising my hand to freeze him in place. The spell wrapped around him like invisible chains, holding him firmly as he tried to regain his composure.

He shook his head. "If you want to know, we have to make a deal."

"What?"

He straightened slightly, his usual smirk struggling to return. "A truce of sorts," he rasped.

My eyes narrowed. "A truce?"

"You don't kill me," he said, his voice hoarse but steadying, "and I'll help you find Carrow."

***

I returned home later than I intended, my steps heavy as I walked to my room. August said he had heard of the first vampire—Carrow—but he didn't know much. He said he would ask around, to find something that could lead us to more. I just needed to give him a few days. I also needed to trust him.

I didn't.

But I had no other option than to try. As infuriating as he was, I had never met another vampire as controlled as him. He might have been my only chance to find Carrow.

I'd just have to suffer at the mercy of the mark for a little while longer. But no matter the truce we had now, I would kill him after Carrow.

Dropping the bag of soiled clothes near my door, I caught my reflection in the mirror. The dark circles were back, deeper than before. My hair, once full and vibrant, had thinned, a cruel reminder of the toll these sleepless nights were taking on me.

With a deep breath, I closed my eyes and let my thoughts center on the magic I'd pulled from August. It hummed faintly beneath my skin, warm and foreign but undeniably potent. I placed my hands over my face and willed the energy to flow, erasing the signs of exhaustion. A tingling warmth spread across my skin, and when I opened my eyes, the dark circles were gone. My hair felt fuller, softer, as though vitality itself had been restored.

I studied myself in the mirror, a small, satisfied smile tugging at my lips. Whatever games August thought he was playing, I would ensure he regretted them. For now, though, I allowed myself the comfort of looking and feeling whole again.

16

Chapter 16

Bronwen

"Can you stop?" I snatched the fabric from his hands, glaring up at him. His presence was suffocating, a constant reminder of my inability to keep him away. Why couldn't he leave me in peace?

"I like this *work-for-money* thing," August said, grabbing another shirt from the basket and folding it—completely wrong, of course. "It's keeping me grounded."

I clenched my teeth, trying to focus on the task in front of me. My hands moved mechanically, folding a shirt into neat, precise lines, but my mind was elsewhere—fixated on him, the way his smirk lingered like a challenge I couldn't ignore. Why did he insist on tormenting me?

"What about before you were a vampire? You never worked?" I whispered, barely audible to my own ears, to ensure no one around could hear.

"I'm high born, Winnie," he replied with a sigh.

"Of course you were." I rolled my eyes, but the curiosity

nagged at me. What kind of life had he lived before all this? And why did I care?

A fragile truce may have been in place, but he'd never annoyed me as much as he did now. He'd practically run to our booth when he saw us there and made sure to compliment Mama relentlessly. I would've preferred her to shrug him off, but instead, she held on to every word he said as though he were some noble hero.

He let out a little laugh before placing the terribly folded shirt on top of my perfect stack. My fingers twitched at the sight of the mess. Couldn't he leave anything untouched?

"And is this what you dream for yourself?" he asked, gesturing toward the booth. "A life as a seamstress?"

I shot him a look. "Don't you have someone else you can bother?"

"No, Winnie, I'm all yours." His grin was as infuriating as ever.

I rolled my eyes.

"Winnie, I am going to grab some lavender soap from the Tolberts' booth before they sell out," Mama said, interrupting my brewing argument with August. "Will the two of you be alright until I return?"

I opened my mouth to respond, but August cut me off.

"Oh, Odelia, I will guard Winnie and the booth with my life," he said dramatically, placing a hand over his heart.

I elbowed him in the side, earning a low grunt, and Mama laughed softly before walking away. I turned back to the table, scanning the setup to see what was missing. The weather was growing colder, and I knew women would soon be looking for shawls for extra warmth. Realizing we hadn't put any out yet, I turned to grab a few from one of the baskets.

"Bronwen?"

Lowen's voice startled me, and I jumped slightly, nearly dropping the shawls. When I turned around, his eyes locked on mine, soft and pleading. Before I could say anything, August stepped forward, towering over him with a sharp glare.

"And you are?" August asked, his tone as sharp as a blade.

"Lowen Reeves," he replied, hesitating briefly before looking back at me. "Bronwen, I'm—"

"Lowen?" August interrupted, drawing out the word as if testing its taste. He scrunched his nose. "I've heard that name before. What does it mean?" He stared at Lowen, his masked brown eyes glinting like they were digging into his soul.

Lowen blinked, confusion flashing across his face. "I'm not sure," he said, his voice uneasy before he quickly locked his eyes back on me. "I'm sor—"

"Friend!" August slapped his hands on the table loudly enough to make Lowen flinch and leaned closer. "It means friend," he said with a wicked grin, his tone mockingly cheerful.

Lowen's unease deepened, and he stepped back, glancing between August and me. "Bronwen, I need to talk—"

"Oh, but I think she's already heard enough, haven't you, Winnie?"

Lowen's jaw tightened, his words swallowed as he turned and left.

"What was that?" I asked, turning to glare at August. "I've never seen Lowen back off so easily."

August rolled his eyes. "That is how you choose to spend your time?" He gestured toward the retreating figure. "Truly disgusting."

I scoffed, shaking my head as I placed the shawls on the

table. "How I spend my time is none of your concern."

August's expression turned mockingly aghast. "It is truly disgusting to think that you've touched me with the same hands you've touched him."

I raised an eyebrow, not missing the opportunity to needle him. "I touch him for pleasure for both of us, and you . . . well, I suppose it's pleasure for me and—" I placed my hand on his arm, pulling a small amount of magic, just enough to make his jaw tighten and a low growl escape his throat. "Pain for you."

His eyes burned into mine, and I saw a flicker of something I hadn't seen before he stepped back, his expression smoothing into something unreadable. Leaning close, he whispered, "I love when you talk dirty to me, Winnie."

I opened my mouth, but quickly pressed my lips together when I saw Mama stepping through the crowd, her arms full of lavender soap.

"Oh, Odelia, it was lovely to see you," August said, stepping back with exaggerated politeness. "But I fear I've overstayed my welcome."

I couldn't resist. "When has that ever stopped you before?"

Mama gasped. "Winnie!"

Before I could respond, another voice interrupted, cutting through Market's chatter like a blade. "Odelia, how nice to see you here," a sharp, nasally tone chimed in. I turned to see Mrs. Tralith, a rival vendor whose stall was infamous for poorly made wares and even poorer manners.

Mama stiffened beside me, offering a polite but strained smile. "Good afternoon, Mrs. Tralith."

Mrs. Tralith's eyes darted toward our booth, narrowing as they settled on the neatly arranged shirts and breeches. "I see you're doing well for yourself," she said, her words dripping with sarcasm. "Though I can't help but notice how much business you seem to be pulling from others. Some might call it . . . unfair."

Mama's lips pressed into a thin line, but she said nothing, her gaze fixed firmly on the ground. I felt a flare of anger rise in my chest. How dare she?

"Unfair?" I echoed, stepping forward before Mama could stop me. "If people prefer our work, maybe it's because we put actual effort into it. Unlike some who sell scraps disguised as quality." My voice carried, earning a few curious glances from nearby vendors and shoppers.

Mrs. Tralith's face flushed red, and her mouth opened and closed like a fish gasping for air. "I—I was merely making an observation," she sputtered.

"And I'm making one too," I snapped, crossing my arms. "If you spent less time complaining and more time improving, maybe you wouldn't have to worry about who's doing better."

"Bronwen," Mama whispered, her tone cautionary, but I didn't back down.

"You're just like your father," Mrs. Tralith muttered.

"Oh, you haven't seen my father yet." I leaned over the table. "I suggest you return to your booth before there isn't a booth left."

"Are you threatening me?"

"No—" Mama cut in.

"Yes." I glared at Mrs. Tralith.

Mrs. Tralith straightened her back, her face a mix of anger and humiliation. "Well, I never—"

"And you never will," I cut in, my voice sharp. "So maybe it's best if you never come over here again."

She sniffed indignantly and turned on her heel, storming off without another word. Mama sighed heavily beside me, shaking her head.

"Winnie, you didn't need to do that," she said softly, her eyes flicking toward the onlookers who quickly returned to their shopping.

"Yes, I did," I said firmly, though my pulse still raced from the confrontation. "She had no right to speak to you like that."

Mama placed a gentle hand on my shoulder, her expression softening. "Sometimes strength isn't about fighting back, Winnie. It's about knowing when to let things go."

I frowned. "Not when it comes to you."

Mama said nothing, turning back to the booth to rearrange the stacks of clothing that had shifted in the commotion.

As Market's noise resumed around us, I glanced at August who managed to stay silent during the confrontation. His eyes were on me, and he had a smile plastered on his full lips.

"What?" I bit out.

He shifted his eyes to the crowd ahead. "Nothing."

***

The sun had gone down hours ago. I contemplated if I could handle another conversation with August today, but the curiosity about Carrow was eating me alive. I never got the chance at Market to ask about him, and I didn't want to drag this out longer than I had to. My cloak was used for warmth tonight, but I kept the hood down. He had to find me.

I came to the pond, the air cold and still. The moonlight reflected off the water, casting an eerie glow over the clearing. August appeared from the shadows, his usual smirk in place,

140

his presence an immediate irritation.

"Do we have our own special spot now?"

"Tell me about Carrow," I said before his usual theatrics continued.

"What do *you* know about Carrow?" he asked, leaning lazily against a tree as if we were about to have a pleasant chat.

I crossed my arms, trying my best not to give in. I knew he was trying to get under my skin. "He was some kind of faerie from Alentara that helped a witch with a spell in turn of her completing an immortality spell for him The spell turned him into a vampire. Our entire coven was punished because she messed with the balance of nature in Joveryn which has caused us to no longer be feared and instead we are persecuted."

"That is . . . one way to put it," he said, narrowing his eyes.

"What do you mean?"

His smirk deepened. "Carrow," he said, rolling the name around like a fine wine. "Do you think he'll save you from your nightmares, Winnie? Or did you just fix your little face for my benefit?"

My patience snapped like a dry twig. "I fixed my appearance because I can't afford to look like death warmed over, unlike you," I shot back. "Now answer the question."

He chuckled, his red eyes glinting in the dim light. "Touchy. You really must not be sleeping. Perhaps it's *Lowen* keeping you up?"

I clenched my fists. "Lowen has nothing to do with this."

"He's got everything to do with it," August said, his tone as smug as ever. "A little 'friend' to distract you from what you're really afraid of. Tell me, did he notice those little dark circles before you wiped them away? Or is he as blind as you are to his mediocrity?"

I stepped closer, my patience fraying.

"Have you told him how I am the one you dream of?"

My patience snapped like the twigs beneath my steps. I closed in the distance.

"I changed my mind," I said sharply, reaching for the stake on my thigh. I swung, but he dodged it slightly. It cut through the skin on his arm.

"Winnie," he hissed, clutching the wound.

I swung again, but he caught my wrist. Desperately, I mumbled nonsense words, trying to mimic spells I'd heard Papa use. His eyes widened in confusion, and I used the distraction to sweep his legs out from under him. He pulled me down with him, but I quickly straddled him, gripping his shoulders.

"Do it!" he shouted, his voice filled with equal parts anger and desperation.

I wanted to. The magic beneath my hands called to me, intoxicating and wild. It whispered promises of power and relief from the nightmares. But I couldn't.

My grip tightened as I stared down at him, his red eyes blazing with challenge and something I couldn't place.

"Lost your chance," he muttered, and in one swift motion, he flipped us. Now he was the one pinning me, his hands gripping my wrists.

His gaze swept over me, lingering, and for a moment, he looked at me like I was something more than prey. My breath hitched.

Before I could speak, he was gone.

I sat up, scanning the clearing for any sign of him. Silence pressed around me, heavy and unnerving. I shook my head, trying to banish the flustered thoughts swirling in my mind.

What was wrong with me?

***

"Do you know what I am?" he whispered, his voice a chilling caress against my ear.

"Yes," I whimpered, my back pressed hard against the cold, damp wall of a narrow alley. My heart thundered in my chest. Why had I followed him? What was I thinking?

"Shhhh." He placed a finger against my trembling lips, his touch deceptively gentle. "There's no reason to cry. I'll make it quick."

Tears blurred my vision as my thoughts raced to my family. Mama, her hands too weak to tend to the garden alone. My little brother, relying on me to guide him, even though I was still just a girl trying to figure out how to be enough for all of them.

"Please," I choked out, my voice barely audible. "They need me."

His crimson eyes softened for the briefest of moments, a flicker of something that might have been pity—or amusement. He brushed a stray lock of hair from my face, his touch tender and horrifying all at once.

"Do you think that matters to me?" His voice dropped, resonating with a darkness that made my blood run cold.

Before I could answer, his face twisted into something monstrous. Shadows pooled under his eyes, and his mouth opened to reveal long, gleaming fangs. I tried to scream, but it caught in my throat as he lunged forward.

The pain was instant and excruciating. His fangs pierced my neck, and I felt a searing heat flood my veins. My breath hitched, escaping in broken gasps as he held me in place.

My hands clutched at his shirt, my fingers trembling, but my strength was draining fast. Each second he fed sapped more of my will to fight. My legs buckled beneath me, and I would have collapsed if he hadn't pinned me against the wall.

The smell of blood was overwhelming—metallic, sharp, suffocating. Chills rippled through my body, a cold that burrowed deep into my bones. I was so tired. My eyelids grew heavy, the alley blurring at the edges of my vision.

If I closed my eyes, maybe it would stop. Maybe it would all end. Maybe—

I woke with a violent gasp, my chest heaving as I clutched the blankets to my neck. The room was dark, the faint light of the moon casting shadows across the walls. My heart pounded, echoing in my ears like a war drum.

The need for sleep still clawed at me, but it was useless. The memory of his voice, his touch, lingered like a phantom, refusing to let me drift off again. My hands trembled as I pulled the blanket tighter, trying to ground myself in the present.

Was finding Carrow really worth this? How many more nights could I endure these nightmares before they consumed not just my dreams, but my reality too? How much longer could I keep this up before the fight swallowed me whole?

I had to keep going. For Papa, for Mama, for Adar. For the people who needed me to be strong, even when I felt like I was breaking. Even if this killed me in the end, I had to fight for them.

17

Chapter 17

Bronwen

I adjusted the vase on the mantle for the third time, stepping back to scrutinize the arrangement. No matter how I positioned it, something felt off. Mama had gone to a customer's home to get measurements for a custom dress, and I needed anything to occupy my mind.

I had reorganized all of my dresses, moved things around in the kitchen to the way I thought it made more sense, and rearranged the entire sitting room.

But this vase . . .

Maybe it wasn't the vase. Maybe it was me.

"Winnie," Papa's voice called from the doorway. I turned, surprised to see him standing there. Lately, he didn't return home until supper time. "Would you like to train?"

I blinked, certain I'd misheard. I hadn't sparred with him in years. He was always too busy. A flicker of excitement sparked in my chest, though I tried not to show it. "Yes," I said quickly, setting the vase down. "I'd like that."

Minutes later, we stood in the clearing behind the barn. The crisp air nipped at my skin, but I barely noticed. Papa handed me a sword and held one for himself in his other hand. His grip was firm and confident as always, yet he looked completely relaxed.

"Show me what you've got," he said, slipping into a ready stance.

I gripped the sword tightly and lunged without hesitation, swinging hard. He blocked the strike with ease, his movements smooth and practiced. I pivoted, aiming lower, but he sidestepped like it was nothing, countering with a quick tap with the flat side of the sword to my wrist that nearly made me lose my grip.

"You're holding back," he said. "If you don't commit, you won't land a hit."

My jaw tightened. I adjusted my stance, shaking off the sting of his words. This time, I pressed forward with a series of rapid attacks, each one deflected as if he'd seen them coming before I'd even moved. My arms burned with the effort, but I refused to stop.

Finally, I saw an opening. Feinting left, I spun to strike from the right. For a moment, triumph surged through me—until he caught my blade mid-swing. With a flick of his wrist, he disarmed me. The sword clattered to the ground, and I stumbled back, breathing hard.

"Better," he said, lowering his own weapon. "You're learning. But you're too impatient. Patience wins fights, Bronwen."

My frustration boiled over. "You didn't even break a sweat," I snapped, my chest heaving.

"That's the point," he replied with the faintest hint of a

smile. He gestured toward the barn. "Now, help me clean the stalls."

I groaned, bending to retrieve the sword. "You tricked me into this, didn't you?"

"Of course," he said, giving me a wink before walking toward the barn.

I followed him, muttering under my breath. My pride stung worse than my arms, but I couldn't deny the flicker of satisfaction at having trained with him at all. It was a small victory, even if it didn't feel like one.

The stench was unbearable, a rancid mix of hay and filth that clung to my nostrils no matter how hard I tried to breathe through my mouth. The damp chill of the barn seeped into my bones, and every step stirred up a fresh wave of earthy musk and manure. The shovel's rough wooden handle rubbed against my palms, the friction growing worse with each pass over the filthy floor. My arms ached from the repetitive motion, muscles protesting with every scoop of soiled hay.

Sweat trickled down the back of my neck. It clung to me, mixing with the dirt and grime to create a sticky layer that made my skin crawl. Each scrape of the shovel against the floor seemed louder in the silence, a grating reminder of how far this task was from anything I wanted to be doing. One of Papa's horses let out a disgruntled snort and shifted, knocking against the stall door with a dull thud.

"Move back," I muttered, waving the shovel at it with a weak attempt at authority. The animal huffed at me, almost as if he was mocking my efforts.

As I stepped back to avoid its restless movements, my boot landed squarely in a fresh pile. The sickening squelch was immediate, the warmth of it pressing against the worn leather. A string of curses escaped my lips as I shook my foot furiously, trying in vain to rid myself of the mess.

"Gods be damned," I hissed, my voice echoing in the near-empty barn. The frustration in my tone surprised even me. I glanced toward the open barn door, half-hoping Papa hadn't heard.

"Bronwen!" Papa's voice boomed from outside the barn. He rarely used my real name, and hearing it now made my stomach twist.

I wiped at my forehead, smearing dirt in the process. "I'm sorry, but I'd rather be struck down right now than have to do this any longer," I shouted back, throwing the shovel down with a loud clang. The echo rang through the barn, amplifying my frustration.

Without waiting for his response, I stormed toward Shadow's stall. The dark stallion's ears flicked as I approached, his large eyes watching me with curiosity.

"Let's go," I muttered, lifting the latch on the stall door. Shadow stepped forward obediently, his hooves clacking against the wooden floor. I heard Papa's heavy footsteps entering the barn, his voice calling after me, but I ignored him. With no time to saddle him, I mounted Shadow and nudged his side with my boot, sending us flying past Papa.

"Bronwen, get back here!" Papa's tone was sharper now, but I refused to look back.

"Sorry, Papa," I muttered under my breath. With a nudge of my heels, Shadow took off into the woods, his powerful strides eating up the distance between us and the barn.

The forest was crisp and quiet, the ground softened by the scattered leaves Shadow's hooves kicked up. The wind was brisk but not biting, brushing against my face and sending loose strands of hair flying out of my braid. I regretted not grabbing my cloak, though the coolness of the air felt refreshing in a way, stirring something restless inside me. The familiar rhythm of Shadow's gait usually soothed me, but today it only deepened the ache in my chest.

Adar should have been here. He would have found a way to make this task bearable, or at least distract me with one of his ridiculous stories. The thought of him made my throat tighten. I missed him more than I cared to admit, and his absence only amplified the weight of the responsibilities I felt.

Shadow suddenly slowed, his ears twitching. I tightened my grip on his mane as he came to an abrupt halt.

"Whoa," I said, steadying myself as my body slid forward. Shadow's nostrils flared, and his muscles tensed beneath me. My pulse quickened as I followed his gaze.

A figure stood in the path ahead, silhouetted against the dimming light filtering through the trees. My breath caught as he turned, his dark eyes sweeping over me with an infuriating smirk.

August.

He wore a loose white shirt tucked into brown pants, the simplicity of his attire somehow making him look even more untouchable.

How did he know where I would be? A chilling breeze raised goosebumps on the back of my neck, reminding me that I wasn't wearing my cloak.

My scent had called for him, even though I didn't mean to. He took a step toward me, and Shadow stirred.

"August," I warned, my voice sharper than intended, but the events from the last time he found me on Shadow flashed in my mind—the pain of a mutilated wrist, the anger that he bested me, it all.

He held up his hands in mock surrender, taking a step back. "I just wanted to tell you that I learned something about Carrow."

My heart thudded painfully in my chest. "What? When?"

"Yesterday," he said with a nonchalant shrug, crossing his arms.

"And you couldn't have told me last night?" I asked, the words laced with irritation.

He scoffed, the sound grating. "You didn't give me a chance."

"I gave you long enough, and you chose to waste it," I shot back.

"It's never a waste," he said, his smirk deepening. His eyes lingered on me, their gaze unsettling. "Anyway, I asked around, and I think I may know where the spell was completed."

My pulse quickened, though I tried to hide it. How much could I trust him? His tone was light, almost mocking, yet there was something about the way he held my gaze that made me pause. Was he actually being helpful for once?

I blinked, my frustration momentarily overshadowed by curiosity. "How would that help?"

He shrugged again. "Maybe something was left behind."

"It's been thousands of years," I said, shaking my head. "There wouldn't be anything left."

"Fine," he said, turning away with an exaggerated sigh.

I gritted my teeth, hating myself for what I was about to do. I called after him. "Wait, August."

He turned back, his smirk returning. "Yes, Winnie?" His

voice was laced together like a sonnet, every syllable calculated to irritate me.

"If you're lying—"

"Do you really think I'd waste my time lying to you?" he interrupted, feigning offense. "Winnie, you wound me."

"Take me." It came out like a demand, exactly how I intended. My chest tightened as the words hung in the air between us.

His smile widened, but his expression shifted slightly, almost as if he were amused and perplexed at the same time. Then, he wrinkled his nose. "You should clean yourself first."

My glare deepened, but I couldn't stop myself from brushing the stray hair from my face. The realization hit me like a slap— I wasn't perfectly done today. My hair wasn't pinned neatly, and my clothes weren't pristine. Of course he noticed. And he'd never let me live it down.

"Should we meet tonight?" I asked, trying to steer the conversation back on track.

"Nothing would make me happier," he said with mock sincerity, "but I have other . . . things that need tending to. Besides, it's a long ride. We have to go to Bodaira."

Bodaira. Of course, it had to be Bodaira. My stomach twisted at the thought of it.

"Are we going to ride?"

He let out a laugh, the sound soft but grating. "Do you think a horse would let me close enough to mount it?"

"If we walk, it will take a day just to get there."

"We'll work out the details tomorrow. Meet me at our spot," he said with a wink before disappearing into the shadows.

My heart raced with a mix of anger and anticipation. What was I getting myself into?

I gave Shadow a kick and instructed him to turn back around. He snorted, his way of telling me he didn't want our ride to end, but I had to go home. Especially now that I knew my once private rides where the only thing I may come across was a squirrel was now ruined by the worst possible creature.

And I desperately needed a bath.

Even though it was just August, I could never let him see me like this again.

18

Chapter 18

Bronwen

Our spot.

The pond had become our spot. We didn't need a spot. Even the thought of it made my irritation grow, which was already boiling under the surface at the thought of going to Bodaira. Crawling with witches.

Crawling with judgment.

Something I didn't want August to see. He didn't even know my family's station. He didn't need to know. I could only hope we wouldn't be approached. Though I was sure I wasn't someone they would want to approach if they could avoid it.

The pond looked different in the daylight. The light filtered through the trees, casting dappled patterns over the surface of the water. The once mysterious, shimmering pool now appeared shallow and ordinary. I had never bothered stopping here before considering I'd rather die than step foot into it. Or any body of water for that matter. The thought made my skin crawl.

I should add that to my ongoing list of things August can't know. I cannot swim. And I'm sure that would make him even more enticed to push me in.

The crunching of leaves behind me had me turning around in a hurry. August stood closer than I would have preferred, his head tilted to the side—that odd thing he always seemed to do—and studied me.

"What?" I bit out.

He let out a breath. "So much better than the state you were in yesterday."

He wasn't wrong, though him acknowledging it made me clench my jaw. My dress was a deep brown with sleeves that flared at the elbows into a flowing mess to match the bottom. I am sure he didn't notice that considering the way his eyes stalled at my chest.

Looks like that from men never bothered me. In fact, I welcomed them. Knowing I had a way to fluster them. To take control. But this time, heat rose in my chest. What am I doing?

I had to take his attention away from my body. I didn't like what I was feeling right now.

"How are we going to get to Bodaira considering you're afraid of horses?" I asked.

That brought his eyes back to mine. He let out a gasp and looked as if I had said the most offensive thing to him. "I am not afraid of horses. They are afraid of me."

"You say that."

He studied me for a moment, and something came across his face that he didn't say.

"You could do that magic thing you did on the night we met."

154

"What are you talking about?" That night had been so long ago, and I didn't remember every detail considering I almost died.

"Well, you just disappeared. Did you not take yourself somewhere else?"

"I—I did." The night flashed before my eyes. Before I could set him ablaze, he left. I looked everywhere, and he was nowhere to be found. "But I thought you left."

A smile formed on his full lips. "You'd be surprised all of the times I've been there and you just didn't know it."

He didn't just leave me to die, he hid. He managed to hide and restrict himself from feeding on me. I was an easy target— in the most vulnerable state I had ever been in—and he didn't kill me.

My mind was racing, which caught his attention as his eyes narrowed.

Don't let him catch you vulnerable again, Bronwen.

"I've never done it with another person. I don't know if I could."

A smile swept across his face once more. "Okay, we will do it my way then."

"What—" Before I could finish my sentence, he swooped me into his arms. "August—" The air left my lungs, and the world flew by in a blur. I gripped tightly onto him, too afraid to make him stop. If I fought back, would he drop me? What would it feel like to hit the ground at such a speed? I didn't want to know.

The wind lashed at my face, sharp and cold, making it hard to catch my breath. The trees blurred into streaks of green and brown, their forms twisting and stretching as we moved at an impossible speed. My heart pounded in my chest, each

155

beat a frantic echo in my ears. Trying to focus on anything other than the suffocating velocity made my stomach churn, so I squeezed my eyes shut and buried my face into his chest.

Finally, the rush slowed. The wind softened, and the air I inhaled no longer burned my throat. I dared to open my eyes and found August staring down at me, amusement dancing in his expression. My arms were locked tightly around his neck, my chest pressed to his in a way that made heat rise to my cheeks. I couldn't decide if it was the adrenaline or sheer embarrassment.

His hands, one firmly supporting my back and the other gripping beneath my legs, felt too steady. Too comfortable where they were. I swallowed hard and glanced around, realizing with a jolt that the vibrant blues and greens of Bodaira's coastal buildings were ahead of us.

How did we get here so quickly? I knew he was fast . . . but *that fast*? It couldn't have been more than a minute that I clung to him like my life depended on it. Or did time not feel the same when he moved?

"Put me down," I muttered, loosening my arms from around his neck.

He rolled his shoulders as if my grip had caused him discomfort. "But you seem so comfortable, Winnie."

I ignored him and pressed my palms against his chest to push away, but the moment my hands made contact, I froze. The raw magic beneath his skin thrummed in time with his heartbeat, strong and alluring. It pulsed under my fingertips, intoxicating in its sheer power. My breath hitched.

"Do you like what you feel?" he asked, his voice low and taunting.

His remark snapped me back to reality, and I wrenched

myself free from his grip, nearly stumbling in the process. I smoothed my dress with trembling hands before running my fingers through the tangles in my hair, desperate to reclaim some semblance of composure.

"Do not do that again," I said firmly, though my voice betrayed a slight tremor.

"Were you scared, Winnie?" he asked, his smirk widening as his eyes gleamed with mischief.

I narrowed my eyes, trying to mask the warmth creeping up my neck. "Of course not," I said quickly, too quickly. "It was just . . . I didn't like that."

August chuckled softly, his lips curling into a grin that only deepened my embarrassment. "Didn't like it? Or didn't like that you had to hold on to me?" His voice was low, teasing, and the glint in his eyes made it clear he was enjoying my discomfort far too much.

I crossed my arms as I tried to focus on the town behind him. "Can we just go?"

His playful expression shifted slightly, a flicker of something more serious crossing his face as he glanced at the path ahead. "We'll need to walk from here. The next spot is further along the coast."

The streets of Bodaira weren't bustling, but there were still enough people milling about—merchants pulling carts, fishermen hauling nets, children running barefoot near the edge of town. Their curious glances trailed us as we moved past, and I adjusted the sleeves of my dress, straightening them as I kept my head high.

The farther we walked, the quieter the town became. Cobblestones gave way to uneven dirt and pebble paths, and the hum of voices faded beneath the rhythmic crash of the waves.

Each step felt heavier, the path narrowing and twisting as the ocean loomed closer.

"Have you ever killed?" August's question came abruptly, breaking the tension of the silence as we walked along the uneven path.

"Are you kidding? You've watched me kill two vampires."

He shook his head. "Vampires are already dead. You can't kill what's already dead, Winnie. I mean have you killed the living?"

"A human?"

He nodded.

The crunch of pebbles beneath our feet echoed louder than it should have, as though the land itself was listening. The faint cries of gulls overhead seemed distant and eerie, and the occasional gust of wind whispered through the jagged rocks that lined the path.

"No."

"Would you?"

"If it was necessary."

The words left my mouth without hesitation, but the moment they hung in the air, a shiver ran down my spine. Would I really? What would it take for it to feel necessary? My hands instinctively clenched, and I wondered if August could see through my response as easily as he seemed to see through everything else.

He seemed rather satisfied with my answer, which gave me more unease. His faint smirk carried something darker, something unspoken, and I couldn't help but feel like I had just failed a test I didn't know I was taking.

"Here we are."

I glanced around at the beach where we had stopped. Gray

rocks lined the dunes, flowing into pebbles that gave way to the sand beneath our feet. The waves crashed furiously, each one a warning not to get too close. The air here felt colder, harsher, and the relentless roar of the sea drowned out any lingering thoughts.

On the other side of Joveryn, you could spend hours in the water, swimming and playing without any fears. Boats were free to travel to the other human kingdoms without worry of storms above or anything below to put them in danger. The sun always seemed to shine, and the waves were calm.

But here, on the northeastern side of the kingdom, we were met with nothing but unforgiving waters and certain death.

And it was all from pure magic.

"The bridge was here?" I asked.

"Yes."

I walked along the edge of the water, careful to keep my feet just out of the waves' reach. There was nothing to hint at the past, though I didn't expect there to be. Any piece of a man-made structure had been consumed by the waters long ago. The crashing waves seemed to mock my search, their endless movement a reminder of time's erasure.

"This was a waste." I threw my hands up as I turned to walk away, the frustration bubbling in my chest like a storm waiting to break.

"Wait—" August placed his hand on my arm but I quickly snatched it away as I turned back to him. "You're just looking. You need to feel."

"Feel?" That has got to be the dumbest thing he's ever said. "Shall I grab a handful of sand?" I scoffed as I turned once again to walk away.

In a blur, he was in front of me. "You're a witch. A big spell

159

happened here. So big it caused the earth to shift and the tides to change. Gods, an entire species was created from it! There has to be something left you can feel. Close your eyes. It's always connected."

I let out a breath and humored him, squeezing my eyes shut, though I had never heard of this before.

"Now clear your mind, take in the smells, the sounds beyond the crashing waves and distant thunder. Find the things that a human wouldn't notice because they are not gifted."

Gifted.

I bit my tongue at that, but I still did what he said. I slowed my breath, ignored the various sounds of nature and truly listened.

A tapping noise formed, rhythmic beats three on, silence; and three once more. It sounded almost like the tapping of one's fingers on a table. With the sound came a pull within me. A tug from my deepest self, the part bound in magic and formed by the gods themselves.

My eyes shot open to August, who stood in front of me carefully studying me. I turned to listen for the sound and feel for the pull I locked into only for it to grow fainter with my movement.

I turned back, and it all became stronger once more.

It was August. The sound, the feeling. The incessant creature I couldn't get rid of standing only a foot in front of me.

"You are going to have to back up."

He tilted his head.

"The only thing I can sense is the magic in you *begging* to be pulled out."

He opened his mouth to say something but quickly stopped

himself—unable to hide the smile that formed—and took several steps back.

I closed my eyes again and tried once more.

I still heard August's magic, but much fainter now. Turning my head to listen in another direction, I drowned out his sound and calmed myself.

It was different this time. Gone was tapping and now it was replaced with a low hum. Almost like a fly buzzing around your ear on a hot summer day. But there were no flies this time of year.

My eyes shot open, and I turned towards the sound. The humming grew louder with each step I took. Carrying me to a small gate that surrounded a rather overgrown area. I looked around trying to pinpoint the sound only to see small pieces of gray stone sticking out every few feet. The noise came from past what I could see so I lifted the latch rusted from the salt air and pushed the gate forward, its hinges fighting against me and creaking as if it hadn't been opened in years.

As I stepped in, I could feel August, his own type of magic tapping closely behind me. Gods I'd hoped I wouldn't hear this every time I was around him now.

I kept walking until a small stoned building stood before me. But it wasn't just a building. It was a crypt. I glanced around at the stones overtaken by dying weeds I had dismissed. They were headstones of graves. Graves that I could only imagine how old they were.

"Whatever it is, it's in there," I said, pointing toward the large moss-covered stone door. The door loomed before us, ancient and imposing. Dark moss crept along its edges, and the stone was marked with age. The air around it felt heavier, tinged with a faint metallic tang that made the hairs on my arms rise.

A rusted lock hung from a bolted piece of metal, oddly out of place against the weathered stone—as if it had been guarding secrets for centuries.

August stepped forward and placed his hand on the lock. The moment his fingers made contact, he hissed and yanked his hand back. Red welts bloomed across his fingertips, and his jaw tightened.

"What happened?" I asked, my voice sharper than intended.

"It's been spelled to keep vampires out," he said through gritted teeth. "I can't break the lock. I can't even touch it. You have to do it."

I hesitated but placed my hand on the lock, bracing for the same burning pain. Instead, all I felt was cold, rusted metal. I frowned. While magic had lashed out at August, I couldn't sense any lingering power in the lock. It felt mundane, inert. I tugged on it, but it held firm, the chain rattling mockingly.

I glanced between August and the lock before quickly grabbing his arm. The heat of his magic hummed beneath my fingertips as I quickly pulled a small amount. He yanked his arm away with a sharp growl.

"Fuck, Winnie." His voice was low and taut, a mix of irritation and something else I couldn't place. The brown eyes that met mine were narrowed in suspicion, as if he was studying a puzzle he couldn't quite solve. But I didn't let him linger long on the thought.

The stolen magic surged through me, potent and vibrant, and I channeled it into the lock. A faint crackling sound echoed before the lock turned to dust, its remnants falling to the ground.

I glanced back at August, expecting him to step forward, but he was watching me intently, his gaze heavy.

"What?" I snapped.

He tilted his head. "Why did you do that?"

"What do you mean? You wanted me to open the lock, and I did."

"No," he said, his voice quieter now, edged with something unreadable. "I mean why did you do *that* to me?"

I opened my mouth, but the words caught in my throat. His gaze pinned me in place, his eyes probing for something I couldn't let him find. He didn't know I couldn't use magic without a source, and I couldn't afford for him to figure it out.

"It's more fun that way," I said with a forced smirk, masking my unease with a casual shrug. Before he could press further, I turned to the door and pushed against it, but it refused to budge. I shoved harder, my pride warring with the reality that I wasn't strong enough to do this alone.

I turned back to August, ready to ask for his help, but his expression had shifted. The suspicion in his eyes had softened, replaced by a smile that made my stomach tighten.

Before I could speak, he was suddenly in front of me, his movements too quick for me to register. He pinned me against the stone door, his hands braced on either side of my head. The cold stone at my back only amplified the heat of his presence, his closeness overwhelming.

I clenched my jaw as August leaned closer, his smirk dripping with the same smugness that made my blood boil. He always had that look—like he knew something I didn't. Like he enjoyed keeping me on edge. And I hated how much it worked.

"Winnie *needs* me," he teased, his voice low, his tone maddeningly self-assured. He lowered his head until his face was close enough that I could feel his breath on my lips. My heart raced, and heat coiled low in my belly, betraying me. His dark eyes bore into mine, and for a moment, the world around us seemed to shrink, leaving only him.

"Stop calling me that," I said, quieter than I meant to.

His grin widened. "What should I call you then? Something softer?" He moved his lips to my ear. "Sweeter?"

Before I could respond, the stone door began to tremble, and I nearly stumbled as it shifted behind me. August stepped back, his hands falling to his sides, though his gaze never left mine.

The door had moved effortlessly for him, the weight of the ancient stone no match for his strength. I quickly turned as I felt the heat rise to my cheeks on my betraying body.

19

Chapter 19

Bronwen

The air inside the crypt was damp and suffocating, carrying a musty scent that clung to the back of my throat, thick and unrelenting. The stone walls wept with condensation, their surfaces cool and slick under my fingertips. The faint carvings etched into the walls seemed to shift in the dim light, worn down by centuries of neglect. Every breath I took felt heavy, as if the crypt itself resisted the intrusion of life. I found myself grateful that I wasn't alone—even if it was just August.

The floor beneath us was uneven, a patchwork of cracked stone slabs and loose gravel that shifted underfoot with every step. The faint scrape of our movements echoed briefly before being swallowed by the oppressive silence. A chill hung in the air, carrying the metallic tang of damp stone and the faint, sour scent of decay. But it was the weight of the place—a tangible pressure that seemed to sink into my chest—that truly set my nerves on edge.

I paused, straining my ears. The faint drip of water echoed

in the distance, each droplet striking like the tick of an unseen clock. Beneath the sound of August's boots scuffing the gravel and his magic tapping, there it was again—the humming. Low and insistent, it resonated in the air, a vibration that seemed to seep into my bones, tugging at the edges of my awareness.

"Do you hear that?" I asked, my voice barely above a whisper.

August stepped closer, his eyes narrowing as he scanned the darkness. "I hear nothing but your heartbeat, Winnie."

I ignored his comment and took another step forward, my pulse quickening as the humming grew louder. I closed my eyes, letting the sound guide me as I moved deeper into the crypt.

The path sloped downward, the walls narrowing until we emerged into a small chamber. The air here was colder, the darkness heavier. At the center of the room stood a pedestal, its surface cracked and weathered, as though it had been forgotten for centuries. And there, placed neatly on the top of the pedestal, was a small box.

The humming intensified as I made my way to it, the sound now a steady vibration that seemed to sync with the rhythm of my own heartbeat. The box was unassuming—made of dark wood, its edges reinforced with tarnished metal bands.

"Careful," August said from behind me, his tone sharper than usual. "Whatever it is, it's bound to be cursed."

I shot him a look over my shoulder to see a smile gleaming on his face but didn't hesitate as I reached for the box. The wood was cold beneath my fingers, the metal bands biting into my palm as I lifted it. The humming seemed to quiet the moment I held it, as if the box itself had been the source all along.

166

With a deep breath, I pried the lid open.

Inside, nestled within a layer of decayed velvet, was a leather journal. The cover was worn and cracked, its once-rich brown color faded to a dull gray. Faint symbols were etched into the leather, their meanings lost to time. I hesitated for a moment before picking it up, the pages crinkling softly under my touch. The weight of it felt strange, heavier than the worn leather and brittle paper should account for, as though the secrets inside had a presence of their own.

My pulse raced as I flipped open the journal, its fragile pages filled with spidery handwriting that I couldn't quite decipher in the dim light. Each word looked like it had been scrawled in haste, yet the precision of the symbols hinted at a careful hand. What was in these pages? And why did it feel like it had been waiting for me?

"What does it say?" August asked, his voice close to my ear now.

"I don't know," I admitted, turning the pages carefully. My fingertips brushed over the ink, which seemed to shimmer faintly, though I wasn't sure if it was a trick of the faint light. "But whatever it is, it's important. I can feel it."

August stepped closer, his presence unnervingly close. "Important," he repeated, his voice thoughtful but tinged with something else—something I couldn't place. Distrust bubbled up in my chest. Why did he care so much about this journal? Had he known it was here all along? Was he leading me into this for his own gain?

"Why don't I take it and see what I can figure out about the language?" he asked, his hand extending toward the journal. His tone was calm, almost too calm, as if he were trying to disarm me.

I quickly snatched it away, pressing it tightly against my chest. "I asked you to help me," I said, my voice sharp, "but why do I feel like you wanted to find this just as much as I did?"

His eyes narrowed, and a muscle ticked in his jaw. The reaction was brief, his expression quickly morphing back into that maddening, easy smile. "I'm just trying to help, Winnie. It's written in the old tongue. Do you know how to read it?"

I didn't.

His smile widened as though he'd guessed my answer. "I could translate it for you, but it might take some time. It would be much easier for me to take it home and work on it. Unless, of course, you'd rather spend even more time with me?"

No. I couldn't handle more time with August.

"Here," I said, shoving it into his chest before moving around him to leave this suffocating place. The cool air from the crypt's entrance beckoned me like a promise of relief.

Behind me, August let out a low chuckle, his amusement echoing softly in the confined space. His footsteps followed close, the steady rhythm a reminder that I wouldn't be rid of him so easily.

As I stepped outside, the bright daylight struck my eyes like a blinding glare. I squinted against the sudden brightness, my vision struggling to adjust after the oppressive darkness of the crypt. August groaned, pinching the bridge of his nose as he squinted his eyes shut against the daylight.

"I thought sunlight didn't bother you," I said, my voice laced with curiosity.

"Sunlight doesn't set me aflame like most, but it's still a nuisance. It gives me raging headaches and weakens my senses."

That little revelation sparked a fresh wave of curiosity. I couldn't resist pressing further. "Why can you come out during the day while others can't? And don't say it's because you're special, because you are not."

He studied me intently as if he were calculating just how much he should reveal. The silence stretched between us, heavy and taut. I half-expected him to deflect with one of his cryptic, infuriating remarks—something designed to confuse me or divert the conversation entirely.

But instead, he stayed silent, which only annoyed me more.

"Oh, now you choose not to speak?" I snapped, folding my arms tightly against my chest.

His eyes softened, the sharpness in his gaze dulling, but he still offered no explanation.

Frustration burned under my skin as I turned and walked out of the cemetery, the crunch of dead leaves and loose gravel marking my steps. Even though he stayed silent, his footsteps followed close behind, unrelenting in their steady rhythm. I didn't stop until I was standing on the beach once again, the sea air doing little to cool the heat of my growing irritation.

August's silence infuriated me more than his usual infuriating remarks ever had.

"I'm ready to go home," I said sharply, spinning to face him just as he tucked the journal into the pocket of his jacket.

That journal . . . I had done all the work to find it. I was the one who wanted it. And yet, there it was, in his possession, as if he had any right to claim it. He couldn't even answer one question that I had, and yet he expected me to trust that he would translate it for me?

"Come here," he said, stretching his arms out as if ready to scoop up a helpless child.

My anger boiled over. "Oh no. That is not happening again," I snapped, taking a firm step back.

"What do you suggest then?" he asked, tilting his head, his voice edged with amusement.

I stepped forward, narrowing the gap between us until I was close enough to feel the faint hum of his magic. "Payback," I muttered.

Before he could respond, I gripped his arm, pulling the magic from him in a single, fluid motion. His body stiffened, a low sound of protest escaping him before he fell motionless. The magic coursed through me, sharp and electric, setting every nerve alight. It bent to my will, responding to my command as the world around me blurred and shifted.

When I opened my eyes again, I was standing in the comfort of my small room, the journal clutched tightly in my hands.

Without August.

A faint smile tugged at my lips. He could bring himself back from Bodaira.

20

Chapter 20

Bronwen

"Where were you yesterday?" Mama chopped carrots, her knife moving methodically as she tossed them into the pot already boiling over the fire. The soft crackle of the fire and the rich aroma of simmering broth filled the small kitchen, mingling with the faint chill of the morning air. "With Lowen?"

Her question caught me off guard. It wasn't the first time I'd stayed gone all day. Though I rose early and never told her what I was doing, she had never questioned me before. The sound of the knife rhythmically hitting the cutting board filled the silence as I scrambled for an answer.

She pointed at the onion on the counter, motioning for me to bring it to her, though she never looked up.

"Yes," I lied, my voice steady despite the tightness in my chest.

"No, you weren't. Lowen came by yesterday looking for you."

The weight of her words pressed down on me. I kept silent, my fingers brushing against the wooden counter as I tried to appear unbothered.

"August, then?"

My stomach twisted into knots.

"I like August. He's very handsome and seems smitten with you, though I don't know much else about him or his family."

If only she knew.

"But you shouldn't lead Lowen on," she added, her tone light but firm, the way she always delivered her wisdom without judgment.

"I am not leading him on," I replied, frustration creeping into my voice. "I have told him my intentions. He has told me his. Many times. And I have denied him. Many times. But he will not leave me alone."

Mama's knife paused mid-chop, the soft scrape of the blade against the cutting board suddenly absent. She finally looked up at me, her expression thoughtful and measured. "Sometimes, kindness can feel like encouragement to someone who doesn't want to listen."

The words struck deeper than I wanted to admit. I bit my lip, unwilling to concede that she might be right. Lowen's persistence wasn't my fault, but a small part of me wondered if I should have been firmer—cruel, even.

Mama shifted her weight, reaching for a sprig of thyme on the counter. She stripped the leaves with deft fingers, the rhythmic motion calming in its simplicity. "People often cling to what they think they deserve, Bronwen," she said, her voice quiet but purposeful. "You can't control how they feel. Only how you respond."

I glanced at her, her face illuminated by the warm light of

the fire. She moved with practiced ease, her hands steady despite the slight tremor age had begun to bring. She looked so grounded, so sure of herself, and I envied that.

I wish I could have seen her before I broke her . . . before *we* broke her.

Her magic began fading while we grew inside her. She told me once that it felt like trying to grasp smoke, the power slipping further away each day. Everyone assured her it was temporary, just her body changing, and that once we were born, her magic would return.

But when my brother and I came into the world and her magic didn't return, the truth became undeniable: we had taken it.

They didn't understand exactly what we were until Adar wrapped his little hand around Papa's finger and pulled magic from him. Luckily at the mere age of a month old, he couldn't form the thoughts to do anything with the magic. Papa ripped his finger away immediately and because it was such a small amount, it didn't affect him.

Stories of witches like us—those without a natural connection to magic but with the ability to take it—were thought to be myths until we came along.

She had never blamed us or mistreated us, but I see it in her eyes sometimes. When Papa lights the fire by saying one word or when he gives the wilted leaves of the plants in her garden new life, I see the hurt in her eyes.

The sound of a log shifting in the fire drew my attention. I reached for the kettle, pouring hot water into two mugs, grateful for something to do. Steam curled lazily from the cups as I added dried mint, stirring absently as my thoughts raced. The pale morning light streaming through the window cast soft shadows over the worn wooden table. Beyond it, the world beckoned—chaotic, demanding, and full of the questions I couldn't yet answer.

"Is there something you're not telling me, Bronwen?" Mama's voice cut through my thoughts, gentle but probing.

"No, Mama," I said quickly, though the tightness in my chest remained. I turned away, feigning interest in the kettle by the fire. The journal hidden in my room felt like a weight pressing against my mind, its secrets threatening to spill over into the quiet of our home.

Her gaze lingered on me for a moment longer, as though she could see straight through my feigned composure. Then, with a small nod, she returned to her chopping. But her silence spoke volumes, and I knew she wasn't convinced.

As I picked up a rag to wipe the counter, the faint hum of the journal echoed in my memory, a reminder of the path I was walking. One misstep, and everything I loved could crumble around me.

***

As the sun dipped lower, casting the room in hues of gold and amber, I stared at the strange markings and scribbles filling the pages of the journal. The flickering light made the symbols dance, but no matter how long I studied them, their meaning remained just out of reach. My temples throbbed with a growing headache, a dull ache that mirrored my frustration.

I traced one of the symbols with my fingertip, the ink slightly raised as if it had been etched with intention. Who had written this? What kind of mind had created these cryptic words? My fingers itched to pull at the threads of magic

174

humming faintly from the pages, but I knew it wouldn't help—not without knowing what I was looking for. The journal's secrets felt locked behind a wall I couldn't see, let alone break through.

I reached for my mug, now-lukewarm and barely worth sipping, but it gave my hands something to do. The tea's faint aroma lingered, a mix of dried herbs that couldn't quite calm the tension winding tighter in my chest.

I leaned forward again, resting my elbows on the table as I pressed my palms against my forehead. I wasn't getting anywhere—not alone, at least. But the idea of asking August for help sent a fresh wave of frustration rippling through me. My mind replayed his smirks, his cryptic remarks, the way he always seemed to hold his knowledge just out of reach. Trusting him felt like reaching into a fire and expecting not to get burned.

Still, he knew things. More than he let on, certainly more than I did. The truth nagged at me, a sharp and insistent reminder that whatever lay within these pages wasn't meant to be ignored. I clenched my hands into fists, the cool wood of the table grounding me for a moment.

The journal had to stay with me—there was no way I'd let him keep it. Still, the realization settled over me like a weight: I'd have to spend more time with him to figure out what the journal says.

Gods help us both.

***

The night was heavy with silence, the kind that pressed against your ears and made every sound feel sharper, more intrusive.

The moon hung low, its silver light threading through the dense canopy of trees as I slipped into the woods, clutching my cloak tightly around me. The journal felt like a weight in my bag, its presence both urging me forward and filling me with doubt.

The cool air stung my cheeks, and the ground beneath my boots was damp, each step muffled by the soft moss and leaves carpeting the forest floor. Crickets chirped faintly in the distance, their song a lonely reminder of how far I was from home.

The woods had always felt alive to me, but tonight, they seemed to hold their breath, watching, waiting.

Each step carried me deeper into the dark embrace of the forest, and with it, the familiar tapping in my mind grew louder. Not the journal this time, but the memory of his presence and how I had learned that his magic called to me. It was as if the very trees whispered his name, urging me forward despite the weight in my chest.

When the faintest shift of air reached me, I stopped, my heart leaping into my throat. The clearing ahead glowed faintly under the moonlight, the still water of the pond reflecting the stars above. Our spot, though I hated thinking of it as such.

And then, as if summoned by my thoughts, there he was, leaning casually against a tree at the edge of the clearing. The faint glow of his pale skin caught the moonlight, and his dark eyes gleamed as they fixed on me.

"Winnie," he drawled, his voice a low hum that sent a shiver down my spine. "I was beginning to think you'd never come."

He took a step into the opening and my eyes followed until they stalled at an unexpected sight. Bound and on their knees next to him were three men, bloodied and bruised. They had put up a fight, but it wasn't enough to stop him.

"Please, join us, Winnie," he said, motioning for me to come out of the woods.

"What are you doing?" I asked as I took a step closer. I glanced down to see the small emblem on the men's cloaks. Legion soldiers.

August had captured three Legion soldiers.

21

Chapter 21

Bronwen

My breath caught in my throat, and for a moment, I couldn't move. The sight of them—bloodied, bound, and kneeling—sent a wave of unease rippling through me. My eyes darted over the soldiers, taking in their injuries: the gash across one man's temple, the bruises blooming along another's jaw, the way their shoulders sagged under the weight of defeat. The emblem on their cloaks gleamed faintly in the moonlight, a stark reminder of who they were and the danger their presence brought.

I forced myself to take another step, the damp earth cold beneath my boots. "What is this, August?" I asked. My fingers curled into fists, tension knotting in my stomach.

August crossed one leg over the other and leaned against a sword—a sword I hadn't noticed him holding before. "Two options here, Winnie. You kill them, or you let them go."

"What?"

"You said you'd never killed before. I want to watch you

do it for the first time." His eyes gleamed with a manic light, his grin stretching wider than it should have. He shifted his weight forward, almost bouncing on his heels like an excited child waiting for a show to start.

"I am not killing them." I walked to them and pulled the blade from my arm.

"Oh Winnie, I didn't know you had a heart."

"I am not a cold-blooded killer like you." Without a second thought, I ripped through the ropes and freed the first man. He didn't move. Didn't react to me freeing him.

"Three bound for Winnie to choose," August began, his grin widening like a madman savoring a private joke. "One free. Two bound. A game of balance, isn't it, Winnie? Every choice tips the scale. I wonder . . . can you keep it steady?"

I ignored him as I moved to the second soldier.

"Two freed. One bound."

"Do you ever stop talking?" I shot a glance at him, my patience already worn thin.

He tilted his head, feigning innocence. "What? I'm merely admiring your technique. It's almost like . . . you enjoy it." His tone dipped into something darker, something taunting. "Doesn't it feel good, Winnie? To hold their lives in your hands?"

"Stop calling me that," I said through gritted teeth.

"But it suits you," he said with a soft chuckle. "Winnie. It's endearing, really. Don't you like it?"

I shook my head, the anger at a tipping point as my knife ripped through the ropes that held together the last man's wrists.

"Three freed. But Winnie may still lose," August whispered.

The men stood in unison and rubbed their wrists, looking

around like confused animals.

They now knew August was a vampire. If they saw him during the day, what would they do? And me? What did they think I was? One looked oddly familiar, but I couldn't place it exactly. If I recognized him, did he know me? Did he know my name?

I shook the thought away. August would not risk himself. He would handle it. And whatever he did with them, well, that wasn't my concern.

It wouldn't be on me.

The men paced around in complete delirium.

"One last thing, gentlemen." The men stopped and stared at August. "She's a witch."

I turned and glared at him. "Are you fucking kidding me?"

"Woah, Winnie, I didn't know you had such a dirty mouth." August's face lit up in fascination.

The men, as if blind to the fact that a vampire was only a few feet away, drew their swords and pointed them at me.

"So you want to watch them kill me? I would've expected you to do it yourself." I took a step back, glancing between August and the Legion soldiers that seemed to stare straight through me.

He shrugged his shoulders. "You're a witch. Use your magic to kill them. Unless . . ." August let out an exaggerated gasp, covering his mouth. "You can't do that."

I glanced back at the soldiers who were inching their way closer. "August."

"*Tell me, tell me, tell me, tell me, Winnie.*" The words came quick.

"I can't," I said through gritted teeth.

A sinister smile grew on his lips. "Can't what?"

"I can't practice unless I have a source." The words tasted bitter on my tongue, like a confession I never wanted to make. Admitting it to August felt like a defeat, a crack in the armor I had carefully built around myself. My magic had always been my power, my secret edge, and now, laid bare before him, it felt like a vulnerability he could exploit. The hollow ache of not being able to access that power without a source gnawed at me, a reminder of how dependent I was—and now he knew it.

August let out a satisfied moan at my confession as if he had known all along. "Here. You might need this then." He tossed me the sword he had used to prop himself up, causing me to drop my satchel and the journal to fall out. His eyes widened when he saw the journal lying in the dirt.

I swore at him under my breath as I pulled the strings on my cloak to allow it to fall on the ground. I turned my attention back to the three men in front of me . They were significantly larger than me, each with muscles in their arms that were larger than my thigh. It would be a useless fight if they all came for me at once. I would have to be swift, and even then, my chances were slim.

"We had a deal." I glanced at August as I stepped back again, only for the step to be matched by the men.

"The deal was that we didn't kill each other until we found Carrow. Nothing was said about others killing you."

"Fuck you, August."

"Winnie. What would Odelia think if she knew her precious daughter just asked to fuck me?"

Before I could respond, the first man advanced, as the other two stood frozen in place. Their eyes seemed to be glazed over like they were waiting for a signal to take them out of the state they were in.

The soldier swung his sword low, but I met it with mine. The sound of metal clinking together filled the air, sharp and jarring. Our swords met each time, and I strained to match the force that was given to me. My arms ached from the weight of his strikes, and my breaths came short and quick. I wouldn't last long playing defense.

Thank the gods Adar taught me the Legion's techniques. I knew how to spar with them. But I had one thing on them.

They didn't know my techniques.

I feigned a swing high, my eyes intentionally marking a spot, before slicing much lower, straight through his stomach. His grunt of pain was drowned by the sound of steel against flesh. He fell, but I didn't give him a moment to recover. I pierced his chest before he hit the ground. Blood sprayed over me, warm and metallic, the sharp scent filling my nose. My hands trembled as I pulled the sword out, my mind screaming at me to process what I'd just done.

The first human I had ever killed.

But there was no time.

The second soldier lunged, his sword slashing down toward me. I ducked and rolled to the side, reaching for the fallen man's sword to even the odds. My fingers closed around the hilt just as the second soldier's blade crashed down where I had been a moment ago. The ground shook beneath the force of his strike.

I sprang up, gripping the second sword tightly. He swung again, but I parried with one sword while driving the other into his leg. His scream echoed through the clearing, raw and guttural. He stumbled back, his leg buckling as he reached for the blade embedded in his flesh. I didn't wait. Lunging forward, I drove my sword into his chest, the force of the blow knocking him off balance. He crumpled, blood pooling beneath him.

My breath came in ragged gasps as I turned to the last soldier.

The man I thought I recognized hesitated, his sword trembling in his hands. His eyes darted between the bodies of his comrades and my own blood-streaked form. Fear radiated from him, and for a moment, I thought he might flee. But then he lunged, his swing wild and untrained. I sidestepped easily, using his momentum to disarm him. The clang of his sword hitting the ground echoed like a death knell.

I pressed my blade to his throat, the sharp edge biting into his skin.

"Please," he whispered, his voice trembling.

My hands shook as I hesitated, my breath coming in shallow gasps.

August's voice cut through the moment, low and menacing. "Finish it, Winnie."

My mind raced, the weight of the blood already on my hands pressing against my chest. My fingers tightened on the hilt, but I couldn't bring myself to push the blade forward.

August stepped closer, his presence a suffocating shadow. "If you can't do it, I'll gladly help," he whispered in my ear, his voice dripping with mockery.

Before I could respond, August moved swiftly, stepping behind the soldier like a predator savoring its prey. "I'd hate for all of this blood to go to waste," he murmured, his voice low and almost reverent. His hand gripped the man's shoulder with deceptive gentleness, tilting his head to expose the vulnerable curve of his neck.

My breath caught as August's mouth brushed against the man's skin. The soldier's trembling form froze, his wide, terrified eyes locked on mine. I couldn't look away, even as August's fangs pierced flesh, the sound a sickening yet intimate whisper that seemed to echo in the clearing.

The soldier's body jerked, a choked gasp escaping his lips, but August held him firmly, his fingers flexing like he was savoring every moment. My stomach churned at the wet, visceral sound of feeding, yet a part of me—one I couldn't name—was transfixed. It was grotesque and hypnotic, the way his muscles tensed and his eyes fluttered closed, as if the act brought him something more than sustenance.

His gaze flicked to mine, crimson streaks smudging his lips. He didn't speak, but the challenge was clear: watch. I should have looked away, should have turned my back on the horror unfolding before me, but I didn't.

I couldn't.

August exhaled sharply as he pulled back, his chest slowly rising and falling. His lips glistened with blood, and his tongue darted out to catch a stray drop, the motion so deliberate it made my breath hitch. The man in his grasp sagged, his skin pale, his eyes glassy as the last shreds of life left him.

August let the body drop unceremoniously to the ground and straightened, the dark amusement in his expression giving way to something I couldn't quite place. His eyes flicked to my neck, lingering just long enough to make me feel exposed. My heart raced as his gaze returned to mine, sharp and knowing.

For a moment, the clearing felt smaller, the air thicker. I wanted to move, to run, to do something, but my legs were heavy, rooted to the ground beneath me. If he chose to attack, I wasn't sure I'd stop him.

But he didn't.

He let out a quiet, satisfied sigh, his lips curling into a faint smile as he turned and disappeared into the shadows.

The clearing was silent, the moonlight casting an eerie glow over the blood-soaked ground. I fell to my knees, my hands trembling as I stared at the bodies around me. My chest tightened, the enormity of what I'd done crashing down on me.

And yet, beneath the horror and exhaustion, a small, shameful part of me reveled in the chaos. In the power.

In the sight of August feeding.

I sat there for what felt like hours, the moonlight illuminating the crimson streaks on my skin. Finally, I forced myself to stand, my legs unsteady beneath me. I went to grab my cloak and satchel, only to find the journal gone.

Panic surged through me as I frantically searched the ground around me. My satchel lay open, its contents scattered, but the journal was nowhere to be found. I froze, my mind racing. My stomach churned as realization dawned.

"August," I hissed, my voice low but filled with venom. Of course, he had taken it. I should have known the moment his gaze lingered on it earlier. That smug, infuriating bastard. My hands clenched into fists as anger coursed through me.

The cold night air bit at my skin, but it did little to cool the heat rising in my chest. I stumbled back toward the woods, my thoughts swirling with frustration and determination. The clearing and its ghosts faded behind me, but one thought remained clear: I would get that journal back, no matter what it took.

22

Chapter 22

Bronwen

Market was a lot slower today than it had been. The air carried a biting chill, and the faint scent of roasting chestnuts mingled with the sharper tang of freshly dyed fabrics. Vendors called out half-heartedly to passersby, their voices weary, as if they too could feel the storm rolling in.

August was there, like always, but I refused to look at him. What happened two nights ago was weird, almost too intimate. And more than anything, I was mad. He took that journal, and I wanted it back. He came to our booth, did his usual flirting with Mama, and tried to get under my skin though I ignored every advance.

He eventually seemed to give up and leave our booth, though he didn't go far. I could hear his laugh at the woodworker's booth and him "accidentally" knocking over several glass items at the poor old woman's glasswork booth. The tinkling sound of breaking glass cut through the chilly air, followed by the old woman's exasperated sigh. But through it all, I never gave him one glance.

The streets had grown less crowded as the clouds grew thick and gray, so we decided to pack up the booth early and go home. I grabbed the last basket of scarves and began to carry them to the wagon.

Someone grabbed me by the arm and pushed me against a wall in an alleyway, causing me to drop the basket. Just before I reacted, I realized it was August, and the fear left me, replaced by annoyance.

The alley was dim, shadows pooling in the corners where the sunlight failed to reach.

"What?" I spat out, watching his eyes trail all over my face.

"Why haven't you looked at me today?"

I took my eyes away from him, noticing the dark green door with a gold fox plated on it that I had seen a few times in my nightmares.

"I didn't feel the need." I tried to leave, but he pulled me back in place.

His eyes raced over me.

I let out a sigh. "What do you want, August?"

He grinned, a dangerous glint in his eyes. "Are you upset that I made you kill?"

His words hit like a stone. The soldiers—their faces blurred in my memory, like a distant, unpleasant dream. I should have felt something for them, but all I could focus on was the journal. Why did their deaths feel like nothing more than a passing inconvenience? Why did August command so much of my attention, pulling me away from everything else?

Something was wrong with me.

"I want the journal back," I said, forcing my voice to stay steady, hoping it would mask the crack forming in my resolve.

187

"You took it from me first, Winnie. You know, after you pulled magic from me and sent boiling metal through my veins."

"I took it to find Carrow. Don't play games with me. Give it back."

His grin deepened, his voice lowering to something almost menacing. "And what do I get in return?"

"The satisfaction of not being turned to ash," I snapped, though my confidence faltered under his intense gaze.

"Hmm." He leaned closer, brushing his fingers against my cheek, his tone now silky and dark. "How about this? I'll return the journal . . . for a taste."

"A taste? A taste of what?"

He brushed the hair from my neck away and ran his fingers over my scar, lingering just long enough to make my breath hitch. "*You*, Winnie."

"Absolutely not," I hissed as I pushed his hand away, though my heartbeat betrayed my conviction. "I'm not yours to barter with."

"Oh, but you are," he whispered, his voice like silk. "You enjoyed it when I marked you. You *let* me bite you. Admit it, Winnie. You like it."

My heart rate quickened as he leaned into my neck and inhaled. I couldn't do anything. Not right now when anyone could walk by at any moment. If he was discovered, I had no doubt he would bring me down with him.

"Admit it. You're curious about how it may feel now that you're marked. I saw it in your eyes the other night. I know you've heard the stories. How euphoric it is after you've been marked. But just know that I am the only one that can make you feel that way. *You're mine*, Winnie."

I pushed him off of me. "I am not yours."

He came back, pressing his body close against mine and bringing his mouth to my ear. "Imagine how I feel. The taste of your blood consuming my mind. I could tear through the entire Market and never feel satisfied because nothing tastes like you. And here you are . . . so close. Just let me have a taste."

I couldn't move. I blamed it on the public setting but I couldn't deny that I was curious. I *did* let vampires bite me when I hunted them. But was it really different after you were marked? Was the committed woman truly insane, or was it so much more than that?

He brushed his lips down my neck, leaving goosebumps in its path. The hand I had between us, pushing against his chest, grew weaker in its restraint. I wanted to move, but my body wouldn't do it.

His teeth sunk into my neck, and I let out a gasp. After the initial sharp, cutting pain, my entire body warmed. A wave of something I couldn't place rippled through me. There was no way I should feel this . . . this heat, this strange comfort. I should have hated every second of it, but I didn't. Instead, my thoughts tangled in confusion and shame. What was wrong with me? Why couldn't I make myself stop him?

August gripped my sides with his hands. Somehow, my hand ended up in his hair, gripping it and fighting the urge to pull the magic I felt in him. A moan escaped my lips and any other time, it would have mortified me. But right now, I didn't care and I didn't want this to end.

My eyes drifted to the street to see two ladies staring at us with their eyes wide. Though they couldn't see exactly what he was doing, I knew what they were thinking. And the last thing I needed was for them to run screaming vampire.

With the hand gripping his hair, I pulled his mouth from my neck and brought it to my own. I'd rather those ladies think I was a whore than know what was really happening.

August tensed after what I had done, his eyes widening slightly in shock. For once, the ever-composed vampire seemed stunned, caught off guard by my boldness. But he recovered quickly, relaxing almost immediately and bringing a hand up to cup my face. I pushed aside the thought that I could taste my blood in his mouth as I deepened the kiss, trying to make it as believable as possible.

I allowed it to go on for possibly a moment too long when August's hand started trailing down my back, but after I glanced back to the street and saw that the bystanders were gone, I pushed him off of me.

He looked at me with an uncertainty in his eyes that I hadn't seen before. I paused for a moment as I looked at him before I brushed the thought off. I grabbed his arm and pulled a small amount of magic from him, just enough to heal the bite. Even after that, he stood silent, his gaze flicking between my lips and my eyes as though trying to make sense of what had just happened.

A small laugh escaped my lips at the thought that something as simple as a kiss had managed to leave him speechless. The one person I never thought would shut up.

"A couple of ladies stopped to watch the show. I just gave them a different one to protect your secret." I turned to walk away, but he grabbed me by my hand and brought me back close to him, gentler than he's ever been.

He singled out my thumb and brought it to my lips, rubbing it across them before showing it to me. It was covered in blood.

I was about to walk into a street full of people with blood on my mouth. My blood, yes. But I'm not sure how I could've explained my way out of it.

August brought my thumb to his mouth and sucked the blood off of it. My breath grew shallow at what he had done and the memory of his lips on my neck came flooding back.

"Red looks good on you, Winnie."

His sly words snapped me back to reality. I snatched my hand from his before storming off without saying another word.

As I disappeared into the crowd, my mind refused to settle. Anger surged first—at him for his audacity, his constant need to manipulate and control, and at myself for letting him. My hands clenched into fists as I replayed the encounter, each word, each smirk, igniting the simmering rage inside me.

But anger wasn't all I felt, and that was the worst part. Beneath the frustration was something darker, something I didn't want to name. A pull, a curiosity, an undeniable intrigue that made my chest tighten. His touch lingered on my skin, his words echoing in my ears, weaving through my thoughts like a thread I couldn't untangle.

Why couldn't I ignore him? Why did his presence feel so overwhelming, like he filled the air I breathed, leaving no room for anything else? It wasn't just hatred—it was fascination, and that truth burned hotter than my anger.

I stopped in the middle of the street, the hum of Market fading into the background. My fingers brushed against my neck, the scars still there. I should have hated every second of it, but instead, a wave of warmth rippled through me at the memory. It wasn't just the physical sensation—it was the way he looked at me, like I was both prey and partner, an equal and a conquest all at once.

That's what made me hate him the most. He saw too much. He knew how to twist every moment, every feeling, until I couldn't tell where my anger ended and something else began.

I touched my lips absentmindedly, the ghost of his still lingering there. The kiss—it had been my way of taking control, of protecting his secret, but the way his eyes widened, the way his hand hesitated on my back, told me I'd done more than distract him. For once, I'd caught him off guard, and part of me reveled in it.

But then he'd smiled, that infuriating, knowing smile that made my stomach twist. He knew. Somehow, he always knew exactly what I was feeling, even when I didn't.

Why couldn't I ever keep control of the situation?

I shook my head and forced my feet to move. Whatever this was, whatever hold he thought he had over me, I wouldn't let it control me. I'd get the journal back, and I'd make him regret ever thinking he could toy with me.

And yet, as I walked away, the memory of his voice lingered, low and teasing, wrapping itself around me like a whisper I couldn't shake.

"Red looks good on you, Winnie," his voice echoed faintly in my mind.

23

Chapter 23

I never realized just how much self-control I had until I let her walk away. The only thing my body had been craving for weeks just walked away.

She walked away.

If she hadn't pulled me off her when she did, I might not have been able to stop myself from draining her in broad daylight right in front of those nosy women.

Each step up the stairs grew heavier. My body begged me to go after her while my mind pushed me forward until the door closed behind me. The dim light filtered through cracks in the shutters, casting jagged lines across the room. The air was thick with the scent of old wood and damp stone, suffocating as the rage inside me boiled over.

Go go go go go. The voices grew louder, insistent, until I grabbed a chair from the small table and hurled it across the room. The crash of splintering wood echoed, but it did nothing to quench the fire roaring inside me. My chest heaved as

I picked up one of the broken legs and, without hesitation, plunged it into my stomach.

The sharp, excruciating pain bloomed, grounding me just enough to stop the spiral. I collapsed onto the ground, my back hitting the cold floor, and closed my eyes. The agony was a small mercy—a barrier between me and the overwhelming urge to chase her down and take what I wanted. My mind whispered dark thoughts, but the pain kept me tethered.

I needed something to prevent me from going after her with the taste of her blood still in my mouth. It was too much. But gods, I needed to feel it again. I begged the pain to knock me out, to carry me through the night without another thought.

***

When the first light of morning crept through the cracks, I stared at the ceiling, exhausted and empty. I hadn't dreamed. Could it be that I've lived and died through every vampire she had killed? No. It was more than that. I fed on her. Gods alive, I have never felt something like that. Her taste set every fiber of my being on fire with need.

I shouldn't have done it. It made the unrelenting craving for her infinitely worse. She was all I could think about—not just the image of feeding on her, but everything else. The scent of her hair, the way she looked at me like she's plotting every possible way to kill me.

She didn't just make my mouth water anymore. She made my fucking cock hard.

My body craved her blood, but my mind—it craved something I didn't dare name. She wasn't just prey; she was a force that could unmake me.

And fuck I think I'd let her do it.

I stood, the broken chair leg still embedded in my stomach, and pulled it out with a grunt. The wound closed almost instantly, but the pain lingered in my mind like a dull ache. As I paced the room, my thoughts spiraled further. Why was feeding on her different? Why had the dreams stopped?

The silence of the night before was unnerving, like a missing piece of a puzzle I didn't know I was solving. Why did feeding on her feel like . . . more? It wasn't just blood. It was her.

And I hated how much I wanted her again.

As the memory of her blood filled my mind, I clenched my fists. Her taste was unlike anything I'd ever known. It wasn't just sustenance—it was euphoria, fire, and something that clawed at the edges of my control. It was her defiance, her fury, the way she looked at me as if she could burn me to the ground with a single glance.

She doesn't just consume my thoughts; she ignites something primal, something I can't suppress.

And then there was the kiss. The moment her lips met mine, everything shifted. For a brief second, she'd taken control, and it had stunned me. Even now, the memory of it lingered, her taste mingling with the faintest trace of blood.

I shouldn't have let her walk away. But I did. And it was the second time I'd made that mistake.

I stopped pacing and stared at the closed door. The room felt too small, the air too thin. My mind screamed at me to stay put, to fight the urge clawing at my chest. But I couldn't.

The storm had left the ground saturated and muddy, muting the world outside. When I opened the door, the damp air hit me like a whip, but it wasn't enough to ground me. I couldn't smell her—not in this rain-soaked atmosphere and certainly not near her home, where her father's magic masked their scents. The absence of her scent was maddening, but it also told me one thing: she was home.

The distance to her house from town was long, but my speed made it feel like nothing. The ground squelched faintly beneath my boots, a reminder of the storm that had drenched everything in slick, dark mud. As I reached the treeline near her home, I paused, staying hidden among the towering trees. From the treeline, I saw the cottage bathed in the faint, damp glow of morning light. Shadows moved in the yard—Winnie and her father. I stayed hidden, my body pressed against a tree, watching them.

She was training. The sharp clang of steel rang through the heavy air as she parried her father's blows. Her movements were precise, her posture rigid yet fluid. Even from this distance, I could see the determination in her eyes, the way she refused to back down, even when he pushed her harder.

Her hair was pulled back, but a few strands had come loose, clinging to her face with the moisture still in the air. She fought with an intensity that made my chest tighten. I couldn't look away.

Her father said something I couldn't hear, his tone sharp but instructive. Winnie responded with a quick retort, her lips curling into a faint smirk before she lunged forward, forcing him to step back. Even in this, she was defiant, unyielding.

My eyes traced the lines of her figure, the way her breath clouded in the cool, damp air, the flush of exertion on her cheeks.

I tightened my grip on the tree, forcing myself to stay hidden. To her, I was the monster in the shadows, and maybe she wasn't wrong. But watching her now, something shifted in me again, a pull I couldn't ignore.

What was she doing to me?

I stayed until the sun began to set, the light glinting off the damp ground as her father called an end to their training. As she turned to follow him inside, a flicker of hesitation stopped her. She paused at the door, her head tilting slightly. I recognized the motion instantly—she was listening.

Her head snapped around, her sharp gaze sweeping the treeline. What sound my magic made was too subtle for most, but she had learned to hear it. I held still, but it was too late; she'd sensed me. Her green eyes narrowed, and without a word to her father, she stepped off the porch and began walking toward the woods.

I stepped out from the shadows, letting her see me. Her expression shifted, a mixture of irritation and curiosity crossing her face. She didn't hesitate, closing the distance between us with purposeful strides.

"What do you want, August?" she asked, her voice sharp, but there was something else there too—a challenge.

"Just checking in," I said smoothly, letting a slow smile spread across my face. "You seemed . . . preoccupied."

"Did you bring me the journal?" she asked, her voice sharp, cutting through the cold air.

The journal. For a moment, it had slipped my mind, replaced entirely by thoughts of her. The way she moved earlier, the fire in her eyes—it had consumed me.

"No," I said smoothly, letting a slow smile spread across my face. I leaned against a tree, feigning calmness to hide the truth. "I've been dealing with some other things."

Her expression darkened, her irritation flaring instantly.

"We had a deal, August. You feed on me, and I get the journal. Or have you conveniently forgotten?"

"I haven't forgotten," I said, pushing off the tree and stepping closer. "But it's not as simple as handing it over. That journal isn't some bedtime story, Winnie. It's filled with things that could change your perception of the truth."

Her eyes narrowed, her jaw tightening. "And you're the expert now?"

I tilted my head, letting the playful menace creep into my voice. "I might be. At the very least, I'm the only one who can help you decipher it."

"I don't need your help."

"Don't you?" I asked, stepping close enough to see the defiance flicker in her gaze. "I'm not keeping it from you. I only want to help. But if you'd rather find another vampire old enough to understand this lost language, then by all means."

Her anger faltered slightly, replaced by hesitation. I could see the war inside her, the conflict between her pride and the possibility I might be right.

After a long pause, she crossed her arms tightly. "Fine. But I want it back."

"Of course," I said, smiling faintly. "We can meet tomorrow at our spot to study it."

The mention of the pond brought an immediate shift in her demeanor. Her shoulders stiffened, and her gaze turned distant. She didn't say anything, but I knew exactly what she was thinking. The soldiers. The blood.

"You're thinking about them," I said softly, watching her closely.

Her eyes snapped back to mine, her expression guarded. "They are dead. I killed them. Should their deaths not bother me?"

I let the silence stretch between us, the weight of her question hanging in the cold air. "Does it truly bother you? Or do you just think it should?"

Her lips pressed into a thin line, but she didn't respond. Without another word, she turned and began walking back toward the cottage, her boots squelching softly against the wet ground. I watched her go, every step drawing her further away yet leaving me more tethered to her than ever.

24

Chapter 24

Bronwen

The scream that ripped through my throat startled me awake, a cold sweat clinging to my skin. I clutched the blankets tightly, my chest heaving as I tried to shake the remnants of the nightmare.

Disappointment flooded me. The night before last, for the first time in weeks, I had slept soundly. No nightmare. No new victim that I had to live through. I didn't know why, but the night full of sleep felt like a gift. Now, it was gone, and the return of another nightmare felt like a cruel reminder of my failures.

I pushed the covers back and swung my legs over the side of the bed, the cold wooden floor biting against my feet. The room was dim, the pale morning light filtering through the curtains. My mirror caught my eye, its surface reflecting the disheveled mess I had become.

With a sigh, I stood and made my way to the washbasin. I splashed my face and began the familiar routine of preparing myself for the day.

I left my room and padded softly down the hall. The scent of wood smoke greeted me, leading me to our small sitting room rather than the kitchen. The fire crackled warmly in the hearth, its golden light dancing across the stone walls.

My steps faltered as I saw them—Papa and Mama sitting close together on the worn loveseat by the fire. His arm was draped protectively over her shoulders, and her head rested against his chest. They were speaking in low voices, their words indistinct but filled with a tenderness that made my chest ache.

Mama's laughter, soft and melodic, broke through the quiet. Papa leaned down to press a kiss to her temple, his expression uncharacteristically gentle. It was a rare sight—one that I cherished even as it left me feeling like an intruder.

I hovered in the doorway, uncertain whether to interrupt. My parents had always been a team, their love a constant in our lives. But seeing it so openly displayed, in the quiet intimacy of the morning, was something else entirely.

Mama noticed me first, her gaze lifting to meet mine. Her smile widened, warm and inviting. "Good morning, Winnie. Did you sleep well?"

"Good morning," I replied, stepping into the room. "Well enough."

Papa's eyes shifted to me, his usual sternness softened by the glow of the firelight. "Come, sit with us," he said, patting the space next to him.

I hesitated for a moment before crossing the room and sinking into the space next to him. Papa wrapped his arm around me and pulled me into his chest. I stiffened briefly, but the familiar scents of leather and pine washed over me, soothing the tension in my shoulders. With a quiet sigh, I let myself lean into his warmth, my hand unconsciously curling against his chest as the fire's glow danced across the room.

The next few hours passed uneventfully, but the weight of anticipation hung heavy in my chest. As the afternoon stretched on, I grabbed my cloak and headed outside. The air was brisk, carrying the sharp chill of the season. As I made my way to our spot, the sun's weak rays pierced through the sparse canopy, warming my skin just enough to stave off the cold.

He was already there, leaning casually against a tree at the edge of the clearing, his dark coat blending into the shadows. The sunlight glinted off his hair, and his expression was somewhere between smug and amused as I approached.

"You're late," he said, straightening as I stepped closer. His voice carried a lightness, but there was an edge to it—as if he'd been waiting longer than he wanted to admit.

"Did you bring the journal?"

He smirked, holding it up. "I did."

I rolled my eyes, adjusting the cloak tighter around me. "You could've picked somewhere warmer for us to meet."

"I'm not the one who needs to worry about the cold," he replied, his tone teasing. He turned the journal over in his hands, his fingers brushing the aged leather. "Shall we?"

With a nod, I settled on a fallen log near the pond. August crouched beside me, his presence a reminder of the strange partnership we'd formed, and handed me the journal. As I opened it, the faint scent of aged leather and ink drifted up, mingling with the crisp air.

"Have you looked at it already?" I asked, glancing at him.

"Of course," he replied, his tone casual. "But it's not exactly a quick read."

"What does it say?" I asked as my fingers brushed over the markings.

"It's a mix of old dialects, some magical script, and a few things even I don't recognize. But this—" he pointed to a passage near the center of the page. His fingers grazed mine causing me to jerk my hand away. "—mentions Carrow."

I followed his finger, my heart skipping at the name. "Can you translate it?"

"Not all of it," he said, his brow furrowing. "But enough to know it's important."

He nodded towards the journal. "This mentions a curse."

"A curse? I thought he wanted to be immortal?"

"He did. He was at one point. He was fae, which are immortal beings. He upset the wrong witch, and they cursed him with a slow, painful death. A very old fae to now become mortal being forced to feel what it was like to be hundreds of years old until his body eventually gave in.

"He traveled to Joveryn and found a witch to find a way to reverse what was done to him. And trying to reverse a curse, well, it always has its consequences."

The word "curse" felt like a blow, reverberating through my mind. A curse. My fingers brushed over the faded ink on the page, the spidery script mocking me with its incomprehensibility. This journal was supposed to hold answers, not more riddles. I clenched my fists, the rough edges of the leather digging into my palms as a wave of frustration surged through me.

"How does this help us?" I snapped. "It's all just . . . fragments. Words that don't mean anything without the full context. We need something solid, something we can use."

August's gaze flicked to me. "Patience, Winnie," he said, his tone infuriatingly calm. "The answers are here. You just have to be willing to dig for them."

I glanced at him, suspicion flickering in my chest. "Why are you helping me?"

He smirked, his gaze meeting mine. "Why do you want to kill him?"

My attention was drawn back to the journal. "I have my reasons."

"And when you decide to share your reasons with me, maybe I will share mine."

"This doesn't help me find him."

"We have an entire journal to search through. Something is bound to give us a hint eventually."

I let out a breath as I scanned the area. My eyes came to a halt at the blood-soaked ground on the other end of the clearing. The rain had washed away most of the blood, but a few spots remained.

A flicker of satisfaction surged through me, quickly followed by guilt. The soldiers' deaths had been necessary—*hadn't they*? But the memory of their faces, their screams, intruded like an unwelcome guest. What kind of person felt triumph in that?

August shifted beside me, his gaze following mine. "How does it make you feel, Winnie? Knowing you defeated three warriors."

I shot him a look, heat rising in my chest. "I don't owe you an answer."

His smirk deepened, and he leaned closer, his voice a low murmur. "No, but it doesn't take away my curiosity."

His breath raised the hairs on my neck, sending a small flutter through my belly that I desperately tried to ignore. The conflicting sensations of fear and fascination tangled within me, leaving me unnerved. Why was he beginning to have this effect on me? I turned to him, my eyes shifting for a second to his lips reminding me of the feeling of them on mine only days ago. I wanted to say something to ease the tension, but the words caught in my throat. His deep brown eyes, which usually felt like two endless pools of darkness peering into my soul, now shimmered with an otherworldly warmth. The sunlight revealed caramel hues streaked with flecks of gold that seemed to dance and swirl, mesmerizing me despite my best efforts to look away.

"Tell me, Winnie," he paused for a moment, his gaze lowering, "Did you dream about me last night?"

That was enough to have me almost fall off the log as I tried to put some distance between us.

"Gods, August, are you that vain? I do not dream about you," I snapped, though the heat rising to my cheeks betrayed the unease his question sparked.

He titled his head and smiled. "Not like *that*. Though I don't think Lowen would satisfy you anymore if you ever dreamt of me."

Him bringing up Lowen caught me off guard. Was he . . . *jealous*?

"Then what did you mean?" I asked.

"I meant the nightmares."

I crossed my arms. Why did he have to phrase it like that, as if he knew exactly how to get under my skin? "Of course I did."

"And the night before?"

"No," I admitted reluctantly. "Though I had just assumed I'd gone through all of your killings."

It was a refreshing change to go from a few hours of sleep to uninterrupted relaxation. Though the peace caused me to sleep far later in the day than I ever had. I may have slept through the entire day if it wasn't for Papa slinging my door open and practically flipping me out of the bed to spar with him.

"It's been forty-two days. You are far from the amount that I've killed."

"Then why did it skip a night?"

"I have a theory."

I waited for an answer. Had he found a loophole? A way to get me out of this torture?

"I fed on you, and we both got a good night's sleep for the first time in weeks." His words hung in the air like a challenge. My breath hitched as I processed the implication, my mind reeling with the mixture of anger and confusion.

Him feeding on me brought more than I could handle with it. It made me lose control, something I had to have. Especially around him.

But the thought of not having to die every time I closed my eyes? Tempting.

He smiled as he leaned a little closer to me, as if he could hear the conflicting thoughts I was having. He brought his hand up and toyed with the strings that kept my cloak wrapped tightly around my neck, his fingers grazing the soft fabric in a way that sent a shiver down my spine.

"N—no." I pushed his hand away, my voice faltering as I fought to regain control over my racing thoughts.

"Winnie, I—" His eyes darted sharply to the woods, his

entire demeanor shifting in an instant.

Before I could react, he wrapped his arm around me, and the world blurred as he moved us swiftly into the shadows of the woods. In a single motion, he had me pinned against a tree, his hand pressed firmly over my mouth. The solid pressure of his body against mine left no room for escape, and my heart pounded in my chest.

"Someone is coming," he whispered, his voice barely audible but edged with urgency.

His eyes held mine for a moment, warning me to stay silent. The weight of his hand over my mouth, combined with the intensity of his gaze, sent a mixture of irritation and fleeting fear coursing through me. I grabbed his arm, my nails biting into his skin, and he seemed to understand the unspoken message. Slowly, he lowered his hand, though his body remained pressed against mine.

The voices grew louder, drifting through the trees with a commanding edge. August's gaze was locked intently on the direction of the voices, his body tense and unmoving. My curiosity surged, and I wriggled free from his grip, and turned to follow his line of sight.

"I know I heard someone," a gruff, authoritative voice muttered, the sound sending a jolt through me. It was deep and laced with suspicion, each word deliberate as though the speaker was accustomed to issuing commands.

A second voice responded, softer but no less resolute. Their footsteps crunched through the underbrush, growing louder with each passing second. My pulse quickened as I strained to make out their silhouettes.

Finally, a figure emerged through the haze of trees, a Legion soldier with a graying beard and a hand resting on the hilt of his sword. His eyes scanned the area, narrowed in focus. Another man stepped forward behind him, his broader frame partially obscured by the shadows. The air left my lungs in a rush as recognition hit me like a blow.

Adar.

My brother's familiar features came into view, his sharp jawline and bright green eyes hardened in a way that made my stomach twist. His presence was a jarring collision of relief and dread.

I instinctively stepped back, colliding with August, who stood unwavering behind me. His body tensed, a protective edge radiating from him that both annoyed and unsettled me. My mind raced, grappling with the shock of seeing Adar here, of all places, and the consequences that might follow.

August's gaze flickered to mine briefly, his eyes calculating. He leaned closer, his lips brushing the shell of my ear as he whispered, "Stay quiet, Winnie."

The older man crouched at the blood-stained ground, his knees creaking audibly as he leaned closer. His gnarled hands hovered over the crimson stains, fingertips brushing the dirt as if searching for some hidden truth. A string of curses escaped his lips, low and bitter, his breath forming small clouds in the cold air. His face twisted in frustration, the lines etched deeply into his weathered skin revealing a lifetime of duty and suspicion.

Adar's head turned in my direction, his sharp eyes scanning the treeline with an intensity that made my breath catch. August tucked us further behind the tree as I struggled to stay silent. The cold air seemed to cling to my skin, every inhale sharp and shallow as if even my breathing might give me away.

I wanted to move, to run, to do something—but my body

refused to obey. My heart slammed against my ribs, its rhythm loud enough that I was sure Adar could hear it. The underbrush crunched beneath his boots as he stepped closer, the sound like thunder in the oppressive quiet of the clearing.

Adar's gaze swept past me, lingering for a heartbeat too long before moving on. I clenched my fists, my nails biting into my palms to keep my focus. But the weight of his presence was suffocating, his every movement a reminder of how close I was to being discovered.

I turned my head just enough to catch August's expression. His body was taut, like a coiled spring ready to snap. His gaze flicked to me briefly, his eyes hard, before returning to the clearing.

The sharp snap of a twig broke my thoughts, and my eyes shot back to Adar. He crouched low, inspecting the bloodstains on the ground with a furrowed brow.

A wave of guilt crashed over me, threatening to drown out the fear. I wanted to call out to him, to explain everything, but the weight of my secrets pressed down on me, locking the words in my throat. If he knew—if he found me here—it would all unravel.

Adar straightened, his gaze drifting once more toward the trees. His jaw tightened as he took a cautious step forward. My knees threatened to buckle as I fought the urge to bolt. The shadows shielded us for now, but the distance between us felt impossibly small.

I swallowed hard, turning back to August. My voice was barely a whisper, trembling with urgency. "Get me out of here."

Without a remark, a playful smile, or any type of torture he loved to give, he nodded and scooped me up.

25

Chapter 25

Adar

Something stirred in the woods.

I froze, my hand instinctively tightening around the hilt of my sword. My breath fogged in the crisp air, the only sound the crunching of leaves beneath my boots. My gaze fixed on the shadows between the trees, and for a fleeting moment, I thought I saw movement—a shape, dark and swift, slipping deeper into the forest.

"Delvaux!" The gruff voice of my superior snapped me back to the present. He crouched near the blood-stained ground, his weathered face etched with suspicion as he gestured for me to come closer. He'd insisted on reviewing the scene himself, muttering something about "missing pieces."

I shook off the lingering unease and strode back to him, forcing my focus to return to the task at hand. The clearing reeked of death, the metallic tang of blood lingering even though the bodies had been removed. Dark stains marred the ground where the soldiers had fallen, the churned-up earth telling a grim story.

"Look at this," my superior muttered, his calloused fingers pointing to the disturbed ground near one of the former bodies. The churned ground was clawed and torn, as though something had fought violently for survival. "There was a fight here. Not just any fight—whoever did this was quick. Precise."

I crouched beside him, my eyes scanning the area. The patterns in the ground painted a vivid picture: a struggle, brief but brutal. Deep gouges marred the dirt, and patches of dried blood shimmered faintly in the weak sunlight. It was clear that this was no ordinary attack.

My mind flickered back to a few nights ago—the initial search.

Three soldiers had gone missing during a routine sweep, and their silence had been enough to send a ripple of unease through the Legion.

We found the first signs of a struggle not long after entering the area they were designated to patrol that night. The ground was churned and bloodied, faint impressions of footprints in the dirt. A Legion cloak laid abandoned at the base of a tree darkened by dried blood.

"Spread out," I'd ordered, the wind biting at my face as the patrol fanned into the trees.

My group was the one that found them. Two soldiers fallen close to each other, one with one of our swords embedded in his leg, both gashed deeply and covered in blood. Was this some sort of ambush? Did it have to do with our coven? Our men in the coven are trained, but Papa would have found a way to send me a message if it had to do with the coven so I

211

could ensure no one would suspect us.

"The last one is over here!"

I turned to the soldier's direction but froze in my tracks when I saw who it was.

There, with no gash marks, no sign of struggle, lay Rhydian. My breath caught in my chest, tightening like a vise as I took in his face. His once vibrant, full-of-life expression was now hollow, his skin pale as ash. No one told me he was one of the missing soldiers. No one warned me what I was fucking walking into.

My hands trembled as I crouched next to him, my gaze fixed on the puncture wounds on his neck. A vampire had been here. And Rhydian was the only one bitten.

The realization hit me like a blow, and anger surged through me, hot and consuming. He didn't even want to join the Legion. I remembered his hesitation, the way he laughed nervously whenever we sparred, always saying he'd rather be hunting or working the fields. He wasn't meant for this life. He wasn't meant to die here.

I wasn't there. I didn't protect him. What kind of friend— *what kind of soldier*—was I?

A vampire that fought the first two with a sword? A vampire that managed to restrain himself from feeding despite all the bloodshed? It didn't make any sense.

Unless . . . he wasn't alone.

The thought twisted like a knife in my gut. Rhydian had no chance, no way to defend himself against something like this. And I hadn't been there to protect him.

"Adar!" One of the men's voices broke through my haze, but I couldn't tear my eyes away from the blood-soaked ground. Anger and guilt twisted in my chest like a blade. Why had he been bitten while the others seemed to have fought? Why him?

"Sir!" The voice came again, sharp and urgent, pulling me back to reality. I clenched my fists, my determination hardening. Whoever had done this would pay.

"Delvaux?" My superior's voice dragged me back to the present. He was still crouched near the blood-stained ground, his sharp eyes scanning for any missed detail.

"Do you think they're still nearby?" I asked, glancing back toward the treeline, my grip tightening on my sword.

The older man followed my gaze, his expression hardening. "If they are, they'll regret sticking around."

***

My superior gave me leave for the night, knowing how close we were to my family's home. I trudged up the steps, knocking the mud off of my boots before pushing the wooden door open. Mama dropped the pot on the counter when she saw me.

"Adar! What a wonderful surprise," she said as she wrapped her arms around my neck. Wrapped in her small frame, I felt the first bit of relief I'd had in days. Papa stood and placed a hand on my shoulder. I glanced at him to see his forehead creased. He knew better than to think I was just home for a friendly visit.

Mama pulled away and looked between the two of us. Her touch lingered on my arm for a moment longer than usual, as if she could sense the weight pressing down on me. The warmth of her embrace still clung to me, a fragile barrier against the cold that seemed to have seeped into my bones over the past few days. It was the first moment of solace I'd felt in weeks, a flicker of something resembling peace. But it was fleeting, and I knew better than to hold onto it for long.

"We can talk about it later." I nodded to Papa. "Where's Bronwen?"

"Winnie!" Mama yelled down the hall.

As she emerged, I couldn't stop my eyes from scanning her. My gaze softened for only a moment before concern overtook me. Her vibrant green eyes, mirrors of my own, were clouded with dark circles. Her usually radiant complexion was pallid, her cheekbones sharper than I remembered. I straightened, my jaw tightening, a hard line forming on my lips as I tried to tamp down the growing knot of worry in my chest.

"You look like shit."

Fuck, why did I say it like that?

Bronwen raised an eyebrow, crossing her arms tightly over her chest. "Well, you look as charming as ever, brother," she snapped, her voice dripping with sarcasm. "Glad to see your time away hasn't softened your sharp tongue."

I sighed, pinching the bridge of my nose. "I'm serious, B. You look . . . worn down."

"Gee, thanks," she shot back, rolling her eyes. "Maybe I should've taken beauty tips from the Legion. You all seem to thrive on sleepless nights and bad lighting."

I couldn't help the exasperated groan that escaped me. "Can you, for once, take something seriously? You're clearly not taking care of yourself." I turned to my parents. "I've been gone for a few weeks and the two of you let this happen to her?"

I walked to Bronwen. "Have you slept? Have you eaten?"

Her gaze narrowed, and she stepped closer, her chin tilted

defiantly. "And where were you, Adar? Off playing soldier while the rest of us are here, keeping everything from falling apart? Don't lecture me about responsibility."

The tension between us crackled like a live wire, but before I could fire back, Papa's calm yet firm voice cut through. "Enough, both of you. This is not how we greet each other after weeks apart."

Bronwen turned away, her jaw set tightly. I felt a pang of guilt gnaw at me, but I buried it beneath my frustration.

This wasn't over, not by a long shot.

26

Chapter 26

Bronwen

Adar's concern for my appearance did nothing but irk my nerves. I should have been thankful he didn't notice anything else—the shadows of my secrets that clung to me, threatening to unravel at any moment. What I did. What I kept hidden. But leave it to Adar to make me want to punch him in the face instead of embrace him after weeks apart. How dare he comment on my appearance when he had no idea of the weight I carried?

The worst part was, I had a solution. A solution that sickened me as much as it tempted me. I hated that I needed August—that he had become the one thing that could quiet the relentless torment of my nightmares. Yet, here I was, wandering the woods, hoping August would sense me and grant me the elusive rest I so desperately craved. Each step felt heavier, not just from exhaustion but from the weight of my reliance on him. It gnawed at me, the bitterness of needing someone like him—someone I should hate—mingling with the shame of the relief his presence brought.

Our spot had been ruined, thanks to August and his games. Yesterday after he took me away, he brought me to the edge of the woods near my home and I quickly left him after the unsettling closeness and nausea from the speed swept through me. No decision to meet again—or where, and I didn't leave last night with Adar home.

I waited all day for him, taking Shadow for a ride, pacing the woods, but he never came. After warming by the fire and waiting for my parents to fall asleep, I changed into my leathers and went out into the darkness, hoping to finally find him.

I changed my direction today, leaving from the front of our cottage and walking down the small road that led closer to town. The recent rain had left the path damp, and the cool air carried the faint scent of wet earth. As I passed the Miller's house, I remembered that one of their mares had just given birth. My curiosity piqued, breaking the monotony of my wandering, and I turned toward their barn.

The Miller's barn was grand compared to ours, with its freshly painted beams and carefully organized stalls. Inside, I crept quietly down the aisle until I found the mare and her foal. The foal was nestled close to his mother, his tiny body trembling as he adjusted to the world. He was a pretty thing, delicate and small, with a tawny brown coat and a sleek black mane that glinted faintly in the filtered light streaming through the slats of the barn.

I stayed a while, running my fingers along the rough grain of the stall doors, marveling at the strength and beauty of the other horses. Their glossy coats and steady eyes spoke of careful tending—something that seemed worlds apart from the chaos I carried.

When I finally stepped back onto the path, the barn fading into the distance, a sharp pain raced through my scars, stealing the breath from my lungs. The sensation was unlike anything I had experienced before, like a warning bell ringing deep within me. My hand instinctively flew to my neck, brushing against the fabric that concealed the marks. Most days, I forgot they were even there, hidden by carefully placed fabric and willful ignorance. But now, they burned as though reignited by some unseen force.

I froze, my heart pounding in my chest, and then another wave of pain ripped through me, forcing a strangled cry from my lips. My knees buckled, and I clutched a nearby tree for support. The unsettling sensation churned in my chest, a mix of fear and urgency I couldn't ignore. Something was wrong, horribly wrong.

I straightened with effort, forcing myself to move. Whatever was happening, I couldn't afford to stand still. The forest around me felt darker, the trees leaning in as if they, too, sensed the weight of my unease. I had to find him. Had to understand what this pain meant before it consumed me whole.

"What are you doing out here alone?" A sinister voice from behind me spoke.

I couldn't think. I had to do something fast.

Just as the vampire advanced towards me, I turned around and placed my hand on him, feeling the familiar surge of power that came with siphoning his life force. The euphoria was immediate, a heady rush that made my skin hum with energy. It was as if every nerve in my body awakened, vibrating with life that wasn't my own. I relished the control, the way he crumpled before me, completely at my mercy. For the first time in what felt like forever, I felt whole, like this was how I was meant to be all along. The intoxicating sensation made my heart race, even as another wave of pain tore through me, grounding me back in reality.

I focused on the vampire in front of me, his magic draining into me like water through parched soil. The rush of power surged through my veins, warm and electric, as though I was being filled with pure vitality. It was overwhelming, but I didn't care. I reveled in the sensation, feeling unstoppable, untouchable—finally myself. When his strength waned and his eyes dimmed, I grabbed the stake strapped to my leg and plunged it into his heart with calculated precision. I couldn't use fire on him like I loved to do once before. I had to spare every ounce of power I could because I knew whatever I was about to walk into, it wouldn't be good.

But it didn't matter what danger I'd be stepping into. Every part of my being was telling me, *pulling me* to save him.

After pulling the stake out of the vampire and strapping it back to my leg, I ran back to the horse stable. Another wave of pain had me falling to my knees, but I pushed myself up to take a few more steps to get to the stable.

After mounting the brown mare from the first stall, I raced through the woods following a magical pull that was forcing me to find him. As I went deeper into the woods, I heard a faint, familiar sound. The chants grew louder, low and rhythmic, and I realized what it was.

Spells.

As I emerged from the cover of the woods, the clearing stretched out before me, bathed in pale moonlight. A dozen or so witches formed a tight circle, their bodies swaying in unison as their chants filled the air. The air felt charged, thick with magic, and each step forward sent a shiver down my spine. At the center of it all, I saw him—August—on his knees, his usually commanding figure reduced to something frail and broken. Blood soaked his shirt, streaking down his arms and pooling beneath him. His skin was paler than usual, a stark contrast to the crimson staining him, and his chest rose and fell with labored breaths as though every movement pained him.

I dismounted the horse and gave her a hit to send her away. I pulled the strings that kept my cloak on, allowing it to fall to the ground. Before I could comprehend what I was doing, the few witches that were blocking my view of him were screaming as they burned into nothing. August's eyes raised to mine, and he smiled when he saw it was me.

I took a step forward and stabbing pains shot through my head as I could feel someone's magic being used on me. I raised my hand to my head and grabbed the invisible flow of magic and gained control of it. This magic was nothing like I've felt before. A woman with brown curly locks screamed when she felt only what I could imagine as someone ripping an organ out with their bare hands. Her screams grew louder as I ripped her connection to magic away from her. Her terror was palpable, her wide eyes brimming with fear as she scrambled backward.

"Siphoner!" someone yelled, the word laced with panic, and the witches began shifting uneasily, their confidence fracturing as they realized what I was.

One man, perhaps more foolish than the rest, pulled a sword from his belt and charged at me, his movements reckless with desperation. With a single thought, I formed two swords and prepared for his advance.

His sword came down hard but I met him with the defense of the sword in my right hand as I pushed the sword in my left into his abdomen.

Another man came to my right and cut through the fabric on my arm before I moved out of the way. Blocking his next advance with one sword, my other ripped through his stomach all the way to his neck. Blood splattered across my face when I pulled the sword to me as he fell to the ground.

A sharp wave of pain seared through the scar on my neck, and I glanced back to see the remaining women huddled closer, forming a tighter circle around him. Their chanting grew more frantic, the words an unintelligible blur that reverberated through the clearing. Whatever they were doing, it was clear they weren't finished.

My swords disappeared and with one motion, I had them flying up into the air before they hit the ground with such force that I could hear the crack of their bones from the distance I was from them.

Another woman, hidden in the shadows until now, darted forward and wrapped her arms around the curly-haired witch, trying to lift her to her feet.

Her voice cracked as she screamed at me, "You don't understand what you're doing!" Her tone was a mix of fear and pleading, as if hoping her words could stop the inevitable.

I lifted my hand, my fingers curling with purpose, and gave them nothing but a single motion. The sound of their necks snapping echoed through the clearing, sharp and final.

I stood frozen, my breath catching as I took in the aftermath of my actions. The blood-streaked ground glistened under the pale moonlight, and the acrid scent of burned flesh stung my nose, mixing with the bitter tang of iron that clung to the air.

My hands trembled, slick with blood and trembling from the amount of magic I had wielded, yet my gaze stayed locked on him. Guilt simmered just beneath the surface, battling with an unspoken triumph I didn't dare acknowledge.

But more than anything, I was worried. Worried for him.

It took him a moment to stand, his movements slow as if each subtle moment pained him. Blood still oozed from the wounds the witches had inflicted, the stark red dripping onto the earth with every shaky step. His shoulders sagged under an invisible weight, and his chest rose and fell with labored breaths, each one seeming to cost him more effort than the last.

As August began walking toward me, I noticed the slight limp in his stride, the way his hand briefly pressed against his side as if to hold himself together. His usually sharp, mocking gaze was dulled, clouded by pain and something else—something I couldn't quite name. His silence unsettled me as much as his battered appearance.

For once, there were no biting remarks, no infuriating smirks or cryptic quips. The air between us was heavy, charged with everything left unsaid. The closer he came, the more I could see the toll the fight had taken on him. His pale skin seemed almost translucent under the moonlight, and the shadows under his eyes were deeper than I'd ever seen them.

August stopped a few feet away, his lips twitching as if he wanted to respond, but no words came. Instead, he simply looked at me.

"August," I said. "What—"

Before I could finish, he reached out, his hand brushing

against my cheek. His touch was cold, trembling slightly, but there was an urgency in the way his fingers lingered. It caught me off guard, stealing the rest of my words.

Then, without warning, he pulled me closer, his lips crashing against mine with a raw intensity that made my breath catch. It wasn't calculated or teasing, like I would have expected from him—it was consuming, frantic, like he was pouring every ounce of himself into this single moment.

After the initial shock faded, I was left with utter panic. My heart raced, each beat a furious reminder of how good this felt. Anger surged through me—anger at him for crossing a line, but mostly at myself for feeling anything but revulsion.

I had kissed him before, yes. But that kiss was nothing more than a distraction. Nothing more than to keep us both alive.

But when he kissed me now, it wasn't the same. There was a desperation in the way his lips moved against mine, a hunger that was both foreign and terrifying. This wasn't the usual predatory desire I had come to expect—it was something deeper, something that made my chest tighten with emotions I didn't want to name. It couldn't mean anything. It couldn't.

It couldn't.

So I did the only thing I could do. I pulled the stake off of my thigh and stabbed him in the leg.

He stared at me, eyes wide with a mix of shock and . . . amusement? His lips twisted into a faint, almost imperceptible smirk, even as he collapsed to the ground. The glint in his eyes made my stomach churn with frustration, and before he could utter a word, I disappeared with the little magic I had left.

27

Chapter 27

Bronwen

I couldn't explain why I saved him. I could say it was self-preservation. That I worried his death would bring mine. But I knew better than that.

To be free of a marking, one of the two must die, and the other will live their life as if it never happened to begin with.

I hated to read, so when Mama taught our lessons, she would read aloud and make me repeat it over and over again until I had it memorized. Reading it myself would have just been easier, but I was stubborn.

A dark part of me savored the absolute power in that moment, even as a flicker of unease crept in at what I'd become capable of. The more I thought about last night, the more I remembered. The witches wore dark green cloaks, with a strange symbol on the back. The sun? Stars? I wasn't sure. They weren't a part of our coven, but that didn't matter. I killed witches.

To save a vampire.

I didn't even second guess myself once. The only thing on my mind was saving August.

And today at Market, he didn't even come. I should be relieved. But instead, a restless energy had taken hold of me, an incessant need to scan the crowd for a familiar face. Every customer became a potential him, every flash of blonde hair set my heart racing before disappointment settled in. My stomach churned, a tight knot of nerves I couldn't shake, and my fingers tapped a restless rhythm against my side. Was I waiting for him, or dreading him? I couldn't tell anymore.

Was I worried?

No. It was the mark, wasn't it? Twisting my thoughts, making me dwell on him when I should have been focusing on anything else. It *had* to be the mark, because the alternative was something I couldn't face. And yet, the nightmare last night, vivid and relentless, made his absence all the more unbearable.

It wasn't until the noise of Market grew fainter that I realized I had walked away, but even then I didn't stop myself.

When I found myself standing in front of the deep green door with a fox on it, I barely paused before twisting the handle and pushing it open. I didn't even know for sure if he would be here, but it was the only option I had.

And I was right.

The room was dimly lit, the only source of light coming from a fire roaring in the hearth on the right wall. Shadows flickered and danced across the rough stone walls, creating shifting patterns that felt almost alive.

Sparse furnishings filled the space, practical but worn. A heavy wooden table stood in the corner, its surface scarred with deep grooves and faint stains from years of use. Beside it, an empty chair was pushed haphazardly, as though someone had left in a rush. The firelight reflected off a tall bookshelf to the left, its shelves lined with leather-bound volumes that looked as though they hadn't been touched in decades.

August sat in a cushioned chair facing the fire, his posture stiff and unnatural. His shoulders were drawn tight, and his fingers gripped the armrests with white-knuckled intensity. The usual smirk that teased at the corners of his mouth was absent, replaced by a cold, distant expression. I removed my cloak and hung it on a hook near the door. As I took a few hesitant steps closer, the confidence that had carried me this far began to crumble, replaced by a gnawing uncertainty.

"What do you want?" His voice cut through the room, low and sharp, like a blade honed to perfection. He didn't turn to look at me, his gaze fixed on the fire as if I were an afterthought.

A step closer. "You weren't at Market."

"Was I supposed to be?"

I scrunched my nose. "It seems like you're avoiding me now."

He stayed silent for a long moment, the crackle of the fire filling the space between us. His gaze remained fixed ahead, unmoving, as if he were weighing the weight of his words before letting them out. The quiet stretched, and just when I thought he wouldn't answer, he finally spoke.

"Yes, Winnie. I am." His voice was low and devoid of the usual teasing lilt.

Was he . . . *pouting*?

"Did you not like me saving you? It seemed, in the moment, you were very happy to see me." My voice wavered slightly, but I pressed on, taking cautious steps closer. Though I knew I was pushing my luck, the silence between us felt heavier with every moment, until I was standing next to his chair, close enough to feel the heat of the fire and the tension radiating off him.

He stayed silent, seeming more interested in the waves of oranges and reds in front of him.

"Look at me when I am speaking to you." I went to grab his face and turn it to my direction but before I could, he grabbed me by the waist and pulled me into his lap.

I straddled him on my knees, and this time he had his eyes locked on mine, still with the same emotionless face.

"Is this better?" he whispered.

My heart raced, pounding against my chest as if it might break free. His hands gripped my waist tightly, grounding me even as my thoughts spiraled. His piercing gaze held me captive, and I couldn't tell if I wanted to pull away or lean in closer.

"What is wrong with you?" My voice came out quieter than I intended, an attempt to mask the way my stomach twisted in knots.

He said nothing, his silence a weight pressing down on me. I shifted, trying to move off of him, but his hands only tightened their hold.

I grabbed his throat with my hand, ready to pull magic and force him to let go of me when he tilted his head back and let a smile escape his lips.

Was he playing with me?

I opened my mouth to say something but before I could conjure up words, his hands left my waist and trailed gently down my thighs.

"August." His name came out breathlessly.

He let out a grunt. "Do not say my name like that."

I shook off the thought and tightened my hand on his neck. His hands came back up my thighs, only this time he brought my dress with them. The rough texture of his fingers against my skin sent a shiver through me, one I didn't want to acknowledge.

I reached down and grabbed his hand with mine, stopping him from exposing me any further. "What are you doing?"

He looked at me through furrowed brows before he sighed and closed his eyes. "You've made me feel things. Things I didn't think I was capable of feeling."

I shook my head vigorously. "You—you're not making any sense."

In an instant, he had me pinned against the wall, his movements swift and fluid, as though he'd done this a hundred times before. One of his hands rested on the wall above my head as he leaned into me while his other hand rested against my hip, anchoring me in place. His eyes raced over my face, searching for something, and the intensity of his gaze sent a shiver rippling through me.

The cold stone pressed into my back, its unyielding surface a sharp contrast to the searing heat radiating from his body. My skin prickled where his fingers grazed me, and a strange war raged within—part of me recoiled at his closeness, at the dominance of his presence, while another part, traitorous and undeniable, leaned into the heat, into the safety his grip seemed to promise.

"I am making perfect sense, Winnie, and you know it. You feel it too," he murmured, his voice low and unrelenting, each word a tether pulling me closer to something I wasn't sure I wanted to face.

I hated him. I hated the way his touch lingered on my skin like a brand, the way his voice curled around my defenses and pulled them apart piece by piece. I hated how he made my heart race, made my breath catch, and made my knees weaken with every deliberate movement.

But more than anything, I hated myself. For letting him in.

The firelight flickered against the walls, casting shifting shadows that seemed to mimic the chaos inside me. His gaze held mine, unrelenting, and I felt the mark pulse like a second heartbeat demanding my attention. It wasn't just a pull—it was a command, a quiet whisper in the back of my mind telling me to give in, to let go.

My body leaned forward before my mind could stop it, closing the space between us, drawn by something I couldn't name. I told myself it was the mark. It *had* to be the mark. But the thought of stepping away, of breaking this connection, felt like ripping apart something vital.

"August," I whispered, his name trembling on my lips like a prayer and a curse all at once. My hands hovered just above his chest, the heat of him radiating through the space between us. "I can't . . . I shouldn't . . ."

His hand squeezed my hip, grounding me even as my thoughts spiraled further out of control. "Winnie," he murmured, his voice a low rasp.

I wanted to scream at him, to tell him to stop, to tell him to let me go. But instead, my fingers curled into his shirt, clutching him like he was the only thing keeping me from falling apart entirely.

My heart raced, and I knew he could hear it. There was no point in denying it any longer. I felt it. I felt it when he drained the Legion soldier. I felt it when he fed on me. I had been able to fight it, and I thought I still could until last night. The thought of losing him ripped through me to the point that I was no longer in control of my own body.

It was the mark. I knew it was the mark. I felt it deep in my chest, a pull I couldn't fully explain, as if an invisible thread bound us together. It wasn't just physical—it was emotional, a hum that resonated through my veins, calling me to him even as my mind screamed to resist. But I couldn't stop it.

And I didn't think I wanted to anymore.

"What do you want?" I asked, hoping he would snap out of this before it was too late.

His eyes locked on mine. "Ruin me. Take what you want from me. I'll be yours to do whatever you desire. Drain me of my magic, leave me with nothing, over and over again. Whatever you want." His voice dipped, carrying a dangerous edge, as if he relished the vulnerability. "Just let me touch you. Let me feel you. Let me *taste* you."

"It's the mark making you want such things," I said, trying to reason with myself more than him. "Nothing more."

"And if it is? Why shouldn't we take full advantage of it? Feel everything it wants us to feel." His words were a heady mix of charm and menace, each syllable weaving a spell around me. There was a daring glint in his eyes, as if he was testing just how far I would let him go.

He pulled the hem of my dress up and grabbed my thigh, his touch igniting a warmth that spread through me, both thrilling and terrifying. The mark seemed to hum in agreement, a subtle vibration that blurred the boundary between him and me.

I let out a sharp breath. "And when I change my mind? When I come to my senses?"

He smiled and brought his lips close to my ear. "When you grow bored of me, you can kill me yourself."

"Promise?" I asked breathlessly as the hand on my thigh continued to move higher, leaving a trail of goosebumps.

He brought his face back to mine, our noses almost touching. He brought his other hand that was on the wall down and grazed his fingers over my lips before tracing them down my neck all the way to my chest. The heat of his breath lingered on my skin, sending an involuntary shiver through me.

"Cross her heart," he whispered, tracing an X over my chest.

28

Chapter 28

Bronwen

August's breath was warm against my lips, his forehead resting lightly against mine as his hand slid further up my thigh. Each movement was slow, as if he were savoring the moment. My fingers gripped his shirt tighter, the rough fabric grounding me against the rising tide of heat and confusion.

The room was quiet save for the faint rustle of fabric as he shifted closer and the uneven cadence of our breathing. Even the creak of the floorboards beneath us seemed distant, swallowed by the crackling tension in the air.

His hand brushed my thigh again. His touch sent a shiver coursing through me, unbidden but undeniable. I arched into him instinctively, my breath hitching as his lips quirked into a faint, maddening smirk.

"You can't even admit it, can you?" His voice was soft, carrying a dangerous edge of amusement that only stoked the embers burning beneath my skin. "What you feel."

I swallowed hard, my throat constricted with unspoken

words. "I hate you," I whispered, the lie trembling on my lips even as I forced it out.

His smirk deepened. "Then ruin me, Winnie," he murmured, his voice low and heavy as his lips brushed against the shell of my ear. "Take everything you hate and make it yours."

The pounding of my heart drowned out any rational thought. My chest heaved with shallow breaths, my body betraying me as I fought to keep control. I hated how he made me feel—hated the way he unraveled me with just a touch, a look, a word. But what I hated most was how much I didn't want him to stop.

"Do you think this is a game?" I asked, desperate to push him away from the place he had drawn me into. "That I'm just some—some plaything for you to toy with?"

His expression darkened, the playful smirk vanishing as his hand stilled against my skin. "A game?" he repeated, his voice dropping to a dangerous whisper. He leaned in closer, his eyes locking onto mine with an intensity that sent a chill through me. "No, Winnie. This is survival. And you—" His hand moved again, sliding around to rest possessively at my bottom, his fingers curling slightly as though to stake his claim "—are the only thing keeping me alive."

His words snapped something in me. With a frustrated growl, I grabbed his face, pulling him into a kiss that was as much defiance as it was surrender. He let out a low, guttural sound, pushing me harder against the wall as if he needed the contact to keep himself tethered.

I kissed him harder, threading my fingers into his hair. It was softer than I'd remembered, slipping between my fingers like silk. The hum of his magic brushed against my palms, a faint, electric vibration that sent a thrill down my spine.

"Fuck, Winnie. Why are you doing this to me?" he mumbled against my lips, his voice ragged and strained.

His lips left mine, blazing a trail down the column of my neck. I gasped, my head tilting back to grant him better access as he lifted me and wrapped my legs around his waist. The floorboards creaked beneath us as he carried me across the room, his movements steady and confident. The warmth of his breath against my skin mingled with the faint scent of cedar and earth that clung to him, intoxicating and wholly him.

"Tell me to stop," he murmured, his voice softer now, almost pleading. His words ghosted over my skin, daring me to push him away even as his hold on me tightened.

I couldn't find the words. My throat felt raw, constricted by the storm of emotions raging inside me. Instead, I let my hands slide from his hair to his chest, fingers brushing against the hard planes of muscle beneath his shirt.

"Damn you," I whispered, barely audible, as his lips found the hollow of my throat.

He chuckled softly, the sound low and dangerous. "Haven't you figured it out yet, Winnie? You've already damned me."

His words hung between us, heavy and unyielding. My hands moved to the buttons of his shirt, fumbling slightly as I tugged them free one by one. Each undone button revealed more of him, his pale, unblemished skin taut over the hard lines of his muscles. My fingers trailed over his chest, and the texture of his skin—impossibly smooth—sent a jolt of electricity through me.

His gaze burned into mine, something raw and unguarded flickering in his eyes as I pushed the fabric off his shoulders.

His smirk returned, softer this time, tinged with something almost vulnerable.

"This changes nothing," I said as I rubbed my hands against the muscles in his shoulders and arched my breasts into his chest.

"Keep telling yourself that," he said quietly, his voice carrying the faintest edge of a challenge. Then, with a swift motion, he threw me onto the bed.

In an instant, he was on top of me, pulling at the strings that held my dress together. I grabbed his pants and tried to push them down.

"Not yet," he mumbled as he pulled my dress over my head.

Before I could protest, he kissed me and whispered, "I want to taste you first."

I let out a gasp as the words caught me off guard, but I wouldn't fight him. Every bit of my will had given into him, and deep down, I wanted to feel his bite again. I waited as he kissed my jaw before trailing kisses down my neck, heat forming in my lower belly until my breath hitched as he continued down. Kissing my breasts. Kissing my stomach. Kissing my—oh gods. He nibbled down, sending a jolt of pleasure through my body.

"August!" I screamed as he slid a finger inside me, continuing the motions with his tongue. His pace quickened as he sucked and nibbled. Tension built as warmth spread through my core, and I arched my back as I gripped the sheets. I rocked against his mouth and fingers, chasing release, but before I could reach it, August raised his head, his eyes locking on mine.

"I want to see exactly what I do to you, Winnie."

He slid a second finger in, and I tilted my head back as he

thrust harder, drawing a sharp gasp from my lips. I rolled my hips to meet his motions, my body tightening around his fingers, desperate for more.

Just as the tension started to build again, his thrusts slowed, causing a desperate whimper to escape me. "Look at me, Winnie."

I had never listened so easily, but I'd do anything he said right now. August's eyes darkened as he brought his thumb to my sensitive spot and circled it in cruel, taunting motions.

"August," I begged, my voice breathless as I rocked against his fingers.

That was all he needed to hear.

His thumb stroked harder as he curled his fingers, sending me over the edge. His eyes never left mine, watching every bit of me unraveling and giving into him.

He stared at the mess he made of me as he stood and pulled his pants down, exposing his long length. "I can't wait to feel you come all over my cock."

My body ached in anticipation. I had relentlessly denied Lowen—and every man before him—this part of me. I had never done this, but I had never wanted someone the way I wanted August. It isn't just a want, it was a need.

And there wasn't one part of me that wanted to deny August this part of myself.

If he could make me feel like he did with just his fingers, what was this going to do to me?

In an instant, he was on top of me and took my mouth again, sliding his tongue against mine. He slid his hands along my body as his chest pressed against mine.

The tip of his length nudged against my entrance. He reached down, inserting it partially causing a gasp to escape my lips. He took slow, shallow strokes, giving me a moment to adjust.

"Winnie." His body tensed as he took deep breaths, as if he was trying to hold himself back.

"Stop fighting yourself." I arched my back. "I want it all."

The little bit of restraint he had left seemed to fade away as he pushed in as deep as he could. I moaned as I adjusted around him. Trailing kisses down my neck, he pounded into me. Our bodies slapping together mixed with our breaths growing more ragged filled the silence of the room.

He turned me over, gripping my neck as he brought me onto my knees and thrusted into me hard from behind.

"Say you're mine, Winnie," he whispered into my ear.

I bit my lips as I tried to stay silent. I wasn't his.

I couldn't be his.

He pinched my nipple with one hand as he kept his other gripped tightly around my neck. I cried out as the pain warped into pleasure.

"You want to come again?" He pulled his length out slowly before slamming into me again. "You want to clench around my cock? Then say it."

Warmth spread to my lower belly again, begging to be released with each taunting thrust.

"I'm yours," I whispered.

He reached around me, rubbing his thumb over my sensitive spot as he pounded into me so much force that the bed shifted against the floor.

"August!" I screamed as release shattered through me again. My body went limp, but he held me tightly against him as his strokes grew quicker, and he followed me into release.

The warmth of his body against mine left me in a hazy lull,

my breaths slow and deep as I stared at the ceiling. The quiet after felt heavier, tinged with something neither of us dared put into words.

Then, as my fingers trailed absently over the sheets, I noticed how much the sun had dropped. The golden light that had once streamed through the window had faded. Now, a dim orange glow stretched long shadows across the room.

Panic surged through me.

"I have to go," I gasped, sitting up abruptly. My heart pounded as I swung my legs over the side of the bed and reached for my dress.

August propped himself up on an elbow, watching me with a lazy smirk, but his eyes held curiosity. "Leaving so soon?"

I ignored him, my thoughts consumed by the realization that Mama must be worried sick. She had no idea where I was.

August mumbled something snarky under his breath as he pushed himself up from the bed. He reached for his pants, sliding them on before making his way to the fireplace.

I walked to the door, pulling my cloak onto my shoulders and began tying the strings. "I still want to find Carrow. That is my priority."

After securing the knot, I looked up at him. He was crouched down next to the fire and moved the logs with an iron poker. The flames made his messy hair seem almost iridescent and the sweat on his chest glistened, making me want to walk back over to him and never leave.

When my eyes reached his, I realized he had been watching me the entire time with a smile stretched across his face.

"Why don't I come get you midday tomorrow and bring you back here? That way, you don't have to freeze, and I don't have to deal with a headache from the sun."

I nodded before almost running out of the door.

Chapter 29

Bronwen

The streets were eerily empty, the kind of silence that makes even the faintest footstep echo like a thunderclap. The sun hovered low in the sky, casting long, golden shadows across the cobblestones. There were only a few hours left before darkness swallowed the town.

I walked toward the town gates, each step crunching against the uneven stones. My fingers brushed the soft fabric of my dress, a futile attempt to soothe the unease prickling at the back of my neck. The distant caw of a lone crow overhead seemed to mock the stillness, its cry fading as quickly as it came.

"Did you think I had forgotten about you?" I murmured as I trailed my hand down Shadow's side. He shifted restlessly beneath my touch, his dark coat glistening faintly in the dying light. His unease mirrored my own, his movements jittery as he stomped the ground and flicked his tail. Only a few horses remained throughout the woods, their nervous whinnies barely audible over the rising wind.

I mounted Shadow in one fluid motion, the leather of the saddle creaking beneath me. The reins felt cold and stiff in my hands as I guided him onto the path leading home. The quiet pressed in, broken only by the rhythmic crunch of his hooves against the dirt road.

August's face flashed in my mind, unbidden and unwanted. The memory of his voice, his touch, and the twisted interplay of power between us sent a shiver coursing down my spine. What I did with him, what I allowed—no, *invited*—flooded my thoughts, and the shame of how much I had liked it burned deep. Guilt gnawed at me, not for what I had done, but for the undeniable truth that I wanted more. That bitter taste in my mouth wasn't regret—it was self-reproach for the dangerous, intoxicating thrill I had felt in his presence.

The weight of it pressed against my chest, each breath feeling heavier than the last as I stepped inside my home. The smell of roasted herbs and warm broth filled the air. Mama and Papa sat at the table, bowls of stew steaming in front of them, their quiet conversation a soft murmur against the crackle of the fire.

"How were the Finches?" Papa asked, looking up as I entered.

"What?" I asked, caught off guard by the question.

"Did they like the jackets I made for the boys? It is starting to get cold, and I didn't want them to wait any longer. Thank you for taking them for me." Mama smiled, though her eyes pleaded for me to understand.

She had covered for me.

I nodded slowly, forcing a small smile as I moved toward the table. "They loved them," I said, my voice steady despite the guilt twisting in my stomach. "The boys refused to take them off."

Mama's smile softened, the worry in her eyes easing. Papa grunted in approval, returning his focus to his meal. The room fell quiet again, but the unspoken tension lingered, heavy and suffocating. I picked at my food, the stew's warmth doing little to thaw the icy weight in my chest.

***

The sound of a crack—splintering wood, or perhaps bone— rang through the black void of my nightmare. A scream followed, distant yet familiar, the kind that clawed its way into your soul and refused to leave. I jolted awake, gasping for air as my heart hammered against my ribs.

Moonlight spilled through the small window, casting silver streaks across the room. My chest heaved as I clutched the blanket tightly, the phantom echoes of the nightmare still lingering in my ears. My neck throbbed faintly, and my hand instinctively brushed over the scars that August had left.

The nightmares had haunted me for weeks now, each one more vivid than the last, leaving me restless and raw. Except for that one night. The night he cornered me and I let him feed. That had been the only night I'd slept peacefully.

The memory burned, as much from the shame as from the unsettling truth that I hadn't hated it. Yesterday, I thought he was going to bite me again. When he didn't, I felt something close to disappointment. My stomach twisted at the admission, but there was no denying it.

I swung my legs over the edge of the bed, my feet meeting the cool floorboards. The air in the room felt heavy, pressing against my skin like a tangible weight. I couldn't stay here, trapped in my thoughts. Not with the way they spiraled toward him, toward the things I couldn't afford to admit.

Pulling on my cloak, I stepped into the hallway, the soft creak of the floorboards breaking the silence. I needed air, a distraction, anything to escape the war waging within me. But no matter how far I walked, I knew the truth would follow.

I had wanted him to bite me. And that terrified me most of all.

The woods were dense with shadows, the remnants of last night's rain clinging to the underbrush. My feet moved automatically, the path familiar even in the dim light of early morning. The stillness was almost oppressive, broken only by the occasional rustle of leaves or the distant call of a bird.

Then, through the trees, I caught sight of movement. A figure emerged, his steps heavy. It was Papa. He carried his hunting gear slung over his shoulder, the crossbow strapped across his back a stark reminder of what he had been doing. He didn't hunt often—not vampires, at least—but the sight of him now, blood staining the hem of his cloak, sent a chill through me.

"You're out early," he said, his voice rough from exertion. His gaze swept over me, lingering for a moment as if searching for something.

I swallowed hard, forcing myself to meet his eyes. "Couldn't sleep," I replied, my voice steady despite the unease curling in my chest. "You?"

"Same," he admitted, his expression unreadable. "I thought I'd see if the woods were quieter last night. They weren't."

I glanced at the blood on his cloak, my stomach twisting.

"Vampires?"

He nodded, his mouth a grim line. "Two."

My heart sank at his words, guilt prickling at the edges of my thoughts. I should have been the one out there. Not him.

"Did you get them both?" I asked, my voice quieter now.

He hesitated, just for a moment, before nodding. "They weren't together."

The weight of his answer hung between us, unspoken questions and concerns pressing against my chest. But he didn't elaborate, and I didn't push. Instead, I fell into step beside him.

The warmth of the fire greeted us as we stepped inside, and the sound of Mama humming softly from the sewing room drifting through the air. I paused briefly in the doorway, watching as she bent over her work, the golden morning light spilling across the table. Papa patted my shoulder as he headed toward his room, leaving me to follow the sound of scissors slicing through fabric.

"Pass me the blue thread, will you, Winnie?" Mama asked, her tone light but distracted as she focused on hemming a dress.

I reached for the spool and handed it to her. "This one?"

She nodded, her fingers deftly threading the needle. I sat beside her while she went through the rhythmical motions. For a moment, the only sound was the soft pull of thread through fabric. Then, without looking up, she asked, "Lowen or August?"

My hand stilled, the piece of fabric I had been folding slipping from my fingers. "What?"

Mama glanced up briefly, a knowing smile playing on her lips. "Lowen or August. Which one was it?"

I hesitated, my throat tightening. "It wasn't Lowen," I said finally, my voice barely above a whisper.

Mama's smile softened, her gaze returning to her work. "I thought so."

The silence stretched between us, comfortable yet charged. I could feel her waiting, giving me space to say more if I wanted to. For a moment, I considered telling her everything—the nightmares, the bite, the way August's presence unsettled and intrigued me in equal measure. But the words caught in my throat, too heavy to let go.

Instead, I reached for another piece of fabric, focusing on folding it neatly. Mama didn't press me further, but her quiet understanding lingered, a calm against the storm brewing inside me.

30

Chapter 30

Bronwen

I adjusted the neckline of my dress in the mirror, my reflection pale and a little too tired. After spending the first half of the morning helping Mama in her sewing room, I anxiously got ready to meet August. No matter how hard I tried to focus on anything other than him, my mind always went back to him. His silky hair between my fingers. His smooth, muscular chest pressed against my body. His full lips on *every* part of me.

Gods! If I can't get your mind away from that, how am I going to focus on the journal?

I reached for my cloak, draping it over my shoulders as the soft knock came at my door.

"Come in," I called, my voice steady.

Papa stepped inside, his presence filling the small space. His weathered face was drawn tight, a hint of worry etched into his features as his eyes swept over me.

I stiffened under his gaze, pulling my cloak tighter around

my shoulders. He didn't look like that this morning.

"Where are you off to?" he asked, his tone casual, though his eyes betrayed his concern.

"Just meeting a friend."

"A friend," he repeated, his tone carrying an unspoken question. He stepped closer, his brows furrowing. "Be home before dark."

I tilted my head, studying him. "Why? What's wrong?"

His lips pressed into a thin line before he finally spoke. "I just got word that a group of witches were found dead. It looked like they were killed in the woods a few days ago." He shook his head. "I don't think it's safe for you to go hunting right now."

My breath caught, but I forced myself to keep my expression neutral. A wave of guilt churned in my stomach. I swallowed hard. "Our witches?" I asked carefully, though I knew they weren't.

"No," he said, his tone heavy with frustration. "But we are looking into it. I sent a letter to Adar, but we are keeping this quiet. There is no reason for more of the Legion to be snooping around right now. Until we know more, I want you home before dark. Promise me."

"I promise," I said quietly, though the words felt heavy on my tongue.

Papa's gaze lingered on me for a moment longer before he turned to leave. "Be careful, Winnie."

As the door closed behind him, I let out a shaky breath. My fingers tightened around the edge of my cloak, my mind racing. The memory of those witches burned vividly in my mind, their faces frozen in terror as the flames consumed them. I had done it to save him. To save August. But no one else would see it that way, and I couldn't blame them. How could I justify taking the lives of witches to protect a vampire?

The guilt twisted in my chest, clawing at the edges of my resolve. It wasn't just the witches. It was the way I had wanted him to live. The way I couldn't bear the thought of losing him, even when I knew what he was—what he would always be. My actions had blurred the lines of who I was supposed to be, leaving me adrift in a sea of conflicting emotions.

I had betrayed everything I was supposed to live for. My family. The coven. The mission to protect our kind. And yet, the weight of that betrayal was nothing compared to the pull I felt toward him.

Toward August.

***

This was a mistake. I should have stayed home, kept myself busy with Mama, but my feet had carried me here of their own accord. To this place. To him.

I had to keep my focus on the goal. Find and kill Carrow. But now the lines were blurred. Did he now have something he could hold over me? Is this going to change things? I didn't want it to.

But I also wanted to feel him again. Gods alive I had never felt something like that.

I stopped near the clearing, the pond shimmering like glass in the sunlight. The water was still, undisturbed, as though it were holding its breath. I stood there, hands tucked under my arms, and waited.

"Punctual as always," his voice broke the silence.

My heart lurched, though I kept my expression steady.

August stepped out from the shadows, his pale hair catching the light and giving him an almost ethereal glow. His steps, though confident, had a slight hesitation, as if he were bracing himself. His hands remained loose at his sides, but I caught the faint clench of his jaw—a crack in his usual composure.

He stopped a few feet away, his gaze sweeping over me with a look that made my skin prickle. And then, as if he knew exactly what I was thinking, he relaxed and a smug smirk formed on his lips.

I clenched my fists, wanting to take that look right off of his face.

My annoyance towards him was still there. At least that didn't change.

"So," he drawled, "are you ready to go, Winnie?" He extended his hands toward me.

I took a step back. "How about I draw from you to get us there faster?"

His smirk faded slightly, replaced by a look of mild irritation. "Oh no. You're not drawing magic from me again."

"It's the easiest way," I argued. "I've never done it with someone else, but I'm sure I could. If you'd just let me—"

"No," he interrupted, his tone sharper now. "I'd prefer not to have my blood boiled today."

I took a step closer, the frustration bubbling over. "Then what? You carry me like some—some sack of potatoes?"

He tilted his head, amusement creeping back into his features. "Yes, Winnie."

I scoffed, shaking my head. "What about what you said yesterday? *I'll be yours to do whatever you desire.*"

"I say a lot of things when I'm horny."

My mind shot to me saying I was his. "Me too."

249

A smirk crept on his lips. My hands itched to grab him, to force him to comply, but before I could make a move, he was behind me.

His hands closed around my wrists, pinning them together effortlessly. For a moment, his fingers trembled, barely perceptible, before his grip steadied. I froze, my breath catching as his presence loomed close, too close. His voice was a whisper against my ear, low and laced with amusement.

"What will you do now, Winnie?" he murmured, his breath warm against my neck. "No hands, no magic. Are you still so sure of yourself?"

A shiver ran down my spine, my heart pounding so loudly I was sure he could hear it. I tried to pull away, but his grip tightened just enough to remind me of his strength.

"Let me go," I said, though the words came out shakier than I intended.

He chuckled softly, the sound sending another shiver through me. "Ask nicely."

I turned my head slightly, just enough to catch his gaze. "August."

His eyes darkened, the playful glint replaced by something more intense. "Maybe if you moan my name like you did yesterday, I'll comply," he said, his gaze dropping to my lips.

Betraying heat formed in my lower belly. Though I wanted to protest further, I knew it would do no good.

And I knew of a better way to get my way.

I closed my eyes, swallowed my pride, and said his name, barely above a whisper.

He immediately released my wrists but stayed hovering above me.

Before he could say anything to fluster me more, I grabbed

him. The world around us seemed to tilt and blur, the clearing dissolving into a rush of shadow and light. My feet hit solid ground, but the air felt heavier, warmer—a stark contrast to the crisp forest air we had left behind. The familiar scent of smoke and cedar enveloped me, grounding me as the dim light of his home came into focus.

As my eyes adjusted to the dimly lit room, August grunted and staggered back, grabbing his chest. His other hand briefly brushed the edge of the table for balance, the movement small but telling.

"Fuck, Winnie."

I walked toward him, my hand gliding down the soft fabric of his shirt. "Let me make it up to you."

"What?" His voice cracked, uncertainty laced heavily through it.

I didn't know where it came from—whether it was the room and the memories it held, being so close to him again, or the faintest trace of his magic still humming through me—but I wanted him. Needed him. My mind screamed at me to stop, to consider the implications of what I was about to do, but my body moved with a confidence that belied the turmoil within me. And I knew I wouldn't be able to focus on the journal until I felt him again.

I pushed him down into the cushioned chair. Slowly, I dropped to my knees, my gaze fixed on his. My heart pounded in my chest, every beat a reminder of the risk I was taking. The vulnerability in his expression wavered, giving way to something darker, something unsure. I could see it—the flicker of doubt, the hesitation just beneath his facade. It mirrored my own uncertainty, the quiet battle between wanting to take control and fearing what it would cost me.

"Winnie . . ." he began, his tone hesitant.

"Just let me," I whispered, my hand trailing down to rest on his knee.

The silence that followed was deafening. I could feel the weight of his gaze on me, his breath uneven as he hesitated. For the first time, the tension between us felt fragile, like it could shatter at the slightest provocation.

I stayed there, waiting, my own vulnerability pressing against the air between us. Whatever came next, I knew there would be no going back. And that thought thrilled and terrified me in equal measure.

Once? A moment of weakness. A mistake.

Twice? *It was so much more.*

31

Chapter 31

August

Winnie struggled with the button on my breeches, her fingers fumbling slightly before she glanced up at me, a flicker of determination crossing her features.

I gently moved her hands to the side so I could unbutton them for her as I took deep breaths trying to calm myself.

When my cock bulged out, she took in the sight before raising her eyes back to mine. Her emerald, siren-like eyes made my breath hitch in my throat. A smile formed on her lips as if she knew exactly what she was doing to me.

She dragged her tongue slowly up my length, her movements deliberate, her gaze flicking up to meet mine, a mixture of mischief and intent in her eyes.

Fuck me.

Her grip tightened on my thighs, her nails digging in just slightly as she opened her mouth and took me in. Her lashes fluttered briefly, and I caught the way her shoulders relaxed, as if settling into the moment.

Yeah, she knew exactly what she was doing.

Her motions were slow, and it had me gripping the arms of the chair to keep myself from unraveling. Every touch from her ignited a part of me that had never felt so alive. She grabbed the base as she quickened her motions causing some of her hair to fall into her face. I reached down to sweep it away, and when I did, her eyes locked onto mine. My grip on her hair tightened, forcing a moan from her lips, and I couldn't hold back any longer.

I grabbed her by the waist and pulled her on top of me, pushing myself into her with one quick thrust. I groaned when I realized just how ready she was for me. She wrapped her arms around my neck and kissed me so deeply that I forgot how to breathe for a second. She matched my pace as her fingers trailed into my hair.

"Harder," she moaned against my lips.

Fuck, my Winnie liked it rough.

Our ragged breaths mixed together as she clenched around my length and yelled, "August!"

Gods alive, my name had never sounded so good. I could listen to her say it a million times and never grow tired of it. My pace quickened as I trailed kisses up her neck. I could smell only her scent for the rest of my existence and never want anything else.

Between the kisses, I ran my teeth across her neck, fighting for control of that part of myself that wanted nothing more than to taste her again. Every inch of her seemed to pull me further into something I couldn't name—something dangerous. She was fire and gravity all at once, and I hated the way she unraveled me. My grip on her waist tightened, not just to hold her closer, but to steady myself. I wanted

254

to lose myself in her, to let her consume every thought and impulse, but the darker part of me whispered caution. A line was forming between want and need, between control and surrender. I wasn't sure which side I stood on anymore.

"Do it," she panted as my teeth grazed her skin.

"What?"

She pushed my head into her neck, urging me to bite her, and it was like every wall I'd built around myself cracked. My fangs extended, instinct roaring louder than reason, and for a moment, I wondered if I would stop once I started. I bit her and something between a gasp and a moan escaped her lips as she pushed my cock deeper into her. Her blood sang to me, rich and intoxicating, and I hated myself for how much I craved it.

How much I craved her.

Her grip tightened in my hair as her body grew still, and she clenched around me once more. Between her moans, her blood, and her wrapped around me, I followed her into release.

After our breaths slowed and the warmth of her body faded slightly, I sat in silence, staring at her. The fire's glow cast flickering shadows across the room, but my focus remained entirely on her in my lap. She looked impossibly serene, yet the chaos she brought into my life was anything but. Her dark hair shimmered like raven's wings, her emerald eyes sharp and piercing, and her full lips, soft and inviting, curved as if she knew more than she let on.

I knew I should speak, should address the swirling thoughts tangling in my mind, but for a moment, I simply let myself exist in the quiet tension that always seemed to surround her. Every time I looked at her, I felt that dangerous pull— the one that made me forget everything except her. But tonight, I couldn't let that pull blind me. Not again. I inhaled deeply, steadying myself as I stood, bringing her with me, and wrapping a blanket around her.

After walking to the desk, I spread the journal open on the desk and flipped to a section near the middle, running my finger along a line of cryptic script.

"I was going through this last night," I said as Winnie came to stand at my side. "I think these are spells. I can't make sense of them, but I thought you might be able to."

Last night after Winnie left me and I regained a sliver of composure after what had happened, I fumbled through several pages of Carrow's life before he came to Joveryn. My hands had trembled as I turned the pages, her presence still a hum in my veins. Each passage I read seemed to echo with a truth I wasn't ready to face, the words blurring as my thoughts drifted back to her.

A fae who was once immortal but powerless, consumed by greed and determined to find a way to become stronger. He stole from a witch in Alentara who eventually found him and cursed him. He spent the next year trying to find a witch to help him, but word had gotten out about him, and no one in Alentara would help.

His knowledge of magic was extensive, and he understood the spell required to regain immortality. Yet, without the necessary tools or power, he remained unable to perform it, his ambitions thwarted by his limitations.

She leaned over my shoulder as she scanned the text, her brows knitting together in concentration. Her fingers lightly traced one of the symbols, her movements hesitant but purposeful, as though she were trying to unravel its secrets. Her scent wrapped around me, jasmine mingling with the faint remnants of our earlier closeness, clouding my thoughts. The tension between us hadn't faded—it clung to the air like smoke, impossible to ignore. I wanted her again, and that terrified me. I tried to focus on the symbols, but the pull she had on me made it nearly impossible.

She nodded, her lips pressing into a thoughtful line. "They're spells," she said, her voice quiet, almost reverent, as though speaking the words aloud carried weight. Her finger brushed over a strange symbol. "But they aren't any I've studied before. These must be the spells Carrow brought with him from Alentara. The ones he used to make himself immortal."

I stilled, a sense of relief forming over me after finally finding something that might be helpful. "So this is it," I murmured. "This is how he did it."

Winnie turned the page, the parchment crackling softly under her hand. The next set of symbols was more intricate, woven together in a pattern that felt both ancient and danger-ous. Winnie's eyebrows furrowed, seeming to not understand anything on the page, but one symbol had me placing my hand on hers, preventing her from turning the page again.

My heart pounded, the weight of the moment pressing heavily against my chest as the realization took shape. The air between us felt charged, the unspoken truth hanging there, ready to shatter whatever fragile balance we'd maintained. My lips parted, the words catching in my throat as I fought against the storm of emotions threatening to consume me. A thousand thoughts raced through my mind—what this would mean, what she would do—but I knew I couldn't hold it back any longer. Finally, I whispered, "Delvaux."

Winnie stiffened beside me, her heart rate racing. "What

did you say?"

I turned slowly as I studied her. "Delvaux," I repeated. "Your ancestor . . . she was the witch who cast this spell. She's the one who made Carrow immortal."

She shifted her eyes to the candle burning on the desk, her hand curling slightly against the edge of the journal. Her breath hitched, and for a moment, I thought she might deny it, might try to bury whatever truth I'd just uncovered. But the flicker in her eyes betrayed her—a mixture of guilt and resolve she couldn't quite mask. Her heart rate continued to climb, a subtle tremor betraying the calm expression she tried to maintain.

I realized it then—the way her shoulders tensed, the flicker of hesitation in her movements, and the way her lips parted slightly, as if preparing to speak but deciding against it. The name I had spoken wasn't a revelation to her; it was a wound she'd carried in silence, festering in the shadows of her determination. She already knew. She'd known long before I said the name. The guilt and resignation were written all over her face, even as she tried to focus on the flame. It was the kind of knowing that weighed heavy, a burden she had carried in silence, and now I had spoken it aloud, leaving no place for her to hide.

"You knew already," I said, my voice sharper than I intended.

Her shoulders straightened, her gaze snapping to mine with a sharpness that caught me off guard. Her emerald eyes burned with defiance, but beneath it, I saw the edges of vulnerability—the fear of what this connection might mean, of what I might think of her now. "Yes. Why does it matter that she is my ancestor? All that matters is that I find and kill

Carrow."

I stopped, running a hand through my hair, frustration bubbling to the surface. I took deep breaths to calm myself because no matter how much it aggravated me that she kept this from me, all that mattered was that I knew now.

And it wasn't like I was telling her the entire truth either.

I turned to her again, her features sharp as if she was waiting for me to say something so she could explode on me. Instead, I cupped her face, the connection making her slightly jump in surprise before I whispered, "And to think you couldn't be any more perfect."

32

Chapter 32

Bronwen

I took extra time to ready myself this morning, feeling a lightness in my heart. If it was because of August, I'd never admit it. I decided it must be because we were finally making progress in finding Carrow.

Or maybe it was because I didn't have a nightmare last night.

I didn't even plan on having him bite me. And I didn't do it because I wanted a full night's sleep again. I did it because I wanted to feel the weird sensation that it gave me.

And it was better than I was expecting.

Not having a nightmare was just a plus.

The biting chill in the air had been growing stronger by the day, leaving only a few hours of warmth when the sun hung highest. Today was one of the more pleasant of those days. I left my cloak behind, not wanting it to cover my deep red dress, before walking out the door to meet with August.

The woods felt alive as I walked, the crunch of fallen leaves beneath my feet mingling with the distant chirping of birds.

Shafts of sunlight filtered through the canopy, dappling the path ahead in patches of gold. My steps were slow, measured, as though savoring the calm before the inevitable tension of meeting him.

About halfway to the pond, a subtle shift in the atmosphere made me pause. The light seemed dimmer here, the shadows thicker, and the rustling of the leaves overhead felt more like whispers than the wind. A chill unrelated to the weather slid down my spine, and for a fleeting moment, I wondered if August had decided to arrive early and watch me from the trees.

Shaking the thought, I pressed on, my heartbeat quickening.

"There you are."

I whipped my head around at the familiar, deep voice, my heartbeat quickening. The air around me grew heavier as Lowen stepped out of the shadows, his face contorted with anger. The woods, usually a haven, felt smaller, the trees pressing in around us.

"Lowen?" I scanned the woods for any sign of August, my unease mounting. He had to be close.

"Who are you looking for? The man I've seen you with at Market? Is that why you've refused to see me?" His voice was sharp, cutting through the quiet with bitterness.

"You know why I haven't seen you, Lowen," I said through gritted teeth, my body tensing.

"The day in the barn? When you had me begging you to marry me just to bid me away?" He scoffed, his tone dripping with resentment. "Oh, I'm far from that now."

"Then what do you want?" My voice wavered, though I tried to steady it.

"I want what is due to me." He stepped closer, his eyes

darkening with intent.

Before I could react, someone grabbed me from behind, pinning my arms tightly against my sides. The sudden force stole my breath, and I struggled against the grip. Lowen's lips curled into a cruel smirk as he approached.

"Let me go," I hissed, thrashing against my captor. Desperation gave me strength as I reared back, my head slamming into the person's face. A sharp, wet crack followed, and they let out a pained scream, releasing me. I spun around and saw one of Lowen's friends gripping his nose, blood streaming between his fingers.

"You bitch," he mumbled, venom in his tone. "You're going to regret that."

I stepped back quickly, positioning myself to keep both Lowen and his friend in view. The air seemed to thrum with tension, my mind racing through my options. Running crossed my mind, but it wasn't in my nature to flee from a fight. My hand hovered near the blade strapped under my dress, ready to defend myself.

Lowen's friend lunged first, his steps heavy and uncoordinated, but before he could reach me, a blur shot between us. In the next instant, his body was airborne, crashing against a tree with a sickening crack. The sound of his fall was muffled by the eerie stillness that followed.

My breath hitched as I saw August emerge from the shadows, his eyes darkened with fury as he watched the blood pooling beneath the lifeless body. He took a slow breath, regaining his composure before turning his cold, piercing gaze to Lowen.

In an instant, August was behind him. He gripped Lowen's neck, his fingers curling with a controlled ferocity that betrayed his calm demeanor as he forced Lowen to look him in the eyes.

"What were you planning on doing?" August's voice was low, almost conversational, but there was a chilling edge beneath the surface that made the hairs on my arms stand up.

Lowen's face twisted in defiance, though fear flickered in his eyes. "I was going to take what she should've given me years a—"

Before the words could fully escape his mouth, August's grip tightened, and with a swift, effortless motion, the sickening crack of a broken neck echoed through the clearing. Lowen's body crumpled to the ground with a heavy thud. I stared at the body, trying to make myself feel sad. But I felt nothing other than he had gotten exactly what he deserved.

"Winnie." His voice brought me away from the guilt that formed because I didn't feel sad for Lowen or his disgusting friend. August was stiff, his eyes wide.

"What?" I asked.

"You—you've never—" his voice trailed off.

What was his problem? He almost looked remorseful, but there was no way he regretted what he just did.

I was going to take what she should've given me.

Oh no.

"Do not make something out of this." I turned to avoid his stare but he was in front of me again.

He pinched my chin between his fingers and forced me to look at him. "Winnie."

I pushed his hand away. "Yes, August. You were my first."

He shook his head. "You should have told me. I would've—"

"You would have what? Been more gentle? Made it special? I know, and I didn't want that. I wanted to feel exactly how

263

you are. I didn't want you to hold back."

August straightened slowly as he slid his hands into his pockets, his expression blank save for the faintest hint of satisfaction lingering in his smirk. "Winnie, that was me holding back. I fear if I did what I wanted to do to you . . . you might break."

Heat rose to my cheeks, not because of what he said, but more because of how bad I wanted to know what he meant. What he could do.

I had to move my mind from that. I turned, my eyes locking on the bodies again. One thrown against a tree in a way only a vampire or a witch could do. Adar already had me worried, and now there was another incident that made the woods less safe.

I clenched my hands into fists. "Dammit, August." I turned away, my steps quick as I followed the direction I had come from.

"Where are you going?" Wind whispered through the trees, brushing against my hair as he moved in one quick motion to be standing next to me. "You're welcome," he added, his tone infuriatingly casual.

I gritted my teeth, doing everything in my power to ignore him. As the familiar silhouette of our old wood barn appeared ahead, I silently prayed Papa wouldn't be there.

Why do you need a shovel, Winnie? Who is that man lurking in the woods watching your every step, Winnie?

August halted at a safe distance from our yard, his sharp gaze scanning its boundaries. I wasn't sure if he understood the full extent of the protective spells Papa had placed, but he seemed to know enough not to press his luck.

I cracked the barn door open just enough to peer inside, the creak of the hinges causing the horses to stir. They settled once they saw it was me—all except for Shadow. He neighed impatiently, bumping his stall door with an insistent nudge, demanding my attention.

"Not now, boy," I murmured, stepping into the barn. I ran a hand along his neck, his familiar warmth grounding me for a fleeting moment before I turned back to the task at hand. I grabbed the shovel and stepped outside once more.

August stood waiting, his foot tapping a slow rhythm against the ground. His expression was a mix of impatience and amusement, as if my delay had personally inconvenienced him. "Took you long enough," he said, his smirk deepening as he watched me approach.

I walked past him, ignoring the sharpness in his gaze that seemed to demand acknowledgment, his smirk fading just slightly as I brushed by. The tension hung between us, thick and unyielding, as though he were daring me to stop and meet his eyes. But I didn't give him the satisfaction.

I made it back to where Lowen and his friend's bodies still lay, lifeless and heavy with the weight of what had transpired. The sight of the bloodstained ground brought a wave of emotions crashing over me—anger at their audacity to attack me, guilt over their deaths despite not being the one to kill them, and frustration that I now had to deal with this mess. My hands trembled, a mix of adrenaline and rage, as I tried to steady myself. The memory of their actions, Lowen's threats, and the ease August had with killing them when I was being threatened. The conflict churned in my chest, the guilt clashing with the grim triumph, leaving me breathless and hollow.

I cursed under my breath as I plunged the shovel into the

soil, the cold metal slicing through the hardened ground with a dull crunch. Each push sent vibrations up my arms, and the dirt clung stubbornly to the blade, forcing me to stomp on it with my foot to drive it deeper. The motion was mechanical, a futile attempt to silence the whirlwind of thoughts raging in my mind.

"Are you upset that I killed your lover?" His tone was casual, almost bored, though his eyes glinted with something darker. "He didn't seem like a very nice person."

I glared at him, my frustration bubbling over as I swiped the sweat from my brow with the back of my hand. The hours of digging had left my arms aching, the shovel slicing into the cold, unyielding earth as I worked to create a hole deep enough to keep scavengers at bay. Meanwhile, August stood there, perfectly still, his sharp eyes watching my every move with an infuriating air of detachment.

"I do not need you saving me. I can handle myself." My voice was sharp, but I hated how unconvincing it sounded, even to my own ears.

"Oh, I'm well aware, but I didn't want you to get your pretty dress dirty." His eyes swept over me, lingering just long enough to make my skin prickle. "Though you still managed to ruin it."

I glanced down and grimaced at the dirt smeared across the fabric. A pang of irritation surged through me—not at the dress, but at him for noticing.

I pressed the shovel into the ground again, hoping to mask my unease.

"It's nearing sundown. You could have left the bodies and made it look like a vampire did it."

"A vampire did do it," I mumbled, but I kept my eyes on the task, focusing on the rhythm of digging. The earth was heavy, resistant, but at least it didn't talk back.

He laughed before stepping down into the hole with me, his presence invasive and too close. Before I could react, he yanked the shovel from my hands and tossed it aside with effortless force.

"Do not pretend you are sad," he said, his voice cutting through the tension like a blade. "I saw your face when I killed him, remember? You may not have realized it, or maybe you don't want to admit it to yourself, but you smiled. Just like the victory that covered your face with the Legion soldiers. You've spent a week trying to guilt yourself into feeling bad for what you did. And yet you feel nothing, no matter how much you try to deny it. You're just as sick and twisted as I am."

His words landed like blows, each one hitting harder than the last. I bent down, grabbing the shovel with trembling hands, my anger flaring hotter than before.

"Is this what you wanted? To make me just like you?" My voice cracked, but the fury behind it didn't waver.

"Oh no," he said, his smirk deepening. "You do not get to blame this on me. You've been this way. Do you remember how we met? With your little ways of killing? Wanting to watch a vampire burn alive?" He stepped closer and gripped my throat with his hand, pulling my face closer to his. "I just want you to admit it to yourself. We're no different from each other."

The words pushed me past the breaking point. My grip tightened around the shovel as I swung it with everything I had, the motion fueled by equal parts rage and desperation. The metal edge connected with his side, eliciting a low grunt from him as he staggered slightly but didn't release me.

His grip on my neck only tightened, his darkened eyes burning into mine with an intensity that made my stomach twist. "Admit it," he hissed, his voice laced with equal parts menace and challenge.

My breath came in shallow gasps as I dropped the shovel, my hands flying to his arm. Summoning the magic I needed, I pulled sharply. The force of it wrenched a startled growl from his throat, and he released me instantly. I hated him in that moment. Hated the way he could read me so easily, the way his words twisted inside my mind like barbed wire. But more than that, I hated how much I *still* wanted him. The thought struck like a lightning bolt, and before I could stop myself, I closed the space between us and kissed him.

I was just as sick and twisted as he was.

I shoved him back, putting as much distance between us as I could manage. "Either help me, or get out of my way," I spat, my voice trembling with anger.

He tilted his head slightly, the smile on his face fading as he glanced around the clearing. His nose wrinkled slightly, as though weighing his options and finding them all distasteful, before finally stepping out of the hole with ease.

I rolled my eyes, the tension in my chest easing just enough to let me take a steadying breath.

33

Chapter 33

Bronwen

The morning air was crisp as I stepped into the barn, my boots crunching against the frosted ground. Shadow's stall was the first on the left, his black coat catching the pale light that filtered through the slats in the wooden walls. He neighed softly when he saw me, his dark eyes watching as I approached.

"Good morning, boy," I murmured, reaching out to run a hand down his neck. His warmth was a welcome contrast to the chill that clung to the barn, and I could feel his muscles relax under my touch. "It's getting colder, isn't it?"

He nudged me gently, his way of agreeing, and I couldn't help but smile despite the weight of the previous day still lingering in my chest. I set the basket I'd brought on the ground, pulling out a thick blanket I'd stitched together last night. The soft fabric felt reassuring between my fingers as I draped it over the railing of his stall.

"This should help keep you warm," I said, arranging the blanket along the side for him to nuzzle into when the nights grew colder. I added extra hay to his stall, spreading it out evenly to create a thicker, softer bedding. Shadow watched my every move, his ears flicking as I worked.

It was a relief to focus on something simple, something tangible, after everything that had happened. Lowen's death. August's words. Another nightmare after forgetting to ask August to bite me. The weight of it all pressed against me like the icy air outside, but here, with Shadow, I could let it rest for a little while.

When I finished, I stepped back to admire my work. "There. You should be comfortable now," I said, leaning against the stall door. Shadow snorted softly, nudging my shoulder with his nose.

I chuckled, rubbing his muzzle. "You're welcome."

But the peace didn't last long. My thoughts drifted back to August, to the journal we hadn't touched yesterday. We'd been too consumed by the chaos of the day, and now, with the morning stretching ahead, I knew I couldn't put it off any longer. The answers we needed were somewhere in those pages, and despite my frustration with him, August was the only one who could help me find them.

I sighed, giving Shadow one last pat. "I'll be back later," I promised, grabbing the empty basket and heading toward the barn door. The sunlight outside was brighter now, the frost beginning to melt, but the chill in the air remained.

***

The streets of town were bustling despite the chill in the air, but I barely noticed. My jaw was set, my lips pressed into a tight line as I walked beside August, refusing to meet his gaze.

His presence loomed beside me, silent for once, though the tension between us was thick enough to cut.

I hadn't said a word to him since we'd left the woods. I was still fuming, my arms crossed tightly over my chest to keep from shoving him. When I'd been walking to meet him, he'd appeared out of nowhere, grabbing me before I had a chance to protest. Without warning, he pinned my wrists together, rendering me unable to pull magic to take us to his home. Then, he'd carried me—*ran with me*—all the way to the edge of town.

"You can't just do that," I snapped under my breath, finally breaking the silence.

His lips quirked into a faint smirk, but he didn't look at me. "You're the one who can't be trusted not to drain me dry."

I stopped abruptly, forcing him to halt and turn to face me. "You didn't even give me a choice, August! You just decided what was best and did it."

His smirk faltered, a flicker of something unreadable passing over his face before he recovered. "We got here, didn't we?"

"And now we're walking through town because people are everywhere," I shot back, gesturing to the bustling streets around us. "Some plan."

He didn't respond, his gaze drifting to the cobblestones as if he were searching for an answer there. The silence between us was heavy, but I didn't care. Let him stew in it. I wasn't going to let him get away with pulling that stunt without consequences.

His gaze shot to a small trinket shop. "Be right back," he said before darting inside.

I glared at his retreating figure. "Are you kidding me?" I

271

yelled after him, drawing a few curious stares from passersby. My cheeks burned, but I held my ground, crossing my arms tightly.

When he emerged, a grin plastered across his face, I knew trouble was coming. He knelt in front of me with a dramatic flourish, holding up a simple ring as if it were a priceless treasure.

"Please forgive me, Winnie," he said, his voice dripping with exaggerated emotion. "I can't bear for you to be angry with me. Think of our kids! What would they do without me? Please let me come home."

A crowd was beginning to gather, drawn by his antics. August, ever the performer, even managed to make his eyes glisten with fake tears. My face burned hotter, but not from embarrassment. This was infuriating.

Without a word, I turned on my heel and strode away, leaving him kneeling in the street. The sound of muffled laughter followed me, but I didn't look back. Let him explain himself to the gawkers. I had better things to do.

I pushed the door open to his home, the creak of the hinges echoing in the unsettling silence. The air inside was damp and chilling, biting through the fabric of my dress. Shadows lingered in every corner, stretching and shifting as I stepped inside. Shivering, I went straight to the fireplace to start a fire, my hands fumbling slightly as I gathered the kindling.

Striking the flint, I focused on coaxing the flames to life, the small sparks catching until a faint glow began to illuminate the room. The warmth spread slowly, chasing away the lingering chill and the oppressive darkness.

The front door slammed open with a force that made the hinges groan, and I spun around, startled. August strode in, his coat swirling dramatically as he stepped inside. A mournful expression overtook his face, his lips pulling into an exaggerated pout as he met my gaze.

"You didn't like my performance," he said, his voice dripping with mock sorrow. "I poured my heart out in the street for you, Winnie. Do you know how many people laughed at me? Laughed!"

I sighed. "What are you talking about?"

He flung himself into a nearby chair with all the grace of a sulking child. "You left me there, kneeling in front of everyone, broken-hearted and humiliated. Do you even care how much that hurt me?"

I straightened, brushing the soot from my hands, determined not to feed into his nonsense. "I started a fire. It's freezing in here."

"Ah, of course," he said, sitting up straighter as his eyes flicked to the fireplace. "My poor, shivering Winnie, forced to warm herself in my cold, lonely home. What a tragedy."

"August," I said, crossing my arms and fixing him with a flat stare. "Do you have a point, or are you just trying to make me regret every decision I've ever made?"

He smirked, his faux sadness evaporating in an instant. "You wound me. Truly. I'm just here to make sure you know how deeply you've bruised my delicate ego."

I rolled my eyes, gesturing to the desk. "Can we please just work on the journal?"

He huffed dramatically, but obliged, making a show of trudging over to the desk like a man carrying the weight of the world. Dropping into the chair with an exaggerated sigh, he looked up at me expectantly. I ignored his theatrics and sat next to him, flipping the journal open to the page where we'd left off.

As I leaned over to study it, August's hand brushed lightly against my shoulder. The touch was warm, his fingers slightly rough as they swept my hair to the side, exposing the back of my neck. My breath hitched, the heat of his palm lingering against my skin as his lips teasingly ghosted over my neck.

"What are you doing?" I whispered, my voice catching despite myself.

"Nothing," he murmured, his tone low and unapologetic. His breath was warm against my skin, sending shivers cascading down my spine as his lips pressed gentle kisses along the curve of my neck.

I turned my head to glare at him, but the look in his eyes stopped me. Mischief danced there, softened by something deeper, something almost tender. "August," I said, my tone half a warning and half a plea.

"Yes, Winnie?" he replied innocently, his lips brushing against my skin as he spoke.

I forced myself to focus. "No. None of that." I pushed him gently away. "You're being punished."

"Punished for what? For saving you yesterday? For not letting you drain me just to get us here? Or for my grand gesture?" His smirk widened as he added, "Which, by the way, had several women wanting to make me feel better after you left."

I tensed at his words, narrowing my eyes. "For inconveniencing me. Always."

"Winnie, I can think of far better ways for you to punish me," he said, his voice low and teasing as his hand slid slowly up my thigh, deliberate and unhurried.

Before he could go further, I caught his hand, holding it in place. "No," I said, my tone steady as I placed his hand firmly on the journal. "Read this to me."

He sighed as he straightened, his fingers brushing lightly against the edge of the journal.

"I found one," he began, his voice quieter now, "A witch with a vengeance. One with her own personal motives, though I don't care enough to know them. But I still needed a place to inhabit. Somewhere protected by an army, a fortress where thousands would bow before me. A place where I could live eternity and rule. I had to be the—"

August's voice trailed off abruptly as his eyes caught on the next line of text, his jaw tightening.

"Had to be the what?" I glanced at him, but his silence stretched. His shoulders stiffened, and I could see the hesitation in his expression, as though he'd said more than he intended.

My gaze dropped to the page, but the ancient language was nothing more than incomprehensible symbols to me. Still, a sketch at the bottom drew my attention. The lines were bold yet precise, forming an unmistakable image. A black raven on a deep red banner.

"That's—that's the royal banner," I breathed, my stomach twisting with a mix of recognition and dread.

August's jaw tightened, his fingers curling around the edge of the journal as though anchoring himself. His eyes flicked to the window, avoiding mine, but the tension in his posture spoke volumes.

"He had to be the king," I murmured, my voice barely audible as the realization settled over me like a heavy weight. "Carrow is the king of Joveryn."

Chapter 34

Bronwen

It couldn't be.

My father had always spoken of the king as a protector, an ally to our people. But this—this was a betrayal that ran deeper than anything I could comprehend. The air felt colder, sharper, as if the realization had sucked the warmth from the room.

I had grown up believing the king was a distant but benevolent figure, untouchable in his castle yet a presence that loomed over us all. But now I saw the truth for what it was—a carefully woven lie. He was no different from the creatures we hunted. Worse, he had ensured his survival by hiding behind his crown, behind a kingdom that unknowingly protected the monster within.

The weight of it all pressed against my chest, suffocating in its enormity. This wasn't just about vengeance anymore. This wasn't just about undoing the past. How could I kill someone who had built a throne out of his immortality? How could I fight someone who never left the protection of his castle walls?

A tremor ran through me. The realization settled deep in my bones, thick and suffocating.

There was no way I could kill him.

Frustration boiled over as I pushed myself from the table, grabbing the journal and hurling it across the room. But August moved in a blur, catching it mid-air before it hit the wall. He carefully closed it and set it on a shelf, his calmness only feeding my growing despair.

I shook my head as I began pacing the room, my steps quick and uneven. No matter what I did, I would never reach Carrow. It was a lost effort. We would never be free from the curse Papa believed was on us.

I would never be fixed.

August stood in front of me before I even realized he'd moved, his hands firm but gentle as they cupped my face. His touch grounded me, even as my mind raced with defeat.

"Winnie," he said softly, his voice steady despite the storm brewing in my chest. "It's okay. We can find a way to him."

"No." I shook my head, my voice breaking. "No one is allowed inside the castle walls. And I've never used magic to go to a place I've never been before. We can't get to him."

His thumbs brushed lightly against my cheeks, wiping away tears I hadn't realized were falling. "Then we find another way," he said, his tone resolute. "You don't have to do this alone, Winnie. We'll figure it out together."

I wanted to believe him, to let his words wrap around the crushing doubt that threatened to drown me. But all I could feel was the weight of the impossible task ahead, and the creeping fear that there might not be a way forward.

"Let's do something to take your mind off of it. Let's go out into the woods tonight."

I shook my head, though the thought of the cool night air and the freedom it promised was tempting. "Papa asked that I not go into the woods at night right now."

"Why not?"

"They found the witches," I said, my voice quieter. "And he's worried about my safety."

August's lips curled into a smirk as he leaned against the desk. "Winnie, you killed those witches. You are the scariest thing in the woods."

A reluctant smile tugged at my lips despite myself. "That's not the point. I'd like to respect his wishes for at least one night."

"Well, we still have a few hours before the sun goes down. Why don't we take a walk through town?"

I hesitated for a moment, my mind still tangled in the weight of everything I had learned. The frustration, the helplessness—it was suffocating. But sitting here and letting it consume me wouldn't change anything. If August could pretend nothing had shifted, maybe I could too, even if just for a little while. I glanced toward the window where the sun still hung high in the sky. The thought of sitting here, drowning in my own frustration, was unbearable. With a sigh, I nodded. "Fine."

August grinned like he'd won something, pushing off the desk with an easy grace. "Excellent choice."

I grabbed my cloak and followed him out of his home

The world outside my worries still moved—vendors still called out their wares, the scent of fresh bread still drifted from the bakery, and children still ran through the streets, laughing as they chased one another.

August walked beside me, hands tucked into his coat pockets, eyes scanning the people around us with something bordering on amusement.

For a moment, I let myself forget. I let the normalcy seep into me, dulling the sharp edge of my thoughts, until the sound of the banner flapping in the wind above pulled me back with a violent jolt.

My gaze lifted, locking onto the raven stitched in black across the red fabric. My stomach twisted, my breath hitching as a surge of anger burned through me. That symbol had always meant something distant, something unreachable, but now, it was a mark of betrayal, of deception that stretched beyond what I had ever imagined. My hands clenched at my sides, my nails digging into my palms. The world around me blurred, the voices of Market fading beneath the sound of the banner cracking in the wind, like a taunt I couldn't escape.

A touch to my arm made me jolt. August. His hand was light, grounding, his gaze flicking between me and the banner before settling on my face. He had noticed. Of course, he had noticed.

"Winnie," he said, his voice quieter now. "Come on. You're glaring at that thing like you want to set it on fire."

I exhaled sharply, forcing my fists to relax. "Maybe I do."

His smirk was softer this time, lacking its usual sharpness. "Tempting, I'm sure. But unless you're planning on taking my magic and outing yourself in front of town, I suggest we keep walking."

I tore my eyes away from the banner, inhaling deeply to steady myself. The anger still simmered beneath my skin, but as August tugged me forward, guiding me away from the towering insignia, I let the tension slip from my shoulders.

For now.

A sudden force slammed into August's side, jolting him mid-step. A young boy, no older than ten, had barreled straight into him while chasing another child through the street. August barely stumbled, but the sharp glare he shot at the boy could have stopped a grown man in his tracks.

The child froze for a moment, wide-eyed, before muttering a quick, "Sorry, sir," and darting off before August could say anything.

I pressed a hand to my mouth to stifle my laughter, but the amusement was impossible to contain. "Oh, the great and terrifying August, bested by a child," I teased.

He exhaled sharply, straightening his coat with a dramatic sigh. "He's lucky I'm feeling merciful today."

I shook my head, grinning. "Or maybe he's just faster than you."

He narrowed his eyes at me before they softened. "See? This is better than sulking in that room," he said. "I'd even buy you something sweet if I thought you'd accept it without suspicion."

I scoffed. "I'd assume you poisoned it."

He clutched his chest as though I had wounded him. "Winnie, I'm offended that you'd think I would kill in such an . . . impersonal way."

A small laugh escaped me before I could stop it. The tension I had been carrying all day loosened, if only slightly. "Is that supposed to be comforting?"

He smirked. "You tell me."

Without thinking too much about it, I turned toward the bakery, the warm scent of freshly baked bread pulling me in. August raised an eyebrow but followed without a word as I stepped inside. The interior was cozy, the wooden shelves lined with golden loaves, pastries dusted with sugar, and sweet rolls dripping with honey. A woman behind the counter gave me a kind smile as I ordered two small fruit tarts, their crusts flaky and filled with dark berry preserves.

I carried the treats over to a small table by the window, the glass slightly fogged where the warmth inside met the cold air outside. August sat across from me, watching with mild amusement as I slid one of the tarts in his direction.

"Can you eat actual food?" I asked, taking a bite of my own. The sweetness burst across my tongue, and for the first time today, something felt easy.

He twirled the tart between his fingers, then finally took a bite. "Yes," he said after swallowing. "But it does nothing to curb my hunger."

I paused mid-bite, my eyes narrowing. "Then why bother?"

He shrugged, licking a stray bit of jam from his thumb. That small motion made my belly warm, and I cursed myself silently. "Maybe I just like the taste." He tilted his head, watching me with something unreadable in his gaze. "Or maybe I just wanted an excuse to sit here with you a little longer."

I rolled my eyes, but my lips twitched with the hint of a smile. I let the warmth of the bakery settle into my bones, the scent of fresh pastries lingering between us. Anything to keep my mind away from Carrow. I traced the rim of my tart absentmindedly before speaking. "What about other vampires?"

August paused, the pastry halfway to his mouth, before tilting his head. "You want other vampires to sit here with you?"

I shot him a glare. "No. I mean, can vampires feed on each

other?"

He set the pastry down and leaned back, tapping his fingers against the edge of the table. "They've tried. But vampire blood is poison to other vampires. Doesn't exactly make for a good meal."

I frowned, absorbing the information. "So fire, stakes to the heart, and vampire blood?"

August smirked, watching me with amusement, but there was a knowing glint in his eyes. "It doesn't kill them," he said. "It puts them in a paralytic state. Long enough to make them completely defenseless." He leaned in slightly, his voice dropping just enough to make me shiver. "But nevertheless, add it to your arsenal, Winnie."

As the warmth of the bakery lingered, we eventually rose from our seats and stepped back out into the cold streets. August walked beside me, his usual smirk present but subdued, as if he too was reluctant to let the moment end.

When we reached the town gates, I slowed my pace, hesitating before turning to him. "So . . . does this mean our truce is over?"

He raised an eyebrow. "What?"

I crossed my arms, studying his face. "Our truce was for you to help me find Carrow. We found him, and we can't get to him. That means it's over, right?"

August's expression darkened slightly, his jaw tightening before he shook his head. "I'm not giving up, Winnie. I don't think it's over."

I searched his face for any sign of doubt, but there was none. His confidence—his stubborn belief that there was still a way forward—made my chest ache. I wanted to believe him, but all I could feel was the weight of reality pressing down on me.

Still, I found myself nodding. "Alright."

It wasn't agreement—it was something else. A reluctance to let go of this strange, infuriating thing between us. Because despite everything, despite knowing how dangerous he was, I wasn't ready for this to end either.

"I have something to do tomorrow, but let's meet after your father is asleep."

"You're taking what I said about respecting his wishes for one night quite literally, aren't you?"

August smirked, tilting his head slightly as he studied me. His eyes flickered with something, his gaze dipping to my lips for the briefest moment before snapping back to mine. There was always a careful balance between us, a pull I wasn't sure either of us entirely understood—or wanted to admit. He stepped closer, just enough that I could feel the lingering warmth of the bakery still clinging to his clothes, the contrast against the crisp winter air sending a shiver through me. He extended his hand toward me, palm up, his fingers brushing against mine for just a second longer than necessary. The touch was fleeting, barely there—yet it sent a pulse of warmth through me. He noticed—I knew he did—because the smirk that followed was slower this time, more deliberate. "Take just enough to get home. I'll be waiting tomorrow night at our spot."

35

Chapter 35

Bronwen

Footsteps.

They echoed through the alley, slow, deliberate. My breath came in ragged gasps as I pressed myself against the cold stone wall, desperate to disappear into the shadows. But I knew it was useless.

A whisper of movement. A flash of silver in the moonlight. Then—

A hand clamped over my mouth, the grip unyielding as my body was wrenched from its hiding place. Panic exploded in my chest as I clawed at the fingers digging into my skin, but they held firm. My vision swam with terror as I was pulled against something solid, something unbudging.

"Shhh," a voice purred, smooth as silk, laced with something dark and intoxicating. "I'll be quick. I promise."

Fangs sank into my throat, and a white-hot pain ripped through me. My body convulsed, my scream swallowed by the night. Every heartbeat slowed, my limbs growing weak, my struggles useless.

The world blurred, edges fading into nothingness.
I was dying.
And then—I was gone.

I gasped awake, my body jerking upright in bed, drenched in sweat. My heart slammed against my ribs, my breath coming too fast, too shallow. My hands trembled as I pressed them to my face, willing myself to calm down. It was just another nightmare.

But the feeling of death still clung to me, wrapping around my limbs like chains. My skin tingled where the fangs had pierced in my nightmare, phantom pain lingering even in wakefulness. It was jarring—how different he was at night, how monstrous. The August that haunted my nightmares was a creature of hunger and cruelty, a shadow in the dark that felt nothing for me. But when I was awake, he was something else. Still dangerous, still manipulative, but there was something more. Something human.

"Damn it," I muttered, swinging my legs over the side of the bed. I braced my elbows on my knees and dropped my face into my hands.

I had forgotten to get him to bite me.

With a growl of frustration, I shoved myself up, crossing the room to grab a piece of charcoal from my dresser. Without hesitation, I yanked up my sleeve and scrawled the words onto the inside of my forearm in bold, smudged letters.

Make August bite me.

If I had to carve it into my skin to remember, I would. Because I couldn't do this anymore. I couldn't keep dying in my sleep.

***

The woods were quiet as I walked alongside August, the chill in the air biting at my skin through my cloak. Frost clung to the edges of fallen leaves, glittering faintly in the moonlight. The smell of damp earth and decaying foliage lingered in the air, grounding me in the moment despite the turmoil swirling in my thoughts.

"What are we going to do out in the cold that will make me feel better?" I asked, my tone edged with skepticism as I tugged my cloak tighter around my shoulders.

August glanced at me, a crooked smile playing at his lips. But there was something else there—something fleeting, like he was holding something back beneath the playful exterior. "Patience, Winnie. You'll see."

I rolled my eyes but followed as he led us deeper into the woods, ducking under low-hanging branches and stepping carefully over gnarled roots. Despite my irritation with him, a part of me welcomed the distraction.

"I want to see you do it again," August said suddenly, his voice breaking the quiet.

I glanced at him. "Do what?"

"Kill a vampire."

I raised an eyebrow, a flicker of amusement breaking through my guarded expression. "I could kill you," I said, trying to bite back a smile.

"In due time," he replied with a wink, his grin sharp and teasing.

I shook my head. "So you want me to kill a vampire. Do you not care about your kind?"

"They mean very little to me."

286

I didn't respond immediately, his words striking a chord I hadn't expected. I understood that feeling more than I wanted to admit. Other than my family, everyone else felt distant, unimportant. Witches shunned me, humans feared me, and vampires were monsters.

Except August.

I wasn't sure what he was to me.

"How about that one?" I whispered, pointing toward a shadowy figure in the distance.

August followed my gaze, his smile fading as his eyes landed on the vampire. He was tall, with curly blonde hair tied back, his posture predatory as he fed on a young woman. The scene was grotesquely intimate, the girl's body limp in his arms.

"Not that one," August said firmly, his voice low. The teasing edge was gone, replaced by something hard, something almost wary. His usual smirk had vanished, and for the first time ever, he looked genuinely unsettled.

"Why?" I asked, my curiosity sharpening at his sudden shift in tone.

"Winnie, not that one." He reached out, grabbing my arm to pull me away, his grip tighter than necessary. His eyes flickered with a hesitation I wasn't used to seeing in him. "Let's go."

I bristled at his command, his touch igniting a spark of defiance. Who did he think he was, telling me what to do?

Fuck. That.

I grabbed his hair and pulled him down, yanking magic from him in the process and sending him sprawling to the ground.

The woods around me seemed to close in, the dense canopy overhead letting only faint streaks of moonlight illuminate the narrow paths. Every sound seemed amplified—the rustling leaves, the distant cry of a bird, the snap of a twig underfoot.

As I approached the vampire, I pulled the hood of my cloak down, letting the cool night air brush against my face. I slashed the palm of my hand on a jagged branch, the sharp sting grounding me as blood trickled onto the forest floor. The vampire dropped the lifeless body he'd been feeding on with a sickening thud, his eyes locking onto me.

He appeared before me in an instant, faster than I could track. His hand brushed a loose strand of hair from my face, his touch cold as he tucked it behind my ear.

"Such a pretty, pretty face," he hissed, his words laced with malice. "A shame."

I held his gaze, unflinching, even as chills ran down my spine. Something about his presence was wrong, his energy darker than anything I'd felt before. He must have been old— ancient, even. A part of me, reckless and insatiable, wanted to feel the rush of magic that would come from siphoning him. But another part, the one that whispered warnings I refused to heed, knew this was a mistake.

Just as he leaned in, his eyes darkening with intent, some- thing shoved me back. I stumbled, catching my balance as a tall figure stepped between us. August.

"What are you doing?" the vampire growled.

"This one is mine," August said in a tone I had never heard from him before. Authoritative. Unwavering. Powerful.

The words held no humor, no playfulness—just a quiet, dangerous certainty that made even the other vampire pause. It was the first time I had ever seen August as something other than infuriating. In that moment, he was terrifying.

I grabbed his arm and turned him to me, my frustration bubbling over. "I didn't need your help. I thought you wanted—"

August silenced me with a hand over my mouth, his gaze darting past me. His eyes darkened, until his expression shifted to something closer to fear.

I turned to see what had caught his attention. Vampires emerged from the shadows, one by one, until we were surrounded. Their eyes gleamed with menace, their postures tense as they encircled us. The air grew heavier, the oppressive tension pressing against my chest.

The blonde vampire's gaze shifted to me, his lips curling into a mocking smile. "You've marked her, Augustus. And she's still alive."

Augustus?

August stiffened beside me, his fingers twitching slightly as if resisting the urge to reach for me. "I'm having a little fun with her," he said, his tone forced. "But when I am ready, I will kill her. No one else."

The vampire sneered. "Her blood smells unlike anything I've encountered. Let me taste it."

"No." August stepped in front of me once again, using his arm to tuck me tightly behind him.

The vampires around us took a synchronized step forward at August's rejection, their movements unnervingly precise. Their eyes glinted with quiet menace, their postures tense as if waiting for a single command to act.

"I don't think you heard me correctly. I gave you a command. A simple one at that. Let me taste the girl, and I will be on my way."

"No, Fa—" August paused, glancing around, seeing there was no way out. I could pull a little more magic from him and have us disappear before they could react, but the way he held

289

my closed hand tightly in his told me he didn't want me to do that. Barely above a whisper, he said, "Father, please."

The word hung in the air like a death knell. *Father.*

The vampire . . . August's father's demeanor shifted, curiosity melting into something colder, sharper—an anger that seemed to drain the air from the clearing. August didn't flinch, but I saw the subtle way his shoulders tensed, his jaw tightening as though he were bracing for a blow. His usually smooth demeanor cracked, revealing something raw beneath it—a quiet fear he couldn't quite mask.

August hesitated before pulling me to his side. When he took my hand, his grip was firm but trembling slightly, as if the act itself cost him more than he would admit. The blood crusted on my skin made the gesture feel grotesquely intimate, a sign of reluctant surrender as he extended my hand toward his father. His fingers lingered for a moment too long, as if silently pleading for forgiveness he would never ask for aloud.

"What are you doing?" I asked as I tried to pull my hand free. August's eyes met mine, wide with something that looked like desperation. It was the quietest, most vulnerable I had ever seen him, the air between us heavy with unspoken words. I could read the message in his gaze as clearly as if he'd shouted it: *Don't fight. Please don't fight.*

I stopped fighting, allowing August to hold me with his arms wrapped around me as his father took a step closer. He grabbed my hand and slowly brought it to his face.

Every natural instinct inside of me told me to wrap my hand around his face and stop him, but I fought it. I knew even if I managed to stop this vampire, I wouldn't be able to stop the six others that were waiting for one wrong move to attack.

And knowing that this was somehow August's father, I

couldn't count on him if I was to fight back. It was his father after all. And I wouldn't hesitate to kill anyone who hurt my father.

He sank his teeth in, and sharp, searing pain shot through me, stealing my breath. He drank alarmingly fast, his movements precise and methodical—the mark of someone who had done this countless times before. A twisted mix of terror and betrayal churned in my stomach, each pulse of my blood a reminder of how powerless I was in that moment.

I kept my glare fixed on August, a fiery mix of pain and betrayal coursing through me. How could he let this happen? My mind screamed at him, but my body was too weak to do more than endure. And yet, as much as I wanted to hate him, the sheer panic in his eyes pierced through my anger. There was no triumph in his expression, no satisfaction— only desperation and fear, as if he were watching something he couldn't stop, something that terrified him just as much as it terrified me.

"That's enough," August said as he kept his eyes locked on mine.

His father didn't listen, and my eyelids grew heavy. All I wanted to do was go to sleep.

"Enough!" August yelled as he ripped my hand from his father's grip. The strength in my legs disappeared, but August caught me just as I closed my eyes.

36

Chapter 36

Bronwen

The first thing I felt was the ache in my veins, a hollow emptiness that made it hard to move. My head throbbed in time with my pulse, and every breath felt shallow, as though even the air had been taken from me.

I blinked slowly, my vision blurry as I tried to take in my surroundings. The room was dimly lit, the soft glow of the fire flickering in the hearth casting waves of warmth against the cold stone walls. The heat from the flames seeped into my skin, chasing away the lingering chill that had settled deep in my bones. I recognized the space immediately—August's room. The familiar scent of smoldering wood mixed with the faint traces of him, grounding me in the moment despite the ache in my body.

When my eyes finally adjusted, they landed on him. August sat in a chair near the corner of the room, his elbows resting on his knees and his hands clasped together. He was staring at me, his expression cool, though there was a tension in his posture that made my stomach twist.

"You're awake," he said, his voice low, almost cautious.

I swallowed hard, my throat dry. "What happened?" My voice cracked, and I winced at how weak I sounded.

He didn't answer immediately, his gaze dropping to the floor before returning to me. "You lost a lot of blood," he said finally, his tone clipped. "You're lucky you're alive."

Memories of the night before flooded back, the sharp pain of his father's bite, the suffocating weakness that followed. Anger flickered in my chest, faint but growing. "You let it happen."

August's jaw tightened, and he stood abruptly, pacing to the other side of the room. "I didn't have a choice," he said, his voice sharp. "If I hadn't . . ." He trailed off, his hand raking through his hair. "If I hadn't done what I did, you'd be dead."

"And this is better?" I croaked, gesturing weakly to myself. My arm felt like lead, but I forced myself to sit up, the movement making my head spin. "You handed me over to him, August."

He stopped pacing, his back to me. "I know." The words were quiet, almost a whisper. "I didn't have a choice."

I nodded slowly, though the motion made my head spin. "Because he's your father. You love him."

He turned, his eyes narrowing with something between disdain and pain. "No. I do not *love*." The words were clipped as though he'd rehearsed them a thousand times.

I blinked, the weight of his declaration hitting me harder than I expected. But no emotion compared to the anger I felt towards him right now. A father. August had a father and never mentioned it. "How do you even have a father?"

August's expression didn't shift, but I saw the way his hands

293

curled into fists, his knuckles whitening as if he were holding something back. His jaw tightened, his gaze flickering toward the fire before he forced himself to meet my eyes again. "I just do," he said, his voice clipped.

"That's not an answer." My irritation flared, my patience thinning with every vague response. "You've had plenty of opportunities to mention this, and yet, somehow, it never came up?"

He turned away from me again, his shoulders rigid. "It wasn't relevant." His voice lacked its usual smoothness, like the words felt foreign even to him.

I scoffed. "Not relevant? You have a father who is powerful enough to command other vampires—who almost killed me—and you're telling me it wasn't relevant?"

His shoulders tensed, fingers twitching slightly at his sides before curling into fists. "I didn't think you'd need to know." His voice was quieter this time, almost as if he were trying to convince himself as much as me.

I clenched my fists, ignoring the way my body ached from the movement. "So what else aren't you telling me?"

At that, August turned sharply, his eyes flashing in warning. His posture stiffened, but his fingers tapped restlessly against his thigh, betraying his agitation. "Drop it, Winnie."

"No," I snapped, pushing myself up further. My head spun, but I refused to back down. "You dragged me into this. You let him sink his teeth into me. You don't get to tell me to drop it."

He didn't respond, his silence heavy, and I let out an exasperated huff as I threw the blankets off me. "I'm done with this. I'm going home."

The moment I tried to push myself off the bed, my legs

buckled beneath me, the room tilting dangerously. Before I hit the ground, August was there, catching me with ease. His arms wrapped around me firmly, his expression a mix of worry and guilt.

"You can barely stand," he said, his voice softer now, almost pleading. "Stop being so stubborn."

"Then tell me," I demanded, my voice trembling with both exhaustion and anger.

His jaw tightened, and for a moment, I thought he would refuse again. Then, suddenly, he ran a hand through his hair and let out a bitter laugh. "You really don't let things go, do you?"

"Not when they almost get me killed," I shot back.

He let out a slow breath, his fingers raking through his hair before settling on the back of his neck. His gaze darted away, as if weighing his next words before exhaling heavily. "I was born a vampire," he admitted, voice tight, like the words pained him. "Not turned into one."

I froze. My body felt too heavy, as if the weight of his words had pressed me deeper into the mattress, pinning me in place.

"What?" My breath caught in my throat, my mind scrambling to process what he had just said. Born a vampire. Not turned.

He didn't look away this time. "I was never human, Winnie. I was born this way."

The words hung between us, heavy and suffocating. The very foundation of what I understood about vampires cracked beneath me, shifting and rearranging itself into something I wasn't sure I could accept. I struggled to process them, my pulse hammering in my ears. It wasn't possible. It shouldn't be possible. Vampires were dead things, cursed things, creatures that clawed their way out of the darkness, feeding on the living to sustain their unnatural existence. And yet, August stood before me—just as real, just as alive as I was.

"That's not possible," I said finally. "Vampires are—are dead. They can't procreate."

August's gaze darkened. "My mother was human," he said, his tone low and steady.

A chill ran down my spine. "Human?" The word felt foreign on my tongue, as though saying it aloud would make it more real.

August. Half vampire. . . Half human.

No. No, that didn't make any sense. My mouth opened, but no words came out. My throat was dry, my stomach twisting. The logical part of me screamed that this was wrong, that he was lying, but deep down, I knew he wasn't. He was still a vampire, but it made him different. He could move freely in the daylight, his eyes could shift between a deep, mesmerizing brown to a blood-curdling red, and his restraint—his control—was like nothing I'd seen in any other vampire. It explained so much, yet left even more questions swirling in my mind.

His jaw ticked as he carefully placed me back on the bed, his touch firm yet gentle, as though I might break. "If you want answers," he said, his voice quieter now, tinged with an uncharacteristic vulnerability, "then you have to lay down and rest."

He avoided my gaze, his tension palpable as though speaking these truths had cost him something he couldn't get back. I sank into the bed, my body too weak to argue, but my mind raced, piecing together fragments of a puzzle I hadn't known existed.

He sat on the edge of the bed, his elbows resting on his thighs, and let out a deep breath before turning to me. His expression was a mix of weariness and determination, as if preparing himself for the weight of what he was about to say.

"Vampires are a lot more civilized than you think," he began, his voice calm but carrying an edge of something defensive, as if he had explained this before and been dismissed. "There's a hierarchy in our society, just like in yours. And my father? He's old—very old. With age comes benefits: power, influence, protection. Like what you saw in the woods. That wasn't just a coincidence." He paused, his gaze flicking to the floor for a moment. "The night we met, someone was with me. My father sent him to follow me, to ensure his . . . interests were protected."

I scoffed, crossing my arms despite the ache in my limbs. "So, it's not just a bunch of bloodthirsty monsters lurking in the dark, waiting for their next meal? That's what you're telling me?"

"No," he said, the corner of his lips twitching upward, but there was no real amusement in it. It was more like a mask, something to hide behind. "Vampires can go weeks without feeding if they choose," he continued, but I didn't miss the slight hesitation before he said it, like he was carefully measuring how much to reveal. "And when they do sustain, they indulge in other things. Excessively. Parties, sex, decadence— it's all a performance, a ritual to prove to themselves that they still have control. That their only thought isn't blood." His expression darkened slightly. "Not all of them succeed.""

I tilted my head, watching him. "And yet, here you are," I said, arching an eyebrow. "Living amongst humans. Pretending to be one of us."

He hesitated, his eyes flickering with something unspoken before he replied, "Something took my attention."

"So," I pressed, "are there half-vampires walking around everywhere?"

"No," he said simply, his tone growing quieter. "Not every male can procreate. It's tied to certain lineages, specific bloodlines. Mine happens to be one of them."

We sat in silence as I tried to take in everything he told me. But nothing I learned was as terrifying as what had happened to me.

A knot of worry tightened in my chest. "Has he marked me now?" My voice barely rose above a whisper. "Will it be him who kills me every night instead of you?"

He shook his head. "I already checked. My mark is still there. I don't think you can be marked twice."

He brought his hand up and brushed his fingers through my hair. "No more going out into the night," he added, his voice heavier now. "I don't know how this will affect him, and he isn't someone to provoke."

I nodded slowly. No part of me wanted to fight him on this— it was clear this wasn't a suggestion but a plea born of fear.

"What happened to your mother?" I asked quietly, the question hanging between us like a fragile thread.

He hesitated, his gaze dropping to his hands. His fingers twitched slightly, as if grasping at something invisible, something lost. "She left a long time ago," he said finally, his voice even but not emotionless. There was something there, something buried beneath layers of practiced indifference. His fingers tightened into a fist before he forced them to relax. "My father became too much for her." His voice was quieter now, almost detached, but the way his throat bobbed told me more than his words ever could.

My heart ached at the thought of a young, vulnerable August. "She left you?" I whispered, the words catching in my throat.

His jaw tightened, and he nodded once, but the motion was stiff, as if he were forcing himself to acknowledge it. "My father would have killed her before letting me go." His breath came a little shallower, his shoulders tense like he was bracing for something that had already happened long ago. "No matter his disdain for me," he paused, his tongue running over his teeth as if debating whether to continue. "The lineage ensured my survival." His voice lacked the usual arrogance— it was hollow, resigned.

I reached for him instinctively, pulling him down to lie beside me. His tension didn't fade immediately, but the weight in his eyes softened slightly as he settled next to me and wrapped his arms around me, pulling me into his chest.

"Rest, Winnie. Market starts in a few hours, and I'm sure Odelia will be looking for you."

I brought my bitten hand to his face, my fingers trembling slightly as I pressed it toward him.

"Bite me."

August's eyes flickered, his jaw tightening as he studied me. "You're too weak right now."

"You want me to rest? I can't with the nightmares."

His fingers twitched around mine, his gaze darkening as if he were waging a silent war with himself. He dragged his thumb over the delicate skin of my wrist, almost absently, before sighing. "You always do this," he muttered. "Push until you get what you want."

I held his gaze, unflinching. "Then stop making me push."

His gaze flickered between my face, my hand before he let out a slow, measured breath. Whatever battle raged inside him, I could feel it in the way he lingered, grounding himself before surrendering.

August bit down, the sting sharp and immediate. His touch remained careful, but I felt the restraint in the way his grip tightened, the way his breath hitched ever so slightly. His lips lingered against my palm before placing a gentle kiss and pulling away.

"Now heal yourself."

"I thought you didn't like me pulling from you," I murmured, my voice quieter now.

August let out a slow breath, running a hand through his hair. As his gaze met mine, something softer flickered beneath the usual sharpness.

"You could set me on fire right now, and I wouldn't try to stop you, Winnie."

Chapter 37

Bronwen

I walked beside August, my steps measured but steady. I felt far better than I had hours ago, though a faint ache still lingered in my limbs. My cloak was wrapped tightly around me, not just to stave off the cool breeze but to conceal the leathers I still wore beneath—a stark reminder of the events from the night before.

"So . . . *Augustus.*" I glanced at August to see his jaw tick before he quickly changed his expression.

"I thought you might have missed that," he mumbled.

"No, but it was the least important thing I heard, Augustus."

"Please do not call me that."

I raised an eyebrow. "So you can call me Winnie, but I can't call you by your real name."

He stopped and turned to me. "My mother called me August, and my father calls me Augustus if that tells you anything about the opinion I have on those names."

I looked at him for a moment, realizing now more than I

301

ever have why he had been so adamant with calling me Winnie.

Market was alive with activity. Booths lined both sides of the street, their colorful awnings flapping in the gentle wind. Merchants called out to passersby, their voices blending into a symphony of bartering and chatter. The scent of fresh bread and roasting meats filled the air, mingling with the sharper tang of herbs and spices displayed in woven baskets.

My eyes drifted over the bustling stalls. One was stacked with an array of wooden carvings—miniature animals, intricate figurines, and delicate ornaments that seemed to come alive in the sunlight. Another displayed an array of polished trinkets and jewelry, the metal gleaming as the merchant gestured animatedly to a customer. A few steps away, a booth brimming with jars of honey and jams drew a small crowd, the golden contents glinting enticingly.

It seemed like everyone was here, knowing the unforgiving winter would soon limit their chances to buy and sell goods.

Despite the lively atmosphere, I kept my focus forward, my hand brushing the edge of my cloak. My muscles were tense, and I was acutely aware of August walking close beside me. His presence was steady, his gaze scanning the crowd with quiet vigilance.

Mama's smile brightened as we approached, giving me a sense of normalcy that I so desperately needed.

"Oh, I see where you have been." She glanced at August. "I was worried considering Shadow was still in his stall."

My stomach dropped so fast it felt like the ground beneath me had vanished. How could I have forgotten Shadow? The one thing Papa always checked on first. The one thing that would give away my early departure. I had carefully thought out what I was going to say when seeing Mama, but this had my lie crumbling. A dozen excuses tumbled through my mind, each one faltering before it could form properly. I opened my mouth, but the words tangled in my throat, a lump of fear blocking any coherent thought.

Just as the panic threatened to bubble over, August stepped in smoothly, his expression shifting into something effortlessly charming. "I came and got her this morning," he said, his voice carrying a teasing warmth, laced with just enough casual arrogance to sound believable. He tilted his head slightly, his smirk just shy of smugness. "Couldn't possibly let her make the trip alone, could I? What kind of gentleman would that make me?"

Mama's brow furrowed for a moment, her sharp eyes flicking between us. August met her gaze evenly, offering an easy grin that softened the suspicion in her expression. After a beat, her lips twitched, and her smile returned, though it didn't quite mask the lingering concern.

"Well, next time, bring her back with a full wagon to save us both some work," she said with a teasing lilt, though the hint of exasperation remained.

August nodded, a faint smile tugging at the corner of his mouth as he placed a hand lightly on my back.

"I'll make a note of that." He steered me around the booth with an ease that made my earlier panic dissipate slightly. His hand lingered for just a moment, a quiet reassurance that he had things under control.

Mama began sorting through bundles of material, her movements quick and efficient. I glanced back at August, his calm demeanor unshaken, and felt a flicker of relief. It wasn't often that someone could deflect Mama's questions so effortlessly.

"Winnie," he said, picking up a crate loaded with folded clothes. "Why don't you handle something lighter while I deal with this?"

I rolled my eyes but complied, reaching for a smaller basket filled with spools of thread. The weight was manageable, but the distraction it provided felt heavier, grounding me as I busied myself with the task.

As the morning wore on, a handful of customers came by, browsing through the bundles of fabric and admiring Mama's work. It felt almost normal, the familiar rhythm of Market calming me. But the spell of normalcy was broken when I noticed Mrs. Reeves heading in my direction.

"Bronwen," she called out, her voice trembling slightly as she approached. Her hands clutched the sides of her shawl as though trying to hold herself together. "Have you seen Lowen?"

My stomach sank, my breath catching in my throat. "No," I said carefully.

Her lips pressed into a thin line, and she glanced between me and Mama. "It's been a few days since he came home. The last time I saw him, he said he was going to see you."

The weight of her words pressed down on me, my mind scrambling for an answer that wouldn't betray me. "No," I said quickly, the denial falling from my lips before I could think twice. "I haven't seen him in weeks."

Mrs. Reeves' eyes narrowed, flicking to August standing silently by my side. Her expression hardened, anger seeping through the cracks of her worry. "It must have something to do with you," she snapped, her gaze piercing me. "He was fine until he mentioned coming to see you."

My heart twisted, but not with guilt. Lowen had made his

choices—dark ones—that had nearly cost me everything. I forced myself to keep my face neutral. "I don't know what you mean," I said, my voice steady despite the storm brewing in my chest. "We haven't spoken."

If only she knew what her son had tried to do to me—what August had stopped.

She glared at August, as though his mere presence was further evidence against me. "And who's this? A new friend of yours?" she spat, her tone sharp enough to cut. "It's no wonder Lowen's upset."

August shifted slightly, his posture rigid. He didn't respond, letting her words hang in the air like a challenge. The silence stretched, thick and suffocating, until I finally spoke, unable to let her leave without a response.

"You've got some nerve, Mrs. Reeves," I said sharply, my tone cool and measured, but the edge in it was unmistakable. My fingers tightened around the fabric of my cloak, nails pressing into my palms as I forced my expression into something neutral, something controlled. I wouldn't let her see how deeply this affected me. "Lowen's a grown man. If he's upset, maybe it's because he realized he can't live under your thumb forever."

"How dare you!" Her eyes widened in shock before narrowing into a glare. "You think you know my son better than I do?"

I crossed my arms, tilting my head slightly as I met her glare without flinching. "You'd be surprised," I said, my voice calm, almost indifferent. The truth was, I did know her son—better than she ever could. Better than she was willing to admit.

Her nostrils flared. "Watch your mouth, girl."

I tilted my head. "Or what?"

Mrs. Reeves shook her head sharply, her face reddening, but I saw the flicker of doubt that passed through her expression. She didn't know the truth, but she sensed it—something had shifted, and she didn't like it. "If you hear anything," she snapped, her voice trembling, "you know where to find me."

"Oh, I'll let you know," I replied, my words dripping with sarcasm. "Wouldn't want you losing more sleep."

She stormed off without another word, disappearing into the crowd. Mama watched her retreat, then turned to me, her brows knitting together in disapproval.

"Was that really necessary, Bronwen?" she asked.

I crossed my arms. "She came here accusing me of upsetting Lowen. What was I supposed to do? Smile and nod?"

"You could have handled it with a bit more grace," Mama replied, her tone sharp enough to make me flinch. "That woman is worried about her son. You don't have to like her, but you could have shown a little compassion."

I let out a huff, turning away slightly. "She had no right to come at me like that."

"And you had no right to speak to her the way you did," Mama shot back. "I raised you better than this."

I looked down at the ground, guilt prickling at the edges of my frustration.

Mama sighed, her voice softening slightly as she added, "Just think before you speak next time. She's a mother worried about her child. You understand that, don't you?"

I nodded reluctantly, but part of me rebelled against the idea of giving Mrs. Reeves any pity. Lowen wasn't an innocent victim. He'd been dangerous, and if August hadn't intervened, I might not even be standing here.

Mama studied me for a moment longer before turning back

to the booth. I glanced at August, who had remained silent through the exchange. His expression was blank, but there was a glimmer of something in his eyes—approval, perhaps. I couldn't tell.

As Market began to wind down, August stayed close, helping load the wagon with the last of the goods. His strength didn't go unnoticed, drawing curious glances from other merchants. After grabbing the final crate from our booth, we made our way to the wagon where Papa was waiting, his arms crossed and his face as stern as ever.

His sharp eyes immediately landed on August, his gaze cool and assessing. "And who's this?" he asked in the kind of tone that could make grown men shift uncomfortably.

August stepped forward slightly, but instead of offering his hand, he clasped them behind his back. "August," he said smoothly, nodding politely. "W—Bronwen's friend."

His hesitation before saying my name was barely noticeable, but I caught it—and so did Papa.

Papa's eyes flicked down to August's hands, his brow lifting slightly. His expression didn't change, but I knew that look— the subtle shift of someone testing for weakness. "Not one for handshakes?"

August's lips curved into a small, measured smile. "I've never been a fan of germs," he said lightly. His fingers twitched slightly, then flexed once before settling, as if resisting the urge to shift under Papa's gaze.

Papa didn't move, but something about his presence sharpened, his stance becoming subtly more rigid. "A strange thing for a young man to worry about," he said, his voice carrying a quiet suspicion, like he was weighing August's words against something unspoken. His fingers drummed once against his

307

forearm before stilling, his stare unwavering.

I stepped forward quickly, forcing a smile. "Papa, he's just helping me out. Don't scare him off."

"Scare him off?" Papa said, his tone feigning innocence as he looked up at August, something he's never had to do to another man before. "I'm just trying to get a sense of the company you keep."

August met Papa's gaze evenly, not a flicker of unease betraying him. "I'd do the same if I were you," he said, his voice steady, unhurried. "It's good to be protective of your family."

The tension between them hung in the air like a taut rope. Finally, Mama cleared her throat, breaking the moment. "We'd better get going," she said, her tone pointed. "August, thank you for your help."

Papa gave August one last measured look before turning to climb into the wagon.

August leaned in, his voice a quiet promise. "Go home and rest, Winnie. I'll come for you tomorrow."

With no sense of objection left in me, I nodded.

As I began to walk to the front of the wagon, I glanced back at August, who offered me a faint smile. There was something in his expression that made my chest tighten. Whatever game he was playing, he was good at it. But I couldn't shake the feeling that Papa wasn't done trying to figure him out.

38

Chapter 38

Bronwen

August waited just outside the magical barrier surrounding our yard, leaning casually against a tree. His usual air of confidence was present, but there was something different today—something quieter. I couldn't tell if it was his mood or mine that had shifted.

"Ready?" he asked.

I nodded, tightening my cloak around me as I stepped closer to him. "Where are we going?"

He smirked. "You'll see."

We walked side by side through the woods, the cool air filling the silence between us.

After a few minutes, August glanced at me. "Do you trust me?"

I narrowed my eyes. "Should I?"

His smirk widened, but there was something softer behind it. "Let me carry you."

I blinked. "What?"

His smirk deepened. "Come on, Winnie. We both know you've been through worse. Besides, it's not like this is your first time."

I tensed, remembering the last time he had carried me—how fast he had moved, how the world had blurred into nothing but motion and wind. I had barely been able to breathe, my body reacting in ways I hadn't understood at the time. But I had refused to let him see it. Refused to admit that, for a moment, the speed had unsettled me.

"You were reckless last time," I muttered.

"I was efficient," he corrected smoothly. "I'd let you take us, but you've never been there."

I hesitated. He was waiting, patient, but I saw the challenge in his eyes, the way he was testing me.

With a sigh, I nodded. "Fine. But if you drop me—"

"I won't."

Before I could respond, he stepped closer, lifting me effortlessly into his arms. The movement was so smooth, so natural, that I barely had time to react before he took off. The world blurred around us as he moved, the trees merging into streaks of green and brown. The wind whipped past my face, sharp against my cheeks, but August's grip was firm, grounding me even as the world shifted at impossible speed. My heart pounded—not just from the movement, but from the feeling of being so close to him, held so easily in his grasp.

Then, as suddenly as it had started, we stopped.

I sucked in a breath, the ground solid beneath my feet again as August set me down gently. I stumbled slightly, but he steadied me with a hand on my arm.

"See?" he said, voice laced with amusement. "Told you I wouldn't drop you."

I shot him a glare, but it lacked heat. "I'll be the one bringing us back."

His lips twitched, but he didn't argue.

I turned, taking in our surroundings. We were no longer in the dense forest but in an open, hilly expanse. The land stretched far in every direction, the rolling hills covered in golden grass that rustled softly in the wind. In the distance, a few scattered trees stood like sentinels against the sky, their bare branches reaching upward. It was breathtaking, a view so open and endless that it made me feel small in the best way possible.

Then, slowly, snow began to fall.

I watched as the first flakes drifted down, delicate and silent, melting as they touched the warm earth. But the temperature was dropping, and soon the snow would stick, covering the golden grass in a thin layer of white. A chill crept through me, not entirely from the cold. I wrapped my arms around myself, unease curling low in my stomach.

"The first snow of the season," I murmured, more to myself than to August.

He glanced up at the sky. "You don't like it?"

I shook my head, watching the snow swirl through the air. "It always feels like it brings something with it." I exhaled, the white mist of my breath vanishing almost instantly. "Something bad."

The snow will soon fall so heavily that it will leave little room to leave your home. No way to town, no way to get what you need, so you'd better be prepared before you're trapped. Winter had always felt like a warning to me—a reminder of how easily the world could turn unforgiving. It wasn't just the cold or the isolation. It was the way it stole things, the way it

311

left the weak behind.

Shadow had been one of them.

His mother had abandoned him, maybe sensing he was too small, too weak to last through the brutal winter.

So, no, I didn't like the snow. Because it always took something, and I never knew what it would be until it was too late. It was a thief, silent and cruel, and I had spent too many winters watching it steal away things that were too small, too fragile, too forgotten to fight against it. Even now, as the flakes dusted the hills, that same familiar dread curled in my stomach, whispering that this winter would be no different.

I barely noticed August step beside me until he spoke. "My mother brought me here once."

His voice cut through the spiral of memories, pulling me back to the present. I blinked, my arms still wrapped around myself. "She did?"

He nodded. "I was a child. She took a risk sneaking me away from my father. We sat right here, just looking at the hills and the sky."

I stayed silent, sensing this was something he didn't share often.

"It was one of the happiest moments I ever had," he continued, his voice softer now. "Until he found us."

My chest tightened. "What happened?"

August let out a slow breath, but he didn't speak right away. His fingers flexed at his sides, then curled into loose fists before he forced them to relax. He shifted his weight, his gaze flickering toward the horizon as if searching for something in the distance.

For a long moment, I thought he might change his mind, that he would brush past it with one of his usual smirks and some deflective remark. But instead, his shoulders stiffened, and when he finally spoke, his voice was quieter than before.

"He took me back," August said, the words carrying the weight of something that had long settled into his bones. "Made sure she never did it again."

He exhaled sharply, running a hand through his hair before shaking his head. "It wasn't just about control. It was about punishment. She had defied him, embarrassed him. He couldn't allow that." His jaw tightened, a muscle ticking as he stared at some unseen memory. "I never saw her the same way after that. And she never looked at me the same either."

A heavy silence stretched between us, but I didn't fill it.

Finally, he scoffed, though there was no humor in it. "Funny, isn't it? One of the happiest moments of my childhood ended with a lesson in obedience."

I swallowed, my throat tight. "She tried," I murmured. "She did what she could."

For the first time since he started speaking, August looked at me. Really looked. His gaze was sharp, assessing, but beneath it, I caught something else—something unguarded. He held my stare for a moment, then nodded once. "Yeah," he said quietly. "She did."

A silence settled between us, heavier than before. I looked back at the hills, imagining a young August sitting here, his mother beside him, both of them pretending—for just a little while—that they were free.

Without thinking, I reached for his hand. His fingers twitched at the contact, but he didn't pull away.

"Now you're here again," I murmured. "And no one's taking you back."

He glanced at me, something unreadable in his eyes before

313

he gave my hand a gentle squeeze. "No," he said quietly. "Not yet."

We lingered on the hills until the sun began its slow descent, casting long golden shadows across the land. The snowfall thickened, dusting the earth in white. It was beautiful, but the unease in my chest never left. I had him bite me again the moment the idea ran through my mind. Nightmares had to be a thing of the past now. As the last rays of daylight threatened to disappear, I took a slow breath and reached for August's arm.

"Time to go," I murmured.

He nodded, but neither of us moved for a moment. Then, with a steadying inhale, I focused on the familiar pulse of magic beneath his skin. The world folded inward, the biting chill of the hills vanishing in an instant as we reappeared deep within the woods, far enough from my home that no one would witness our sudden arrival.

The forest was quieter here, the thick canopy above muffling the distant wind. A thin layer of snow coated the ground, crunching softly beneath our boots as we steadied ourselves. August's gaze flickered around as he adjusted to the shift in surroundings, brushing a bit of stray snow from his sleeve.

We began walking, the trees thinning as we neared the outskirts of my home. The familiar sight of our yard was just coming into view when a figure emerged from the shadows ahead. My breath caught in my throat as I recognized him.

"Adar?" I said, my voice a mix of disbelief and joy. He stood tall, his familiar frame clad in the uniform of the Legion, his dark hair tousled as though he'd been traveling for days.

His face broke into a warm smile as he approached. "B! You're a sight for sore eyes."

I hurried forward, wrapping my arms around him. "What are you doing here? I thought you were still at the camp."

"It was my turn to spend winter at home," he said with a chuckle, pulling back to study me. "I wanted to surprise you."

August lingered a few steps behind me, his usual confidence subdued as he watched the exchange. Adar's gaze shifted to him, his brow lifting slightly. "And who's this?"

I stepped back, gesturing between them. "Adar, this is August. August, my brother Adar."

August inclined his head politely, but his eyes flickered over Adar in quick assessment. "Pleasure to meet you."

Adar extended a hand, his smile easy and genuine. "Same here. Any friend of Bronwen's is a friend of mine." His posture remained relaxed, but there was something measured in the way he watched August, waiting for his response.

For a split second, August hesitated, his fingers twitching ever so slightly before stilling. "Forgive me," he said smoothly, his tone as calm as ever. "I'm not much for handshakes. It's . . . complicated."

Adar's eyes narrowed slightly, a flicker of curiosity passing through them. He let his hand fall to his side, but not before his fingers curled briefly into a loose fist. "Well, I'm glad you're keeping an eye on her," he said lightly, though there was a protective edge to his words. "She can be a bit of a handful."

I rolled my eyes, shoving Adar playfully. "I think I handle myself just fine."

"I don't doubt it," Adar said, grinning. "Still, it's good to see you safe."

"It's good to see you, too," I replied softly.

As we reached the edge of the magical barrier, Adar paused, glancing at August. "Are you staying for dinner?" he asked.

August shook his head with a faint smile. "Not tonight. I just wanted to make sure Bronwen got home safely."

Adar nodded, seemingly satisfied, and stepped aside to let me pass. I glanced back at August, who stood just beyond the barrier. "Goodnight," I said softly.

"Goodnight, Winnie," he replied, his voice warm despite the distance growing between us.

"*Winnie?*" Adar whispered, amusement dripping from his face.

I shot him the look of death before shoving him off of the porch step.

***

I sat at my dressing table, brushing out the tangles from my hair as the soft glow of the single candle flickered in the mirror. The soft creak of the door behind me made me glance up, and Adar stepped in, closing it gently behind him.

"Do you ever knock?" I asked, trying to mask my surprise with irritation.

He smirked, crossing the room and sitting on the edge of my bed. "Do I need to? It's not like you're hiding anything."

I raised an eyebrow at him through the mirror but didn't respond, turning my attention back to my hair. "Why are you really home, Adar?" I asked after a moment, my tone casual but curious.

He leaned forward, resting his elbows on his knees. "Lowen and one of his friends have gone missing." Adar's voice was calm, but I felt the weight of each word settle like stones in my chest. "Word reached the Legion a few days ago, and I volunteered to come home for the winter to investigate."

I stilled, my fingers tightening around the brush handle. "Missing?" I echoed, forcing the word past the sudden lump in my throat.

"Yes," he paused, watching me carefully. "The last time anyone saw Lowen, he mentioned coming to see you."

My stomach clenched, the weight of his words settling like ice in my chest. I forced myself to move, setting the brush down deliberately, meeting his gaze in the mirror. "I haven't seen him," I said, forcing my voice to stay even.

Adar didn't blink. "You're sure?"

"Of course I'm sure," I replied, spinning around to face him directly. I tried to hold his gaze, to meet the weight of his scrutiny with unwavering confidence, but my pulse hammered in my ears. "Why would I lie about that?"

He didn't answer right away. Instead, he studied me, his silence stretching just long enough to make my skin prickle. Then, finally, he leaned back slightly. "It's not just Lowen," he said, his tone shifting, sharpening. "A couple of Legion soldiers were killed recently. And those witches they found in the woods."

I swallowed hard, forcing my hands to remain steady at my sides. "What are you saying, Adar?"

His gaze remained locked onto mine, unrelenting. "Some of the witches were killed by swords," he said, his voice quieter now but no less heavy. "Not all of them, but enough to raise questions."

I forced my expression to stay neutral, but inside, every nerve was on edge.

"You're good with a blade, B," he continued, his voice measured. "Better than most."

My fingers curled into the fabric of my dress. "And you think

317

I had something to do with it?"

His silence was more damning than any accusation. He exhaled slowly, tilting his head slightly as if he were trying to see past my words, past my carefully crafted calm. "I think," he said carefully, "that you've been keeping secrets. And secrets have a way of coming out."

The air between us felt too thick, too suffocating. I turned my back to him, reaching for the items on my dressing table more forcefully than I intended. "If you're here to accuse me, Adar, you can leave."

For a moment, I thought he might press further. That he might demand the truth. But instead, the bed creaked softly as he stood. I heard the quiet inhale, the hesitation before he spoke again.

"I'm not accusing you," he said finally. "I'm just saying . . . if there's something I should know, you can tell me. It's me and you, remember?"

I kept my back to him, my fingers trembling slightly as I adjusted a brush that didn't need adjusting.

The door clicked softly shut behind him. Only then did I let out the breath I'd been holding, my hands gripping the edge of the table as I stared at my reflection in the mirror, my own face unfamiliar in the flickering candlelight.

39

Chapter 39

Bronwen

I left earlier than usual, the snow crunching beneath my boots with each step. The cold air stung my cheeks, but I welcomed it. I needed distance from the house before August found me. Adar had caught me off guard yesterday, and I hadn't given myself the chance to process the fact that he and August had met. He hadn't seemed suspicious at the time, but the weight of his questions in my room had left me uneasy. I didn't want him to see August again. Not right now. At least not until things settled down.

Even if it meant the nightmares would start again.

Once I felt far enough from the house, I lowered my hood, letting the crisp air bite at my skin. I took a different path today, veering away from my usual route to keep as far from Lowen's grave as possible.

The silence stretched, pressing against me in a way that made my skin prickle. The wind whispered through the trees, rustling the brittle branches overhead. My fingers twitched at my sides, curling slightly into my cloak. Where was he? We hadn't agreed to meet, and maybe I shouldn't have assumed he would come. A flicker of embarrassment warmed my face.

"Winnie, what are you doing?"

Relief flooded me as I turned, my breath easing—but it was short-lived. The moment I saw his face, the tension snapped back into my chest. His expression was tight, but there was something dark lingering in his gaze.

"I told you I didn't want you to be alone," he said.

A flicker of irritation rose in me, cutting through the cold. I squared my shoulders, meeting his stare. "I am fine. I can handle myself."

He shook his head, stepping forward, his voice quieter now. "Not with *him*."

I opened my mouth to argue, but the words faltered on my tongue. His jaw was set, his usual smirk nowhere to be found. There was no amusement in his eyes, no teasing lilt in his voice. Just quiet, steady concern. My frustration wavered, replaced with something I didn't want to name.

My voice softened, but the weight behind my words remained. "I just wanted to tell you that we need to stay apart for a little while." My fingers twitched, as if resisting the urge to reach for him.

August's eyes darkened slightly. "What?"

"Adar is suspicious." I flicked my gaze toward the trees for a brief moment before settling back on him, as if expecting someone to be listening.

His brow furrowed. "He didn't seem suspicious yesterday."

"Not of you. Of me." I exhaled through my nose, a slow, measured breath. "He thinks I did everything that has happened lately."

August's lips curled into something, not quite a smirk but not far from it either—like the accusation amused him, even if it was dangerous.

"I didn't realize how sharp your brother was." There was something almost thoughtful in his tone, as if he were reassessing Adar entirely.

I shook my head, exhaling sharply. "That isn't the point. I am just going to stay home until Market in hopes his suspicions will die down."

August studied me for a long moment before finally nodding. "Okay." But it was too easy—too simple. My chest tightened as I searched his face, waiting for the argument, the teasing remark, the challenge I had expected. None came. Instead, he just stood there.

It should have been a relief, but instead, unease curled in my stomach. August never let things go this easily.

"That's it?" I asked, my voice quieter now.

He tilted his head slightly. "You expected me to fight you on it?"

I hesitated, pressing my lips together. "A little."

A slow smirk tugged at the corner of his mouth, but it didn't quite reach his eyes. "I always find a way back to you, Winnie. Whether it's tomorrow or next week, we both know this isn't the end."

My breath hitched at his words, but before I could react, he stepped forward, his hands brushing the edges of my cloak before settling against my arms. He pressed a lingering kiss to my forehead, his touch warm against the cold, grounding me even as my thoughts raced. His breath fanned against my skin, and for a fleeting moment, I let myself close my eyes, let myself forget everything else but this.

By the time I returned home, the scent of herbs and simmering broth filled the house, the warmth wrapping around me like a blanket as I stepped inside. The kitchen was alive with movement—Mama stood near the stove, stirring something in a pot, while Adar sat at the table, peeling an apple with slow, deliberate motions. His knife glided smoothly, peeling the apple in a single, perfect spiral. His gaze flicked to me as I entered, lingering a second too long. He didn't speak, but something about the way he watched me sent a prickle of unease down my spine—like he was waiting for me to say something first.

"You're back just in time," Mama said without turning. "Lunch is almost ready."

I slipped off my cloak, hanging it by the door. "What are you making?"

"Stew," she replied. "The two of you will need something hearty for the next few days."

I frowned, glancing between them. "Why?"

Mama wiped her hands on her apron before finally facing me. "Your father and I are leaving for a few days. We need to travel south before the roads get worse to pick up extra grain and supplies for the winter."

Adar sighed, setting the apple down. "You couldn't have sent someone else?"

"We could have," Mama said, giving him a pointed look. "But we didn't."

I crossed my arms. "How long will you be gone?"

"Three, maybe four days. We're leaving tonight."

Something uneasy settled in my chest, twisting tighter the more I thought about it. Traveling at night this late into the season was dangerous enough—but not just because of the cold or the roads. The woods were darker in winter, the shadows stretched longer, and I knew too well what lurked beyond them.

"You're traveling at night?" I asked, my voice sharper than I intended, my fingers curling against my arms.

Mama turned, her expression calm but firm. "You forget who your father is," she said with a knowing smile. "We've done this before, and we'll do it again. He's more than capable of handling anything that comes our way."

I glanced at Adar. He leaned back in his chair, fingers drumming lightly against the wood—not in boredom, but in thought. His eyes remained on me, calculating, assessing, as if he were trying to piece something together that I couldn't see.

"Everything will be fine while we're gone," Mama assured us, as if sensing my hesitation. "Just keep the house warm and don't get into trouble."

Adar smirked. "That depends on her."

I shot him a glare, but Mama ignored us, turning back to the stove. "I expect you both to be alive when we return. That's all I ask."

Her words were light, but the weight behind them lingered. I swallowed hard, trying to shake the nagging feeling that things wouldn't be that simple.

"What about Market?" I asked, forcing my voice steady, hoping the shift in conversation would quiet the unease curling in my stomach. Market was in a few days, and three to four days meant they wouldn't be back.

Mama stirred the pot before glancing over her shoulder. "I would say we could skip this one, but it could be the last one before the snow prevents us from going, and I want to make sure everyone has gotten what they needed."

She was always thinking of others.

She wiped her hands on her apron before turning fully to face us. "Can the two of you handle the booth on your own?"

Adar scoffed. "We'll be fine."

I nodded, though my mind was still caught on the thought of them traveling at night. "We'll manage."

Mama gave a satisfied nod. "Good. Just don't let your bickering scare off the customers."

I watched as she turned back to the pot, humming softly as she stirred, as if she hadn't just told us she'd be gone for days. As if everything was fine. The steady scrape of the wooden spoon against the pot filled the silence, comforting in its familiarity. But something in my chest remained tight, restless.

Adar said nothing, only continued peeling his apple, his knife gliding smoothly through the fruit. He wasn't worried. Mama wasn't worried. Maybe I was overthinking it.

But I couldn't shake the feeling that when they left, something would change. And I wasn't sure I was ready for it.

Chapter 40

Bronwen

The wooden table between us felt wider than it ever had before. I traced the edge of my bowl with my spoon, dragging it through the untouched broth, while Adar chewed in silence. The clink of his knife against the ceramic plate filled the room, an unwanted reminder of how empty the house felt without Mama and Papa. The weight of their absence pressed heavily on us, filling the air with unspoken thoughts neither of us wanted to acknowledge.

Adar cleared his throat, the sound abrupt in the quiet room. He shifted in his chair, stretching his fingers before finally speaking. "Want to spar tomorrow?"

I glanced up at him. "Sure."

The awkwardness remained, stretching between them like an invisible barrier neither knew how to cross. The fire crackled in the hearth, but the warmth it provided did little to melt the tension in the room.

I finally sighed, setting my fork down with a clatter. My

fingers curled against the worn wood of the table, knuckles tightening. "You think I did it, don't you?"

Adar didn't look at me, but the muscle in his jaw tensed. "Did what?"

"The witches. The soldiers. Lowen's disappearance. You accused me."

His fingers curled around his knife, grip tightening. "I had to ask."

"I didn't do it."

Silence fell again, heavier this time. The fire crackled, a log shifting in the hearth, but it did nothing to dispel the cold knot forming in my stomach. Adar exhaled through his nose, his fingers tapping idly against the handle of his knife, a restless movement that made my skin prickle. Adar brought his gaze to meet mine, as if he could will the answers out of me. I gripped the edge of the table, resisting the urge to look away, to shift under the weight of his suspicion.

I couldn't let him see the truth beneath my denial.

Adar exhaled, rubbing his temple. "It wasn't you?"

My pulse pounded in my ears. The words sat at the edge of my tongue, threatening to spill free. If I told him now, it would be over. No more secrets. No more carrying this alone. But then I saw the way he was watching me—waiting, measuring, looking for the moment I cracked. If I gave him one truth, he would start pulling at every other thread, and eventually, it would lead to August. I couldn't let that happen.

I swallowed, my voice firm. "No."

A beat passed. Then another.

Adar leaned back in his chair, nodding once. His fingers drummed against the table before stilling. "Okay." But his eyes never left me, and I knew the conversation wasn't truly over.

***

The morning air was crisp, a thin veil of snow clinging to the grass as I tightened the grip on my sword. Adar stood across from me in the clearing behind our house, rolling his shoulders as he stretched. The tension from last night still lingered between us, unspoken but present, but here—in the familiarity of sparring—it felt easier to ignore.

He lunged first, blade flashing in the morning light. The force of his strike jolted through my arms as I parried, steel grinding against steel in a sharp clang that sent vibrations up to my shoulders. I pivoted sharply, boots skidding slightly against the frost-laced grass as I dodged his next strike. My muscles coiled, and I thrust forward in a quick, precise motion—he barely deflected in time, our swords scraping together with a grating hiss. His brows lifted slightly, but he said nothing as we reset.

The dance continued, each movement growing sharper, more aggressive. The crisp morning air burned in my lungs, sweat slicking my grip despite the cold. My muscles screamed with exertion, but I ignored them, anticipation thrumming through me with every clash of our blades. I saw it in his eyes—the flicker of realization, the moment he understood I wasn't the same fighter he'd faced before. His grip adjusted, his footing shifted, his movements becoming less practiced and more reactionary. I blocked his attacks with sharper precision, anticipating his movements before he made them. I pressed forward when I knew he expected me to falter. I twisted my wrist, knocking his blade aside with a forceful parry. The impact reverberated through me, but I pressed forward, forcing him off balance. He stumbled, catching himself just in time, his breath coming a fraction faster now. He let out a short laugh, shaking his head.

"You've gotten better," he admitted, rolling his shoulders as he straightened. "A lot better."

I fought to keep my face neutral, shrugging like it was nothing. "Papa sparred with me twice."

Adar narrowed his eyes, gripping his sword hilt. "You don't improve this much from two lessons."

I hesitated. He was right. I knew he was right. But I couldn't tell him the truth—not all of it, at least. So I offered him a different one. "I've been sparring with August."

Adar stilled, his stance shifting, as if those words alone had altered the entire fight. His fingers flexed around his blade, suspicion creeping back into his gaze.

"August?" He repeated the name slowly, testing it. "I've never heard you mention him before. Where did you meet him?"

"Just someone I met in town." The words came out too quickly, too rehearsed. I could tell from the way Adar's expression tightened that he noticed.

Adar scoffed. "I've never seen him before. And I know most people in town. He must be new."

I lifted my chin, gripping my sword tighter. "Oh, so now you know every single person in Joveryn? Should I start listing names and see if you remember them all?"

His eyes narrowed slightly, his grip on his sword tightening. "What family is he from? I doubt he's from town if I've never seen him."

"I don't know," I lied smoothly, forcing a casual shrug. "He

328

doesn't talk about them much. And I never asked."

Adar's frown deepened. "That's suspicious." He studied me for a long moment, as if he was trying to decide whether to press further or let it go.

"Or maybe he just doesn't like talking about his past," I countered, trying to keep my voice even. "Not everyone has a home like ours."

Adar studied me, his lips pressing into a thin line. "How long have you been seeing him?"

I shrugged. "A while. We train, that's all."

"Why didn't you tell me before?" His tone was edging toward something firmer now, more insistent. "You've been training with him for a while, and you never thought to mention it?"

I let out a slow breath, keeping my expression carefully neutral. "Do you really want to get into this?" I snapped, lowering my sword and stepping back. "Did you want me to write a letter? You're never here, Adar. When exactly was I supposed to bring it up?"

"You're right." His voice was quieter now, but there was an edge to it. "But I'm here now. And this time, I'm paying attention."

41

Chapter 41

Bronwen

"Do you have any more scarves?"

"No, I'm sorry. They sold pretty quickly this morning. I am hoping we will make it to one more Market before the snow is too thick, and I will be sure to set a few scarves to the side for you, Mrs. Verusha."

She nodded before walking away, disappearing into the thick crowd of Market-goers moving between the stalls.

"Wow, B. I've never seen you so nice," Adar mumbled next to me as he organized the coins we'd collected.

I elbowed him in the side, causing him to chuckle.

"We should bring more gloves next time," I said, glancing at the dwindling pile of winterwear on our table. "They're selling faster than anything else."

Adar nodded, squinting at the coins in his hand. "That, and shawls. Everyone's worried about the snow this year. Did you hear Mrs. Verusha going on about how last year's blizzard trapped her inside for weeks?"

I laughed softly, the sound surprising even me. "She'll need more than scarves to survive that."

Market continued in a steady hum around us, voices rising and falling as vendors called out their goods and customers haggled over prices. A merchant beside us bickered with an older man over the price of salted fish, their heated exchange blending into Market's lively chatter. Nearby, a group of children rushed past, laughing as they clutched warm rolls wrapped in cloth, their breath misting in the cold air.

As the crowd ebbed and flowed, my eyes kept drifting toward the edges of Market, searching for a familiar face. We had been here for a couple of hours, but August hadn't come. I shifted my weight, my fingers idly smoothing the fabric of a wool shawl. He had been reliable about showing up, lurking in the shadows, always watching. But not today. My stomach tightened slightly at the thought. When I told him not to come around a couple of days ago, he agreed without a fight. I thought he was just being easy for once, but maybe I'd misread the situation.

Was he pouting next to the fire again?

The thought made me smile, and I tried to think of a way to make my escape to him. I'd hate to leave Adar alone, though. We'd promised our parents that we would handle it.

A woman paused at our table, her fingers grazing the edge of a thick woolen shawl. "This one?" she asked, her voice hesitant.

Before I could respond, bells rang throughout Market, loud and urgent, splitting the winter air.

The sound jolted through me, sharp and unrelenting, making my fingers twitch as I dropped the basket in my hand. Around me, Market shifted in an instant. Conversations halted mid-sentence, stalls left unattended as merchants and customers alike turned toward the source of the bells.

"Shit," Adar whispered before grabbing me and pulling me with him.

A ripple of excitement spread through the streets like wildfire, voices overlapping in a frantic hum. People surged forward, feet scraping against the cobblestones, breath misting in the cold air as they jostled for a better view. Someone bumped into me, nearly knocking me off balance, but they didn't stop to apologize. The urgency in the air was suffocating, the energy shifting from curiosity to something far more primal.

The stage was in a form I had never seen before. Usually it was open with an empty noose waiting to be wrapped around a witch. Today, a wall on wheels had been pushed in front of the platform, keeping part of the stage hidden.

The energy of the crowd was electric, bordering on frenzied. Hands clutched at cloaks, elbows jabbed as bodies pressed together, the air thick with murmurs of speculation. Some people craned their necks, others climbed onto crates and barrels, desperate for a glimpse of whatever had drawn the kingdom's attention. The collective anticipation was suffocating, a mass of humanity shifting as one, driven by a mix of fear and exhilaration. People shouted, creating a deafening roar that echoed through the narrow streets. Adar and I stood in the spot our family always had, somewhere in the middle of the fray, surrounded by townspeople whose excitement bordered on frenzy.

Through all the noise, a familiar tapping of magic had me turning to the right, and I saw August on the far end trying to push his way through the crowd. He seemed out of character. He was no longer the cool, collected August he usually pretended to be. His hair was in disarray, and he wore nothing but a loose-fitting shirt, making him stand out among the cloak-filled streets. He was still far from me, having no luck getting any closer until he stilled as the streets grew quiet and he turned his attention to the stage.

I followed his line of sight to see several Legion soldiers walking onto stage in a weird formation. In the front was the older man that I saw with Adar at the pond that day.

Once they stopped on stage, the older man spoke. "We are about to witness something no one in our lifetime has seen before. With our greatest capture yet, we have a very special guest. The Joveryn King has joined us!"

Cheers erupted through the crowd at the announcement. The sound felt like a sharp slap to my senses, my pulse quickening as dread coiled in my chest. I clenched my fists, trying to steady myself against the suffocating wave of panic and anger that threatened to consume me. The jubilant cries around me seemed to mock the tension knotting in my stomach. I dug my fingernails into the palms of my hands. This was it. I was about to see Carrow.

The soldiers began to step away as a hooded man walked to the front of the platform. The crowd fell silent, the excitement morphing into a palpable tension. I could feel the weight of their collective breath, held in anticipation. Every creak of the wooden stage seemed amplified in the stillness, the sound cutting through the dense air like a blade. My heart thundered in my chest, every beat a countdown to the revelation of the vampire beneath the hood. His movements were deliberate, his steps unhurried, as if savoring the power of this moment. My hands clenched tighter, my nails biting into my palms as dread and curiosity waged war within me.

The hood obscured his face completely, a dark shadow that made him appear almost otherworldly. The moment stretched unbearably, the silence so oppressive I could hear the faint rustle of fabric as he reached up to pull the hood back. I ran scenarios through my head. If August could just get to me, I could pull from him and set Carrow aflame without anyone knowing it was me. If August would just—

My breath caught in my lungs as the man removed his hood.

It was August's father.

Carrow was August's father.

The realization hit me like a thunderclap, freezing me in place. The world around me dulled, sound and movement fading into a distant blur. My mind raced, piecing together fragments of memory, hints I'd overlooked, all pointing to this impossible truth. My fingers went numb, my limbs suddenly weightless, as though the very ground beneath me had shifted. The roaring crowd, the winter air, even the heavy scent of burning torches—it all became secondary to the fact that Carrow was August's father.

I turned back to August, desperate for answers, only to see the anguish on his face as he fought to get to me. August wasn't just pushing through the crowd—he was fighting. His breath came in sharp, visible bursts in the cold air, his muscles tensed like a predator caught in a snare. He slammed into the man blocking his way, sending him stumbling back, but before he could move forward, another man threw a punch, catching August in the side. He barely reacted, twisting away before another set of hands grabbed at him, pulling him back into the chaos.

I had never seen him like this before. His desperation was

raw, unrestrained, carved into every line of his face. He wasn't thinking—he was just trying to get to me. But the crowd was relentless, swallowing him whole, dragging him further from me instead of closer.

"People of Joveryn!" Carrow's sinister voice brought my attention back to him. "We are coming to a new age. An age where we will no longer have witches among us. This capture will go down in history."

He nodded to someone, and the wall began to roll away. A heavy groan echoed through the air as the mechanism engaged, the hinges creaking in protest, dragging the moment into unbearable suspense. The tension in the crowd shifted, the breathless anticipation thick enough to choke on. I could hear the faint shuffling of feet, the sharp inhalations of those around me, but my own body refused to move. The creaking stretched on, agonizingly slow, each passing second a cruel extension of whatever horror lay behind it.

The energy of the crowd sharpened, breaths coming faster, bodies leaning forward, as if drawn toward the platform by some invisible force. Excitement clashed with unease, the pulse of the gathered mass teetering between thrill and dread. It felt like watching the sky fracture before a storm, an overwhelming sense of inevitability suffocating the space around me. Gasps and whispers crashed over the crowd like waves, the exhilaration from moments ago curdling into something sharper, something almost sickly. Some recoiled, others pressed forward, hands clenching at their cloaks, their breath misting in the frozen air as shock took hold.

My vision tunneled, locking onto the platform as the last barrier slid away, the final inch unmasking the nightmare I hadn't dared to consider. The world tilted, my breath caught somewhere between my lungs and my throat, strangling me from the inside out. The air turned dense, pressing against me, suffocating and cruel. My heart pounded, each beat a hammering warning that what I was seeing was real, that there was no turning away now.

Because Mama and Papa hung above the platform.

Chapter 42

Bronwen

No. *No*, that wasn't right. That wasn't—

The world blurred at the edges, sound warping into a distant hum as my gaze locked onto the figures hanging above the platform. Not them. It couldn't be them. But the familiar lines of their faces, the unmistakable presence of Papa, of Mama—

A ragged breath escaped me. Their lifeless bodies swayed gently from the nooses, the rope taut against their necks. The color had drained from their faces, their eyes closed as if in final defiance of the spectacle they had been made into. Blood rushed in my ears, drowning out the gasps and murmurs of the crowd. My knees buckled, but I forced myself to stay upright, the reality of what I was seeing sinking into my chest like a blade. The cheers of the crowd turned into a deafening roar, their delight a twisted contrast to the agony tearing through me.

And it was all because of August.

A game. It's always been a game to August. He said he

was going to drag this out, push me over the edge. And now, standing here, I could feel the full weight of his cruelty. I had been nothing but a pawn, led along by my own arrogance. He played me perfectly, let me believe I had any control in this, let me think I was clever enough to keep up with him. And I fell for it. Every single step.

My anger churned violently with my despair, a storm raging within that threatened to pull me under. How could he have orchestrated something so vile, so personal? Had he planned this all along? Had every touch, every smirk, every calculated look been leading to this moment? My stomach churned as the realization took root—this wasn't just manipulation. This was execution, a trap I had walked straight into with my eyes wide open. But all of this was on me. The nightmares warned me. They showed me exactly who he was, and I ignored them.

I let his words wrap around me like a spell, let myself believe in something that was never real. I had wanted to trust him. I had wanted to believe I wasn't alone in this fight. But in the end, I was nothing more than entertainment to him. Every fiber of my being burned with hatred and grief. I had trusted him. I had let him get close. I had given him the chance to shatter me, and he took it. I clenched my fists so tightly my nails bit into my palms, grounding me in the searing pain. It wasn't just grief twisting through me—it was fury. White-hot and blinding.

I glanced at August, my eyes filling with tears. He stood frozen, still far away in the crowd, his wide eyes glistening with what looked like horror and disbelief. His mouth opened slightly as if to speak, but no words came. His shoulders, usually squared with confidence, sagged under an invisible weight, and his hands hovered at his sides, clenched and trembling as though he were fighting an internal battle he couldn't win.

Why wasn't he smiling?

He won.

Was this not the moment he had been waiting for? Hadn't he told me he would break me? That he would drag me under, make me like him? But his face—there was no satisfaction in it. No cruel smirk, no triumphant gleam in his eyes. Just horror.

Liar.

"We have captured the leaders of the witch coven!" Carrow's voice boomed. "Now, where are their children? The twins?"

A hush fell over the crowd, the collective energy shifting from frenzied delight to tense anticipation. People craned their necks, eyes darting from face to face, searching for the next act in this grim spectacle. Some murmured to each other in hushed, hurried tones, while others stood frozen, their breaths held as if afraid to draw attention to themselves.

Adar snatched my arm, his grip firm and unyielding. "We have to go," he hissed, his voice low and urgent, the edge of panic sharp enough to cut.

Around us, the crowd surged. Hands clutched at sleeves, eyes darted between strangers. Adar scanned the shifting mass of bodies, searching for a way out.

"Now, Bronwen," he growled, tugging me closer as the chaos of the crowd pressed in around us.

I kept my head down, gripping my hood tightly as we pushed through the crowd, but the pressure around us was closing in. Elbows jabbed against my ribs, bodies shifted too quickly, blocking every possible exit. The once-celebratory energy of

Market had turned—curious whispers became accusations, and the weight of a thousand watchful eyes sent ice through my veins.

We were almost free when a sudden yank wrenched me backward. My hood ripped away, cold air biting at my exposed skin. Gasps rippled through the crowd like wildfire, a single moment of stunned silence before the hysteria began.

"Witch!" the old woman shrieked, her voice cracked with age but loud enough to carry.

Before I could react, a man grabbed me from behind, his grip bruising as he yanked me toward him. I staggered, my heartbeat pounding in my ears. A second hand gripped my arm, another set of fingers clawed at my cloak, desperate hands trying to pull me down. The world spun in a blur of movement, of snarling faces and grasping limbs. Somewhere in the chaos, I still searched for August—searching for the smirk, the satisfaction—but all I saw was panic in his frozen stance.

A flash of silver, and then hot blood splattered across my arm. Adar's blade carved through the man's throat in one clean, decisive motion. He crumpled, gurgling, and the iron scent of blood filled the air.

"Bronwen!" Adar roared, his voice cutting through the growing hysteria.

His words snapped me back, and I moved without thinking. I ripped my arm free from the man's slackening grip, shoved past the old woman, ignoring the way her nails scraped across my wrist as she tried to hold on. The crowd swelled, bodies pressing closer, the feverish excitement morphing into full-blown panic.

We ran as fast as we could to the town walls, only to be met with Legion soldiers standing at the gate. Their armor glinted in the sunlight, and their blades were drawn, a clear warning that there was no escape.

Adar didn't hesitate. He charged the larger of the two soldiers, slamming his shoulder into the man's chest with a force that sent them both crashing to the ground. The soldier's sword flew from his grasp, clattering across the cobblestones.

I darted forward and snatched the blade. Its weight settled comfortably in my hands, a reassuring reminder of all the training that had been drilled into me over the years. The second soldier turned his attention to me, his eyes narrowing with determination as he lunged. I parried his strike with practiced ease, the clash of steel reverberating up my arms. He pressed his attack, but I sidestepped fluidly, my movements swift and calculated. Feigning a retreat, I twisted my wrist and delivered a sharp strike across his thigh, forcing him to stagger. With one final thrust, I drove the blade into his side. His scream cut through the chaos as he crumpled to the ground, and I stood over him, my breath steady despite the adrenaline coursing through me.

Adar was already on his feet, grappling with the first soldier. He drove his knee into the man's stomach, forcing him to double over with a pained gasp. Without hesitation, Adar grabbed him by the head and drove his knife into his neck. The soldier collapsed, gurgling, before falling limp at his feet.

"Bronwen, more are coming!" he shouted, his voice strained but steady.

I turned to see reinforcements flooding toward the gate, their armor gleaming ominously in the sunlight. My heart pounded as Adar grabbed my arm, pulling me toward the woods.

"To the horses!" he barked, and we ran, our breaths visible in the frigid air.

The woods offered some cover, the dense trees muffling the sounds of pursuit. My legs burned as we pushed forward, the looming threat of the soldiers driving us onward. Finally, we reached the small clearing where the horses were tethered, their eyes wide with fear.

Adar untied a dark bay mare and shoved the reins into my hands. "Go!" he ordered.

I climbed onto the mare, the unfamiliar saddle biting into my thighs. Adar spurred his horse forward, and I followed, the sound of hoofbeats pounding against the frozen ground.

The icy wind lashed at my face, biting through my cloak and chilling me to the bone. The trees blurred into streaks of green and gray as we pushed deeper into the forest, their skeletal branches clawing at the sky. Behind us, the distant shouts of soldiers still echoed, a grim reminder that our pursuers weren't far.

"Keep up, B," Adar called over his shoulder, his voice strained but firm.

"I'm right behind you!" I shouted back, gripping the reins tightly as the mare's hooves slipped briefly on a patch of ice. My heart thundered in my chest, fear and adrenaline warring for dominance.

The hours stretched endlessly as we rode, the forest growing denser with each passing mile. My mind raced, refusing to stay still as I replayed the image of Mama and Papa hanging from the nooses. Tears stung my cheeks, freezing against my skin as the cold wind whipped past. What had happened? They weren't supposed to be in town—so why were they there? My chest tightened as guilt gnawed at me. All of this was my fault.

The path became a winding maze of narrow trails, flanked by towering trees that offered both cover and disorientation. But no matter how far we rode, I couldn't outrun the suffocating guilt pressing against my chest. Their lifeless faces, pale and haunting, hovered in my mind's eye. I had led them to this. Had they known they would be caught? My stomach churned violently, bile rising in my throat. Did they suffer? Did they call out for us? My thighs ached from the unfamiliar saddle, but I dared not stop.

This was my fault.

I had ignored the warnings, let August into my life, let him distract me while he orchestrated my family's execution. The sharp edges of my grief pushed me forward, but it wasn't just grief—it was self-hatred, raw and unrelenting. The thought of the soldiers closing in spurred me onward, but it was the unanswered questions, the gaping hole in my chest where my parents had been, and the unbearable truth that I had let this happen that truly drove me. If I had been stronger, smarter, less reckless—would they still be alive?

As twilight descended, the first signs of exhaustion began to creep in. The horses' breaths came in heavy puffs of steam, their pace slowing as the terrain grew rougher. Adar glanced back at me, his expression grim. "We're close," he said, though his tone betrayed his own weariness.

Finally, we emerged into a small clearing. At its center stood an unassuming stone cottage, half-hidden by overgrown ivy and surrounded by dense thickets. The air felt different here— still and heavy, as though the forest itself guarded the place. Adar dismounted and gestured for me to do the same.

"Is this it?" I asked, my voice barely above a whisper.

Adar nodded, his eyes scanning the perimeter. "The coven's

safe house. Only the most trusted witches know about it."

I slid off the mare, my legs nearly buckling beneath me. Adar caught my arm, steadying me before leading both horses to a makeshift stable tucked behind the cottage. The structure was crude but functional, its wooden beams weathered with age.

Inside the cottage, the air was warmer, carrying the faint scent of herbs and aged wood. A single lantern hung from a hook near the ceiling, casting a soft, golden glow over the sparse interior. Shelves lined the walls, filled with jars of dried ingredients and ancient tomes. A fireplace nestled on the back wall, the idea of the warmth it would bring a welcome reprieve from the bitter cold outside.

I turned to Adar, his lightheartedness and happiness shattered, replaced by a hollow look that broke my heart. His shoulders sagged as if the weight of what we had seen had crushed him. Without a word, I pulled him into my arms, and we both collapsed to the ground. The rough wood of the cottage floor pressed into my knees, but I barely noticed.

Adar clung to me, his body trembling as silent sobs wracked his frame. My own tears burned against my frozen skin, the weight of our loss settling like a stone in my chest. Each sob felt like it tore through me, raw and unrelenting.

"They weren't supposed to be there," I whispered hoarsely, my voice breaking.

Adar shook his head against my shoulder, unable to respond. His grip tightened as though holding onto me was the only thing keeping him grounded. The weight of the day pressed down on us like a heavy shroud, and for the first time, I felt the full depth of our loss—a vast, aching void I wasn't sure we could ever escape.

43

Chapter 43

Adar

The room was small and dimly lit, the wooden table in the center scarred from years of use. Around it stood my father's closest friends, men who had once been his confidants, allies in the hidden war against the Legion and vampires. These were the same men who had helped him smuggle vampires to Bronwen when we were children, ensuring she could pull without exposing herself to danger. Now, they stood here, voices raised, their faces lined with worry and anger.

Bronwen and I sat side by side at the table, though it felt like we were worlds apart. She hadn't spoken in days, not since that night when everything fell apart. Her gaze was fixed on the vase in the middle of the table, its chipped edges and faded flowers an anchor for her distant thoughts. Her hands rested motionless in her lap, her fingers curled slightly as if even moving them took too much effort. Every so often, her chest rose and fell in a slow, measured breath, like she had to remind herself to keep breathing. The yelling and arguing swirled around her, but she remained utterly silent.

Questions raced through my mind constantly. What happened? How were they discovered? Did we have a traitor in the coven? Papa was always careful, and Mama—Mama couldn't even practice magic anymore. She lost her connection when she was pregnant with us. We somehow pulled magic from her within the womb. Our first victim.

I couldn't get the image of them hanging from the platform out of my head. Their lifeless faces would be forever engraved in my memory. The entire reason I joined the Legion was to protect our witches. And I wasn't there to protect the two most important ones.

"You have to leave," Jonah said, slamming his hand down on the table. The sound echoed sharply, cutting through the noise. "The Legion is tightening its grip. They're interrogating anyone they think might know where you are. It's only a matter of time before they find this place."

"And what happens to the coven if we do?" I shot back, my voice sharper than I intended. My fingers dug into the edge of the table, the rough wood biting into my palms. "They've already lost their Father. If we run, they'll be left defenseless. No one else can lead them."

"This isn't about the coven," another man, Darrin, countered. His voice was calmer but no less urgent. "This is about survival. If they captured you, I would never forgive myself. Think about the bigger picture."

"The bigger picture?" I spat. "What about the people here? The ones who look to us for guidance? You expect me to abandon them?"

The argument grew louder, voices overlapping as each man tried to make his point. Threats were made, accusations thrown, but through it all, Bronwen never said a word. Between the yelling, arguing, and threats made, she remained silent. The firelight flickered across her face, but she didn't seem to register it. Even as the men's voices rose around her, she didn't flinch or shift in her seat. It was as if she was somewhere else entirely, her mind locked away where none of us could reach her.

I stole a glance at her, the hollow look in her eyes twisting something deep inside me. Her face was expressionless, but the way her shoulders slumped, the way her lips barely pressed together, told me enough. She wasn't just quiet—she was drowning in something I couldn't pull her from. She looked like a ghost of herself, and I hated that I didn't know how to fix it. I hated that I didn't know if I even could. It had been days since our parents died. The day after, I had tried to grieve, but there had been no time. There was never any time.

Every moment since had been spent making decisions I wasn't ready for, trying to hold everything together when I barely knew how to keep myself from falling apart. We'd been too busy dealing with the fallout—organizing the coven, managing fears, and pretending we had control when, in reality, we were barely holding on. Every day felt like trying to plug holes in a sinking ship, and the water was rising fast. It felt like there was no space left for grief, only action.

"If we leave, the Legion might stop hunting, but they might not," I said, raising my voice to regain control of the room. The men quieted, their eyes turning to me. "And if they don't, then what? They'll pick this kingdom apart while we're gone. And even if we do get away, what kind of life would that be? Hiding, running forever? I won't live like that."

Jonah slammed his hand on the table again, his frustration

boiling over. "You think I want to send you away? You think I don't know what that means for the coven?" His voice cracked, and for the first time, I saw more than anger in his eyes—I saw fear. "I had a brother, Adar. The Legion took him three years ago. They dragged him through the streets and hung him just like your parents, leaving his body to rot. You think they won't do the same to you?"

His words hit like a punch to the gut, but before I could answer, Darrin spoke up, his voice quieter but no less urgent. "I have a wife and daughter. They're already packing what little we have in case we need to flee. If they find out we've been helping you, we won't just lose our homes—we'll lose our lives." He exhaled sharply, rubbing a hand over his face. "We all loved your father. We all loved your mother. But this fight doesn't just belong to you anymore. We have families too."

I clenched my fists under the table. The weight of their words pressed down on me. I had been thinking about survival in broad strokes—what it meant for Bronwen and me, what it meant for the coven as a whole. But these men weren't just names on a list of allies. They had families, people who relied on them. And by staying, we were putting them all at risk.

The silence that followed was suffocating, pressing against my chest like a weight I couldn't shake. The crackle of the fire seemed distant, swallowed by the enormity of what we were facing. I had no answers, only the overwhelming certainty that no matter what choice I made, people would suffer for it. I looked at the men around me, the ones who had stood beside my father for years. Their loyalty was unquestionable, but their fear was winning. I couldn't blame them.

"I can end this."

The words were barely above a whisper. Every head turned toward Bronwen. Her voice—after days of nothing—cut through the tension like a blade.

"What?" I asked, my heart hammering in my chest.

Bronwen slowly lifted her eyes to mine, like it took effort just to move. And for the first time in days, I saw a flicker of something behind them—not just exhaustion, not just grief, but resolve, cold and certain. "I can stop this," she said. "But you have to trust me."

44

Chapter 44

Bronwen

The sun hung low, casting long shadows behind the buildings, its golden light waning and signaling that nightfall was imminent. Jonah had spelled my cloak to render me invisible, as long as I kept the hood up. The spell hummed faintly against my skin, a constant reminder of the lengths we had to go to for safety.

Once I slipped into the alleyway, I pulled the hood down and let the cloak fall to the ground, the soft fabric pooling around my feet.

I ascended the narrow wooden steps, my feet making no sound against the weathered planks. Silence was a habit I couldn't break, even though I knew he could already sense me. He would smell me coming, just like always.

The door flew open before I reached the top step, slamming against the wall with a loud crack. August stood there, gripping the sides of the doorframe as he looked down at me, a mixture of relief and anguish etched across his face. His hands trembled slightly as they clutched the wood, and his shoulders sagged under an invisible weight. His lips parted as though he wanted to speak but couldn't find the words, his breath shallow and uneven.

The tension in his posture hinted at the storm of emotions he was barely holding back. His eyes, once full of mischief and fire, were now dark hollows, rimmed with exhaustion and grief. His skin, paler than I remembered, seemed almost translucent, stretched thin over his shirtless form. He looked like he hadn't fed in days.

I stared at him for a moment, taking in the way his breath came fast and uneven, the way his fingers twitched as if he wanted to reach for me but didn't dare. This wasn't the August I had prepared myself to fight. But the memory of my parents' lifeless faces burned in my mind, and the hesitation melted away.

"You lied to me," I said, shoving him hard in the chest and stepping past him. My voice trembled, a crack betraying the fury bubbling inside me, but I pushed through it. Each step forward was an assertion of my anger, my grief, my need to make him feel even a fraction of the pain clawing at me. Heat flushed my skin as my breath quickened, my body vibrating with a mix of rage and betrayal. He staggered back, his expression crumpling with guilt.

"I did," he admitted, his voice barely above a whisper.

"You tricked me!" I shoved him again, harder this time, and he stumbled back, barely catching himself against the edge of the table. He exhaled sharply but didn't push me away.

"I didn't—"

"It was a game to you. Just like you said." My voice broke, but I pushed through it, the anger surging to keep the tears at bay. "A game to see how far you could push me."

Before he could respond, I drew my dagger in a smooth motion and swung at him. He leapt back, but not fast enough. The blade grazed his chest, slicing through his skin and leaving a shallow, bloody line. He winced, his jaw tightening, but he didn't move to defend himself.

"No, Winnie, I—"

"You don't get to call me that!" I hurled the dagger at him. He dodged at the last second, the blade embedding itself into the wall just inches from his head.

His chest rose and fell too fast, his breath uneven, his hands twitching as if fighting the instinct to react. "I had nothing to do with it!" His voice cracked as he raised his hands, palms out, his body tense as if bracing for another attack. "I would never let something like that happen to you."

"You had everything to do with it!" I lunged at him, fists flying.

This time, I felt him flinch under my touch. My blows landed—one to his ribs, another to his jaw—his head snapping to the side from the impact. But he stood there and took it, his hands clenching into fists at his sides as though holding himself back.

"Fight back!" I screamed, slamming my fists into his chest. His breath left him in a sharp exhale, his body staggering slightly under the force of my strike, but he didn't retaliate.

Tears streaked down my face, hot and unrelenting, blurring my vision as I lashed out again—as though striking him could erase the horrors I couldn't stop reliving. He sucked in a sharp breath, his body jerking with the force of my rage, but he never lifted a hand to stop me.

My chest heaved, my knuckles burned, my body trembled

from the sheer force of it all. The weight of everything—the lies, the loss, the betrayal—pressed down on me, fueling every strike. "They are dead because of you!"

His knees almost buckled beneath him, his body folding inward as if I had struck something deeper than flesh.

"They are," he whispered, his gaze dropping to the floor. "He couldn't torture me anymore—not until he found you. And now he's hurt me more than he ever has before. Because he hurt you."

I had come to kill him before nightfall. I'd planned every step, every word. But now, standing here, seeing the wreck of him, I couldn't do it. I had expected to find him reveling in victory. Him taunting me with his words with a smirk plastered on his face or finally trying to drain me dry.

But not this.

He stepped forward, then stopped. His hands twitched at his sides, his fingers curling into fists, as if he wasn't sure he had the right. For a moment, he just stood there, his breathing ragged, his gaze flickering over my face like he was searching for something—permission, forgiveness, maybe even absolution. Then, as though something in him finally broke, he reached out and wrapped his arms around me. I stiffened, my breath catching, but he didn't let go. His grip was firm yet trembling, like he was afraid I might slip away if he loosened his hold even a fraction.

"Winnie," he said, his voice cracking. "I didn't know."

I let him hold me, if only for a moment. The anger that had burned so brightly in me just minutes ago seemed to fade, leaving a hollow ache in its place. His arms around me felt both foreign and familiar, a fragile connection in the midst of so much chaos. His body trembled against mine, and I could feel his grief as keenly as my own.

No one had ever made me feel the way August did. Even with the lies, the pain, and the chaos, there was a gravity to him I couldn't escape. It was the way his presence filled the room, steady and unyielding, no matter how shattered he seemed. The way his voice softened when he said my name, like he was speaking to every broken part of me. I remembered the rare moments of honesty between us, the glimpses of vulnerability he let slip when he thought I wasn't looking. Despite everything, there was a part of me that felt seen by him, in a way no one else ever had. And in this moment, I wanted to hold onto that feeling, no matter how fleeting it might be.

I stepped back, my fingers trembling slightly as they gripped the fabric of my dress. I knew what I was about to do. And I knew, after this, he might never touch me again. But for this moment, I needed to feel him. To remind myself that I was alive, that I could still reach for something that wasn't pain or loss. This wasn't just about him—it was about me. Reclaiming something in a world that felt like it was spinning out of control. Pulling the dress over my head felt like shedding the weight of the past few days—the grief, the betrayal, the helplessness. It was claiming something for myself, even if it was fleeting. Even if I had to pretend, just for tonight, that everything didn't fall apart. I needed to feel grounded, to hold onto something familiar amidst the chaos.

"Winnie, I don't think . . ." he started, his words faltering as I undid the strap holding the stake to my thigh. It clattered to the ground between us.

His eyes roamed my body, his breath hitching as I stripped away the last barriers between us.

"I don't think . . ." He ran a hand through his hair, his voice breaking. "You . . . fuck, Winnie."

"Can you just stop talking for once?" I asked, my voice low but steady.

He hesitated, his hands clenching at his sides. "I just . . . I don't think this is what you really want right now. You've been through too much."

I stepped to him, hesitating just long enough to meet his eyes, to make sure he understood. My fingers trembled as they reached for his face, the warmth of his skin grounding me in this moment. I knew what I was about to do. I knew what it meant. And yet, I still whispered, "This is what I need right now."

I kissed him. For a moment, he remained tense, like he was still fighting himself. But then I felt it—the moment he gave in, the quiet surrender as he exhaled against my lips, his body melting into mine. His hands slid down my thighs, gripping tightly as he lifted me effortlessly. I wrapped my legs around him, my hands tangled in his hair, refusing to let there be space between us. He carried me to his bed with a quiet desperation, as if he needed this just as much as I did.

August laid me down gently, hovering over me as if uncertain, before pushing his pants down and climbing on top of me. He kissed the side of my chin, slow and careful. I grabbed his face, pulling his lips back onto mine, refusing to waste this moment on anything other than feeling every part of him.

His touch was softer than ever before, his hands tracing down my sides in gentle motions, like he was trying to hold onto something slipping through his fingers. I arched into him as I felt his tip near my entrance, a hesitation in his breath before he pressed his forehead against mine. Then, finally, he

355

pushed inside me.

He moved inside me with slow, deliberate strokes, his body pressing against mine as if he were trying to memorize every inch of me. His lips found mine again and again, his kisses deep and unrelenting, as though he was afraid to stop. I clung to him, my fingers digging into his back, holding on to this fleeting moment where nothing else existed—no grief, no lies, no war—only us. But this wasn't like we had done it before.

This was so much more.

The pressure built inside me, a slow, winding coil that tightened with each thrust, each ragged breath we shared. I tried to hold on, to drag this out for as long as I could, but the pleasure coursed through me like a storm I couldn't contain. A cry tore from my lips as my release crashed over me, shattering through every thought, every restraint. My body trembled beneath him, my heart hammering as he groaned against my neck, his movements growing erratic before he followed, his own release wracking through him in shuddering waves.

I gasped for breath, my body still trembling, as he pressed his forehead against mine, his chest rising and falling in time with my own. For a moment, there was only silence, the weight of what we had done settling between us. Then, with slow, trembling hands, I reached up, tangled my fingers in his hair, and pulled his magic.

A sharp breath escaped his lips, his body jerking slightly as he raised his head. His dark eyes searched mine, like he knew this wasn't just about us.

"Winnie," he breathed, his voice barely above a whisper.

I didn't release my grip. Instead, I pulled harder, my nails pressing into his scalp, anchoring myself to the feeling of him.

Tears blurred my vision as his breaths stilled, his skin paling to an unnatural gray as every bit of magic I could take was stripped from him.

Chapter 45

August

She had left me dead . . . or asleep. I didn't know. But I felt everything I had experienced in all of those dreams. She had taken so much from me that my body had been too drained to do anything else. But I didn't expect her to leave me—not like this.

Not when she didn't have a home to go to anymore.

I'm not sure how long it had been, but her scent still lingered in the room—faint, like a whisper of jasmine and warmth, clinging to the edges of my senses. My limbs felt sluggish, a dull ache thrumming beneath my skin as if my body were still recovering from the magic she had stripped away. I felt hollow, slow, like I was moving through water, the absence of my power leaving me weaker than I had ever known.

My heart began to race as the sweetness of it twisted into something metallic and sharp. Her blood. My hands trembled, the weakness in my limbs making every movement feel unsteady. I fumbled to throw on my clothes, frustration flaring at how much effort it took, but the urgency in my chest only grew sharper, overriding the exhaustion weighing me down. Opening the door to the alley, the smell of her blood hit me like a punch. It was so strong that my already unsteady body faltered, my knees nearly buckling as I stumbled back, gripping the frame for support. The dizziness from my drained magic mixed with panic, twisting my stomach into knots.

What the fuck happened?

Sheer panic took over, my mind racing with possibilities I didn't want to consider, and I bolted down the street, chasing the trail of blood that led me into the woods. With each step I took, I could feel myself growing stronger and faster once more.

The forest was eerily quiet, the snow underfoot crunching with each frantic step. Moonlight filtered through the twisted branches, casting sharp, uneven shadows that seemed to reach for me. The bitter cold bit at my skin, the air thick and heavy, as if the woods themselves were conspiring to slow me down.

I stopped when I saw her standing under the moonlight, her glowing green eyes locked onto mine. A strange stillness settled over the clearing.

Something was wrong.

Her posture was too controlled, her expression blank. She wasn't scared. She wasn't even tense. She was waiting.

My stomach twisted, but I forced myself forward. "What are you doing?" I asked, my voice sharp with unease.

She didn't answer.

The wind stirred the loose strands of her hair, but she didn't react—didn't blink, didn't shift, didn't move at all. The

359

silence stretched between us, thick and suffocating, and for the first time, I truly felt like prey.

I took another step forward, something dark curling in my gut. Why isn't she moving?

Then, a voice came from the shadows behind her. "What are you doing out here alone?"

My father.

A cold dread slithered down my spine.

Bronwen didn't react. She didn't turn to him. Didn't flinch.

Because she wasn't surprised.

No—

"Winnie, no."

I moved to stop her, but the moment I stepped past the shadows, I slammed into something invisible.

Fucking witches.

The air around me crackled with unseen power, locking me out of the circle. The realization hit me like a gut punch. She planned this.

I slammed my fists against the barrier. "Father, it's a trap!"

He didn't react. He couldn't hear me.

A slow smirk curled at the corner of his lips. "Are you giving up so easily?"

Then he reached for her, his fingers curling around her throat.

She didn't resist.

Because she wanted this.

As soon as he sunk his teeth into her, she grabbed the arm he had wrapped around her and brought him to his knees.

The guards who always accompanied my father emerged from the darkness, but the same invisible shield kept them from reaching him.

I glanced around looking for any sign of where the witches could be until I saw a glimmer of something reflecting off of what looked like nothing. I ripped a branch from the tree and threw it as hard as I could to where the glimmer once was.

A woman with long gray hair formed out of thin air and fell to her knees with the tree branch sticking out of her chest. As the circle broke, the witches' cloaking spell vanished, their forms emerging from the shadows. Dozens stood in a perfect ring, their faces partially obscured by deep hoods, but the glow of their magic illuminated the frost-covered ground. Some held their hands aloft, fingers twitching as faint trails of light spiraled upward.

I turned back to Winnie and my father to see her raising her flaming hand, just as she did with me so long ago, except this time she was prepared for the guards.

As soon as the guards tried to reach my father, fire caught them, and they fell to the ground screaming, their cries piercing the cold night air. The flames consumed them quickly, turning their bodies to ash even as their screams faded. One guard managed to lunge toward a witch, claws bared, and took her down with a feral swipe before he too succumbed to the flames. Another darted through the chaos, striking at two witches with swift, deadly precision, their bodies crumpling to the ground before his own erupted in fire.

The clearing was a chaotic blur of glowing magic and burning ash, the acrid smell of scorched earth and flesh thick in the air. Amidst the carnage, I caught a glimpse of Adar tucked in the shadows, one hand on a vampire I hadn't seen before to pull magic from, and the other pointing to his next victim.

I took a small step forward, a movement that made her twin

look at me. His eyes widened when he saw me as if the pieces of a puzzle were finally coming together. I guess Winnie never told him, even after everything. He raised his finger to me, and I winced before realizing nothing happened. When I glanced back at Winnie, her eyes were still locked on me. She was using the magic she had pulled from my father to protect me—even as she betrayed me.

I ran to her, stopping only a few feet in front of her. Her eyes, the ones I had seen every time I closed mine, were devoid of any emotion. They were cold and unyielding, a stark contrast to the memories I clung to. She was no longer the girl I had known. She was something sharper, harder—someone who had carved away every trace of weakness, burying her pain beneath cold resolve. And in that moment, the realization crashed over me like a tidal wave, leaving me breathless.

She had also planned everything that happened mere hours ago—every word, every glance, every touch. The warmth of her body pressed against mine, the intimacy I thought we shared—it had all been a lie. My chest tightened, a mix of anger and heartbreak coursing through me. I wanted to scream, to lash out, but the betrayal cut too deep, leaving me paralyzed.

She came to me, fucked me, took my magic, all to kill my father.

"Don't do it." I gritted my teeth. "You will regret it, Winnie."

She kept her eyes on me as she brought her hand down, the flames erupting from her palm with a ferocity that seemed almost alive. My father's screams ripped through the night, raw and guttural, before cutting off abruptly as the fire consumed him. The acrid smell of burning flesh filled the air, turning my stomach. For a moment, everything seemed to slow—the crackle of the flames, the wavering light that cast Winnie's face in harsh shadows, the ash drifting upward like snow.

Her expression didn't change. There was no triumph, no satisfaction, only a cold, calculated resolve. Her hand didn't waver, even as his body turned to ash and crumbled into nothing.

Chapter 46

Bronwen

August's scream pierced through the woods as his father crumbled into nothing, leaving only ashes between us.

"B! What are you doing?"

I glanced at my brother who frantically waited for me to end it all. To kill August. I wanted to—*I think.* My mind screamed at me to move, to finish it, but my body betrayed me, frozen in place. I could feel the weight of my brother's expectation, the heat of August's presence, but still, I couldn't force myself to act. And protecting him when my brother tried to kill him? I didn't mean to do that.

I never thought to protect him. Never told the magic to shield him. But somewhere deep inside, in a place I couldn't control or even understand, I didn't want to see him hurt. My mind fought against it, rationalizing all the reasons he didn't deserve my protection. Yet, the magic hadn't listened to reason.

An arm wrapped around me, and the world tilted. A flash

of light, and then darkness. When my feet hit solid ground again, the air was colder, sharper. I blinked, trying to adjust, and saw the trees around us—taller, denser, their gnarled branches entwining above like skeletal hands, casting oppressive shadows that danced with every gust of wind. The moonlight barely pierced through the canopy, and the silence here felt different—heavier, as though the forest itself was holding its breath. The snow underfoot muffled every sound, but the cold bit into my skin, a constant reminder of how isolated we were. Each shadow seemed to move, closing in, amplifying the tension that crackled between us.

August paced frantically in front of me, a slur of mumbles coming from his mouth that I barely understood. He glanced at the moon as he whispered, "It's only a matter of time now." He ran his hand through his hair. "You don't understand what you just did, Winnie."

"I know exactly what I did," I paused as I watched him whisper more things I couldn't understand. "Your grace."

He turned to me, and a broken, hollow laugh escaped his lips—short, sharp, and devoid of humor. Before I could react, he was in my face, his hand closing around my throat. His grip was firm but trembling, tightening briefly before loosening again, his fingers twitching like he couldn't decide whether to crush or release me. His thumb pressed just enough to make me gasp, but then his hand flexed, his pulse hammering beneath his skin, a war raging in him that he was barely keeping at bay. His eyes, dark and bloodshot, burned with a mix of desperation and fury, but there was something worse lurking beneath—the kind of unhinged devastation that came when a man lost everything and had nothing left to fear.

In an instant, he slammed me against a tree, pressing his

full weight against mine as he hovered above me. There was a weight in his gaze, a deep well of betrayal that threatened to pull me under. His breathing was ragged, erratic, his chest rising too fast, too sharp, as if his body couldn't keep up with his unraveling mind. His chest heaved with the effort, and I could feel the tremor in his arm as his emotions teetered on the edge of control.

"I don't want to be king." His words were sharp. Just as he stared at me like he was ready to kill me. "You have no idea the series of events that you have just started."

I stared into his eyes, feeling the weight of everything that had passed between us—the lies, the anger, the shattered trust. My voice barely a whisper, I said, "Kill me."

The words hung in the cold air, fragile yet heavy, as though they could shatter at any moment. I didn't flinch, didn't look away. I fully expected him to end it right there, to let his rage and grief take over. After everything I had done, after the revenge I had claimed, maybe I deserved it.

But he didn't move. His hand loosened, his fingers ghosting over my skin as if trying to remember the feel of it before he let go completely. His lips parted, and for a moment, it seemed like he might say something else, something real, but then the darkness in his gaze solidified. "Oh no. You're not getting out of this so easily."

I looked up at him, confused. He glared at me a moment until his signature smirk formed on his lips. But this time, the smile didn't reach his eyes.

"You made me king." He leaned in closer, his lips inches from mine as he whispered, "I'll make you my queen."

www.ingramcontent.com/pod-product-compliance
Ingram Content Group UK Ltd.
Pitfield, Milton Keynes, MK11 3LW, UK
UKHW031032120325
456161UK00006B/445